Ah, Mida! Ever shall the sight of blood upon my blade stir me to burning life, take all reason from my mind, and fill me with the joy that battle brings. A quick leap brought me within reach of the champion of the High Seat, and then did my blade begin the dance of death, a twisting and cavorting the male was hard-pressed to parry. Slash and cut, stab and slice, foot by foot was the male pressed backward, his arm working frenziedly to protect him from harm, his bewilderment so thick it nearly took my notice.

The battle was ended far sooner than I would have wished. Surely had I thought the male one to stand firmly before me, his sword a true challenge to mine, yet did he prove himself no more than the others. Panting, covered in sweat and blood, his backing across the grass was halted by a loss of footing, sending him sprawling to his back with arms flung up above his head. Quick as thought was I upon him, my sword raised high above his throat. Fiercely, proudly, did I stand above the body of he who had challenged me, and raised my arms and sword to the skies.

"For you, Mida!" I called in triumph.

CHOSEN OF MIDA

Sharon Green

DAW BOOKS, INC.

DONALD A. WOLLHEIM, PUBLISHER

1633 Broadway, New York, NY 10019

First Printing, January 1984

1 2 3 4 5 6 7 8 9

 DAW TRADEMARK REGISTERED
U.S. PAT. OFF. MARCA
REGISTRADA. HECHO EN U.S.A.

PRINTED IN U.S.A.

Contents

1 Journey's end—and the blood of enemies

The lanthay moved easily through the trees, pacing itself, taking into its mouth those leaves which came near it in its passage. Unlike much of our journey till then, the land about us was lush and bountiful, warm during the light of each fey, cool and comfortable throughout each darkness. No longer had we snow and chill, empty forests to pass as best we might, and the lanthay, more a beast of the snows and cold, nevertheless seemed to enjoy the warmth as much as I. We had come a far distance in the hands of feyd we had traveled, a distance so great I no longer knew how many feyd I had been upon the trail. The journey had been long—and solitary—yet my thoughts had used the time well to settle about the explanation of what had occurred, understanding each facet of it so that I might more clearly understand where now I stood.

I sighed as I again considered my position, yet the ever-present anger deep within me stirred. From what point would one consider the beginning of the thing? From the time Mida's Crystals were stolen, from the time my clan-sisters the Hosta were taken by males of Ranistard, from the time I, myself, was claimed by the male Ceralt—or the time I was chosen by Mida and dread Sigurr, dark god of males, to stand in their names and see their will done? Each of these things was a beginning of sorts, a beginning of pain and shame and disaster and loss, a beginning of new, misunderstood occurrences which neverthe-less were linked one to the other. My understanding was now complete, yet at what cost?

I reined in the lanthay and dismounted, tethered it to a tree where it might feed, took a cut of meat from its pack for myself, then placed myself where I might watch all about me as I fed. With my return to lands where game was plentiful, it was necessary to recall that predators were also plentiful, children of the wild whose teeth and claws would make short shrift of the unwary. Not three feyd agone had I slain a large yellow zaran, my spear taking it in the chest as it leaped up to strike at my

7

tethered lanthay. The lanthay had nearly torn loose from its rein, so violent was its fear, yet the leather had held and I had been able to calm it. Surely Mida continued to watch over her warrior, for without the lanthay my journey would have been much longer.

I took a slow bite from the meat held in my hand, raw and bloody nilno, freshly killed, sweet and satisfying, chewing the thought as I chewed the meat. Ever had I been wont to think of myself as beneath Mida's protection, yet now the conviction brought many memories of recent happenings and revelations, few of them pleasant. I, who was Jalav, war leader of the Hosta, greatest clan of all the Midanna, had been chosen by Mida as the sole warrior to do the work she had envisioned for me. My sisters of the Hosta she had allowed to be taken by the males of Ranistard as mates so that Jalav alone would be left to lead all of the other clans of Midanna, unprejudiced in this leadership through the absence of all other Hosta. My pain remained great that the Hosta might not be freed of their bondage to males till the strangers had been seen to, the strangers who would come from the skies to touch our lives with the power of their wills. I still knew naught of what they wished of us, yet Mida had assured me they were no other thing than evil.

Evil. Had we true need of evil, there was little need to look further for it than he called Sigurr, dark god males were fond of cursing by. Sigurr, too, had that which he wished me to do, the raising of his male warriors the Sigurri, and in this Mida had concurred. I was to raise the Sigurri as Sigurr wished, to assist in battle against the strangers, yet when the battle was done, the Midanna were then to turn upon the Sigurri and destroy them, doing them before they might do us so. Sigurr knew naught of these designs of Mida, also knowing naught of the hatred for males which Mida had sought to breed in me by placing me in the capture of males, theirs to do with as they pleased. Much had such hatred begun to grow in me at the doings of the male Ceralt—till I discovered that the shame and humiliation given me was deliberate, to see that I felt pleasure rather than pain at the death Ceralt was fated to find at journey's end. Then, for some unknowable reason, the male had changed again, once more becoming the Ceralt whose presence had ever caused me weakness and inner fire, a burning to be held in the strength of his arms, a trembling to feel the touch of his lips, a consuming need to be used by his manhood. At journey's end, with Ceralt's death a certainty and quite near, I had bargained with the dark god for Ceralt's life and health, allowing Sigurr and Mida to believe it was vengeance I sought from the male, a vengeance impossible to claim from one who no longer lived. Sigurr had demanded a price which I had paid and Ceralt's life had been returned to him—yet the price had been so great I no longer was as I had been.

I finished the balance of the nilno between my fingers, sucking up the last of the juices before putting my head back to the tree I leaned upon. My body appeared as it ever had, large of frame, full-breasted, long of leg, the bruises Sigurr had made long gone from my flesh, yet was that flesh now dead to the touch of males. Shortly before my departure from Mida's domain I had sought the truth of the thing, as it had been some time since Sigurr had touched me and I had thought my body recovered. My quarters contained a number of male slaves, large, broad, well-built males—were one to discount the look of perpetual fear in their eyes. I had removed my leather breech and fur boots and had stood myself before them, demanding that they look upon me and feel the need they were not often allowed to see to. Males find pleasure in the look of Jalav and so had it been with the slaves, their desire showing clearly beneath the short, foolish cloth worn about their waists. Their eyes grew bright and their tongues moved to wet their lips, yet when I lay myself upon the fur before them and commanded them to heat my blood, they were unable to do so. Much did the males weep with their failure, so badly in need were they, yet they dared not touch me while my desire failed to be a match to theirs. In disgust and anger I returned them to the wall they habitually knelt before, backs to the wall and hands locked behind their necks, so their need might not be seen to in solitary action. Again the males wept, the strain upon their flesh made more evident by the position they had been commanded to, and then had Mida appeared in her golden mists, to laugh with great delight at that which I had done to the males. She commended the hatred I showed, a hatred she had striven to breed within me, and I said naught of the true motives which moved me to act so. Had there been aught within the males to recall to them their lost strength, surely being shamed and denied so would have brought it forth to battle the fear laid upon them. I sought for a sign in their eyes that they felt a desire for lost freedom of action, yet their continued fear of Mida was as clear as the sign Mida and Sigurr had placed upon me. The males remained slaves, Mida felt pleased, and I—I continued with that which I was destined to do.

The warmth of the lovely fey tugged at me with fingers of drowsiness, seeking to draw me down to slumber amid peace and plenty. It had been nearly two hands of feyd since I had discarded the tent which had kept the life within me in the cold lands, gladly returning to sleeping with naught about me save a lenga pelt. The leathers and furs I had also discarded, retaining no more than the breech about my loins, the leg bands for my dagger, the sword belt for my sword. My legs felt the lighter for the loss of the leg furs called boots, and I gloried in the return of the touch of sweet ground beneath my bare feet. Much had my previously lost freedom been returned to me—should one discount the presence of the sign placed upon me by Mida and Sigurr.

My fingers stole toward the life sign which had hung between my breasts since the time I had first become a warrior, yet memory of what had been done stopped them short of their goal. My life sign was the sign of the hadat, clawed and fanged child of the wild, carved from the tree marked as mine at my birth, stained with the blood of the first enemy I had slain in battle. Ever had it hung upon its leather tie about my neck, yet it, too, was not now what it had been. Its substance was now much like that of Mida's Crystals, seemingly thin and fragile yet possessing great strength. Within it—within it roiled the black mists of Sigurr, marking me as his, showing the rot he had begun in my soul. My life sign had ever been the guardian of my soul, yet now there was little left for it to guard. The Sigurri would know me as a messenger from their master, the Midanna would know I spoke with Mida's voice—and I would strive to forget that which had made it so.

The lanthay raised its head sharply, sensing the approach of danger, and I, too, found the scent brought upon the changing breeze. Lenga prowled the area thereabouts, hunting for prey, seeking intruders within their domain. Resolutely I rose to my feet, untying the lanthay and then vaulting to its back. The Midanna Mida had told me of would not be far distant, for the city of Bellinard, their goal and mine, lay no more than another fey's travel before me. When the Midanna were mine, when Bellinard was taken and the plight of the Hosta known to those who would strive for their freedom, when the Sigurri had risen and come to stand with those who fought the strangers, then perhaps would Jalav be free to taunt the lenga in their domain, courting an end to a burdensome existence. Little else had Jalav to seek, little else had Sigurr—and Mida—left to her.

The fey and the darkness beyond it passed easily and swiftly, the new fey growing to a fine semblance of that which had passed. As the forests began to thin I turned south to remain within them, seeking signs of the Midanna warriors I knew to be in the vicinity. Mida had appeared to Rilas, Keeper of our clans of the Midanna, in a dream, speaking to her of the need to bring the Midanna to the land of males, there to do the work which would be given into their hands. Rilas had no knowledge of who would bring Mida's word to her, yet had we known each other well before the Hosta rode out to seek those who had stolen Mida's Crystal from us. Rilas would know me, and Mida's sign as well, and no more would stand before me than the swords of the war leaders who had led their warriors where Rilas directed.

It took perhaps another three hind before I found the first of the signs left by Midanna warriors to guide other Midanna to them. The signs were composed of little more than twigs bent and broken just so, leaves torn from branches in a particular manner, notches cut in trees above the level of one's eye, and such like, yet to Midanna the trail was clear, the direction unmistakable. Ahead of me lay the warriors I sought, those I had not seen for too long a time. I urged the lanthay forward, eager yet cautious, for to appear too abruptly before Midanna warriors who know themselves surrounded by enemies is hardly wise.

I rode for perhaps five hands of reckid, following trail signs, noting that the forests again began to thin. Had I continued on in the direction I rode, I would have come to the gentle ground slopes which led to the city of Bellinard. My warriors and I had paused behind the last of these slopes before a hand of us had continued on to the city, leaving behind twenty hands of Midanna and four hands of captured males, one of whom had been Ceralt. I had often wondered how the male fared, for I had left Mida's domain shortly after Ceralt and his people had been released, taking a way shown me by Mida which had sent me through other lands than those which the village folk traveled. Though on the mend, Ceralt had been too weak to sit a lanthay, needing, instead, a litter upon which he might lie as it was drawn forward by a lanthay. Lialt, his brother through blood, and Telion, male warrior and brother through choice, had found it necessary to tie Ceralt to the litter, for Ceralt had not wished to use the device he so obviously had need of. The thick-headed male would have clung to a lanthay's back had the choice been his, reopening his wounds and wasting whatever strength he had managed to reclaim. My anger at such foolishness had been great, but Lialt and Telion had seen to the matter without my intervention. I could not have shown my true interest in the males without endangering them all, yet I had watched their departure from a distance, openly in the sight of Mida, my left hand caressing the hilt of the sword she had given me. Much did she believe I longed for the fey I might ride at the males with bared blade; however never again would I seek the males out, for whatever reason. Males and warriors were not meant to mix, a thing which had been well proven to me.

"Hold there!" came a voice out of the woods, causing me to draw rein upon my lanthay, and then were there six warriors afoot about me, each clad in Hitta blue. Their life signs swung as they moved about my mount, four with swords held ready, two with bows as yet unbent, but ready. My hand had moved toward the sword I wore, more in reflex than through desire for defense, yet swords instantly rose higher and arrows held steady in now-taut bows, speaking more clearly than any words. Slowly and deliberately I moved my hand from the sword hilt, then looked upon her who seemed to lead the band.

"I am Jalav, war leader of the Hosta," I informed her, my gaze cool and level, my voice calm. "Take me to the tent of Rilas, for the Keeper awaits what word I bring."

"If you be Hosta, where are your clan colors?" demanded the warrior, eyeing the two silver rings I wore in my ears. She, like the others, wore no more than one, the sign of a blooded warrior. Two rings denote a war leader, as she knew, but yet lack of clan colors still made her suspect a stranger. Each of the Hitta was secure with the blue of her clan about her womanhood, her breasts as free to the air as mine, her feet as bare as those of a child of the wild. Each stood secure with her sisters beside her, yet I had lost the clan which was the source of my pride, the roots of the tree of my life.

"I have put aside my clan colors till the Hosta may be freed from capture," said I, the bleakness in my voice so clear that the warriors before me frowned and withdrew their weapons somewhat. "Now do I ride in Mida's name, doing her bidding, that the Hosta might be succored the sooner. Where is Rilas?"

"Her tent stands deeper in the woods," said the warrior, decision coming to her quickly. She sheathed her sword, surprising the others, then gave free rein to her desire to stare upon the long-haired beast I rode. "What mount do you have, war leader? Never have I seen its like before."

"It is called a lanthay," said I, knowing I had been correct to keep the giant beast. The word I brought would be difficult for many of the Midanna to accept; the lanthay, never having been seen before by Midanna, would do much to awe them into acceptance. By Mida's wishes do all Midanna live, yet many war leaders believe that they alone know the true will of Mida. Then did I dismount and say to the warrior, "Take me to Rilas."

"At once," said she, signing to the others that they were to resume their guard posts. The others obeyed, melting back into the trees, resuming the places they had had before my appearance. The warrior led me through the forest, walking beside me, covertly examining my thigh-length black hair, the matching blackness of my eyes, the loftiness of my height. She, herself, had hair so light it was well nigh as white as my lanthay's fur, falling to her thighs with naught save war leather to keep it from freedom. Her direct and piercing green eyes rose to a lesser height than my black ones, though this warrior had been the largest of those I had come upon. She and I continued on in silence a moment, then her gaze came to study me directly.

"War leader, I know you," said she, her eyes unfaltering. "The fey the Hitta and Hosta met the Silla and Semma in battle. You slew the Semma war leader, and I took the lives of three of the Silla. There was much glory that fey, and I remember you well. Have the Hosta truly been taken captive?"

"Would that it were not so," said I, my voice no more than a mutter, my eyes no longer upon her. "By males are they held, within an accursed city, fated to remain in captivity till Mida's will is seen to. How many clans has Rilas brought to this land?"

"All of our clans answered the Keeper's call," said the warrior in surprise. "Is there a sister clan among us who would refuse? A full nine clans have come to battle the males, yet Rilas knows not where the battle is to begin. Is this the word you bring?"

I nodded without speaking, seeking lost pleasure in the sight which now appeared before me. Through the trees, suddenly growing as though from another world, arose the sight of the tent of Rilas, Keeper of our clans, comprising all of the colors of all the Midanna. The white of the Hirga, the orange of the Hersa, the violet of the Homma, the brown of the Harra, the yellow of the Helda, the gold of the Hulna, the rose of the Hunda, the blue of the Hitta, the red of the Happa—and the green of the Hosta. Also was the tent surrounded by warriors draped in these colors, warriors large and proud and eager for battle. Much did I wish that the Hosta might be among them, yet, had the Hosta been there, Jalav would not have been able to lead them all. So said Mida, she to whom every Midanna looked for direction and approval, she who was mother and leader to all. How foolish a warrior would be, to find fault with that which a goddess did.

Many warriors turned to stare as the Hitta warrior and I came through the trees, some exclaiming aloud as they found they knew me. I had made the acquaintance of each war leader of each clan, and many were the warriors beside whom I had fought. The comments grew louder the closer we came, and then was Rilas in the entrance of her tent, a smile upon her aging face, her lean body as straight as ever it had been. Her hair, falling to her thighs and below, was touched with white, no longer the gold of her youth. Her clan covering fell to her ankles, as befitted her station, and it, too, was of all the colors of our sister clans. I led my lanthay up to her, and quickly did her hands come to grasp my shoulders.

"Jalav, you have returned," she laughed, her warmth flowing through her hands to touch my soul. "It has been too long since last we spoke."

"Aye, Rilas." I smiled, placing my own hands upon her slender shoulders. "Much has happened since last we spoke, and you must know of it."

"What of the Hosta?" she asked at once, searching my face with the sharpness of her gaze. "All here have sworn to tear their prison to the ground, can we but find where they are held."

"Their place of capture must continue to stand the while," I answered, withdrawing my hands as the smile left me. "I come from Mida's domain upon this world, and bring her word and will to her warriors. The Hosta may not be freed till Mida's work is done."

"Jalav, I sense a great change in you," said she, withdrawing a step so that she might look more completely upon me. Her eyes fell on my life sign, a frown touched her, and her gaze returned to meet mine. "Come into my tent," said she. "There are many questions long awaiting answers. Who will see to the war leader's mount?"

Her words had been addressed to those about us, and many warriors stepped forward to offer their services. The giant lanthay, with its long silky white hair, had attracted much attention of its own by its unique appearance. Warriors are ever interested in finding superior mounts, for there are times in battle when one's mount can mean the difference between victory and defeat. The lanthay was taken away by a small knot of those who intended examining it thoroughly, and Rilas turned and led the way within her tent.

"Jalav, seat yourself and take your ease," said she, gesturing toward the dark leather of her tent floor. She herself went to the fire which burned below the roof hole, poured two pots of daru, and returned to where I had seated myself. Animal-fat candles stood about the tent in their tall holders, casting shadows about our doings, pointing up the pleasant lack of clutter. My flesh felt the smooth leather beneath it, remembering it from feyd long past, the aroma of daru filled my nostrils, waking the memory of its flavor; all things I had known so well, all things so long denied me.

"Have you no desire for the daru?" asked Rilas, and I returned to a closer awareness of my surroundings to find that she sat before me, offering the pot which had been poured for me. I took the pot with a small shake of my head, then attempted a smile for her hospitality.

"It seems many kalod since I last sat among my own," said I, sipping at the daru so that it might strengthen me. "Daru was given me in Mida's domain, yet the trail from there was long and without it."

"Tell me what befell you, that the journey became one to Mida's domain," said she, sipping at her own pot, her expression hooded. I knew she reserved opinion upon the matter and I smiled faintly, wishing I, too, might have remained skeptical.

"What befell the Hosta were males from the city of Ranistard," said I, leaning at ease upon one elbow. "These males were womanless, and came in stealth to take the Hosta for their own. Much ill was brought to my sisters by such doing, and now they lie as prisoners to the strength of males, used by them, beaten by them, filled with their seed so that nearly all are with child. They cannot stand beside us in battle, therefore does Mida decree that they must be left as they are till victory is ours."

"And you?" said Rilas, watching with pain as I swallowed down the daru in a gulp. "Were you not also taken by a male? How is it you were able to escape their clutches?"

"I?" I snorted. "Jalav was taken by many males, given by some, used by some, fought for by some. The sight of Jalav finds great favor in the eyes of males, yet the doings of Jalav do not find equal favor. Males are fond of a thing termed mercy, and greatly fond of their concept of punishment. Sooner would I have had death."

Finding the pot of daru emptied, I rose to my feet to fetch more of the drink. I seemed to have a great need of it, and Rilas spoke no word till I again sat before her.

"I have not before seen such bitterness within you," said she, giving me the compassion of her eyes. "And yet you were able to escape these males. Were you forced to go without taking some of their blood?"

"I took the blood of none of them," I whispered, closing my

eyes against the pain. "It was my blood which was taken, and my strength, and nearly my sanity. Rilas—"

"Jalav, you have returned!" said she, a strength in her voice as her hand came to my shoulder. "No longer are you in their capture, no longer need you be concerned by them!"

"The concern will never be gone!" I cried, throwing my head up to look at her. "Rilas, I have done such a thing—"

I had begun the words, yet I could not finish them. I shuddered at the memory, knowing beforehand the condemnation which would be mine. To do such a thing for the sake of a male, to barter my very soul for his life—I shuddered again, nearly spilling the daru, and Rilas moved the closer to take the pot from me.

"Tell me of this thing," said she, a willingness to understand strong in her voice. "The dishonor may not be as deep as you believe."

"The matter goes beyond dishonor," I said in a lifeless voice, lowering my head to bury my hands in my hair. "There was a male called Ceralt, he who took me from the Hosta home tents, he who found me after I had escaped over the walls of Ranistard, he who claimed me as his own despite my objections. Rilas, I cannot describe the feelings the male bred within me—hatred and outrage and humiliation and shame—and the deepest concern I have ever felt for another. Mida's world was bright when he held me in his arms, brighter still when his lips touched mine, brightest and most complete when our bodies were one. It was he who was used by Mida to bring me to her, to the domain she holds beside a god of the males called Sigurr. Ceralt's life was to be forfeit to this god of males, and this I could not allow. I—paid the price demanded by the dark god, and Ceralt's life was spared."

"This thing termed price," said Rilas very softly, her hand to my hair. "This is a male thing, is it not? Somewhat like trade, a value for a value? You received the life of the male—and gave what in return?"

Nearly did I sob, so deeply was I touched by the memory of what had been done to me. I sat cross-legged upon the leather, head bowed. Sigurr, thrice-damned, putrid god of males, bringer of agony, bottomless evil, defiler of life—

"He touched my soul and withered it," I choked, nearly unable to speak of it. "Never have I been used so foully, so—Rilas, I am forevermore marked as his, forever ruined for the pleasures all warriors know. I shall never be the same."

"In time, Mida heals all painful memories," Rilas soothed,

her hand yet astroke upon my hair. "The male whose life is now yours—is it your intention to seek him out?"

"I do not wish his life," I said wearily. "Nor do I wish to see him ever again. I shall never be a part of the life which is his, nor is he able to be a part of mine. He is a leader among his males, and I—I must be a leader among Midanna. It is this which Mida wishes, to give her the city beyond the hills."

"We are to take the city?" Rilas breathed, a great gladness in her tone. "This was told to you by Mida? Speak of her domain, Jalav, tell me of the wonders shown you."

I raised my head to see the glow in her eyes, the need to believe that I had indeed seen that which I had spoken of. Rilas would have preferred remaining unbiased in the matter, yet where Mida is concerned, how might a Keeper remain unbiased? Briefly I considered speaking of my thoughts upon Mida's domain, yet the consideration was idle. Had I not yet been shown the truth of the matter, I, too, would have failed to believe.

"There are a few wonders in Mida's earthly domain, Rilas." I shrugged, forgoing any further indulgence in self-pity. What was, was, and might not in future be undone. "Mida keeps those called Midanna by her, yet not Midanna such as we know. They have no enemies within the caverns which are their dwelling place save for Sigurr's males, and these males they are forbidden to raise sword to. Instead, they use sword and shield upon each other in mock battle, a thing which makes them unfit to face even our youngest warriors. Pets, Mida termed them, and pets they are, much in awe of a true warrior. They strut well and boast well—and use males with true eagerness—yet they cannot stand toe to toe with a warrior."

"These—pets—have males for use?" Rilas frowned, displeased to a great degree. No Midanna warrior is permitted the use of a male till she has proven herself in battle. That Mida allowed unproven warriors males was a disturbing note in a tale of wonder.

"They have slaves and captives," I nodded, speaking no more than the truth. "The slaves are at the disposal of all, to be used when need comes upon them. These males are a sorry lot, well made yet spiritless and empty within. The captives are what travelers are taken, such as the males of the set with which I had traveled." I smiled faintly, recalling the difficulty the so-called warriors had had with those captives. "The males were not pleased, nor of a mind to assist in their use. Without recourse to the sthuvad drug, which Mida refused them, they found it necessary to beg Mida's aid before the males might be used."

Rilas snorted in derision, handed me my pot of daru, then drained her own. Well did I recall the dismay of the child-females in Mida's domain when the males had refused to provide them with sport. Much had they strutted and pranced and boasted of their prowess with blades, ranging themselves before the naked males, who had been taken to a large chamber and chained by the neck to the wall. All the males had been taken there save Ceralt, who remained too deeply wounded to be used. The males looked upon those females who postured before them, sent brief glances toward me where I stood by the chamber's entrance, then proceeded to laugh at wenches who presumed to call themselves warriors. Mida's pets grew furious at such ridicule, yet there was little they might do save slay the males. They had no knowledge of rousing a male save through use of the sthuvad drug, and quickly found that the threat of death brings yielding upon a female sooner than upon a male. Should the male truly be in fear of his life, he will most often be rendered entirely incapable of performance. Throughout the exchange, I found it most difficult to remain sober-faced, and then, when the females were most filled with frustration and venom, the golden mists gathered and Mida appeared. Truly did she seem a goddess in her loveliness, her light, gentle laughter an added spur to the fury of her females. Again they begged for the use of the sthuvad drug, and again Mida denied them, yet the males were not to continue in their amusement. To each of the males did Mida point, one by one, and one by one were they forced to their backs as though chained, their desire touched and quickly begun. Before no more than a hand of reckid, each male twisted upon the floor of the chamber, as furious as the females had been, as prepared for the taking as helpless children. Quickly then did Mida's wenches fall upon them, to use them slowly or quickly, to toy with their need or deny them altogether, to do them as they had thought only they might do females. I watched till Telion and Lialt, in mid-curse, were taken together, then did I turn and leave the chamber, oddly contented. Telion and Lialt had used me as they pleased, yet now had they been put to use, as humiliatingly as had I. The experience would do naught for them, for they would remain convinced of their right till life left them, yet had the experience been given them. Perhaps, in the telling of it, other males, possessed of more reason, would see what they did not.

"The caverns of the domain are vast indeed," I continued, watching Rilas rise to refill her pot and then seat herself again before me. "The males of the caverns, Sigurr's males, have a great deal more battle experience than the females, for it is they who challenge intruders. The caverns of the males are somewhat removed from those of Mida's pets, for the two groups view each other with naught save hostility. Before I was given leave to take to the trail, I was made to face one of these males at Sigurr's request.''

"It is best to remain at a distance from free males," Rilas observed, nodding in approval. "This male you were made to face—was there difficulty from the others when you slew him?"

"I was not permitted to slay him," I informed her, again feeling annoyance at the thing. "The male was Sigurr's, therefore in the dark god's province, save should he transgress upon that which is Mida's. My sword found the heart within him, yet Sigurr restored his life before the blade had been withdrawn. His strength to face me was no more, yet his life had been returned to him."

"Mida!" Rilas muttered, her eyes widened more than I had ever before seen them. "Truly this male god has been given powers to rival Mida's. Does she propose to allow the thing to continue?"

Briefly I hesitated, for I knew not how the query might best be answered. Rilas had not stood in my steps, nor seen what I had seen.

"Mida is—in contest—with Sigurr," I stumbled, well aware of Rilas' gaze sharp upon me. "Sigurr proposes that I raise his legions, the Sigurri, to battle beside our Midanna against the coming strangers, thinking that his Sigurri will best us once the greater battle is done. Mida wishes me to raise his legions as he asks, yet we are to destroy them instead when the strangers have been seen to. This, I assured her, would be done with ease."

"Indeed," nodded Rilas with a gesture of contempt. "These presumptuous males will not stand long before our warriors. Have you been told the whereabouts of these Sigurri?"

"No," said I, a contempt entering me to match Rilas'. "Sigurr fears I will lead our warriors in attack against the city his males dwell in, therefore are we to know naught of the city till I and a small band of our warriors are led there by those Sigurri now held captive within Bellinard. Once Bellinard is ours, the Sigurri may be freed."

"I see there is much set to our hands," Rilas mused, sipping at the daru she held, her gaze distant from the tent. "The city of Bellinard must be taken and held, yet these males termed Sigurri must not be slain. What will occur should the Bellinard males use the Sigurri males to battle against us?"

Rilas seemed vexed at the thought, and it came to me how little she knew of the doings of males.

"The Sigurri will not be used so," I informed her, knowing I spoke the truth. "They are now held as slaves by the Bellinard males, and slaves are not given weapons with which they may free themselves. Do you forget that I, too, was held slave in Bellinard?"

"Indeed had I forgotten," smiled Rilas, a smile of revenge in the offing. "Should those who wronged you survive our attack, their disposition must certainly be yours."

"I shall allow none to deny me the pleasure," I smiled in return, setting the daru pot down so that I might stretch at ease upon the leather. "There are those in Bellinard, both male and female, who shall find my wrath to be no small thing. Should they survive they will regret their survival, for I mean to show them mercy."

Rilas began to reply, then swallowed the words, knowing in some manner that I did not wish to speak of mercy. Mercy was a doing of males, far more cruel than any manner of torture conceived of by Midanna. With the black leather of the tent floor comfortably beneath my back and legs, I allowed the weariness deep within my flesh to flow free. There were many things I had learned among males, yet few would find approval among Midanna. When the city was mine, I would see with what approval the males themselves faced them.

"If you hunger, I would share Mida's bounty with you," said Rilas, and then her finger came to the scar still easily visible upon my thigh. "This mark and the others like it—the thought came earlier that you had perhaps walked the lines for enemies, yet surely this cannot be. You have long been absent from the lands of Midanna, and, most importantly, you continue to live."

My flesh twinged to the touch of her finger, my mind returning to the fey I had acquired the scars. I had escaped over the wall of Ranistard the darkness previous, weak with pain and lack of sustenance, seeking no more than my freedom from the capture of males. Then had I met a small band of Silla, two hands of warriors and one who stood as war leader among them, who had also escaped from the city. To keep from being struck down like a herd beast, I had walked the lines for them, passing each warrior and her spear in an attempt to reach the sword at the end of the lines. The toll taken by the spears had been too heavy, and I had been unable to reach the sword stood so enticingly before me. Wrapped in pain, covering the ground with streams of lifeblood, I had fallen short of the sword, unable to rise again, unable to avenge myself.

"Indeed did I walk the lines for enemy Midanna," I growled, forcing my eyes to the tent roof to keep from sending my lust for vengeance toward the Keeper. "Had Mida not intervened I would now be naught save picked bones, yellowing in the light of the fey, that or crippled beyond hope. It has long been my wish to one fey meet those falth again."

"May Mida hear your prayer and smile upon you," said Rilas, a soft understanding to her tone. Her hand came to me where I lay and touched my shoulder, then she rose easily to her feet to go to the tent entrance. Clearly did I hear her call for provender so that we might feed, yet I felt no urge to rise from my back in anticipation of what might be brought. Once again was I among Midanna, once again was it possible for Jalav to rest secure among her own. Rilas returned to seat herself once more, yet my eyes had closed and did not care to open. The air was fresh and clean, the tent was dim, the fey was early, and I had been upon the trail since before the new light. When Rilas did not soon speak again, another spoke in her place and I slept.

When I awoke there was provender awaiting me, that and freshly brewed daru. Rilas had already fed, yet she sat in silence the while I fed, observing the proper manner in which one partakes of Mida's bounty. She sat cross-legged, as did I, finding her long though slit clan covering no hindrance to the position. When at last I had finished the cut of parvan, she watched a moment as I sipped at my daru, then spoke.

"I would now speak of the greatest change about you," said she, her expression carefully hooded. "For many kalod have I seen the carving which was your life sign, hanging upon its leather between your breasts. I believe I know the lines of it as well as I know the lines of my own, yet those self-same lines now comprise other than that which was. What has been done to your life sign, Jalav, and what meaning does it hold?"

Her face, no longer youthful, seemed strained beneath the careful expression which hooded it. Her hand had crept to her own life sign, communing with it as I had often communed with mine, seeking a comfort her eyes denied her. Much did I wish I might give her such comfort, yet comfort was not for Midanna.

"My life sign has been touched by both Mida and Sigurr," said I, finding an acceptance of sorts in the knowledge that naught might be done to change matters once more. "Its substance now resembles Mida's Crystals, and within it roils Sigurr's breath, a sign to his Sigurri that I ride in his name. I am to lead the Midanna to victory in Bellinard, then am I to seek out the Sigurri. All has been decided by the gods; you and I, mere mortals, have naught else to do save obey.''

Rilas' light eyes came to my face, searching deeply for that which I had no knowledge of, finding naught of that which she sought. Long did she stare in earnest search, then her head shook briefly in negation.

"Truly have you become an instrument of the gods," said she, "yet I find naught of concern within you. Do you not fear Mida's wrath should you fail? Do you not fear disbelief on the part of others whose assistance and obedience you must have? Do you not wish freedom from these tasks so that you might once again take up the life you previously led?''

My laugh was short and nearly bitter, and I rose to my feet to turn from Rilas toward the tent entrance.

"I shall not fail," I informed her, my left hand to the hilt of the sword I wore, "therefore is there naught to fear from Mida. The belief of others is unnecessary to me; I require naught save their obedience. As to the life which once I led, think you one chosen by the gods will be allowed to return to so mundane an existence? Should I somehow find less success than is acceptable, my soul is forfeit; should I succeed in all tasks set to my hand, there will be other things required of me. To believe otherwise would be foolishness.''

A sound came, as of Rilas rising to her feet, and a moment later a strong, steady hand came to my shoulder.

"You are no longer the Jalav I once knew," said she, and a pride of sorts was to be heard in her voice. "You show the strength and wisdom of one worthy of Mida's blessing. There will be great glory in your doings before Mida gathers you to her bosom, and I am honored to be allowed to assist you. Will you walk about the camp with me, so that the others might see you?''

I stood a moment reflecting upon the glory Rilas spoke of, yet bitterness was idle under such circumstances. I nodded in reply to her request, feeling her gratitude in the squeeze of her hand before she withdrew it from my shoulder, and then we two left her tent.

The greened sunshine came through the trees, warming the camp through which we walked. Mida's light was past its highest yet strong for all of that, adding to the new strength I felt within me. I had slept no more than two hind, yet the sleep had been a deep one, untroubled by thoughts of predators on the hunt and enemies stalking my trail. Many and many Midanna were about, each in her own clan color, a large number eager to approach Rilas and myself to ask of what occurred. We walked slowly as I explained that I had forsaken Hosta green till the Hosta might be freed of their bonds, and murmurs of approval came from those who heard my words. For a Midanna to be bereft of her clan colors was a heavy burden, one no warrior took up without good cause. Many of the Hosta's sister clans were eager to set about freeing them, finding disappointment in my assertion that such an act was not yet to be. That we were to take the city they camped near and then battle strangers from the depths of the unknown was something of a distraction for them, yet Midanna find it difficult abandoning their own, especially when their own are in need of assistance. They would do as Mida wished, yet the Hosta would not be forgotten.

With nine full Midanna clans upon the same quest, the camp was large indeed. Each clan numbered greater than twenty hands of warriors, some walking about with Rilas and myself, some taking their ease where they had set their sleeping leather, some practicing at weapons, others gone about the business of hunting for the camp's provender or standing watch about its perimeter. After a few reckid of walking, we came upon a clearing which was guarded by many warriors armed with sword and spear, in the midst of which were more than ten hands of males, bound hand and foot with leather, their throats also circled by leather which held them fast to trees. The captives, city males by the appearance of their cloth body coverings, were for the most part hard used, their cloth coverings slit open to display the sight of male strength, their eyes dull from pain and use of the sthuvad drug. Some moaned in their misery, yet some were recently enough taken that they had not yet learned the proper manner before their captors. They fought the leather which bound them, sweat glistening upon their hard, strong bodies, curses falling in fury from their lips. There were three of those who fought so, and their eyes came to me when I paused to inspect them.

"Hunters from the city we mean to take," said Rilas, indicating the males within the clearing. "We take no others than those who approach our camp too closely, for we do not wish to alert those within. They are far too few for the needs of our warriors, yet must we make do with that which Mida sends us. After the city is ours, our warriors will have the pick of the captives."

"You there!" called one of the three males as I nodded at Rilas' words. "You in the breech!"

"Silence!" snapped one of his guards, a Hirga by the white of her clan covering. "The war leader wishes to hear naught of male prattle!"

"Prattle!" exploded the male, his broad face atwist with anger. "When I speak to a wench, there is naught of prattle about the conversation—for the wench is not allowed speech of her own! By the look of her, that black-haired wench stands high among you, and therefore do I demand that she attend me! She, at least, may comprehend the jeopardy you all stand in!"

The Hirga scowled in insult and raised her spear to attend the male with its haft, yet I stepped forward and stayed the blow. Many males, in supposed superiority, speak freely of that which a warrior wishes to learn, in an attempt to force the warrior to bow to his will. Should this male be as foolish as others, surely would he speak of Bellinard and what changes had occurred since last I had been there.

"You wish to speak with me?" I said, moving farther toward the place where the males lay. The eyes of all three were upon me, their gazes moving from breasts to thighs and back again, finding pleasure in the sight of Jalav. They, among all the others, had coverings which were whole, showing they were as yet untouched.

"I do not speak with females," growled the male who had called to me, his dark eyes attempting to master mine. "I am accustomed to commanding, they to obeying. My men and I are to be released at once, else will it surely go harder for you when the High Seat's guard have captured all of you. I, myself, will buy you when you have been declared slave, and your conduct at this moment will determine what treatment you receive at my hands. Now: have us released, and with speed!"

Closely did the male look upon me, clearly expecting immediate obedience to his will. Easily might it be seen that the pompous oaf knew naught of value, therefore did I turn to the Hirga who stood not far distant.

"I was mistaken in believing this male wished to speak with me," said I to her evident disapproval. "As he commanded, he is to be released at once—in the charge of whichever warriors wish his use. You are to see to it."

"At once, war leader," laughed the Hirga, turning to gaze upon the frothing fury of the male, who had heard my words. I ignored his shouts and demands as I returned to Rilas and the others who awaited me, recalling the hatred which had filled Ceralt and Telion when they thought upon their use as captives. Much had they cursed their time at sthuvad use, recalling naught save humiliation and pain, burning to be avenged against those who had used them so. And yet, when it had come to the use of Jalav, naught save pleasure did they think they gave her, no bitterness, no humiliation. Males are peculiarly sightless in their doings, knowing no more than their own desires, their own needs and wants. To speak with one was an exercise in frustration; to reason with one an impossibility. Males possess no reason, no more than the children of the wild.

"The males seem angered," Rilas chuckled, walking beside me as I continued on. "Males are ever angered when warriors teach them their place."

"They will soon have little strength for anger," I observed, seeing the number of warriors who came at the Hirga's summons. The males themselves no longer shouted and cursed, for the sthuvad drug was even then being forced upon them. They would be made to serve till the drug's lust left them, rendering them incapable of further service till the drug was given the following time. In such a way must males be used when many wished to use them, for males were not like females. No drug was needed by Sigurr's males when they took the use of the females of the set accompanying me, their rightful spoils as the males of the set had been for Mida's pets. Much had the females screamed and thrown themselves about in attempted escape, yet the males, in laughing pursuit, had netted them all. They had each been stripped of the leather they wore, forced to stand bare before the males who meant to take them, then one by one were put to their backs and used before the others. Few had found enjoyment in their use and, as the time passed, true pain was brought to them. The number of Sigurr's males was large, far larger than the number of females to be used, yet each male had taken his full turn before the wretched females were released. I had been made to watch the proceedings by Mida, shown the doings through her golden mists as we sat within her chamber, forbidden to turn and walk from the sight. Shortly thereafter I had been required to face Sigurr's male with blades, and great had been my pleasure when my point had entered his chest. Would that Sigurr had not reclaimed the life of the male.

The walk beneath the trees of the forest continued, Rilas directing our steps to the left of the captives' clearing, toward another small clearing among the greenery. I thought little concerning this new direction, yet once we had neared the place of fewer trees I saw something that captured my attention as a zaran captures its prey. The clan coverings about the bodies of the warriors there appeared to be the red of Silla trash. My head came up as my hand went to my sword hilt, yet Rilas' hand came to cover mine.

"You are not mistaken, Jalav," said she, a hardness having entered her tone. "They are indeed Silla, yet have we agreed upon a temporary truce with them. They have lately escaped capture by males, and have offered their swords in our cause should we allow them opportunity for revenge. I have not yet given my final decision upon the matter for they are, after all, Silla, yet do I feel we must consider their offer carefully before rejecting it."

"There is no more than one thing to be considered," said I, keeping my eyes upon the red-clad forms to be seen through the trees—and my hand upon the sword I wore. "Are they in possession of your word that no harm shall come to them the while they remain here, or are they free to be faced and challenged? This I must know at once, Rilas, for I would not sully your word with my actions. Should the need arise, I will follow them from camp upon their departure."

"For what reason do you ask this, Jalav?" said she, a frown of displeasure in her voice. "Do you have quarrel with them upon other grounds than that they are Silla?"

"Indeed," I nodded, a great, grim pleasure filling me. "It was they for whom I walked the lines, they who took no care to dispatch an enemy before she might fall into the hands of males. I swore they would regret not having taken my life, and now shall they see how Mida rewards the warrior who rides in her name. Speak to me in answer, Rilas, for I will not stand here long in talk."

"The truce was one guaranteed by their actions," said she, her voice filled with anger. "They made no mention of having faced one of our own, an admission of guilt wordlessly put forward. The truce is no more."

"And soon, Mida willing, they will be the same," said I, immediately moving forward toward those hated forms. I strode quickly to the clearing and entered it, drawing no more than a glance from those Silla seated and standing about. What need had they to concern themselves with those who came and went— did they not have a truce to protect them? She who stood as war leader to them conversed with two others without turning, yet I knew her without having the sight of her face. Her features were graven in my memory, the sound of her voice raised in laughter over my agony clear beside them. Never would I forget her—till she lay lifeless at my feet.

"Helis," said I, astand in the middle of the clearing with none between us. My voice, filled with the venom I had so long choked on, reached her and brought her head about with a frown, her eyes searching for the one who called her by name. When her gaze fell upon me she stared in disbelief, then turned full around to face me with that disbelief clear in the stiffening of her body.

"You!" said she, taking one step forward before halting, her hand stopped just short of the sword she wore. "You were not—How is it possible you—"

"I had no doubt Jalav's charge was true," said Rilas, stepping out to my right as she cut into the Silla's stumbling words, "and now you, yourself, confirm them. You stand accused by your own tongue."

"Accused in what manner?" snapped the Silla, anger all through her. "That this one walked the lines for us was no more than what we would have found at her hands had our positions been reversed! Has a Silla never walked the lines for a Hosta?"

"No Silla has ever been denied individual combat while I stood as war leader," I ground out, returning her furious gaze to me. "When one is a true war leader, one does not fear the outcome of such combat. Nor would I have allowed a warrior who had faced me—with swords or through the lines—to fall into the hands of males. It would have been wiser of you to face me that first time, Silla; I could not then have bested you."

"Nor will you now, Hosta," she returned, quickly drawing her blade. "When my point moves close you will recall the touch of the spears, how sharply they entered your flesh and how thickly your blood flowed. You will find yourself different from what you were, Hosta, and then will you find yourself slain."

The smile upon her lips as she moved forward showed how thoroughly she believed the words she had spoken, yet the murmur among the warriors accompanying Rilas and myself was more important by far. No warrior stood in that forest that fey who did not know of some warrior who had returned from a wound less than she had been than before the wound. To feel metal in one's flesh and give drink to the ground with one's blood is not a thing easily forgotten, a thing to be dismissed as though of no consequence. If I were to lead our clans against Bellinard as Mida wished, the warriors and war leaders who had accompanied Rilas must be shown I was not less than I had been. Perhaps, had I not been touched by Sigurr and chosen by Mida, the task would have proven itself more difficult.

Without words, I drew my sword as the Silla had done, moving forward to match her advance, doing naught to bring her attention to my blade. The sword given me by Mida was of a pair with the dagger worn in the leg bands upon my right leg, the blades pale gold, the hilts silver-chased black, the weapons odd enough to give one pause. Never before had I seen their like, with strokes put upon the blades which spoke in a tongue I was sure none knew, and I had no wish for sight of them to strike fear in the Silla's heart. That I used Mida's weapon to face the Silla was of no consequence; it would be *my* skill which bested her, *my* vengeance which took the blood from her as her commands had taken the blood from me. Her life was mine, and it would be I alone who took it.

The Silla, filled to overflowing with confidence and pleasure, awaited my arrival in the center of the clearing. As I approached her, her blade flashed out, a vicious stroke meant to wound rather than kill, an attempt to drive me back in fear rather than a true beginning of combat. I raised my weapon and slipped the stroke with no effort, showing clearly by my failure to return the stroke in kind that I had no interest in engaging in the play of warriors-to-be. The smile and pleasure faded from the Silla's face as her gaze met mine, ending the foolishness of play, bringing a grimness upon her to match that which she saw in me. It had been her choice to stand as war leader to her small band of warriors, to take the place of Zolin, true war leader of the Silla, she whom I had previously bested and slain. Now would she learn the meaning of that which she so ardently desired, the glory of being a war leader to Midanna—and the demands of the state.

Helis' weapon slashed toward me in true attack, and as our blades met I felt the thrill of battle flash through me, setting my blood to singing, bringing me truly alive. So long had been my time of capture by the males, so long had I been forced to swallow the bile of insult unchallenged, so long had I been denied the glory and satisfaction of battle! The weapon I held was perfection for a warrior, beautifully balanced, sharp and strong, able to withstand the edge of the Silla's blade without losing its keenness. Our blades rang again as the Silla's point attempted my flesh, yet was it my edge which gleamed with abrupt crimson as Helis proved herself awkward in guarding after attack. Upon her forearm was a matching line of red which paled her skin with its presence, which shook her body with a brief tremor, which added worry to the look in her eyes. The fear she had hoped for had not found me, yet was there another upon whom such fear might fall. My hand closed more tightly about the hilt of Mida's sword, and then was the battle so eagerly sought by Helis brought to her.

The battle after first blood, which took little time, was much of a disappointment. The Silla brought her sword up to guard against my attack, yet the fury of the assault drove her slowly back across the clearing. Helis was a blooded warrior and therefore hardly one to give over her life before the final swordthrust, yet had she become leader of her sisters through no more than words. Each warrior who wore the second silver ring of a war leader had taken that second ring from the ear of the war leader she had slain and replaced, proving her worth as a warrior and her superiority to she whom she had slain. It had been I, not Helis, who had bested the Silla war leader, and this fact took great toll from what confidence Helis had been able to generate. Her defense quickly grew fearful and unsure, her sword no longer daring to thrust at me lest I discover another unguarded road to her flesh, her body shuddering when my edge or point reached her despite her efforts at defense. The Silla bled from nearly as many points as I had bled, yet she made no more outcry or protest than I had made, warming me to her despite the red of her clan covering. I had been so long among city and village slave-females, those who wept and cried out in their pain and fear, those who cringed and begged for mercy at thought of punishment to be given them by their males; the Silla knew herself bested yet continued to face me, thereby earning the right to a speedier end to torment. I struck hard, with much strength, knocking her blade from before her, then thrust forward to see my blade bury itself in her chest, below and between her breasts. The Silla's eyes widened as her body convulsed, covering my blade with a torrent of red, and then Mida's light was gone from her eyes, showing her soul had already fled. I withdrew from her before her body fell to the sweet ground, then turned with dripping sword to face the others of the Silla.

"Which others among you would stand as war leader?" I demanded, looking from one to the other of them as they stared at the lifeless, untenanted flesh which once had been Helis. "Which of you burn to face me with swords, to prove that I am no longer fit to be called Midanna?"

The Silla stirred at my words, their eyes coming to study me where I stood, feet spread, body and sword readied, head held high. The hands of one or two flexed toward their swords as lips tightened and growls arose in their throats, yet they knew well enough that their skill with swords was not equal to mine. To face me singly would be sure death for her who made the attempt, yet did the Silla trash stand two hands in number. One among them whispered to the others, another added agreement and encouragement, and then were they all rushing forward, sword in hand, voices raised in battle cry, to face me together as they had not the courage to do separately.

The first moments were a flurry of sword thrusts and raging shouts, attack and defense, madness and more madness. I struck away blades thirsting for my blood, taking small toll in counter-thrusts among the number of swords before me, thanking Mida that not all of them were able to join the line of attack at once. And then those others who had walked with me had joined the battle, engaging the Silla and drawing away all save two. The blood thrummed through my body in true battle appreciation, though my lip curled in disgust at the actions of the Silla. To die in battle is the right of all Midanna, yet no other than Silla trash would fall upon a single warrior in numbers where their own safety would be assured. Had they demanded their right to battle, no others save warriors such as they would have come forward to face them, warriors in numbers equal to theirs. Now they faced not one war leader but several, those who had walked with Rilas and myself, those who had no patience with cowardly actions. The Silla were done sooner than they knew, and the doing took little more time than the telling.

The two remaining before me were those who had urged the others to the attack, yet they, themselves, were less than eager to face me. After a moment of hesitation they emboldened them-selves to strike together, one high, at my head, one low, at my legs. I jumped quickly to my right as they struck, blocking the blow to my head, avoiding the blow at my legs, and then another stood beside me, a warrior with hair so pale it seemed nearly white, one whose clan covering was Hitta blue. The Hitta took the Silla to my left, I the one before me, and soon were the two enemy Midanna again one with their sisters, lying upon the ground amid pools of blood. No single Silla had been spared, as was proper, and when all was done, the Hitta turned to me with a grin.

"Since the moment of their arrival have I been praying for such battle," said she, a sparkle in the green of her eyes. "I salute you, war leader, for having rid us of their presence, and for having provided such sport."

"The doing was not mine," said I, looking about the clearing which had once more regained the peace of battle ended. "The Silla falth brought their own ending upon themselves, choosing death in battle over life in captivity. The choice itself was commendable, yet one does not begin an honorable act with dishonor."

"Silla know naught save dishonor," snorted this light-haired warrior, also looking about herself. "Had they remained behind us when we began our attack upon the city, I would not have known in which direction to point my sword."

"Jalav, how do you fare?" demanded Rilas, reaching me with anger all through her. A Keeper is denied the glory of battle for other glory is hers, yet did Rilas recall the battles of her youth and bitterly regret her loss. She, as Keeper to our clans of Midanna, would not refuse the demands of her position, yet did she feel the bitterness of denial.

"I am revenged, Rilas," I smiled, holding my bloody sword away from her. "The doing provided little of the effort I would have preferred, yet am I revenged."

"The effort was great enough for my liking," said she, frowning as she moved her eyes about me. "How badly do the wounds pain you?"

"Wounds?" I echoed, finding I also matched her frown as I looked upon myself, seeking signs of that of which Rilas spoke. Surely, had I been wounded I would have known it, and yet there, in two places upon my left arm and one place upon my left leg, were signs of where Silla swords had reached me. The wounds were not serious, yet it took sight of them to bring me the burning throb of their existence, the flare of pain I had not felt when I had received them. Had I been asked as to when they had been given me, I would not have found it possible to answer.

"Mida continues to hold her shield firmly before you," said Rilas, a grim pleasure to her tone. "Not only were you able to keep their points from you till the others had joined you, you were also made to feel no pain which might dangerously distract you. With such aid as that, the city will surely be yours."

"It will not fall of its own," said I, pondering what truth might lie in Rilas' words. Had it been Mida's hand which had kept the pain from me, or was there another, unknowable reason for the happening? Perhaps the vague suspicions I felt were unfounded, yet so much had occurred in my life which began as unexplained confusion that I now felt I saw some pattern to the thing—which this latest occurrence lacked.

"Certainly it will not fall of its own," Rilas laughed, looking about to see more and more warriors come streaming toward the clearing from all about. "It is we who will cause its fall, and you who will lead us. Come and clean your sword and tend your wounds, Jalav, and then speak to us of the manner in which we are to take that place of males. All here will listen, Jalav, and all will follow.''

"Aye, speak to us, war leader!" came from all about, the voices filled full with agreement and a willingness to obey. Shining faces surrounded me, faces filled with respect and support, and I saw at last the role played by those Silla who were no more. My own ascendancy to war leadership of all the clans had been accomplished through the slaying of hated enemies, their attack upon me the spur which caused the other war leaders to move in my cause. Here, indeed, did I see the hand of Mida, yet little quarrel did I have with the method used. Far better to spill enemy blood to achieve my goal, for each and every one of my sisters would be needed to take Bellinard. Rilas moved off in the direction of her tent, beckoning me with her, and gladly did the throngs of warriors part to let me pass. I would speak and they would listen, I would lead and they would follow, and then, Mida willing, the city would be ours.

2 Bellinard—and a city is captured

Eager discussions sped away the balance of that fey and half of the next. When mid-fey brought the beginnings of Mida's tears, falling slowly at first and then more and more heavily, it was clear to all that the time to strike was at hand. The rains would drive all city folk within their dwellings, leaving no others save those males in leather and metal to bar our way. We awaited the fall of darkness beneath the trees of the forest, pleased by the touch of Mida's tears yet also thoroughly chilled by them. The warmth of the fey had fled with the brightness of Mida's light, bringing discomfort borne in silence to warriors and discomfort loudly and bitterly protested to the males. The captives, of course, knew naught of what was afoot, and took the gags placed in their mouths and additional leather upon their bodies as punishment for having reviled their captors. No more than two hands of warriors were left to guard the males, those warriors miserable at being left behind, and yet the duty was a very necessary one. Should any of the males succeed in escaping his bonds, many Midanna lives would undoubtedly be lost.

Perhaps two hind past the fall of darkness I led the Midanna from the forest, afoot, across an open expanse, and to the walls of the city. The walls of Bellinard contained two gates, one through which males and their slave-females entered the city, and the other, a goodly distance away, through which no others save the males in leather and metal rode. This second gate, beside the immense dwelling called the palace of the High Seat, was of special interest to me, and yet those who entered through the first gate must needs face the greater hazard of traversing the entire city before reaching the dwelling of the High Seat. The groups of armed males making their rounds throughout the city must be seen to before our descent upon the palace, therefore must a portion of our strength enter the first gate; I felt it needful that I lead them through the city ways, and yet I wished to be beside those who entered so near the main objective of our attack. Rilas had laughed at my quandary, suggesting that I pray to Mida to be allowed to exist in two places at the same moment, and yet the matter was not amusing. How is a war leader to lead if she must be in some place other than before her warriors?

Of necessity, the matter was decided by need rather than desire. It was my desire to accompany those at the second gate, yet was it needful that I lead the way through the city. Tilim, war leader of the Happa, and Rogon, war leader of the Hirga, were chosen to accompany me with five hands of warriors from each of their clans, a large enough force to do that which must be done, and yet small enough to move undetected. The other war leaders disliked having to wait at the farther gate, and yet, as I stood in the downpour beside the darkened city wall, seeing them and their warriors slip away into the darkness to seek the place of the second gate, I felt they would obey me and make no attempt to take the glory of victory before our arrival. They well knew my personal reasons for wishing the city to be ours, and knew also that I would have their hearts should they disclose our presence before the proper moment. Mida would be greatly angered at such foolish behavior, yet I and my sword stood a good deal closer to them.

With the departure of those making for the second gate, I directed the throwing of climbing leather to the metal points atop the wall the balance of us stood beside. Fully five hands of warriors threw the weighted, knotted leather, and yet no more than three lines had to be cast a second time. With all lines secure the warriors scaled the wall quickly yet carefully, for the tears of Mida, however welcome, made the ascent slippery and treacherous. I, myself, waited with the others, sunk in a foul humor yet unable to do aught for it. I had fully intended to accompany those warriors who scaled the wall and faced the males who guarded the gate, yet had there been firm protests from Tilim and Rogon. What would become of our attack should the sole warrior with knowledge of the city and its ways fall prey to some foolish mishap in the wetness, they asked. Jalav might lead nine clans, twenty hands of warriors and more to each clan, yet was she forbidden to lead a mere five hands of warriors to take the males beyond the gate. The two who spoke so did not shrink back from my expression at being told such a thing, yet surely was it a near thing. I spoke no words of my own, recognizing the wisdom of their council even while I reviled the need for such care, and the matter was decided. I stood, the safety of a slave-female forced upon me, foul-humored yet unarguing, awaiting the time my sword might drink of enemy blood with none to deny me.

Few sounds were to be heard through the thickness of the wall and gate, yet even had they not been there, the silence would surely have remained near complete. The warriors ascending the wall had been warned to walk upon feet of clouds as they slew the gate guards with swords of swiftness and silence, and this they did. Within moments of their dropping within the wall, the sound came of the gate bar being drawn back, and then the gate itself, ponderous in its movement yet not impossible, opened to admit us. I, astand where the gate halves met, was first within, yet little was left to be done where the males were concerned.

Beside the gate, to either side of it, stood two small dwellings wherein the males of the gate, males of leather and metal, took their rest the while they remained to guard the gate. As I had thought would be the case, the entire number of males had been found within these dwellings, sheltering themselves from damp discomfort rather than keeping watch for intruders. My warriors had sent them to an eternal watch in Mida's chains, their bloody, lifeless bodies giving full testimony to the destination they had already reached. I complimented the warriors upon their doing, designated those who would keep watch from the shadows for the approach of other males, then led the rest to the first of the city's ways.

The city lay in deep darkness, allowing the warriors who prowled behind me no sight of the tall, close, strangely decorated dwellings which lined the ways we trod. With the number of armed males the city boasted, my force was none too large, and yet to move stealthily with so many in one's wake would surely have proved impossible to any save Midanna. From shadow to shadow did we move, seeking to avoid rousing those males who, though armed, were not of the set of leather and metal. To rouse them would have been more than foolish, for their numbers were considerably greater than ours, great enough to cause our defeat should their appearance cause us delay in facing those others who were indeed of the leather and metal ilk. We, as one with the shadows we moved through, avoiding those few sheltered torches upon dwellings remaining lit in the downpour, moved on through the city ways, grateful that the usual stink seemed washed away beneath the tears of Mida, the slime covering the stones of those ways gone from beneath our feet. They who followed disliked the ways we trod, yet I, who knew them from another time, felt savage pleasure at the manner of my return. Once before had I been taken through these ways, bound in leather, stumbling to the snarling push of males, forced to the darkness beneath the dwelling of the High Seat, chained there and left to rot till it was their pleasure to release me—to the further chains of slavery. Aye, there was much pleasure in Jalav at her return, much pleasure and much anticipation.

There was no battle as we moved through the city ways, for battle necessitates face-to-face, blade-to-blade encounters. Slaughter there was aplenty, of each set of males in leather and metal which we came upon, they knowing naught of our presence till our daggers sank into their throats. I find such slaughter distasteful, even of males such as those, and yet was this slaughter necessary to our purpose. We moved between the dwellings, across the broad expanse at city's center which no longer held tents of many colors, beyond further dwellings to the broad, stoned way which led past solitary dwellings, flowing through shadow and rain and approaching each set of males about these solitary dwellings and doing for them that which must be done. It was necessary to leave no living enemy behind us, yet was I greatly pleased when we had approached the immense dwelling of the High Seat as closely as possible and the necessity for slaughter was left behind.

Or so I thought. Long reckid passed with no sign of our sisters without the second gate, yet was it easily seen, even through Mida's tears, that the males to either side of the gate sat comfortably within their small dwellings. We lay belly down in the wringing grass, our hair and coverings soaked through, our bodies chilling quickly due to lack of motion, I, at least, more aware of the wounds I had received the fey previous than I had been to begin with. To wait further reckid would do little good, therefore did I send warriors toward those males who paced on all sides of the immense dwelling, and then myself led others toward the gate. Once these males were done and the balance of our sisters within the city, we would take ourselves a dwelling called palace.

The foolishness of males is great indeed. Those within the small dwellings wore their contrivances of leather and metal, yet their head coverings had been removed to provide them with greater comfort. Their comfort lasted little beyond our entrance, yet was the battle brisk enough to drive away the chill. He whom I faced was able to draw the sword he wore, yet for what reason he wore a weapon I am at a loss to explain. The male knew naught of the proper wielding of a blade, shown clearly by the manner in which he came at me. It took no more than two strokes to down him, one to block his thrust, one to cleave him from crown to chin, and then were the gate dwellings no longer tenanted by any save Midanna.

"These males are a sorry lot, Jalav," said Tilim, who had accompanied me with others of her Happa. Large was this Tilim, nearly as large as I, with hair and eyes of a crisp brown. "Those by the large dwelling came arunning when we struck here, seeing naught of the Hirga who awaited them in the grass till the ability of seeing was beyond them. Should the balance of these city folk be the same, we shall find the need to battle one another to retain memory of sword skill."

"It is said the best of them stand guard within the High Seat's dwelling," I replied, finding it unbelievable and yet totally believable that not a single male had cried out an alarm. To wish to run directly to battle is clearly understandable, yet to fail to give the alert to those whom one calls sister—or brother, as these were males—is an action fit for no other than a male. For what other reason does one post a guard than to give warning of strangers? Of what use is a guard, if not to shout a warning before taking joyously to battle? It had been clear to me for some time that males are beyond all reason, yet each time the matter was proven anew, I found it difficult believing that any could act so.

Quickly, then, was the gate opened to the balance of our warriors, yet even so their numbers disallowed as rapid an entry. As quickly as they entered did they ghost toward the dwelling of the High Seat, moving in and with the shadows of the darkness, disappearing from sight and sensing after no more than three paces. Our main force would attack from all entries to the dwelling, a second force remaining without, in the darkness, to see to any attackers attempting our rear. I felt more than impatient at the passage of time required to admit all of my warriors, yet did I stand with those who had taken the small dwellings with me and force myself to calm. A warrior in haste is a warrior soon slain, a war leader in haste a war leader without judgment.

Despite impatiences, time does indeed pass. With all of my warriors at last within, I saw the gate bar replaced before taking my small force toward the place of the High Seat. Memories of the past are oft-times dangerous to dwell upon when engaged in actions of the present, and yet how might I have forgotten my capture in that place, the leather and chain I had been bound with when marched through its halls, the hunger and pain I had been filled with, the filth I had been covered with. Those city folk about in the halls had stepped from the path of my warriors and myself, their noses wrinkled against the stench of the dungeons upon us, their faces clearly showing how superior they thought themselves to be to mere savages. I trotted gently and quietly through the rain-soaked grass to the pebbled way before the wide stone stairs, once again surrounded by those who were considered savages, yet this time with a sword in my hand. I would not dwell longer upon the past, would not allow the bitterness and hatred to take me; the present promised a great deal of sweetness, and I had come to take payment of the promise.

At the base of the wide stone steps did I halt to send the advance signal about the circle of warriors which had been formed, paused a moment for the signal to make its way toward those who could not see me, then began to mount the wetly glistening steps. The stone of the dwelling, I knew, was the smoothest of pinks, yet little of the color was to be seen in the flickering of the high torches upon the walls. Again I marveled that no alarm arose from the dwelling we approached so closely, that none had seen the lack of guardsmen in their accustomed places, and yet a question occurred which made the situation blindingly clear in the manner in which these males thought. Who was there about that city for the males to fear? Who would brave their walls and dare their wrath, that they must be constantly alert? Surely was it sublime wisdom that the Midanna had enemy clans to keep them ever alert, ever vigilant against attack, well versed in the doings of battle. Easily might it be seen that behind the walls of males lies stagnation, a state Midanna would not allow themselves to fall to.

The oversized entrance to the dwelling now stood before me, warm, beckoning candlelight spilling out into the dampness of the dark. Within was I able to see the blue of the silk hangings upon the walls, the blue of the floor cloth called carpet, the wood of small platforms and seats, the candleholders of silver, the trinkets, the small weaponry, the vastness. Easily and quietly did I enter within, a large number of warriors behind me, none shouting their battle cry nor rampaging about, for what reason is there to give undue warning to an enemy? There would indeed be screaming and shouting and battling aplenty before the darkness came to an end, yet then, at the very beginning, no one of my warriors, at whichever entrance, voiced an unnecessary cry.

"Jalav, in which direction shall we go?" whispered Tilim, afrown at the hall we stood in which swept away left, right and ahead. Large indeed was the dwelling, which contained many males behind many doors.

"We shall go in all directions," said I, attempting in vain to place what little I had seen of the dwelling in its proper place. "This entire keep must be ours, therefore are you to search each corner of it, leaving no enemy behind you to cause mischief. I, myself, shall see to the level above this one.''

Agreement came from the war leaders about me, their faces showing eagerness to get on with the thing, their hands straying restlessly to the hilts of weapons, their eyes roving the emptiness about us with the eyes of their warriors, all seeking to get on with searching out those they might meet with blades. In each direction, left, right and ahead, did I dispatch them, and then, with eager warriors crowding my heels, did I turn to the stairs which led to the next level of the dwelling.

Well did I know, from my time in Ranistard, that the High Seat of that city kept his own private quarters upon the second level of his dwelling, away from those others who served him and bowed to him, guarded by the swords of males in leather and metal. Mida willing, the High Seat of Bellinard did the same, for it was my intention to capture the male rather than slay him, to give him the justice he gave to others rather than allow him the escape of death. The smooth stone of the steps cooled the bottoms of my feet after the warmth of the blue floor covering I had stood upon, yet the high, warm excitement within me was untouched by an equal cooling. Soon, soon would that place of males be mine as it was destined to be, soon would they learn the danger in taking captive a war leader of the Midanna.

Little was to be seen when we had reached the top of the steps, and that little was easily and quickly attended to. A wide corridor stretched away before us directly ahead, showing the doors to many rooms to either side of the area. In the midst of the corridor was a round, high wooden platform, similar to the sort found in the palace of the High Seat of Ranistard, about which knelt three slave-females set to the task of seeing to the needs of the guests of the High Seat. So quietly had my warriors and myself mounted the steps that they knew naught of our presence till we were upon them, the points of swords to their throats to insure their silence. Wildly and fearfully did they look upon us, their eyes wide, their skin pale, their scantily clad bodies frozen in mid tremble lest they move wrongly and precipitate the points of those swords into their throats. One, a light-haired wench of full figure and pretty face, found the threat too great for her senses to allow. Her light eyes rolled up as her body slumped to the floor cloth, and then there were but two who remained to be questioned.

"Which of these rooms contain males with weapons, girl?" I asked very softly, looking down upon the darker haired of the two slaves. She, slender of body within the short blue slave-covering, stared up at me with great fear and trembling upon her, then forced words from a dry and tightened throat.

"Do not slay us, Mistress!" she quavered, her voice held low through effort, her eyes widened yet further. "We are poor, miserable slaves, ignorant of the goings-on about us! I beg you, do not slay us!"

"What ails them, Jalav?" asked a voice at my elbow as I frowned in displeasure at the slave. A glance showed me the pale-haired Hitta warrior who had stood with me against the Silla, she who had been spoken of as Ilvin by others. This Ilvin was known as an excellent warrior among the clans, yet was she ignorant of the ways of city folk.

"See the metal bands about their throats," said I to Ilvin, nodding toward the females who knelt before us. "These females are slaves among slaves, preferring a life of dishonor and abuse to the swift death refusal to serve would bring them. They are bound to give pleasure to any male who seeks their use, for they have no worth other than that." Then did I return my gaze to the dark-haired slave-female, and show her something of my impatience. "What life you retain is of little interest to me, girl. I seek the lives of the males of this place, and will have an answer to the question I have put to you. Speak quickly and truthfully, lest I grow angry at your lack of aid and allow you to share their fate."

"I will speak, Mistress, I will speak!" choked the slave, squirming her body about somewhat before recalling that she knelt at the feet of those who had no interest in her use. "Four masters are in residence in these rooms as guests, yet are they now in the apartments of the Blessed One, sharing a meal and diversion. Should you spare my life I will serve you, Mistress, as loyally as I now serve the High Seat!"

"I have no use for a slave," said I, gesturing my warriors to the doors along the corridors, intent upon testing the truthfulness of the words the slave had spoken. With all in position my warriors burst within at the same moment, yet emptiness greeted their efforts, no males appearing before their drawn swords. A rapid examination of each of the rooms showed no more than the four spoken of to contain belongings and other evidence of occupation, and soon were my warriors returned to the center of the corridor, to assist in seeing to the slave females. Wisest is to leave no living enemy behind one's back, yet slaves are far from the honor of being considered enemies to warriors. The three females, after being briefly questioned as to the whereabouts of the High Seat, were placed within a room, their wrists and ankles bound in leather, their voices silenced by the presence of cloth in their mouths. Then were we able to leave the corridor of rooms, return to the steps of smoothened stone, and turn left, toward the area described to us as that belonging to the High Seat.

This left-hand corridor took us a distance from the steps, yet were we, when turning a corner, at last rewarded with the sight of males in leather and metal, astand before large carved double doors draped in blue silk. Two hands of males were there before us, more than eight paces from the corner we turned, and yet, rather than give the alarm, all but two of the males advanced toward us with grins upon their faces, slowly drawing their weapons. The warriors in my wake murmured in astonishment, failing to understand this foolish lack of proper defense, yet the actions of the males were scarcely a surprise to one familiar with their ways. They saw before them no more than lowly females, prancing about in little clothing, carrying the weapons of males. Surely would these males before us soon teach us the error of our presumptions, taking our swords and then taking their pick among us for their pleasure. That they thought in such a manner was clearly to be seen upon their faces and in their eyes, yet those obvious desires were not meant to be satisfied.

A number of my warriors stepped out from the others, a number sufficient, with myself, to match the number of the males. This the males found vastly amusing, and yet, when their swords crossed ours, the amusement was not long in duration. Large were these males, appearing larger yet in the leather and metal protection they wore, yet they, though somewhat abler with their weapons than those of the small dwellings beside the gate, knew vastly less of the use of a sword than warriors. One does not, when facing an opponent, keep one's guard down till the very last instant, and yet such was the doing of him whom I faced. Filled full with confidence was this male, his eyes moving about my body rather than seeking the movement of my sword, his grin comprising every insult ever offered me in the lands of males. Anger touched me, and grim pleasure as well, and then the sword that had so long been withheld from my grip flamed toward him, impelled equally by the anger and pleasure combined. Startled, the male lost his grin as his weapon flew up in defense, yet his movements proved too slow to prolong his life. A feint at his face raised his sword, a slash at his legs lowered it, and then was my point deep within his throat, above the piece of leather set there to guard it, spilling out his life blood upon the blue floor cloth beneath our feet. No more than a gurgle came from the male as he staggered then collapsed, no more than the sounds from the other males as they joined him by ones and twos. Scant moments passed before all were done so, and then did I turn from this mockery of battle to see the remaining two, before the large double doors, also asprawl upon the floor cloth, one with a dagger in his eye, the other wearing it in his throat. Their positions upon the floor cloth said they had begun to turn toward the double doors when the daggers caught them, thrown by warriors who had not been engaged with swords. It seemed the males had at last been prepared to sound a warning; a pity for them the thought had come too late.

Leaving the dead where they had fallen, we advanced to the large double doors. Deeply carved were these doors, bearing likenesses of males and females and kand and nilnod and all manner of creatures. From within came faint sounds, mainly comprised of laughter above the rhythmic noises I had once heard produced by males with strange devices in their hands. One device was tapped on by fingers, two others were put to one's lips, and it was now no wonder that naught had been heard within the room of the scuffle produced in the corridor by our arrival. The two males at the threshold had been about to push within the chamber; now we, after leaving four of our number to see to our backs, completed the action for them.

Easily did the doors push aside, bringing to view an unexpected sight. Where the balance of the dwelling seemed nearly stark with no more than silks upon the walls, cloths upon the floors, and platforms stood here and there, the chamber we looked upon was more than cluttered. Blue silk hung everywhere in vast amounts about the large chamber, dim in the edge of the glow from countless numbers of candles in silver holders circling the center of the chamber. Deep-piled and incredibly soft was the blue floor cloth beneath our feet, platforms large and small standing in many places upon it, slaves both male and female astand beside and about them, in the shadows, poised ever ready to be commanded to their tasks. Upon these platforms were metal eating boards, golden and bedecked with many-colored glittering stones, tall pots called goblets astand beside them, also of golden metal and cluttered with stones. Four large, carved seats of wood covered with many-colored silks were filled by four males asprawl in them, goblets held in their fists, laughter flushing their faces, naked slave-females in the laps of three. Perhaps seven paces from these males, facing them and looking down upon them, was the fat, bloated creature males called High Seat and Blessed One. Gross was this male in his draping of blue silk, light-haired and light-eyed and thick in the lips, skin of the apparent softness of a city slave-woman. The seat he sat upon was of the sort called throne, seemingly made of golden metal picked out in glittering stones, wide enough for his massive girth, draped in blue silk, astand upon a platform which raised the seat above the level of the others in the chamber. Two naked slave females waved feather fans to cool the male, two others held metal platters with provender for his selection, yet he, like the others of the males, had eyes for naught save that which occurred in the center of the chamber.

A hand of slave males, naked save for the bands of metal about their broad necks, lay flat upon the floor cloth, each male attended by a slave female. The females, though clothed in brief blue slave coverings, had had their wrists closed in chain behind them and their eyes tightly enclosed in folds of cloth, and in such a manner were they attending to the males, upon their knees beside them, lips and tongues caressing the bodies of the males. Each male was clearly deep in his need, their bodies glistening with sweat, their fists clenched in pain, their faces strained with jaws clamped tight and gritted teeth showing. Had the females been able to see them they would not have been as unconcerned as they appeared, laughing lightly as they caressed the males, murmuring insolently and then laughing further, twisting their bodies about to entice the males. That city folk are beyond reason is known to all, and yet was I unable to fathom the reasons for their behavior till one of the four males spoke.

"At them, wenches, at them with a will!" he called with a laugh, pausing briefly to drink from his goblet. "They are chained tight for this punishment you inflict, therefore may you do as you wish without fear of reprisal. At them again, else face punishment of your own!"

At these words the females again applied themselves to the males, happily, laughingly, ignorant of the fact that the males were in no manner chained as they had been told. My warriors and I stood in the shadows produced by the blaze of candles in the center of the chamber, made silent witnesses to the doings of city males which was considered by them as amusement. I, myself, considered the matter low and vile, on a par with the doings of all city males, and yet, before I might step forward out of the dimness and halt the farce, he who was called High Seat raised one round and delicate hand and gestured to the male slaves flat upon the floor cloth.

Immediately was it evident that the males had been commanded to await such a signal before they might attend to their needs. Almost as one did they rise from the floor cloth to sitting, reach for the foolish slave females who knelt beside them, and then began to teach them the stupidity in believing the words of males. Three of the females screamed out their shock as the brief, blue slave coverings were torn from them, baring their flesh to the males they thought themselves safe from. The remaining two, thrown immediately beneath the males they had tended, choked and shrilled in pain and fear as they were brutally entered before having their coverings torn away. They writhed helplessly upon the floor cloth, their wrists tight behind them, their bodies in the possession of those they thought they punished. Another, begging and pleading, was forced to her back, and then another and another, and then all of the females were in the possession of males, their mewling and wheedling and sudden attempts to give pleasure to those they had laughed at sufficient to bring illness to the strongest of warriors. The males in their seats howled laughter at the sudden predicament of the poor, foolish slave females, yet the matter was hardly one for laughter. How low one must be to take amusement from the distress of slaves!

Of a sudden, I had no further desire to stand among shadows, therefore I advanced into the candlelight, my warriors coming forward with me. The sudden light gleamed off my sword where the blood of males failed to cover its brightness, and gasps and screams and a silence of sorts came when those slaves standing about and the males of noise devices spied us. Last of all to see us were the males in silk-covered seats, those four who sat as guests and the fifth who sat as leader to them, and quickly did frowns replace the amusement they had felt.

"Who are you?" demanded the rounded male, he who was called High Seat. "How dare you enter my apartments without leave? Guards! Attend me immediately! Guards!"

"To call for the dead is idle," said I, moving forward more fully into the light. The male slaves continued to use the females at my feet, their doing more desperation than pleasure. "Do you fail to recall the look of Jalav, male, she who was once declared slave by you? Did you find her so commonplace, then, that she has slipped entirely from your memory?"

"You!" said the male, taken aback by my appearance, now clear to his sight. The pale skin of him turned paler still, the narrow, lazing blue of his eyes clearly to be seen, the shrinking back in his seat most obvious of all. Well did this male now recall the sight of Jalav, she who stood before him with head held high and sword grasped tightly in fist.

"No," he whispered, widened eyes most piteously pleading. "I am High Seat of Bellinard and cannot be harmed! Guards! Guards!"

"Blessed One, my sword is yours!" spoke out one of the four males who sat as guest at the gathering, causing me to turn to him as he pushed the cringing slave-female from his lap and struggled erect. Red of face was this male, portly in the manner of he called High Seat, yet not of such immense proportions. The sword he spoke of was dragged clumsily from its scabbard as he advanced upon me, his steps unevenly slow, his eyes unusually bright. "I shall disarm this one for you," said he, "and close her in slave chains at your feet. The wench will provide sport for us all."

"As will the others," said one of the remaining three, he without a slave female of his own. He rose to his feet, gesturing his companions with him, drew his blade as all three stood together, then led the eager attack upon the warriors who had accompanied me.

"Take them all!" screamed the bloated male upon the raised seat to my right, his voice filled with relief and insane anger. "Take them and chain them and you may have your pick of them, and then shall they be beaten and used and sold as—No!"

The final scream of the male was very high-pitched, as though it had come from the throat of a woman, causing the fourth male, he who advanced upon me, to whirl around in an ungainly manner. The sight which met his eyes was that which had caused the High Seat such distress, the sight of the spitting of the three males who had attacked my warriors. One took a sword through the chest, one through the belly, and one through the throat, each having faced no more than a single warrior. These males were poor stuff, less even than the males of leather and metal we had met in the corridor, their slaying providing more disgust than satisfaction to my warriors. The fourth male, he who now held his sword in a trembling hand, stared in disbelief as his companions fell slowly to the floor cloth, their blood pooled beneath them, then tore his gaze from the sight to turn again to me. A pallor had come to his skin as the trembling had come to his body, and the fear he felt stared nakedly from his eyes.

"I am Jalav, war leader of these Midanna," said I, my voice soft as I held his gaze. "Do you propose to face me as those others faced my warriors?"

Abruptly the male started, as though only then remembering the sword in his fist, his eyes darting to it in terror before his hand flung it from him and his head shook in violent negation.

The male had no stomach to face me, a wise decision for one of his undoubted lack of skill.

"Should it then be your decision to retain your miserable life," said I, "remove your covering and go to your belly upon the cloth before me. To stand erect and proud is a privilege reserved for those who prefer death to dishonor."

Had the male been possessed of some vestige of pride, surely would he then have shown a sign of it. My command struck him to the core of his being, and yet, with no hesitation worthy of the name, he began to claw at his covering, removing it with indecent haste. When once he stood bare before me he also hastened to lower himself to the cloth, yet was the gesture of attempted concealment unnecessary. My warriors eyed the unclothed male slaves with considerably more interest than one would expect to find for a male such as the portly one, yet the portly male appeared unaware of the fact. He trembled as he lay stretched out upon the cloth before me, as though he expected the kiss of a blade—or the touch of a hand—to intrude upon his shame, yet were there other, more pressing matters than the shaming of a male to attend to. I then returned my gaze to the male I had come for, he who was called High Seat.

"No!" screamed that male, a rope of spittle dripping down the vastness of his chins, his body again attempting to shrink back in the seat. That rescue would not be forthcoming was beyond belief to him, an impossibility impossible to comprehend. It was obviously necessary to prove to the male that his position was no longer as it had been.

"Take that one and place him in chains," said I gesturing toward the massive male as I spoke to my warriors, then did I nudge the one upon the floor cloth with my toes. "Also, bind this one with leather so that he may not follow and beg to be used. We have not the time for such frivolity."

The male at my feet turned deep crimson as my warriors laughed, perhaps touched with shame that such a thing might be suggested, perhaps touched with shame that a secret truth had been spoken. A moan of sorts escaped from him, yet was it nearly covered by the screams and pleadings and threatenings produced by him called High Seat as my warriors advanced upon him. The massive male cringed within his seat, holding to one arm of it, attempting to resist the will of warriors who had little patience with the foolishness of males. Chains there were aplenty about the chamber, obviously having been taken from the slaves therein, and the placing of them upon the male, ungently and with little care for his comfort, brought outrage to cover his fear.

"You will all be foully punished for this!" he screamed, struggling in the loops of chain, rising at the urging of pain brought him when he attempted resistance. "I will see you more cruelly treated than the lowest of slaves, worked till you drop, beaten till you bleed, used till you scream—No!"

His declamation ended rather abruptly, due to the cuffing he received from a warrior beside him, a Hersa with less patience than most.

"Silence, male!" she commanded, striking the obese captive with the back of her hand, her orange covering dull in the low lighting. "We may find amusement in male prattle at other times, yet now have little interest in it. Should you fail to keep silent, you will quickly find punishment."

Gasps sounded about the chamber, clear indications of the shock touching the slaves who stood fearfully about, hoping to escape notice. These slaves, male and female alike, would not have dared to speak so to those who had enslaved them, a sure sign that they were indeed slaves. To fall slave may happen to any; to remain slave, and conduct oneself in a slavish way, may be accomplished only by one who knows naught of true freedom.

"We must leave here and rejoin the others," said I to my warriors, some of whom led the High Seat in chains, others of whom had already bound the portly male upon the floor cloth in leather. Of the male slaves who had been allowed the use of female slaves, all save one had withdrawn in fear, lest they be struck down by females with swords for attempting the use of females in chains. This last male, though in possession of a moaning female lost to his thrusts, nevertheless regarded me with unwavering gaze, a faint smile touching him when our eyes met. His hands stroked the body of the female he used, causing her to writhe helplessly, bringing her to a higher pitch of frenzied need. My warriors murmured approval of the display, pleased with the strength and ability of the male, their grins telling him of the interest they felt. His hips thrust hard at the female, drawing a cry of pleasure from her, and then his smile widened to a grin of confidence.

"It would be my honor to give you similar pleasure, Mistress," he said to me, his deep voice husky. "Should I be allowed to live, I would serve you well indeed. A body such as yours must have deep needs not easily satisfied. Take me as your personal slave and allow me to serve your pleasure."

Again the slaves about the chamber gasped, the females fearfully for they now realized how small their value would be to female conquerors, the males in anger that another of their number had so quickly claimed the place in the sleeping leather of the leader of the invading warriors. Those males now stepped forward, their voices raised in protestations of their own ability, setting my warriors to chuckling, for never had they seen males so eager to serve. I, to my surprise, felt some faint stirring within me due to the sight of the male who continued his use of the slave beneath him, yet even had my need been great, another need was greater still.

"Before the pleasures of the body come the pleasures of battle," said I, more to my warriors than to the slaves. "When this dwelling is completely ours, then may we dally and sport. Which of you would remain here in sport with males the while we others join our sisters with swords in our fists?"

"Not I!" shouted my warriors in many voices, all stepping forward with laughter and eagerness, some with swords raised high, causing the male slaves who had come forward to back quickly with the cringing females. He in possession of the female upon the floor cloth no longer wore a grin of confidence, and my laughter narrowed his eyes.

"Do not tire yourself completely, slave," said I to him, the amusement I felt strange after so long an absence. "My warriors will return for you all, of that you may be sure, and then will your ability to give pleasure be put to the test. Do not remove the leather from this portly male, for soon he will be a slave just as you are. Remain in this chamber once we have gone, else your lives may be lost through accident."

The silence of fear greeted my words, therefore did I signal my warriors to follow and quit the chamber, returning to the corridor where we had met the males in leather and metal. He called High Seat, forced by his chains in the hands of warriors to accompany us, stared with horror upon the blood-covered bodies of his males as we passed them, his voice stilled more completely by the sight than by the cuffing he had received. We had a distance to go, however, therefore did I pay him no further heed.

When we had at last reached the stairs we had ascended and again descended to the lower level, we found ourselves quickly embroiled in the sort of battle we had not earlier encountered. Many males seemed to have appeared from nowhere, some clad in no more than the cloth covering of males of the cities, the swords in their hands unmatched by empty scabbards at their sides. No more than the swords had the males snatched, it seemed, and these they wielded grimly against the warriors before them. Some few Midanna lay motionless upon the red-stained floor cloth, yet many more males lay so, mute evidence of the skill of warriors. The sounds of battle seemed to come from all about the dwelling, the clash of metal, the screams of pain, the war cries, the curses, all blending with the swiftly moving shadows cast by the candles upon the walls. Leaving half of my warriors to see that the High Seat did not find rescue by his males, I led the others forward to add our swords to the melee.

Truly must hind have passed in the taking of the dwelling. No sooner did we clear an area of defending males and begin to move forward into other areas, than additional males appeared before us, as eager to test our blades as those left lifeless behind us. No scrap of blue silk hanging upon the walls was left unspattered by blood, no shred of floor cloth beneath our feet retained its once-pure color. On and on we fought, through corridors and within chambers large and small, about platforms of wood and bright metal, beside carven figures of males, before the eyes of fear-filled slaves. At last fewer males appeared before us, then fewer still, and then so few we were able to take captives rather than slay them out of hand. This last set the High Seat again to frothing, for much had he hoped to be freed by his males, and such had they truly attempted to accomplish. It was not until all battle was done and the dwelling was ours that I learned that by far the greatest number of males had stood before my set, their desperation prompting them to attempt the freeing of the High Seat in order to rally those males whose courage flagged at thought of facing Midanna warriors. That their leader had been captured was a heavy blow to their confidence, one they were unable to overcome.

With no further males attempting to engage us, we were able to advance more quickly through the corridors. Not long after we had taken captives of our own, we came upon a chamber guarded by Hunda and Homma warriors, a large number of males bound tight with leather within the chamber. To that number did we add the captives we had taken, my warriors making no attempt to mark them for future recognition. The abilities of a male to give pleasure cannot be known from the manner in which he holds a sword, nor even from how well made he appears. There would be adequate opportunity to choose among the best of the males when once all battle was done.

We then continued our advance, yet not without purpose. Mida and Sigurr had demanded that the city be taken, yet was it necessary to bear in mind that the freeing of captured Sigurri was also demanded of me. The Sigurri males had been declared

slave, therefore were they likely to be found in that place where
my Hosta warriors and I had been held, a large chamber containing metal enclosures, chains and whips, and males of leather and
metal who took great pleasure in the indignities they served up to
captives. Should the Sigurri not be found within the confines of
the chamber, the pleasure received from questioning those self-
same males of leather and metal would then be mine.

The vastness of the dwelling at last forced me to the need for
questioning the High Seat upon the whereabouts of the chamber I
sought. A silence had fallen upon the dwelling, one lacking the
sounds of battle no matter the number of lifeless forms we
passed, one enhancing the sound of the labored breathing of the
obese male we kept to our pace. The male found great difficulty
in moving himself about at any pace above that of one aged or
infirm, yet had the presence of chains upon him given him little
choice in the matter. I paused before a large rendering of a forest
glade which hung upon a wall of pink stone, unsure as to
whether the rendering seemed familiar, and then turned to the
male.

"I seek the chamber in which slaves are kept," said I, looking
down upon the panting male where he stood among my warriors.
"As this dwelling is reportedly yours, you shall inform us of the
proper direction."

"Shall I indeed," wheezed the male, looking upon me with a
great deal of his former arrogance returned. His covering hung
sweat-soaked and blood-smeared upon him, his limbs trembled
with fatigue, his skin retained much of the pallor brought about
by having been in the midst of many scenes of battle, and yet the
light eyes of him regarded me as though I were the one enchained.

"You feel you need not do so?" said I, curious as to what had
wrought the change in him. "Do you forget your position among
us?"

"On the contrary, I have only recently begun to understand
my position among you," said he, straightening in his chains.
"It is now clear that I have considerable value to you savages, a
value I need not comprehend to utilize. Had it been your desire
to slay me, the deed would already have been done; I need not
fear reprisal of such a sort for refusing to aid you."

The smirk he sent was gratingly offensive, just as it was meant
to be. The male had sought for safety in his predicament and
believed he had discovered it, and yet his understanding was not
as deep as true wisdom would have made it.

"You are correct in your belief that I do not wish you slain,"
said I with a nod to the two warriors nearest the male. They

immediately stood the closer to him, removing his smirk and replacing it with a frown. "I, however, am able to command obedience from those about me with less than the promise of death. Extend his hand to me."

The male fought my warriors as best he might, yet was the effort useless. For too many kalod had he done no more than gesture slaves to him with his own strength, an activity ill-suited to the enhancement of such strength. Against his struggles was his soft, delicate hand extended to me, and then was my dagger in my fist and advancing toward him.

"A male may live a considerable time with a finger removed," said I, touching him gently with the cold, sharp edge of the blade. "How many fingers will I find it necessary to remove, I wonder, before you speak the words I have commanded?"

"You would not maim me so!" he whispered, his fear and trembling having returned in greater measure, his light eyes widened nearly to bursting. "You are females, and no females may be so savagely brutal!"

"We are warriors of the Midanna," said I, allowing the edge of my blade to part his flesh enough for blood to flow. "Your well-being means naught to me, male, the use I have for you the sole reason for your continued existence. Such use may be had even should you be fingerless, and once fled, my forbearance will not return."

"I will obey!" he whispered, his frantic gaze seeing clearly that I spoke the truth. "Do not harm me further, I will obey you!"

"Obey, then," said I, making no attempt to remove the dagger.

"You must take the first turning to the right," the male babbled, his gaze now firmly locked to the blade at his flesh. "Pass three crossing corridors, and then turn to the left. At the end of that corridor, on the right, is the place you seek."

"It had best be so," said I, at last taking the dagger from his hand. A faint smear of blood lay upon the edge of the sharpened metal, therefore did I first wipe it clean upon the covering of the male before returning it to my leg bands. The male shuddered at the action, his expression showing illness, unaware of the disgust to be seen upon the faces of my warriors. Further comment was unnecessary, therefore did we continue on.

Faint recognition at last came to me when the final turn was negotiated, putting us within the corridor which led to the chamber of slaves. So vast was the dwelling that surely must I have been taken there by another route the instance previous, rendering what few memories I had of the walk worthless to the present time. Our ranks had swelled since I had paused to question the captive male, for other warriors, wandering through the corridors in search of what battle there was to be found, happily joined our search. Their hopes for further battle were dashed, however, when we entered the chamber to find it already taken. The slaves in their metal enclosures, of course, were as yet undisturbed, yet the same could not be said of those who guarded them. Some few lay sprawled upon the stones of the floor, yet by far the greater number lay bound in leather, taken by the Midanna warriors who ranged about the chamber, curiously inspecting the devices the walls and enclosures held. All whirled to face us as we entered, their swords flashing from their scabbards, then grins of welcome replaced the smiles of pending battle they had worn, and swords were put up once again.

"Jalav, you are well come indeed!" called Rogon, the Hirga war leader who had traversed the city ways with me. Not so tall as others was this Rogon, whose dark red hair fell past her thighs, yet her bright dark eyes had seen the end of all warriors who had sought to take her position as war leader. Quick and eager was her blade, as the blade of a war leader should be, and she grinned quite well as we came up to her. "Before returning to this place I have had messengers from those of our sisters about the dwelling," said she. "All battle appears to be ended and the dwelling ours, yet none knew where to reach you with this word. I now see you were in search of the least of the males of this dwelling, and have found him."

"Indeed," I laughed, turning to gaze upon the High Seat as Rogon did, seeing the flush of anger upon his cheeks at her words. "Indeed did I go in search of this male, and now he is mine. As it is not yet time that he be put to use, I shall keep him here, out from under foot."

I directed my warriors to place the male within an enclosure which was to be heavily guarded at all times, then turned my back upon his pleading protests and began a tour of the chamber with Rogon. As it had been when last I had been there, many of the enclosures contained females, a large number of them entirely unclothed. These females, down to the last of them, wept and trembled within the confines of the metal, cringing fearfully back when my gaze fell upon them. The cause of such great fear continued to elude me, for what warrior would be so low as to offer harm to so poor a thing as a city slave-woman? The males within the enclosures, all chained close to prevent attempts at escape, eyed me quite differently, for males find great pleasure in the sight of Jalav. They spoke no word concerning their position, yet their eyes moved about me hungrily, their tongues slowly wet their lips, their bodies stirred with a clank of chain, and their hands circled the obdurate metal refusing them freedom. Male slaves found little opportunity to see to their needs, yet would they find themselves well occupied when once my warriors found the time for pleasure. The slaves were well made, and sure to be deemed of interest.

One enclosure, containing four males, was of great interest to the war leader Jalav. Large were the males, two light-haired and light-eyed, one red-haired and light eyed, the fourth dark-haired yet not so dark as those of the villages I had so recently encountered. Broad of chest were the males, their arms well-muscled, their waists slim, their bodies deeply tanned, their stare direct and filled with interest, the heavy chains upon their wrists and ankles seeming lighter by cause of the unconcern of those who wore them. I examined them as overtly and with as little attention as I had examined the others, yet notwithstanding the fact that I had never seen them before, I knew them at once. All four wore black cloths wrapped about their loins, and all four showed, seemingly impressed within the flesh of their left shoulders, the stroke which stood for the male god Sigurr. The stroke, called letter by males, was one of those taught me by Lialt during our journey to Sigurr's Peak. Black was the stroke upon the bodies of the males, the color of Sigurr, the color of agony well remembered. I turned from the males as their eyes burned into me, denying my hand the wish to reach for my sword hilt. Captives were the males and captives would they remain the while, for other matters needed attending to. When once all else had been seen to, Sigurr's males might then be released. In the interim, they would not stray.

"See our fine collection of captives, war leader," said Rogon, nodding to the bound males we now approached. "My warriors were anxious indeed to return to them, for soon their use will be ours."

The warriors standing guard about the captives laughed softly at Rogon's words, yet the captives themselves failed to share the amusement. The males pulled at the leather which bound them, attempting to break free, yet those bound by Midanna rarely find escape easily accomplished. And then I saw those I had never thought to see again, and I stopped to stare with a great delight filling me.

"We know not why the female failed to be enclosed with the others," said Rogon, following my gaze to the two I stared upon. "She crept about behind these males, attempting to be one of them yet refusing to take sword in hand, and we knew not what was to be done with her. She is undoubtedly slave to him she lies beside."

"I am slave to no man, you bare-breasted hussy!" snapped the female Karil, struggling uselessly in her bonds. She it was who had greeted my warriors and myself when first we had been brought to that chamber, she it was who had attempted to lure males into my purchase as slave, she it was who had brought me shame and pain when I had refused to acknowledge myself slave to her and the male she lay beside. He was the male called Bariose, the one who saw to male slaves as Karil saw to female. It had been his hand which held the lash when it had struck me with fire, and this the male recalled when his gaze met mine. Large was the male, and well used to the ordering about of other males and slaves, and yet that which he saw within my eyes caused him to lay totally unmoving in his bonds.

"There is now a thing to be done with the female," said I, looking upon the indignation of her called Karil without expression. "And the male as well. Unbind their ankles and bring them before me."

"At once, war leader," acknowledged Rogon, gesturing warriors to my bidding as I turned and walked toward the center of the chamber. I knew not whether Mida would care for my taking revenge at that time, and yet, with all battle done, what better time might be found?

In no more than a moment were the male and female, freed of their ankle bonds, brought before me. I stood at the center of the large chamber, surrounded by the enclosures of slaves and the lines of warriors of the Midanna, and looked upon the dark-haired male and female with distaste.

"When last we met our positions were not quite the same," I informed them, folding my arms beneath my life sign. "It was then your choice to accord me the treatment of a slave, denying me the right to stand before you with sword in hand, winning freedom or death in accordance with what skill I possessed. You, in turn, may be accorded the same treatment, for the choice has now become mine, and yet I shall not do so. I offer you the right to face me with swords—should you have the courage to do so."

I looked upon the male Bariose as I spoke, knowing him the more likely of the two to accept my challenge. He returned my gaze directly enough, and yet his sneer of contempt, when it came, rang falsely.

"You think me backward enough to believe I would face only you?" he asked, pulling at the leather upon his wrists as he looked about him. "These others would cut me down when I bested you, giving me no opportunity to declare my victory."

"True victory need not be declared," said I above the angry mutter of the warriors within hearing, disallowing them the opportunity to take insult. "We are not like you, male, not like the folk of cities and villages. The concept of honor is well known to us, therefore would freedom be yours were you to best me. This, I believe, you know full well. Perhaps it would be best to have you face me against your will, then would you find it unnecessary to concern yourself with the matter of backwardness. Would such an arrangement be more to your liking?"

The male stood and gazed upon me, his eyes hard upon the sword at my hip, his skin touched with pallor, his tongue seeking to wet the dryness of his lips. I had recognized the insult for the attempted ruse it was, and now the male stood stripped of it—and dignity as well. His dark eyes, filled with a mixture of fear and fury, rose again to my face as his head shook in negation.

"No, curse you, such an arrangement would not be to my liking," he rasped, torn from the need to speak such words. "I have seen the manner in which these others fight, and know you stand above them. I have no wish to die."

"You would prefer to live as a slave then," said I, showing all of the contempt I felt at such a notion. At his curt, wordless nod I, too, nodded. "May you never forget that the choice was given you. As you have now become a slave, you may reap the fruits of a slave. Immediately."

Curtly did I command my warriors to take the male to a wall, remove his covering, and close his wrists in the cuffs upon the wall. His struggles were great, for well did he know what lay in store for him, yet his struggles, like mine when I had been done so, were useless. His wrists were closed in unyielding metal, his bare body pressed hard against the cool of the wall stone, and then was a large warrior behind him, a lash in her hands. As the lash was shaken out in preparation for use, I turned my attention to the female Karil.

"And you?" I inquired, pulling the female's eyes from the struggling form of Bariose. "Do you also feel you would be wrongly done should you take sword in hand and face me?"

"Face you?" the female snorted, tossing her head in disdain. "I am not such a fool as Bariose. I am a lady, and unconcerned with swords and suchlike nonsense. You will not do me as you do Bariose, for any will tell you I am cousin to the High Seat, much like a sister to him. When he returns with fighting men at his back, he will pay well for my immediate release—unharmed, of course. Should I be harmed, my value will prove much less. That should be clear enough even to savages such as you. Should you wish my value to remain intact, I must not be harmed.''

The female stood with a smirk well upon her, her dark hair somewhat disarranged, her long, city-female covering dirtied and worn, yet her self-concept of value entirely intact. Strange were these city folk and their concepts of value, for what may be of greater value than a truly made sword in one's fist and a clan-sister to guard one's back? Of what value may be a useless, smirking female who delights in the debasement and insult of others?

''You speak of the return of the High Seat,'' said I, again folding my arms. ''You believe he has escaped to gather males to him so that he might return?''

''Certainly,'' said she, again tossing her head. ''He would not have fallen to a female rabble with the best swordsmen in the Guard to protect him. It would be wisest if you were gone upon his return, for his temper is such that he may have all of you slain rather than taken as slave. He is a man of great—''

The words of the female ended abruptly, for I had turned to gaze upon the enclosure which held the High Seat, drawing her gaze with mine. It was clear the female Karil had not seen our arrival, she having been placed upon the stones of the floor at the far wall of the chamber, yet now was she completely aware of the true state of affairs. Her head shook slowly in distant negation as she looked upon the bedraggled figure of the once-mighty High Seat, and her voice, so confident a moment earlier, was no longer filled with scorn.

''No,'' she whispered, her head still ashake, and then did she jump and shudder when a scream of pain was forced from the male Bariose, he who was now under the lash he had so often wielded. ''No, it cannot be,'' said this Karil, turning wide-eyed to stare upon me. ''You cannot have taken him! You are savages! Savages!''

''We are warriors of the Midanna,'' I informed her, feeling something of anger beginning within me. ''Savage'' had I been called by the slave-guards of that city, ''savage'' was I to each of these useless, honorless folk of cities and villages. I had long since wearied of the term, yet this Karil saw naught of my anger.

''Warrior!'' she spat, beside herself with fury. ''Savages have your actions shown you to be, and savages will you remain! I am a high lady, far beyond the comprehension of such as you, far beyond your ability to degrade me! Slay me if you will, yet I refuse to declare myself slave!"

"Excellent," said I, anod in seeming approval of her words. "It is true, I am told, that males much prefer to teach a female her slavery themselves. That you refuse to declare yourself slave should make you of greater interest to males. Remove her covering."

Two of my warriors, widely agrin, caught the female as she attempted to flee, removed the leather from her wrists, and then began the removal of the city slave-woman covering. The female Karil howled and fought, rendering the removal of her covering difficult, therefore did one of the warriors, a Hulna by the gold of her clan colors, produce her dagger from its bands and deftly slit the covering from neck to waist. A deeper howl came from the female as the balance of the covering was torn from her, and then she stood, bare to the eyes of all, in the midst of cloth puddled at her feet. The females this Karil had done in a like manner were undoubtedly numberless, and yet her attempts to keep herself from the eyes of others, and the frenzied weeping and howling, seemed to indicate she felt herself unjustly done. With arms held before her and body bent forward, her head swung this way and that, her eyes searching for an avenue of escape, they finding no more than the laughter of warriors, the appraisal of males. I examined the female in silence a moment, then frowned in mock disapproval.

"The presentation seems amiss," I mused, considering the woman with head to one side. "There is that lacking which I cannot— Ah, now do I have it! The heat. One cannot see her heat."

"No!" whispered the female in horror, her widened eyes immediately coming to me upon hearing my words. "You cannot— It would be bestial—I am not—I cannot be done so! I am a high lady, not for the likes of slave handlers and positionless men! There are none about here worthy of me, not to speak of slaves!"

"She undoubtedly means she is a virgin and cold," called one of the male slaves, causing the others to laugh coarsely and raucously, bringing a deep stain of red to the female's body. "Put her in this cage with me, wench, and I will soon have her hot and hopping—and opened to her teeth."

Again the male slaves laughed, as much at the words of the large, well-made male as at the appalled, disbelieving expression upon the face of the female. She called Karil stared upon the heavily chained male who wished her use, seeing the broadness of his chest, the strength in his arms, the desire of his body, and quickly did she attempt to back from him. She, however, had forgotten the puddle about her feet, and took no more than two steps before stumbling upon the cloth, her arms flailing for balance, a muffled shriek of dismay torn from her lips. The Hulna warrior shot out a hand and caught the female's arm, keeping her from sprawling upon the stone of the floor, yet had the males been well-pleased by the motions of the female's body. Nearly as well-endowed as a warrior was she, soft and rounded and overripe for giving service.

"We must see what heat there is to be found in that one," said I to the two warriors beside the female, speaking so that the slaves might hear me. "Stand her before each of the enclosures of the males, near enough so that they might touch her easily, allowing them all the opportunity of raising her heat. Should Mida intervene and allow so low a thing to be brought about, do not allow her relief till she kneels before the male who asked her use and begs her to serve him. Should she do this, you may then throw her to him."

The female Karil was able to do no more than scream as she was taken by the arms toward the first of the enclosures, yet the males moved about in their chains, eager to have their hands upon the haughty female, eager to have her leap to their touch. Thoughtfully I stood and watched a moment, more to be sure that my warriors kept their weapons—and themselves—from the reach of the males than to witness the female's deep humiliation and fear at the first touch upon her body, then did I turn from the foolishness and pay it no further heed. There were many things yet to be done, perhaps too many things, and though they all must be seen to, I knew not how I, myself, might see to them all.

"War leader, the male is no longer aware of his punishment," said Rogon, indicating Bariose where he hung insensible in the wall cuffs. "Is there reason to continue the lashing?"

I looked upon the male, the blood flowing from the torn flesh of his back, my warrior with the bloodied lash in her hands standing before him, and shook my head.

"No," said I, perhaps sounding more weary than was proper for a war leader. "Take him down, place him in chains, then find an enclosure to hold him. He is no longer of interest to me."

"Jalav, perhaps you would do well to have your wounds tended," said Rogon in a soft voice, her dark eyes concerned.

"Your shoulder has bled heavily, and should you fall victim to the illnesses wounds may bring, we would be leaderless."

That Rogon had mentioned my wounds was a clear indication that I had indeed sounded more weary than I had intended. All those warriors who had accompanied me were wounded, some so far that they now sat with their backs upon the pink stone of the walls, their eyes closed, their wounds given over to the tending of sisters of their clans. That I had not felt the wounds at the time I had received them meant naught; they had long since made their presence fully known, most especially that in my left shoulder. And yet, how might I have had them tended, save that I saw to the matter myself? The Hosta were elsewhere, captives to males, and Jalav stood alone among strangers. Distant kin they were, and obedient to my word—yet nevertheless strangers.

"The wounds must wait," said I, straightening somewhat though I, too, spoke softly. "You undoubtedly have the right of it, Rogon, yet there are many matters remaining which must be seen to first. When this dwelling has been secured, then shall I find opportunity to rest and restore my strength. Have the male removed from the wall cuffs, then send to me runners who have learned their way about this place."

"At once, war leader," said she, a sigh of resignation upon her. "Remain here, and I shall have the runners attend you."

With such words did she take herself off, to see to Bariose and send the runners, yet the runners came bearing a large seat, one of wood and leather with softness beneath the leather, into which I was urged. Little liking had I for seating myself within a device of city folk, yet my strength had ebbed and there was much to do. When once I had sent runners to all war leaders scattered about the dwelling, telling them to assign guards about all entrances before bringing the balance of their sets and clans to the room of enclosures, I then allowed myself the luxury of rest.

Save for the laughter of male slaves, there was little sound to be heard in the large chamber. My warriors, of course, ever alert in hostile regions, spoke only those words which were necessary to what tasks had been set to their hands. The captives taken after battle, males of leather and metal bound upon the stones of the floor, had no wish to draw the attention of warriors to themselves. The female slaves, cowering in their enclosures, wept silently as their masters had taught them to do. The sole cause of what sound there was was the female Karil, she who had been taken before the male slaves to be touched and heated. I had not meant to waste valuable planning time personally observing the punishment I had decreed for her, and yet, once noticed, the doings about her drew me strongly. Much shame had been given me through the actions of this Karil, and much would I have preferred facing her with swords, yet city slave-women were taught solely the manner in which to give insult, naught of the manner which allows satisfaction for insult. With city folk it was necessary for warriors to seek satisfaction by other means, means without dignity and honor.

In the absence of a knowledge of honor, the female Karil had apparently made the decision to attempt to retain something of dignity throughout the ordeal she had been condemned to. The warriors who held her had not immediately thrust her against the lines of metal through which the chained arms of the males reached, most likely to afford the female a false sense of safety. They had held her to the extreme reach of the males, each warrior agrasp upon one arm and a handful of hair of the female, thrusting her gently forward so that no more than the fingertips of the males were able to touch her. In such a manner had they taken her past each enclosure of males, leading her to believe no more would be done than that which had already been done, perhaps a number of times as they had returned to the first enclosure, yet surely no more.

Now, again before the first enclosure, the female Karil had regained some shadow of her former arrogance. Her flesh had felt the touch of males, yet she, it seemed, had not fallen prey to their touch. She had feared she would be made to beg her use, yet this final degradation, it seemed, would not be forced upon her. Had she true knowledge of males and females, her under-standing would have encompassed the fact that the extreme fear she had felt had allowed the feeling of no other sensation, most especially not of desire, yet this thought had not occurred to her. I realized she must truly be as innocent and untouched as the male slave had suggested, and quickly recalled a thing I had forgotten. Though the female Karil had commanded the males in leather and metal to the task of heating the female slaves in her charge, she had not remained within the chamber of display to see the matter done. It was clear the female had quite a lesson before her, yet the sight of the female, stubbornness in the set of her body against the grasp of my warriors, fury in the sharpness of her glances, insolence in the set of her full lips, all spoke of a lesson completely unexpected.

As the two warriors beside the female again thrust her forward, something of surprise was visible upon the features of the city woman. As she had passed the enclosures once before, she well knew the distance she must maintain to remain beyond the easy reach of the males, and yet, to her frowning inspection, the distance seemed incorrect. Petulantly, snappishly, she spoke to the warriors in whose grasp she stood, yet they, with small knowing smiles, made no answer. Instead they merely watched as the arms of the first male, clasped tight in chains, reached through the lines of metal, all fingers of both hands now able to stroke and fondle the female's breasts. The male grinned wide as the female gasped in shock, she attempting to back from the touch, yet finding herself unable to do so.

"No!" came the female's voice, raised shrill and loud as she struggled against those who held her. "Do not allow him to touch me so! He is a slave! A slave!"

"And you are free?" inquired the male whose hands were upon her, his grin turned to laughter. "Run from me, then, high lady. Take your body beyond my reach." The female, stabbed by the ridicule, attempted to do so, yet was her struggle in vain. "Your excellent flesh remains within my grasp, high lady," laughed the male. "It would be pleasant to have you within this cage, so that I might teach a high lady the writhings of a slave. See how well your flesh accepts my touch."

The female whimpered, more than aware of the tightness of her flesh where the hands of the male touched and stroked, also perhaps aware of a new sensation within her body, a burning and need never before encountered. Another male of the same enclosure thrust his arms through the lines of metal with a laugh and a rattle of chain, awaiting his turn at the female, his eyes already upon her. When, after another moment or two, the female was forced against his eager palms, his low exclamation of pleasure mingled with the sob torn from her. The female Karil had indeed begun to writhe, slowly and incompletely, to be sure, yet most definitely a beginning toward heat. Her sense of humiliation seemed to be extreme, and yet she had only begun to learn of that which she had so easily and unthinkingly subjected others to. Among city folk, those most eager to do others in a certain manner are often those who have never been done so themselves. Surely this is a necessary state, for how may one treat others with such unconcern, save they be ignorant themselves of the consequences of their actions? And yet city folk are not like warriors, neither in their manner of doings nor in their thoughts; I moved about in the seat of wood and leather, overly aware of those differences. Would there be greater difficulty upon the new fey than I had anticipated, due solely to my having misread these city folk? Would my journey south to the city of the Sigurri be delayed by cause of this? I knew not, and could do no more than await the happenings of the new fey to know the wisdom or foolishness of my plans.

The female Karil was taken past each of the slave males, after which was she returned to the place from which her journey had twice begun. Lost in thought of plans for the new fey, I knew naught of her return till her scream rang out, bringing much laughter to the slave males within their enclosures. Again had the female been thrust closer to the males, enough so that her womanhood was now within reach, and quickly did the first male accept the offer of her previously forbidden softness. The chains upon his wrists clanged as the female threw herself about in the grip of my warriors, her movement attempting to dislodge the hand between her thighs and the other upon her leg. Her head thrown back, her screams were filled equally with desperation and fear. The male had penetrated her to no more than a small degree, yet she, never having known even so slight a penetration, seemed wildly fearful.

"For shame!" laughed the male, looking down upon the writhing female beneath his hands. "Surely this can be no high lady before me, whose body flows with moisture at the smallest of touches. Surely this is no more than a slave wench, a hot, lusty, helpless female slave sent, to her shame, to serve the needs of men. Your baubles are lovely, little slave. Bring them nearer so that I may examine them more closely."

"No!" wailed the female, beside herself with mortification. "I am not a slave! You lie! You are the slave, and you may not touch me so!"

"Do I lie, wench?" asked the male, penetrating her a bit further. "Is this body I touch dry and unresponsive? Are those pointed breasts I see soft and unexcited? Do you seek to escape that which merely begins to enter you—or to impale yourself upon it?"

Choking and shuddering, caught up in bodily excitement as never before, the female found herself incapable of so much as denying the male's words. How well I knew the sensations brought by the touch of a male, the weakness, the burning, the impossible need to be taken in his arms and used fiercely again and again. It had ever been part of a warrior to desire the use of a male, yet had Mida caused me to feel, during my capture by the male Ceralt, a need so great it had been well-nigh crippling. The least touch of his hand upon my body, the sound of his voice, the mere fact of his presence, the smallest of glances from him, even no more than the thought of him—any of those had made me his upon the instant, filled with shame so great it knew no bounds, yet undeniably, unarguably his helpless slave. Much had the male gloried in such power over me, often using me for his pleasure, at times denying me an end to the agony of need as punishment, through it all taking the decision of which would be done as his alone. Now, after having known the touch of Sigurr the foul, the unnatural need no longer burned within me. No need of any sort for males burned within me, save the need to meet and best them with swords. Males were fools, and blood enemies to Midanna, and wished naught from warriors save their use; much use would they have from this Midanna, yet no more than sword-use.

As the female Karil writhed to the touch of yet another male, I rose from my seat to pace the cool stones of the chamber's floor. The pain of my wounds was not to be acknowledged, yet the throbbing ache of my shoulder had grown despite the lessening of the flow of blood. The thrust had been a cowardly one, from well to the side the while my sword and attention had been engaged with the male directly before me, yet had the male who had done me so ended with my sword in his vitals. The other wounds were mere scratches, beneath the notice of one who had known them many times before, yet the greatest intruded upon my awareness, already stiffening the arm and hand with weakness and pain. There would indeed by much difficulty for me should it continue so to the time of departure upon the journey to the south—

"That wound should be seen to, wench," came the voice of a male, intruding upon my thoughts. "I have seen men die from the blackening sickness, which comes from lack of care of such as that."

Slowly did I turn to regard the male, he who had spoken. In some manner it came as no surprise that it was a Sigurri male, one of the four who stood enchained within their enclosure. The others stood to the far side of the enclosure, their hands upon the lines of metal, their eyes upon the female Karil as she moaned and screamed, their voices raised in laughter and encouragement of him who now toyed with her. This male before me was the red-haired one, his light eyes regarding me soberly, his large left fist about a line of metal, the strength of his broad body disregarding the chains fastened upon him. I felt annoyance that he would speak to me so, as though I were city slave-woman, notwithstanding the fact that the fates of Midanna and Sigurri were entwined.

"I am Jalav," said I, speaking coldly, disallowing the reach of my right hand to my left arm to rub at the pain. "Jalav is war leader to all the clans of Midanna, therefore is she no stranger to wounds. She has no need of the council of males, male, least of all of those who stand in chains."

"The same council was given you by your own, wench," said he, his deep voice calm, taking no note of the balance of my words. "Should you continue to disregard the advice of those about you, you will soon find yourself in the arms of Sigurr, which would be the greatest of wastes. That body of yours was made to give pleasure to living men first, before becoming the eternal property of the dark god. Should you fail to—"

His words broke off as though cut through by my sword, which was poised at his throat between the lines of metal. So great was my rage that nearly did I open his throat, allowing his warm, bright blood to spurt and flow to the flagstoned floor. To say that I would be the eternal property of Sigurr, to serve him forever in the abominations I had once already been made to endure, was to bring the insanity of unbridled rage upon me. Sooner would I see my soul lost forever in the limitless dark, to spread and fade and be no more, than to again face the touch of the dark god.

"You are mistaken, male," I rasped when I was again able to speak, my point having remained at his throat. "Never will I be the property of the dark god, never will I serve his desires. Should you ever speak so again, your life is forfeit. On this you have my word."

The male stood unmoving, no fear to be seen in the light eyes of him, yet was he not so foolish as to tempt my anger with further words. Easily did he see that the fury had not gone from me, and well did he know that my vow was not an idle one. He stood unmoving and in silence till my point was withdrawn and I had begun to turn from him, resheathing my sword, then did his hand rise to the place my blade had rested. A small drop of blood gleamed there, yet was one drop far superior to a greater flow.

Rogon had spied my pacing and had begun to approach me, yet was she still three paces distant when the balance of our sisters arrived. They appeared at the chamber's entrance and walked within in small groups, the silence of the hunt well upon them, yet jubilation upon them as well. Well did they know themselves the victors of the fey, these sister Midanna, and well did this knowledge show in the breadth of their stride and the manner in which their heads were held high. Among them walked their war leaders, filled with pride for the warriors they led, filled with pleasure from the deed they had done. Long would the doing live in the memory of Midanna, long would the story be told about the fires of the home tents. The walled city of males was theirs, said their joy, and would remain so till they saw fit to release it.

"Greetings, Jalav," called Tilim, her words echoed by those about her, her steps bringing her quickly to me. "The guardposts have been set as you directed, and all is secure. Each chamber in this dwelling has been searched, and each male found either captured or put to the sword. Our victory is complete."

"Not quite yet," said I, stilling the murmurs of pleasure about me. "This dwelling and the city is ours, yet they may be lost to us upon the new light when those in the balance of the city arise to find themselves invaded. Their battle skill is naught when compared to ours, yet our numbers are far too few to challenge them. Victory would be far less sweet were there no more than a handful of us remaining to joy in it."

"What, then, shall we do?" demanded another, one Gidon, war leader to the Homma. "Are we to go from dwelling to dwelling, like Sarra trash, and slay them in their sleep? Sooner would I face alone two hands and more of armed males than so dishonor my blade!"

She stood with head held high, golden-haired and green-eyed, amid the growls of agreement of those within hearing. Her gaze was locked to mine, daring me to speak such loathsome commands, and my anger, despite the pain I felt, could not be withheld.

"I would know what prompts the war leader of the Homma to believe I would demand such a deed of her," said I, stepping past Tilim to face the Homma more directly. "Should the war leader Gidon feel that Jalav must be likened to the Sarra, it would be best that she speak more clearly."

I stood before the Homma, my hands at my sides, yet was the desire to draw my blade great indeed. When a captive among the males, it had been necessary that I swallow a great many insults; now that I again rode free, a sword at my side, there were none who might insult me with impunity. This the Homma saw, and my anger as well, and a note of confusion and doubt entered her eyes.

"I—do not know what caused me to speak so," she frowned, her voice now disturbed. "It is known by all Midanna that the war leader Jalav is naught if not honorable. I do not fear you, Jalav, and will face you with swords if you wish, yet it was not my intention to give you insult."

"Then I shall take no insult," said I, feeling my strength drain away with my anger. "We shall not seek out the males of this city, for they are sure to seek us out come the new light. It is for this that we must prepare, with rest and provender, and guardposts fully alert. There is sure to be further battle then, yet is it my hope that no more than a small amount of Midanna blood will be spilled. I shall inspect the guardposts, and then we may speak further of what plans I have formulated."

"A moment, war leader," called Rogon from behind me, halting us all as the others prepared to follow me to the door. I turned to face her, and she stood herself before me to look up into my eyes. "These plans you have formulated for the new light," said she. "Do they require that our leader be in full health and strength, able to do that which is required of her?"

I made no immediate answer to her words, for her meaning was clear in the anger and impatience in her eyes, yet the others were not aware of the exchange which had gone on between us earlier.

"Of what do you speak, Rogon?" asked Tilim, a frown upon her. "Surely does it seem as though you feel Jalav will be unable to stand with us come the new light."

"Should she continue on so, there is little doubt," said Rogon, folding her arms beneath her life sign. "Her wound has already taken a great toll in strength, yet she will not have it tended and rest. Have we come so far, spending the lives of our sisters, to see our efforts come to naught due to lack of judgment?"

"My judgment is as clear as it has ever been," said I above the murmurs of disturbance from the others, standing myself the straighter. "I am hardly an unblooded warrior, new to battle and the wounds it brings. When I feel that rest is required I shall take it. For now there are too many other things which must be seen to."

"Things which have already been seen to by your war leaders," said Rogon, in no whit abashed. "Do you doubt their ability, that you must inspect the guardposts which they have already inspected? As there are plans which must be discussed, why may they not be discussed as your wound is seen to? Do you mistrust the intentions of those you lead?"

Rogon's eyes refused to leave mine, her sharpened gaze saying she knew full well what consternation her words had bred in me. How might I say I doubted the abilities of those war leaders about me when it was not so? How might I say I mistrusted their aid when it was not so?

"I have ever inspected guardposts with my own eyes," said I at last, rather lamely, somehow feeling the child among warriors.

"Never has it been proper to allow others to do the thing for me."

"It is now proper, Jalav," said Tilim, her voice soft with understanding as her hand went to my unharmed right shoulder. "Never before have you had other war leaders among those whom you led. And though there be no other Hosta among us, still must your wound be seen to. Come. We shall find a place you may take your rest, and there you may speak of your plans for the new fey."

They all gazed upon me in silence, these warriors and war leaders, Rogon and Tilim and Gidon and the rest, all awaiting my word upon the matter. I had had no disagreement from them at the time of battle, yet battle was now over and they were war leaders in their own right. Were I to deny their council at such a time, a disastrous rift might well begin to grow between us.

"Very well," said I with a nod, looking about among them. "I will seek the rest you council for I find I do, indeed, have need of it. I will, however, refrain from demanding a similar complete rest for the balance of you, for there are many males about ripe for the taking. Use them with restraint, however, for the new fey will require alertness as well as an easing of need."

The laughter and shouts of approval from the many warriors about the chamber brought smiles to the lips of the war leaders about me. They, too, I saw, would seek out males for their use before taking to their sleeping leather, yet first was it necessary to attend to matters of import. All nine war leaders would accompany me, therefore was it necessary that they designate those who would stand for them while they sat in council with me. As I stood alone awaiting the completion of this task, a warrior of the Hulna approached me.

"Your pardon, war leader," said she, stopping before me. "As you are soon to depart the chamber, we thought it best to ask your wishes in regard to the slave female. She has already been taken past each of the males."

Filled with surprise, I followed the gaze of the Hulna to the female Karil, she who had apparently slipped completely from my mind. The poor wretch now lay crumpled upon the stones of the chamber before an enclosure of males, a warrior standing above her, the males in the enclosure laughing as they looked down upon her. Her body writhed upon the flags as though she lay in the grip of a great need, yet no more than weeping came to break her silence.

"She was given the opportunity to beg the use of the male designated by you," said the Hulna, "yet she refuses to do so.

Her need has nearly consumed her, but she seems to fear the male. How might one feel fear for a male?''

I looked upon the Hulna as she gazed in scorn upon the female Karil, understanding that this warrior, undoubtedly like many others, had no knowledge of males save as sthuvad to their clans. I knew not which would be the greater punishment for the female Karil, to be allowed to go unused, or to be forced to the use of the male, yet did I know which was the more necessary. For the sake of my warriors, then, the female Karil would be thoroughly done.

"Have the male I had designated removed from the enclosure he shares with others and placed within an unoccupied enclosure," I directed. "Leave the female as she is till this has been done."

"At once, war leader," said the Hulna, gesturing two others to her as she strode to the enclosure. They, with swords drawn to keep the balance of the males within, removed the male I had indicated and conducted him to an enclosure not yet in use, his chains arattle as he moved, his anger clear even though his obedience was immediate. The male disliked the points of swords in warrior hands, yet was wiser than to attempt the defiance of them. His anger would undoubtedly mean greater ill for the female Karil, yet had she paved such a path for others many times with her actions. She had cared little for the anger of males when it was others who would bear the weight of it; now would she learn the consequences of such actions.

With the male enclosed as I had ordered, I indicated that the female was now to be taken to him. She cried out as the hands of warriors pulled her to her feet, struggled as they dragged her toward what awaited her, yet I had little pity for her struggles. Others had been denied even so much as the right to struggle, yet had the female been totally uncaring. Now was she being done as she had done others, a state many would benefit from. To know that one will be done as one does others would undoubtedly change the actions of many a city folk. My war leaders, their task seen to, began to rejoin me, then curiously followed as I moved the closer to the enclosure the female had been thrust within.

"Do not leave me in here!" screamed the female, scrambling to her feet from the thrust which had sent her to the floor of the enclosure, turning immediately and running to pound upon the now closed door. Her bare, round body quivered with the fear she felt, a sight not lost to the male who awaited her. He, who had been forced to the far side of the enclosure so that the female might be put within, grinned as he looked upon her and slowly began to advance.

"You shall not be merely left, my pretty," said he, advancing more slowly than his chains accounted for. "I have given my word to have you hot and hopping, and so shall I do."

"Oh, no!" screamed the female, turning to stare upon the male with widened eyes, her back pressed painfully to the lines of metal. The male paused to remove the rag about his loins, baring his excitement, and nearly did the female faint at the sight. "No, do not touch me," whispered the female, edging toward the corner of the enclosure. "I cannot bear the thought that I will be— No! I will give you anything, every silver piece I own, if only you will leave me untouched! I am wealthy beyond your imaginings, and it will all be yours! All!"

"Very well," said the male with a laugh, halting perhaps two paces from her. "I will accept your offer. Go now and fetch the silver pieces for me."

"I cannot!" whispered the female, eyes widened once again. "Those savages and their swords—I cannot!"

"Exactly," nodded the male, his tone dry. "What wealth you possess is now bared before me, already mine to do with as I please. For endless feyd has it been my wish to see you brought so low, you who see yourself so far above those you humiliate and sell. Come and kneel before me, wench, and prepare yourself for the due which has been overlong in coming to you."

The female screamed, undeniably a refusal, and sought to claw her way from the enclosure through the lines of metal. The male growled his anger and strode to her, his step hampered by the chain stretched between his ankles, yet in no more than a moment was his fist in her hair, pulling her toward him. Well did she struggle and beat at his chest, crying out in pain when his fist tightened within her hair, yet was she easily drawn from the corner of the enclosure to its center. Once there her struggles abruptly ceased, no doubt in an effort to ease the pain the male brought with his grip, yet an easing of pain was not to be her lot.

"Your body pleases me, wench," said he, looking down upon the female he held so cruelly. She, fear so strong upon her that the smell was plain, held to the chain between his brawny wrists and did no more than whimper. "Are you not pleased that I find you of interest?" he asked.

"Yes, yes, I am pleased!" she cried in pain, her head undoubtedly ringing from the shake the male had given it. "I beg you, release me, I cannot bear the pain!"

"Please forgive me, high lady!" the male exclaimed, releasing her at once as though bound to do her bidding. "I had not realized you were in such discomfort. I must, of course, immediately make amends."

Those warriors about me laughed aloud, covering the cry of dismay coming from the female Karil as the male, an arm about her waist, sat himself upon the enclosure floor, drawing her down with him and to his lap. Again did she cry out, in more than dismay, struggling to take her bare flesh from his, yet the male took her wrists behind her and held them so with one hand, the other reaching toward her body. The chain which linked his wrists disallowed the matter to be easily seen to, therefore did he bend the female backward, over the width of his thigh, arched like the curve of a bow, in order to have free run of her body. The shock of being done so froze the female briefly, yet was she quickly brought from shock when the hand of the male sought and found her heat.

"Ah, now has your comfort been restored, high lady," said the male, paying no mind to the gasping, gurgling sounds produced by the female. "And yet, it now seems another discomfort is upon you. Your soft, slender body writhes beneath my hand, as though requiring immediate attention. Surely this is so?"

"No, no!" cried the female, indeed writhing well to the slow, rhythmic stroking of the male. "I do not wish to be taken and used! I shall die if you continue to touch me so, I shall die!"

"There will be no death for you, lady wench," laughed the male, continuing his ministrations. "Nor will there be surcease from your need, not till I have deemed you sufficiently punished. Scream if you will, and beg if you wish, yet all will be to no avail."

The male then lowered his lips to her upthrust breasts, drawing the scream he had spoken of, yet was he deaf to that and those following, just as he had vowed. His kisses and caresses continued only a short time, however, before the female indeed began to beg her use. Had she been sent to him cold it would not have been done so quickly, yet she had been sent to him well heated by the touches of the other males. He, however, ignored her pleas for two hands of reckid and more, only then admitting himself unable to continue so, as the strain of his body clearly showed. Quickly, then, was the female put to her back, her legs spread wide, and he had presented himself to her womanhood. Her writhing slowed as fear again possessed her, yet was the fear too late in coming. Of no consequence was the female to that male, therefore did he enter her with a single, savage thrust, causing her to throw her head back with a wild scream of pain, finding less and more than the satisfaction she had craved. Her weeping began in earnest as the male began to satisfy himself fully, and then did I turn and walk from the enclosure.

"Such foolish clamoring," muttered Rogon at my side, shaking her head in scorn. "City slave women are truly low, to feel such fear of males. I, myself, have had many males, yet never would I act so even had I had none."

"Do you truly believe so?" said I, halting to look down upon the war leader of the Hirga, and then to the others about me. "Do all of you truly believe so?"

"Indeed," nodded Tilim, and "Surely!" laughed Gidon, and in such various manners did each of them show their agreement. I looked about me in silence, and then did I nod.

"Very well," said I. "Which of you, then, would be first to have her weapons and clan covering taken, and then be thrust so within an enclosure with such a male. Perhaps you, Rogon?"

"Jalav, I—know not what to say," stumbled this excellent war leader, she who was known for the thirst of her blade in battle. "For what reason would my weapons be taken from me? For what reason could the male not also be armed?"

"For the reason that without weapons you could not best him," said I, seeing the sober regard in all of their eyes, feeling even more of the throb of my wound. "The accursed strength of males will ever best that of a warrior, no matter how bravely she stands in battle, no matter how high her skill with a sword. Never forget the sight you have seen, never forget that you, too, will be done so should you allow a male to cozen you from your weapons. Do not allow yourselves to be captured by them. Death—the final death—would be much the easier—"

I found myself unable to continue, for a great dizziness and weakness had come upon me, of a sudden, dancing my thoughts about. To allow a male to approach too near was the greatest of follies, for how was a warrior to forget his arms, once he was put beyond her reach? And even should he not be put beyond her reach, how was she to find agreement with him, when he sought naught save service and use? A warrior must be free else she withers and dies, yet males must be served and obeyed by their females, disallowing what need they may have to ride free. Warriors had been given no more than the use of males, and in such a doing had Mida been exceedingly wise.

"Jalav, we must find a place where you may take your rest," said Tilim, her voice grave, her arm about me in support, I saw, as vision returned. "Nearly were you upon the flags."

"And quickly," agreed Rogon, who also assisted in my support.

"Have any of you come upon a chamber which would serve? There is naught save slave chambers hereabouts, bare even to sleeping leather."

"Perhaps the chamber of him called High Seat," said Ilvin from among the warriors about us, she of the pale hair and Hitta covering. "As the male was purportedly the highest, would his chamber not be best? And yet it seems a considerable distance from here to the steps we must use to the level above."

"There are steps but two short corridors from here," said a warrior, a Harra by the brown of her clan covering. "Is it possible they may be of use?"

"We shall see," said Tilim, Rogon silently anod. I spoke no word in agreement nor in demurral, for in truth I was able to do neither. I knew full well that Tilim and Rogon strove to keep me from the flags, yet little sensation came to me of their support, no more than the light touch of the cool flagstones beneath my feet to add to it. As quickly as was possible did we depart the chamber of slaves, the cries of the female Karil somewhat muffled from behind, the hastening of warriors sent ahead preceding us. Of no thing was I aware save the throbbing of my life sign where it hung between my breasts, that life sign touched by Mida and the dark god Sigurr. Deeply did it throb, with a hum more felt than heard, occurring in a lack of notice by any save me. Quickly did my surroundings grow dim about me, yet was I able, through great effort, to remain conscious till we had reached our destination. Once there, before the wide portals, but two paces short of the chamber itself, the dimness changed to the black of Sigurr, and then was Jalav swallowed up.

3 A gift—and a champion is named

Sensation returned with an awareness of the fur I lay upon, a fur of great softness and comfort. I moved somewhat upon the fur, by then aware of the second fur which covered me, opening my eyes to look deep within the flames I lay not far from. The warmth of the hearth and the comfort of the furs were a great lure to remaining as I was, yet a sense of impatience and matters unseen to came immediately to move me to sitting. It was not till I had looked about the strange chamber in the hearthlight that I recalled the why of my having no recollection of having entered therein, the why of my having been placed there to begin with. The shoulder wound had taken my strength and senses, an unexplained event I had not then been able to question. That the wound had been painful was true, yet had I had more serious wounds in the past that had not done me so. I turned my head to examine the wound in the hearthlight, aware of the odd fact that all pain now seemed to be gone, also suddenly aware of how great my hunger was—and then sat merely to stare, the while I considered the possibility that I continued to dream.

The wound before my eyes, which had been made by the penetration of a sword to more than finger joint depth within my shoulder, had become no more than a line of pink, tender yet to the touch of my fingers, yet giving no pain of its own, allowing my arm the movement it had not previously allowed. That the arm was clean of all signs of blood was undoubtedly due to the efforts of the warriors who had brought me to the chamber, yet the healing clearly had not had the same effort as its source. For a moment I could not fathom the manner in which this might have been done—save for the possibility that I had lain senseless for feyd rather than hind—and then did I recall the throbbing of my life sign before all consciousness had fled. Had no more than hind been spent in the passing, it was undoubtedly the powers of Mida and dark Sigurr which had seen to my wound, healing me so that I might continue to toil in their behalf. It would take no

73

more than the seeking out of my warriors to learn the truth of the matter, and this I would do with speed.

Climbing to my feet was effortless, filled as I was with new strength and great vitality. The chamber I now stood in was large, too large to be seen by naught save the hearthlight. The outline of an immense platform called bed stood among the shadows upon the far wall, many other outlines less easily discernible scattered all about, all closed within a chamber hung completely about with drapings of silk. Had there been windows in view I might have known how much of the darkness remained, yet the question was not so pressing that I felt a need to seek behind the hangings. My hunger seemed bottomless and growling within me, threatening to turn the newfound feeling of well being to ashes and weakness. The hunger must be seen to first, I knew, that and the matter of seeking out my war leaders; with that done, there would be time enough for other things.

My swordbelt lay upon the floor cloth beside the furs I had awakened upon, the hilt of the blade positioned so that it would be conveniently to hand. Replacing it about my waist took but a moment, as did the straightening of my dagger in its leg bands, then did I stride purposefully toward the sole door to be seen in the chamber. A gentle push swung it outward, immediately giving me sight of the chamber in which he called High Seat had entertained the guests within his dwelling, the chamber which had been well lit within its center by a ring of candles. Some few of those candles continued to burn, illuminating those who occupied the chamber, giving sight to those who had greater desire for things other than sleep. Many slept, it was true, more than a few in chains, yet two of those who remained awake, upon the floor cloth but two paces from where I stood, they and I both well-wrapped in shadow, spoke softly as their shadow-forms moved.

"You are well-made, male," came the whisper of a warrior, her voice breathy and filled with satisfaction. "I shall undoubtedly use you again before we return to the forests."

"It was my hope that I would give you pleasure, Mistress," came the answering whisper of a male, one who was obviously a slave. His arm rose from the floor cloth to the dark shape above him, his hand reaching out with purpose, quickly drawing a gasp of pleasure from the warrior who rode him. "Forgive me, Mistress," he whispered as quickly, his hand retaining its hold. "I mean no insult by touching you so. This lovely breast beneath my fingers drew me so strongly that I could not resist it. How I wish I might be allowed to give you even greater pleasure."

"Greater pleasure?" gasped the warrior, nearly lost to the sensations of her body. "How might such a thing be possible?"

"It would be possible if I were to be allowed to move more freely," said the male, his voice coaxing as his hips rose gently from the floor cloth, drawing a moan which underscored the effectiveness of the motion. "Should you allow yourself to be placed briefly beneath me, your pleasure would easily be increased twofold."

"Beneath you?" echoed the warrior, attempting in vain to duplicate the sensation which the male had given with the thrust of his hips. "I have never had a male in such a way. Would it truly increase my pleasure?"

"Beyond all doubt," said the male, and then were his arms about the warrior, holding her close to his body. "Should I fail to serve you so, I would be remiss in my duties. Slay me if you must, yet first I shall give you the pleasure that is your due."

The male, with one hand at her back and one hand upon her bottom, then rolled quickly to place the warrior beneath him, her possession of him immediately becoming the reverse. The warrior gasped in surprise, her body beginning to struggle in his arms, yet all sound ceased as his lips took hers, a different motion beginning as the male rose to his knees and thrust himself more deeply than he had heretofore been allowed to do. A frenzied moaning began in the throat of the warrior as the hips of the male drove harder and harder, a moaning refused freedom by the lips of the male, a moaning continuing for long reckid and then increasing till her frantic movements were abruptly ended with a deep sigh, a sign the male understood. He withdrew his lips to allow her the breath she required, slowing the thrust of his hips, reaching instead to her breast with his tongue to force a great shudder from her.

"Mida sustain me!" whispered the warrior fervently, her hands upon the broad arms of the male, her body twisting in faint protest against the sensations again building within her. Well she knew that the male had not yet allowed himself to attain release, and therefore would again send her to the reaches she had only just returned from.

"Do you wish me to cease?" asked the male quite softly, his lips moving upon the breasts of the warrior, his hips continuing the thrust of his manhood. "Should you insist that I withdraw I shall do so, for I am a slave and bound to obey. Are you so displeased that you would send me from you?"

"No!" gasped the warrior, grasping the arms of the male as her body opened more fully to his penetration. "It is my command that you continue as you have been doing! I demand that you serve me!''

"Indeed," murmured the male, slowing his movement despite the writhing of the warrior. "I will, of course, obey all commands given me to the best of my ability, yet it seems that I must soon allow myself release. Should this occur, the Mistress will be left with great need unseen to, and I, wretched slave, will undoubtedly be soundly punished. Perhaps, Mistress, this slave might be allowed to suggest a solution to the dilemma."

"Do not withdraw so far!" begged the warrior, struggling in vain with male strength to return him to her. "Do not yet allow yourself release! Mida protect me, I cannot bear to be left so!"

"It need not be, Mistress," whispered the male, again thrusting deep within her. "The Mistress will find herself well seen to, should this slave be given her word that he will be freed from his slavery and this city. I ask no more than to be released unharmed, to go my way quickly and in peace. Speak now, wench, for I mean this slavery to end in one manner or another. Should you wish service, I must be freed to be on my way; should you refuse, I shall find another to serve so."

The warrior, well beside herself with need, choked upon the words which she could not bring herself to utter. To give her word under such conditions would destroy her as a warrior, an agony I knew far too well to doubt. The male seemed well aware of the fact that the warrior would not speak of the shame given her even should she refuse, yet was he ignorant of the memories of she who stood within the shadows and listened. Such memories are not easily forgotten, the seeking of a sworn word in an instance where others sought naught save pleasure. So had Jalav once been done, yet Jalav was no longer captive to males, to be used as they willed and kept without weapons. Jalav was free, to do with males as she pleased.

Silently and easily did I move from the doorway, allowing the door to fall closed in a gentle swing, the silence of my natural tread aided yet further by the depth of the floor cloth, in two paces arriving behind the back of the male. He, attempting to force the sworn word of a warrior, knew naught of my presence till my left hand had taken him by the hair, forcing his head back, exposing his throat to the point of my dagger.

"Should you fail to see to the warrior beneath you, your life is no more," said I in a murmur, pleased with the candlelit gleam of the dagger blade at his throat. "You now perform for your life, male, therefore do I advise the exhibition of great skill."

"I cannot!" gasped the male, frozen in the position to which I had pulled him, fear clearly to be heard in his voice. "In the name of the Serene Oneness, Mistress, I beg you to ease back with that blade! One breath closer and I am gone!"

"You are unable to see to my warrior?" I asked in the mildest of tones, retaining the dagger where I had placed it. "A pity, male, for now she will need to seek the use of another. Do not fail to give my greetings to Mida when your eyes open once again to find yourself in her chains."

"No!" cried the male, a trembling beginning in the broad body of him. "I must not die so! I will serve the woman!"

A brief moment did the male attempt hesitation, seeking, no doubt, an easing of the blade, yet when such easing was not quickly forthcoming, he carefully began the task given him. The warrior beneath him had been silent in her misery, too shamed to speak her desires, yet in but a few reckid was she again writhing wildly, without volition, made slave to a male by the needs of her body. The moment her release came he, too, was taken by the thing, undoubtedly fearing that his release would not be otherwise allowed. The hand of others remaining awake in the chamber, warriors clearly set as guard by Tilim and Rogon and the others, had approached when first I had reached the male, one of their number bearing a large candle from the ring in the center of the chamber. By its light I had been able to see that the male was he who had spoken to me earlier, asking that he be allowed entrance to my sleeping leather. I withdrew my hand and dagger from the male, allowing him to collapse to the floor cloth in defeat, allowing the vision of a well-used warrior to be seen by the others.

"It is fortunate you were awake, war leader," said a Helda, the yellow of her clan covering clear in the candlelight. "That one has shamed us all in her weakness, and would undoubtedly have allowed the male to do you harm."

"Not so," said I, stilling the rumble of anger from the others. She who had been well used lay with face averted upon the floor cloth, shame and self-condemnation strong upon her. "This warrior has done me a service, taking shame upon herself so that I might be spared the pain. It is true this service was done unknowingly, yet has this warrior my gratitude—and that of the male."

"Of the male?" echoed the Helda, afrown in lack of understanding. "For what reason would the male feel gratitude?"

"For such a reason," said I, looking upon the male where he lay beside the warrior, upon one elbow, his head bowed by the defeat he had sustained. "Should this male have attempted with me what he attempted with this warrior, his blood would now be spread upon the floor cloth, staining it as he would have stained my honor. Males must ever attempt the use of warriors, to attain what ends they desire, caring naught for the warrior herself, merely for their desires. Once was I, too, used so cruelly, not for pleasure alone, only to serve the purpose of a male. The need of a warrior burns strong within her, difficult to deny, yet would I have denied it to see myself revenged upon this male. Give thanks to this warrior, male, that you retain what life is in you."

The male looked upon me with pain in his eyes, knowing I spoke the truth; the warrior beside him, a young Harra by the brown of her thrust-up clan covering, also gazed upon me, her frown much like that of the Helda beside me.

"You, too, were done so, war leader?" said she, shock and a good deal of indignation in her voice. "How might such a thing be possible?"

"All is as Mida wills it," I shrugged, beyond the need for further explanations. "It was Mida's will that I learn the soul-destroying agony of service to a male. The touch of this male gave you greater pleasure than any male before him, did it not?"

"Indeed," nodded the warrior, sitting upon the floor cloth and turning her head to regard the male. "Never have I been made to feel such—abandon."

"The thought will come that it would cause no harm to experience such again," said I, without bitterness. "It is this, the desire to know such—abandon—again, which closes the warrior in a trap. You have surely engaged in trading for the Harra. Would you trade the freedom of the forests, the life of a warrior, to follow this male and serve his every need, to insure that this abandon would be yours forever?"

"Never!" gasped the Harra, shock and horror strong upon her, her agitation sending her to her feet and from the male. He, now deeply afrown, stared up at the manner in which she took herself from him, the disgust to be seen upon her face much like a blow delivered him.

"And yet this is the sole manner in which males and warriors might dwell together," said I, pleased to see that those warriors who had earlier condemned the Harra, now stood themselves the closer in support of her. "A male must ever be served by the female he chooses, his word alone to be obeyed, his wishes alone to be seen to. Pleasure alone cannot compensate for the loss a warrior must endure, the loss of the life she has ever known. Should you wish the life of a slave-woman, seek again the arms of a male."

"Would such a fate truly be so terrible?" asked the male, gazing upon the Harra. "To see to the needs of a man is a natural thing for a woman, the thing all women were made for. In turn would I defend your life with mine, hunt for you, feed and clothe you, give you my children to bear. We would each of us serve the other in our own way, and thus would we find happiness together. I see a great loveliness within you, wench, and when I succeed in escaping the chains of this place, it would please me to take you with me."

"You are able to give deep pleasure, male," said the Harra, her tone as sober as the dark of her eyes. "Such a thing would lure me greatly, and yet— Should it be my will to hunt the forests in your stead, to stand with naked blade before those who would challenge me, to leave what daughters I bear in the care of others and ride to battle with the sisters of my clan—how then would stand your views?"

"Such things would be totally unacceptable as well as unnecessary," scoffed the male, rising to his feet to look down upon the warrior. "What need is there for you to hunt when I would do the thing? And how might a man look upon himself, should he allow his wench to stand protection for him? As for the matter of riding to battle—are my sons to be bereft of their mother and I bereft of my woman, due solely to the whim of others to spill blood? A woman's place is by her hearth, not roving about forests and battlefields."

"And not a word of standing together," said I, seeing the shudder of horror touching the Harra, the disbelief and revulsion upon the faces of the others. "The sword of a warrior is unwelcome beside that of a male, the will of a warrior naught beside his. Do you wonder now, that the females of such as these are slaves? To use a male is great pleasure, to speak with him a waste of breath. Never will they see the thing through eyes other than their own."

"In what other way is a man to see?" demanded the male, turning his anger upon me. "Though I now be chained here as a slave, I have not forever been a slave, nor shall I continue so forever. I am a man intending to be free, a man who wishes to see his woman safely beside him, a man who wishes what danger there is to fall upon his shoulders rather than hers. Is this so wrong?"

"And should your concept of safety destroy this female you profess to care for?" I countered, left hand upon sword hilt, anger in my voice. "Should she swear upon her life sign that the safety of your hearth would cause her to waste away, would you then release her? Would you return to her the freedom of the forests, or would you merely assure her that she would soon grow used to naught save caring for your dwelling and serving your needs? Would you release her, male?''

"I—would find it difficult," said the male, his anger covered well by confusion and hurt. "It is difficult to believe such a thing would destroy a woman. I feel you speak through conviction brought about by experience, an experience painful to look back upon. Was it truly necessary to swear such a thing before you were released by the man who had claimed you?"

"I was not released," I spat, then took greater control of my anger. The male before me was not the one who had refused to see my agony, the one who had seen no more than his own desires. That was another male, one for whom I had given away my soul. The male before me backed a pace, seeing that in my eyes which caused him to brace, as though against expected attack; therefore did I shake my head. "I was not released," said I again, "yet the matter is not one to be discussed with males and captives. As this male is so eager to serve warriors, take him to the chamber of slaves and see that he receives the sthuvad drug. It is my command that he is to be used in no other way."

"At once, war leader," said one of the warriors, then did she and another force the male from the chamber at sword point. Twice did he look back, each time at the Harra, yet she, as a warrior, gazed musingly upon the sleeping forms of the remaining slave males, considering their possible use in place of the first male. She, I was sure, would not again heed the words of a male, nor allow him her use and her soul.

"In what way may we aid you, war leader?" said the Helda, not having left her place at my right arm. "Do you wish us to summon any of those who brought you here?"

"You may summon them all when once I have fed," said I, turning to face her. "How much of the darkness remains before us?"

"It is less than two hind to Mida's first light," said the Helda, her eyes upon me. "Provender may be found upon those platforms against the far wall. It is only city-folk provender, yet is it—. War leader! I do not understand what has occurred! Your wound, which I saw with my own eyes, is no more!"

"Calm yourself," said I, placing my hand upon her shoulder to still the upset so plain in her eyes. "Were you not told that I ride in Mida's cause, doing her bidding? It was her hand which healed my wound, so that I might continue her work undisturbed by distractions. Surely you understand the necessity for such?"

"Indeed, war leader, indeed do I understand," said she, hastily yet very still beneath my hand. "Might I be allowed the honor of fetching your provender?"

Great eagerness underlay the Helda's words, a glowing gaze emanating from her eyes, her body quivering as though in the throes of deep emotion held tightly in check. Such a reaction, which I had not expected, disturbed me, yet was there little I might do to dispel it. These warriors knew naught of the doings of the goddess and the god, therefore was it to be expected that they would be much in awe of such. Best would be to pretend it had not happened, yet it was unlikely that such would occur.

"I must first see what there is to be fed upon," I sighed, removing my hand from her shoulder. "I would instead have you send for the war leaders who follow me, so that we may hold council before the new light."

"At once, war leader," breathed the Helda, her left hand to her sword hilt, the childlike eagerness continuing to possess her. "It is my honor to be commanded!"

Quickly, then, did she turn and leave the chamber, intent upon obeying those commands which had become an honor. Ah, Mida! Truly had the goddess full knowledge of the manner in which a warrior might be set completely apart from her sisters. Undoubtedly she thought it necessary to bind me more closely to her will, as she had thought it necessary to breed hatred within me for males; her beliefs were in error, yet how might I instruct her? A warrior cannot instruct a goddess, she may do no more than obey. And this would Jalav do, obey the goddess till life had fled. Jalav was Mida's, with none to deny her, not even the male god Sigurr.

The provender upon the platforms was poor stuff, fit only for city folk who knew no better, yet was it necessary that I feed upon it to restore my strength. The nilno was overdone and awash in cold, thick grease, yet did I swallow each bite of it to the last, and the dark, baked grain as well, and the talta eggs and the lake fish known to warriors as sampa. Those warriors remaining within the chamber stood in awe of the hunger which had gripped me, staring in deep respect as I downed each pot of drink called renth by city males. Clear it was that those warriors had not yet tasted the renth, for it was thin, poor stuff beside the daru of warriors, truly fit for none save males. That, upon the provender which I had consumed, was less than the water to be found in forest streams.

When once I had fed as far as was necessary, I took a pot of renth and stood before the war leaders who had already gathered. That all the candles about the chamber had been relit meant naught, for a great darkness was to be felt in the silence possessed by each of them, a silence brought about by the abrupt healing of my wound. Their eyes lay upon me as I stood before them, left hand upon my sword hilt, pot of renth to my lips, yet no one gaze would truly meet mine, not even that of Tilim or Rogon or Gidon. All knew I had been touched by Mida, and none knew how they, themselves, might touch me.

"For what reason have you come here?" I demanded of them at last, looking to each of them. "For what reason do you stand here before me?"

Frowns touched their faces, indicating deep lack of understanding, stirring them in their places, after a moment moving Rogon to speech.

"We have come in answer to your summons, war leader," said she, less determination in her voice than I had come to expect. "Have you no memory of having summoned us?"

"Indeed have I no memory of having summoned the likes of you," said I, harshly, throwing the renth pot from me so that renth spilled upon the thickness of the floor cloth. "It had been my belief that I summoned war leaders, warriors of the Midanna, those who would sit in war council with me! Had I wished cringing, fearful city slave women, I would have prepared the chains of males for them! Run from me now, slave females, run to the arms of males for the safety you seem so to need! I shall seek for warriors elsewhere."

In great disgust did I turn from them, professing not to hear first their shocked silence, and then the beginning mutters of anger which I had hoped would come. Stiffly did I stride to a platform and take up another pot to be filled with renth, and at that time did the voice of Rogon come again.

"Jalav, you may not address us so!" said she, the cold of insult clearly to be heard. "I, for one, am a warrior of the Midanna, privileged to meet insult with my blade! Should you speak so again, I shall face you with swords, though Mida strike me to the ground for the doing!"

"Though *Mida* strike you?" I snapped, turning quickly to face her, doing naught to cover the fury I felt. "She who faces Jalav will be struck by Jalav, as it has ever been! Is it your belief that I stand not only behind the shield of Mida, but behind her swordarm as well?"

In the face of this demand did Rogon stand in silence for a moment, her anger undiminished yet briefly halted as she consid-

ered her words. To say that a Midanna stood behind the swordarm
of another was to call her a hanger-on, a coward, one unworthy
of the blooding of her life sign. Had Rogon spoken such words
to me before I had been chosen by Mida, her blood would have
long since stained my blade.

"The war leader Jalav does not stand behind the swordarm of
another," said Rogon at last, slowly, reluctantly, unwilling to
give over her anger. "She, like all loyal Midanna, stands solely
behind the shield of Mida—yet farther behind than any Midanna
warrior known to us. We do not fear you, Jalav, and yet—to
face Jalav is not to face Mida."

"Rogon speaks the truth," said I, nodding grimly. "Jalav
wears a sword, whereas Mida wears none. Mida has not Jalav's
need for a sword. Jalav was given a difficult task to see to, yet
was Jalav assured of the assistance of sister Midanna, for Jalav is
not Mida and cannot see to the task alone. Did you doubt that
this task was given me, Rogon, that you and your sisters now
stand in awe of the proof that Mida continues to watch over her
warrior? Has it yet come to you that by cause of the task given
me, I am denied the glory of death in battle? The burden of
Mida's love is a heavy one; must you add to it by seeing me as
that which I am not?"

Rogon's dark eyes gazed full upon me, her stare and silence
well shared by those who stood with her, all anger seemingly
having drained from their bodies. A war leader must have the
obedience of those who follow her, that and their respect; all else
is a drain upon the strength of a clan, a blot upon their battle
spirit. Was I to receive the awe and fear of those about me,
surely would my cause be more easily seen to without them.
This, I felt, was at last understood by those who were called war
leaders, those who would have stood like children before me.
Many of them breathed deeply, straightening their bodies as
befitted warriors of Mida, and then did Tilim step the closer to
stand beside Rogon.

"Jalav, I for one ask that we begin this meeting as though for
the first time," said Tilim, her head held high. "It seems I have
taken too many males for my pleasure, rattling my wits through
the length of their use. I have no memory of that which occurred
when first I entered this chamber."

"And I!" said another with a laugh, and "I, too!" said a
third, and soon were each of them filled with laughter and
agreement, standing about as though in a use tent, rather than in
the presence of a Keeper. Filled with pleasure and pride, I
quickly drained the pot of renth I had taken, gestured to them to

join me upon the floor cloth, then began a discussion of that which I hoped to accomplish come the new light.

It was clear to all that there was little time for lengthy discussions, therefore did they hear me out with no more than frowns to indicate their lack of understanding. Warriors see matters differently than do males, yet was it to be males with whom we were faced come the new light, therefore was it necessary that these war leaders be told of male beliefs. No warrior would be swayed from her purpose on Mida's behalf by a threat to the life of one of her sisters, for her sister's fate would surely be in the hands of Mida. With her purpose seen to, she would then take what revenge was called for, yet would that purpose be seen to first. Also, should a warrior be challenged, that challenge would not be refused though the warrior knew she would undoubtedly be bested and slain. Each instance was no more than that effort demanded by a sense of honor, yet males were well known to have naught of honor within them. My warriors were bewildered and somewhat disbelieving when I rose to my feet to quit the chamber, yet did they follow me without reluctance, intending to find, themselves, the truth of the matters I had spoken of. I felt no insult at their disbelief, for the doings of males must be seen to give proof to the contention that even they might be so low and without honor. My warriors knew little of the doings of males, yet would they learn.

Through the guidance of those who had learned their way about the immense dwelling, returning to the chamber of slaves was not as long a journey as the original search had been. The chamber itself was dimly lit, no more than a hand of torches illuminating the erect forms of the guard I had placed about the enclosure of he called High Seat. The portly male, within his enclosure, slept as soundly upon the metal flooring as any of the slaves longer tenanted within the chamber, unaware of those who stood and regarded him. Once I had seen that he was as I had left him, I looked again about the chamber, for surely did it seem to contain a greater number of males than it had the darkness previous.

"Indeed have we added to their number, Jalav," said Palar, she who was war leader to the Hunda. Her voice, held low, nevertheless contained a chuckle, possibly due to fond memory. "It was discovered that a large number of males had been taken captive, yet had they been left bound where taken. When gathering up these captives, disposition was a considerable problem till this chamber was recalled. When approached by those with captives to be quartered, we who remained here were unreluctant to accept charge of them.''

"How many hind of sleep have you had, Palar?" I asked, continuing to look about. "There shall undoubtedly be battle before darkness comes again."

''I have never yet fallen asleep in the midst of battle, Jalav,'' she replied with a laugh, her voice truly unconcerned. "With so many males available for use, I could not deny my warriors—nor myself. My clan sisters and I believe that one should never enter battle with unused males left behind."

"So that one may find the glory of death as a warrior without regret for that which was left undone," I nodded, my attention elsewhere. "The Hosta believe the same, Palar. What of those four males yonder, they who earlier wore black cloth about their loins? They lie within their enclosure as though felled by blows to the head. Were they used, or merely stripped?"

''Were it possible to point to those who were most used, it would likely be they,'' said Palar, a warm laziness having entered her tone. "In the absence of the sthuvad drug a warrior must make do, yet those four needed naught of encouragement. They fought at being taken upon their backs, as though they were temple slaves set to warrior pleasure, so they shouted, yet were they unable to halt the desires of their bodies. I know not how many warriors tasted of them before they were returned to their enclosure and allowed to sleep."

I nodded silently at Palar's words, piqued that I had forgotten to disallow the use of the Sigurri. They were sure to be displeased over the matter, perhaps even so far as to seek vengeance upon the journey south, yet was the thing done past recalling. Should their desire for vengeance prove too great, they would learn that no more than one of them was necessary to act as guide, and that that one need not be hale and free. I looked again upon their sleeping forms, seeing how their great muscled bodies sprawled in the chains they wore, exhausted, taken, spent, then turned from them to more pressing matters.

"The new light will soon be upon us," said I to Palar, anod toward the portly male, he called High Seat. "Remove yon male from the comfort of his rest and bring him behind me. His presence will soon be required."

"At once, Jalav," said Palar, and then did she gesture to those who stood as guard about the enclosure. With that small chore seen to I left the chamber to seek the others of my war leaders, they who had been sent ahead to arrange matters according to my instructions. Each means of entry was to be guarded, and well, for the conviction had come to me that the males of the city, knowing naught of what they faced, would attempt attack upon the dwelling we held, in an effort to reclaim it. I knew not whether the attack would come before their attempt at parley or during it, yet was I convinced that such an attack would come. Quickly did I see that each set of guards about an entry had had a runner assigned to them, one warrior who would not draw her weapon at an attack, instead taking herself quickly off to draw additional warriors from those stationed in the center of the dwelling. Not all additional warriors would race to the defense of a single entry, for wisest would the males be should they attack a second and perhaps third and fourth point after the initial attack, which would be designed to draw all defenders to the first point. The great majority of my warriors were to be found in the center of the dwelling, most taking their ease upon the floor cloth, some helping themselves to provender which had been found and brought to them, all filled with satisfaction at the thought of further battle. Should the males attack as I believed they would, they would soon learn the folly of facing Midanna warriors.

With all inspections satisfactorily seen to, I then made my way to the large front entrance of the dwelling, that by which I, myself, had entered. All torches had been removed from the walls of the area immediately about the entrance, as had been done with the other entries, yet was I easily able to see the large number of warriors who stood about in readiness. The air from without brought a fresh, dewy smell to raise one from the depths of stale city air and the confinement of dwellings, a small breeze from the still-dark skies wafting about in an attempt to stir the hair of those hidden from it by encircling walls. My spirit rose in protest over the need to remain longer within a city of males who cared naught for freedom, yet was there a task to be completed before the untamed forests might again be mine.

"Jalav, all has been seen to," came the voice of Rogon, her form coming out of the darkness to stand by my side. "Those who had guarded the gates from within now guard them from without, bows in their hands and arrows knocked, their positions difficult to make out even for a warrior. Should the males attempt to flee to fetch the aid of others, none of their number will survive the attempt."

"Well done," said I, moving the closer to the opening which was the entrance to the dwelling. Once there, I was able to stare out at the darkness surrounding us, a darkness filled with more than the stirrings of the feathered children of the wild. The grass,

I knew, was damp and chill with the touch of dew; perhaps it was this discomfort which kept the males who lay within the darkness from remaining still and unobserved. Even as I watched, a patch of shadow lifted briefly before lowering to stillness once more, a gleam of metal momentarily exposed by the movement. Did they think us deaf and blind, that we would be unaware of their presence?

"Their arrival about this dwelling was immediately noted," said Rogon, her eyes seeing what mine had seen. "How is it possible for ones such as they to hunt the forests? Such absence of skill should have seen them dead from lack of sustenance long ago."

"There are those who hunt for them," said I, closing my eyes to the breeze which caressed my face. "These are undoubtedly males who know naught save the ways of a city, naught of that which is necessary to survive beyond these walls. They are males, Rogon; how might they be a match to warriors?"

"How, indeed," said Rogon, scorn heavy in her voice. Our sisters had moved through their ranks both going to and coming from those at the gates, and they none the wiser; how was a warrior to consider them with anything other than scorn? Had their numbers been fewer, the confrontation I anticipated would have been totally unnecessary.

I left the entrance to walk the floor cloth of the corridor, commanding myself to patience as I would have upon the hunt. Our quarry was well within reach, but it was necessary to allow them to strike first. Around and about the waiting warriors I walked, aware of their breathing and mine, aware of the odd feel of a floor cloth beneath my bare feet, aware of how little of the fresh breeze was able to penetrate the dwelling. How was it possible for one to live so forever, locked away from the clean, open air and wide stretches of Mida's true world, walled in through choice rather than imprisonment? It was a matter I had been unable to comprehend, much as I had tried. As well to be beneath the ground in chains, as to be kept in such a dwelling forever.

My pacing had covered much roundabout distance before the faint sounds of distant battle reached us. The beginning of the new fey had just touched light to the skies, clearly the signal the males had awaited. The warriors about me stirred, as though forcing themselves to remain in place, and much did I, too, feel the sharp desire to race toward the battle we knew had begun. It was highly unlikely that any force would attempt entrance at our post, yet the sole male in the area seemed to have little understanding of this point. He called High Seat had stood slumped and silent in our midst, his long covering askew upon him beneath the chains, his entire demeanor one of defeat; now did his features grow anxious and hopeful in the faint light, as though rescue might soon be his. Surely, any with intelligence would see that attack had been expected by us and therefore might not be relied upon as a means of rescue, yet there the male stood, a furtive, crafty, look to his narrowed eye, a sly, evil smile to his fleshy lips, his round, delicate hands turned to fists within their manacles. The male anticipated freedom and subsequent vengeance, yet such would never be his; should the Midanna be in danger of losing that which they had taken, I would see the portly male first to have his throat opened. Never again would a warrior stand in judgment before him, to be declared slave by him, to be lashed for his pleasure. The male was unworthy of life himself, and would no longer be allowed the taking of life from others.

The sounds of battle continued as the light strengthened, yet the males in the grass before the dwelling made no attempt to add to them. They held their positions with as little skill as they had shown in the darkness, heads raising up to peer about, swords glinting in the brightening light, arms and backs and legs in turn presenting themselves as targets. Surely did I begin to believe they meant themselves to be seen, and yet, when a bloodied male appeared from the side of the dwelling, to stagger and fall nearly upon them, they quickly hugged the ground as though attempting invisibility. It was clear the bloodied male was beyond all assistance, yet do I believe they would have broken cover had he merely been wounded. Those who cannot place their wounded in Mida's care till battle is done are bereft indeed, of hope, of intelligent battle, and of all possibility of victory.

With the light of the new fey full in the skies, silence had once again returned. Runners had come to bring word that each of the five points of attack had been successfully defended, the last and farthest entry seeing the greatest number of males in the attempt. In accordance with my instructions, no prisoners had been taken, those coming in attack being either slain or driven off. No warrior had fallen to the blade of a male, and this fact had done much damage to the intentions of the males. They had been taught to fear the skill of a warrior, and this fear would aid in their total conquest.

Much discussion had gone on among the males upon the grass, disagreement rife among their number, yet was their final decision inevitable. All slowly regained their feet to stretch the stiffness from their bodies, all eyes nervously upon the dwelling in which we stood, and then did one of their number, a blue cloth held high above his head, begin to approach us. Slowly and deliberately did the male move, his broad face set in lines of grimness as his arm waved the cloth above his head, his forward movement ceasing only when he stood upon the stones before the wide steps of the dwelling. Clad in a dirt-stained, wet and hanging covering of city males was he, dark red and of mid-thigh length, closing at his side, where hung a blade and scabbard stiff and shiny in their seeming newness. I knew not the meaning of the waving cloth, for surely were we aware of his presence without it, yet the matter was unimportant. The male had come to parley, which was proven by the first of his words.

"You within the palace!" he called, his voice harsh and filled with anger. "Send your leader forth to speak with us, else shall it go harder with you!"

My warriors muttered in disapproval at this, for surely had the males been bested in battle by us, yet the bluster was full familiar to me. Males must ever voice threats to warriors, for true reason is completely beyond them. I nodded to Rogon, indicating that she was to be prepared for that task given her, gestured toward the hand of warriors who were to accompany me, then stepped from the entrance to the length of smooth stone above the waiting male. I paused a pace from the first of the steps, rested my left hand upon my sword hilt, and looked down upon the male.

"What is it you wish?" I inquired, impatiently. The male stared up at me with a frown, his eyes moving from the dagger in its leg bands upon my right leg, to the sword scabbarded about my waist above the breech, to the life sign which swung between my breasts, to the silver rings of a war leader in my ears. His tongue appeared to wet his lips, showing again how well pleased males were by the sight of Jalav, and then he cleared his throat.

"We have come to demand the release of the High Seat," he rasped, the blue cloth still firmly grasped in his fist. "Should you release him now, unharmed, you and your wenches will be allowed to depart unmolested. Our numbers are greater than yours, and sustenance will be denied you should you refuse us. Also, should it be necessary to wrest the palace from you by force, those of you who survive will be declared slave and thrown naked to the men of the city. Wisest would be that you give over this foolishness now, while you are still able."

A moment did I stand regarding him, this male who attempted

to take our victory with talk rather than sharpened metal, and then did I gesture a dismissal of his contention with all the contempt I felt so strongly within me.

"I have little time for the prattle of males!" I snapped, glaring down upon the fool of a speaker. "Do we not both know that you have attempted to retake this dwelling and have failed? You speak of disallowing us provender; we are Midanna warriors, and take what we wish, despite the objections of those about us! Should the matter come to a final battle, we will see this dwelling and all of your city in flames before the last of us falls. Our survivors to be declared slave indeed! Has it not yet entered your head that should our forces meet, there will *be* no survivors?"

The male, having gone ashen at my words, turned in desperation to those who had remained upon the grass. My voice had been pitched so that they, too, of necessity, might hear, yet did I feel much the fool for having spoken as I had. The boasting of males and warriors-to-be was sour upon my tongue, more a gesture of she who has little or no skill, rather than a doing fit for a war leader. It was necessary that these males be dealt with as they were wont to deal with others, yet was the action distasteful.

A hand of others had left their places when my speech was done, and quickly did they join he with the blue cloth. Little brotherly feeling was lost between they who came and he who waited, and much glaring was exchanged before one of the hand addressed himself to me.

"Lady, we ask your pardon for the harsh words addressed to you," said this newcomer, his manner less confident than that of his predecessor. His covering was of a dark gray rather than the red of the first, yet his sword seemed to have had even less use than that of the other. "We seek no battle between our groups, merely the freeing of our leader, our High Seat. We trust that in your generosity no harm has come to him, and humbly ask your price for setting him free. Should your demands be within our power to supply, you shall have them."

Much effort did it take to keep from sneering at this second male. Was this the manner in which to address an enemy, as a slave to a master? Were these males incapable of speaking to one as an equal, rather than with threats from master to slave, or pleadings from slave to master? Had I not stood in Mida's cause, surely would I have walked from all of them, never to allow males within sight again.

"You ask our price for releasing the male you term High Seat," said I, gazing evenly upon the second to have spoken.

"Should our price be the enslavement of every third male within your city, would you meet it?"

"Every third— Unthinkable!" snapped the first male, immediately bristling. "We would not. . . ."

"Hold your tongue!" shouted the second male to the first, his face reddening. When he saw himself obeyed, he again turned to me. "Lady, such a demand must first be discussed among the Council of the city. I, myself, though at their head, cannot speak for them. Is this your sole demand?"

"I have not yet stated a demand," said I, folding my arms beneath my life sign. "Out of curiosity, I merely advanced a supposition. For what reason would you consider one useless, portly male the equal of every third male of your city? The gross creature even appears useless for breeding."

Signs of shock appeared upon the second male's features, yet did one or two of those behind him cough into their hands, as though to hide their own lack of shock. He who had spoken first appeared unsure as to whether to laugh or fall to anger, yet the second was able to find words before the first.

"Young woman, have a care how you speak!" said he, great indignation upon him. "This is the High Seat we discuss, the Blessed One of the Serene Oneness! Contrary to the belief of those who scoff, the Serene Oneness does indeed hear words spoken against his chosen—and punishes them!"

"Ah, now do I see," said I, nodding in thoughtfulness. "You believe the male chosen and protected by your god. Is this so?"

"Indeed," nodded the male in turn, pleased that his point had been so easily grasped. The point, however, understood by me only by cause of a knowledge of the irrationality of males, was still somewhat unclear.

"Among Midanna, one's actions are the sole judge of value," I observed, uselessly, for these were males I spoke with. "However, I fail to see the connection between your assertion and your efforts. Were the male truly chosen and protected by your god, there would be no call for your presence now before me. Should a Midanna be taken by the enemy and her clan fail to free her with a major effort, surely would it be clear to them that Mida had turned her face from that warrior. You view such signs differently?"

"Most certainly," nodded the second male, the sobriety upon him doing naught to firm up the overall weakness of his features. "We consider this disaster as a testing from the Serene Oneness, a seeking for the true depth of our devotion to the Blessed One. Should we fail, we are not worthy of him."

"Again I find your words meaningless," said I, my head ashake. "I had thought no more than a small set of your males would decide upon what price I set for the life of your High Seat, yet now does it seem that all males within the city shall have their say. In what manner will this be accomplished?"

"In no manner," said the male, a small upset appearing within his eyes. "You were initially correct; our Council alone will be responsible for what decision is made."

"Then you speak foolishness!" I snapped, truly losing patience with the oaf. "Should all think themselves tested, all must respond; should only a small portion respond, the testing has failed. Even a child would have the wit to see this. Your response, as the response of all males, is totally lacking in reasoning thought. It has not even occurred to you that you place the burden of testing upon the wrong shoulders."

"What do you say, wench?" demanded the first male, he who continued to clutch the cloth of blue. The second male, unresponsive to my words, stood beside him with a look of deep anxiety. "How might we have misinterpreted this time of testing? Are you not here, deep within our city? Have you not taken the High Seat captive?"

"Indeed." I nodded, now looking down upon this other. "Among the Midanna, Mida will often test her warriors, yet never does the testing fall upon all the warriors of a single clan. No more than a hand of warriors will find themselves done so, more often a single warrior, most often a war leader. To lead others in the name of Mida is a great honor, an honor one must continually prove herself fit for. Is this god of yours less demanding than Mida? When was this Blessed One of yours last tested to prove his worthiness?"

A silence fell upon the males before me, no expression touching them save that their eyes were grim. Each looked briefly upon the others and then looked away, to withdraw within a shell of wordlessness that spoke more clearly than shouting.

"I see," said I, moving my gaze about among them. "He has not been tested since the time he won the glory of his place. Surely, great skill was shown at that time, yet from his appearance, the time must have been many kalod—"

My words broke off at the stir of discomfort and seeming guilt suddenly appearing upon the faces of the males, the manner in which they flushed and looked down toward the ground their leather-shod feet stood upon. A sudden thought came to me, one too foolish to give credence to, and yet. . . . Were these not males?

"It cannot be that the male did naught to earn his place," I said, the flatness of my tone a lash upon the backs of those before me, causing them to flinch as though struck. "You are males, I know, yet even males must demand a gesture from those who lead them. Did the portly one ask most politely for the place? Were his tears of desire heavier than those of other petitioners? In what pale, foolish manner were his merits judged?"

"You may not speak to us so!" blustered the second of the males, he of the weak features and unused sword. "We are not savages, to demand the spilling of blood from our High Seat! The previous High Seat, father to he who currently holds the place, took the weight of spilled blood upon his own soul to keep his son from the necessity! As a true son to his father, the place was his by right!"

"By right," I echoed, still flatly, again resting my left hand upon my sword hilt. "In such unexpected ways are we shown the true wisdom of Mida. It is undoubtedly for this reason that war leaders are denied issue, to keep them from the folly of desiring their daughters, fit or unfit, to follow their steps to glory. Far better to have no issue at all than to foist off upon one's clan a creature of no ability and no sense of personal accomplishment. It is clear that he who came before the gross male was undoubtedly smiled upon by your god, for his cause was supported and victory was vouchsafed him; in no manner might the same be said of his issue."

"That is not so!" began the second male, heatedly and in great agitation, yet the first male, he of the blue cloth, turned upon the second in anger.

"You are a fool, Thierlan!" he snapped, much of a growl edging his voice. "Must the Serene Oneness himself appear before you, to prove your folly beyond all doubt? That you owe your position to the High Seat is known to all; should you now refuse to honor that position and act in the best interests of the city, you may share the fate of that fat, slave-making hanger-on. Speak now, Thierlan: which will it be?"

The second male, he addressed as Thierlan, stared agonizedly at the first, his face working as he stared. The others of those who stood about also stared, yet solely at him called Thierlan, a thing the male was well aware of. A decision has been demanded of him, yet did he seek to delay the voicing of it.

"He is the High Seat, Relidose!" he begged toward the first male, a hand held out in supplication. "He is the Blessed One of the Serene Oneness! After so many kalod of paying him homage, how might we now, in honor, turn our backs upon him? The

Serene Oneness would surely shrivel our souls for such a doing! Had he not been chosen, would he have been allowed so long a reign? Would he not have been brought down much the sooner? We are being tested, I tell you, and dare not fail!''

"And yet the words of yon savage wench have a ring of rightness to them," said this Relidose in answer, looking down and seemingly seeing the blue cloth in his hand for the first time. He cast it from him with a sharp gesture, then looked again upon Thierlan. "I have ever found it difficult to believe that the Serene Oneness would choose one such as Gabilar as the High Seat, yet did it seem that no other thing than that had been done. Now the truth of the matter is in greater doubt, and I am unable to resolve the conflict. Is there no manner of determining the truth where all may see the outcome and know it forsooth?''

"The truth may easily be determined," said I, again bringing their eyes to me. "For warriors who know the reality of Mida, the truth is ever in their grasps. The truth is not as easily reached by males, however, who find reality in naught save that which they may put hands upon."

"Our belief in the Serene Oneness is as strong as your belief in your savage goddess, wench!" snapped this Relidose, Thierlan anod beside him. "The sole difference is the fact that the Serene Oneness truly exists! In what small, female manner would you attempt to resolve our differences of opinion?''

"You seem intent upon offering me insult, male," I said, my gaze held hard to his. "Should this truly be your intent, speak out now and plainly, for I will not overlook your manner again. Do you wish to face me with swords, to determine who will stand and who will fall? Should this not be your intention, I must hear that as well. I am war leader of all Midanna, and will not be spoken to as though I were city slave-woman."

The male continued to meet my gaze, though he frowned as though some matter were unclear. I had spoken softly, as befitted a war leader who had offered challenge, yet the seriousness of my intent was not missed by the male.

"I—did not speak to give you deliberate insult," said he, little friendliness to be heard in his tone. "It would give me great pleasure to face you, wench, if for no other reason than to teach you your proper place, yet this is scarcely the time for such petty squabbles. What suggestion have you?''

"The proper time may indeed present itself, male," said I with a nod. "I shall then be pleased to accommodate you. As for now, my thoughts are as follows: should your god smile upon the male, he will protect him in what battle he faces, giving him victory as he gives him the life of the one who opposes him. Do you agree in this, or do you find the concept too far beyond you?''

"The concept is clear," said the male Thierlan hurriedly, disallowing the heated retort in the throat of Relidose. "It does not follow, however, that the High Seat will agree to personal combat. Should he refuse, it may well be the Serene Oneness speaking through him, frowning upon so barbaric an action. How may we know?''

"The thought comes that those within hearing already have such knowledge," I remarked, then raised my hand to forestall argument upon the point. "In any event, we shall soon see which way the lellin wings. Rogon! Bring forth your captive!''

The males, taken by surprise, immediately looked beyond me to see the appearance of their High Seat, his gross form held in chains, his reluctance to advance overcome by the dagger held in his back by Rogon. She, in obedience to my word, had stood ready to come forth at my command, through the ranks of the hand of warriors who had accompanied me. The gross male blinked at the brightness of the fey as he stumbled forward, urged on by a dagger, and then did his narrowed gaze fall upon those who stared up at him. His shuffling progress came to a halt, his body straightened to its fullest extent, and then did he glare at those who gaped at him.

"Why have I not yet been freed of this odious captivity?'' he demanded, much like a petulant child who has not yet felt the weight of a hand in punishment. "Why do you merely stand there, in easy converse with my enemies, rather than attempting to aid me? When this is done I shall have all your heads, the Serene Oneness strike me down if I do not!''

"Blessed One, we are here for no other purpose than to attempt your release," whined Thierlan, cringing as the others about him frowned. True fear had been well taught me in the realm of Sigurr, yet was it a fear other than that bred by living beings like myself. This Thierlan feared the gross male and his power, a power Thierlan believed transcended that which had been stripped from the High Seat. The fear must be conquered before the male might be commanded by others, and this, Mida willing, would soon be done.

"You have been allowed from the dwelling to answer a challenge," said I to the gross male, drawing his furious gaze. "It has been suggested by these others that you are the chosen of your god, and are looked upon by him as his favorite. Is this so?''

"Indeed is it so!" spat the male, his features screwing up the tighter. "All those who oppose me will fall before the might of the Serene Oneness—and all those who fail to aid me, as well!"

Again did he glare upon the male Thierlan, pleased by the trembling brought to the limbs of the male, knowing full well the fear he put upon him. Indeed was the gross male a maker of slaves, and one who joyed in it as well. It would be pleasant to note how long his joy continued.

"Excellent," said I, the word bringing an immediate frown to the gross male. "I am the chosen of the goddess Mida, sent here to challenge you for possession of this city. You and I are to meet with swords, the survivor of the meeting to be the undisputed possessor of the prize. Are you now prepared to face me?"

"Face you?" shrilled the portly male, atremble with the fury ablaze in his eyes. "I am to face you in chains, the swords of these others at my back and throat, poised to strike when I have won?"

"The chains will, of course, be removed," said I with speed, disallowing the balance of his words which I was able to see poised upon his lips. "My warriors are forbidden to interfere, for that would be contrary to our beliefs. Should you stand the winner, they will each and every one withdraw from the city."

The male sputtered and foamed, all too well aware of the mutter of surprise which came from those males who listened and watched. Their city would be free of those they were unable to best by swords, yet only should their leader face me and stand victorious. To refuse was to give over their city to strangers as a gift, and even to males such a thing would be unpalatable.

"Do you mean to say they would depart without further bloodshed?" demanded Relidose, his suspicions clear in the tone he used. "You would have us believe you have come so far, only to turn your backs upon the accomplishment over the outcome of a single meeting of blades?"

"Certainly." I shrugged, surprised and yet not surprised that the male failed to understand. "Should I be bested, it would show that Mida no longer smiled upon me. My warriors, in all honor, could do no other thing than depart, for our word has been pledged. The word of a warrior is somewhat different from the word of a male."

"Your insolence will be your undoing, wench," growled this Relidose, for some reason annoyed. "I would dearly love to— Well, no matter. The point at hand is the doing of the High Seat. What say you, Blessed One? You will, of course, agree to the meeting and free our city?"

"You dare to dictate to *me*?" sputtered the portly male, now red of face due to his rage. "This decision, like all others, is *mine* to make, you low-born fool! Perhaps you are credulous enough to believe the words of savage sluts! I am not! Attack them now and have done with it!"

"We *have* attacked!" snapped Relidose, dark with anger and impatience. "The attack has come to naught and now are we faced with dealing with these wenches! Should you fail to accept the challenge given you, our city—and your own precious hide— will remain in their capture! Now, how say you?"

"Hold, hold, I pray you, hear my words!" said Thierlan, fearfully interrupting the harsh exchange between the two other males. "It is true, Blessed One, that this may be our sole opportunity for victory, yet is it also true, Relidose, that the Blessed One may be denied the spilling of blood by the Serene Oneness. With such an impasse before us, there is but one suggestion to be made: the High Seat must have a champion."

"A champion!" breathed the gross male, delight replacing the fury he had felt. "Of course! As the Serene Oneness denies me the spilling of blood, I must have a champion! It is all quite simple, you fool, Relidose. I shall have a champion who will best this savage, and then our city will be freed."

"You have not yet inquired as to the acceptability of a champion," growled Relidose, in disapproval. "Perhaps the concept is beyond the ken of these wenches."

"Such a thing is easily done," quavered Thierlan, anxious, now, to see the matter resolved. "How say you, my lady? The High Seat will have another stand in his place against you, one who will stand as though he were High Seat. Will you meet him?"

"This other will stand with the blessing of your god?" I asked, as though unsure of the proper response. "His besting will be looked upon as the besting of this one, complete and uncontested?"

"Complete and uncontested," agreed Thierlan eagerly, the gross male looking on with stiff haughtiness. "He who stands as champion for the High Seat stands with the blessing of the Serene Oneness, of that there is no doubt. Will you accept?"

"I will," said I with a nod. "Go and fetch this—champion, for I would have this foolishness over and done with."

"At once!" shouted Thierlan, his face bright with joy. "I will return immediately with your champion, Blessed One, and you will soon be free."

Quickly did the male take himself off, two of the others

trotting behind him, all knowing there would be no words of thanks nor encouragement from the gross male. As I left the place I had stood before the steps and made my way toward the dwelling, I gestured Rogon to accompany me, first indicating that the hand of warriors were to take her place about the High Seat. Rogon and I entered the dwelling in silence, yet once within her anger could no longer be contained.

"Your words were true, Jalav," said she, whirling to face me with fists upon hips, "and yet I am scarcely able to credit such vileness! To bargain the lives of others for a single life! To allow another to stand for you in a matter of honor! These males are less than the children of the wild!"

"They are males," I shrugged, amused by her anger. "To expect them to behave as warriors do is idle. You must now send runners to those who guard the entrances to this dwelling, warning them that the males may attack again once I have bared swords with the one who will come. Such a dishonorable act, after pledging to abide by the outcome of the challenge, is not beyond the doing of males. They must therefore remain alert."

She stood with mouth agape, staring in disbelief, then shook her head to indicate her feelings before moving off to dispatch the runners. I turned again to the glory of the new fey, the blue of the skies, the freshness of the air, the growing warmth which would soon dry the damp of the darkness. How fortunate was the warrior who might consider no more than such things of joy, untroubled by the dishonors of males and gods. Happily would Jalav have done so, yet Jalav was like the gross male, chosen and blessed and therefore disallowed the simple life. The gross male preferred it so, yet was the gross male demonstrably a fool.

"The runners are sent, Jalav," said Rogon from behind me, anger no longer coloring her tones. "Have you any further instructions?"

"No more than a last word of caution," I sighed, turning from the new fey to look down upon her. "Should it be Mida's will that I be bested, you and the others are to withdraw most carefully, in no manner trusting to the males for safe passage. Hold the portly one captive till all have withdrawn beyond the walls, only then turning him free. I would not have warrior lives uselessly spent."

"Jalav, do you doubt Mida's favor?" Rogon asked, wide-eyed in the dimness and nearly agasp. "Did she not send you to lead us in the taking of this city? Did she not heal your wound? Did she not. . . ."

"Rogon," said I, ending the flow of words. "All you say is

true, and yet—the thoughts of the gods are beyond simple warriors such as you and I. What was earlier desired, may now be displeasing. I do not speak from certain knowledge, merely do I seek to leave no matter of importance untouched. You will remember my words?''

"I shall indeed remember," nodded Rogon, at ease, now, with the thought. A good war leader strove to consider all possibilities before entering battle, and in such a light did Rogon see my commands. I, however, recalled the goddess Mida, and knew not how she would have me serve her desires. Best to be cautious in the face of uncertainty.

With all seen to, I again emerged from the dwelling, Rogon by my side. Across the grass, in the near distance, a set moved toward us, the male Thierlan clearly attempting to hurry their pace. All seemed prepared to obey him save the male in the center of the set, a large male covered in leather and metal, one with an easy stride, one of seeming unconcern. Gazing in curiosity, I moved to the top of the steps, and there was joined by the male Relidose, who climbed slowly to stand beside me.

"If I am not mistaken, that is Hanitor, a captain of the High Seat's guard and the finest sword in the city," said Relidose, turning to regard me. The male stood barely a finger taller than I, a fact he seemed to have been unaware of. "He must have passed the darkness on leave in the House of Heaven Pleasure, else would he have been with the others in the Palace. Were the choice mine, wench, I would sooner pledge myself slave than face him. That you are female will not slow his blade."

"And I," I replied without looking upon him, "knowing full well the mercy given slaves by males, would sooner face *Mida*'s blade than fall so again. Do not speak with no knowledge."

"So you have been slave," he mused, continuing to stare. "He who held you taught you little, wench, for that insolence seems a very part of you. Is this the reason for your hatred of men?"

"I have no hatred for males," I snorted, sparing him a quick glance. "I merely know them for that which they are: without honor and self-seeking beyond belief. I have no need of so useless an emotion as hatred."

"For one with no need of a thing, your supply seems more than adequate," said he, a dryness to his tone. "This Hanitor will feel none of the burn from the flame of your bitterness, girl; his sword will merely seek and find the heart of it. Are there no men among your tribe who might stand for you?"

Annoyance flared within me at his words, yet was it clear that the male made no true attempt at insult. I knew not how it was possible to live so, forever seeking others to stand for one, yet was that the way of males. To offer oneself in place of another is at times a means to glory; to seek another for the doing one should see to, no more than to shame unending.

"For what reason would warriors be so foolish as to wish males among them?" I asked, feeling the warmth of Mida's light bring new strength and pleasure to my body. "Our sets are clans, not tribes, and never would I so dishonor myself as to seek another to hold my place in battle, and surely not a male. Yet, even were I to consider so vile an act, no male has yet proven himself the equal of Jalav in sword skill, therefore would it be impossible to choose such a one."

"It is difficult to credit the calm assurance you speak with," said he, attempting to keep the sharpness from his tone as he eyed the manner in which I stretched toward the rich, blue skies, raising my arms and face to Mida's healing light. "You have announced yourself war leader to this pack of ravening females, I know, yet surely must the number of men you have faced be few. I fear you have little knowledge of the strength and ability men are able to bring to battle. What if you should be slain?"

"Then I will attain the glory of death in battle." I shrugged, at last turning full to face him. "Also, your leader will be assured his position, your city its freedom, and my warriors the knowledge that Mida no longer smiles upon me. Surely, such an outcome would find full approval in your eyes."

"Full approval?" he growled, glowering upon me in something much like anger. "No, my high and mighty war leader Jalav, I do not find full approval in the thought of a wench's coming death. It is enough that men must die in battle. I will stand for you with Hanitor."

Angrily did the male glare at me, broad face grim, brows lowered in menace, fists stiff upon hips. Perplexedly did I return his stare, for I had not the least idea of what he was about. For what reason would this male, this stranger and enemy, offer to stand for me? Was it glory he sought, recognition from his fellow males—or perhaps the freeing of his city through the spilling of his blood? Should the truth lie in the last supposition I would honor him for his courage, yet such a thing might not be.

"You do not have my let to stand for me," I informed him, yet with something of a smile for the loyalty he showed for his city. "The matter is one between Mida and the one who is called the Serene Oneness—and their combatants have already been chosen. Stand aside gladly, male, for the place is not an easy one.''

"Naught is unchangeable till blades have been bared," he maintained stubbornly. "It is not. . . .''

"I see you, Relidose!" came the voice of the High Seat, causing us to turn toward him. The male stood amidst the hand of warriors I had left to guard him, his face screwed up as he peered narrowly at us. "I see how you converse with my enemies in low tones, and I will not forget! When these chains are struck from me, you shall first begin to wear yours!''

"It has come to me that all of us already wear chains, round Gabilar," returned Relidose, standing forth to glare upon the portly male. "Till the coming of these wenches, we were each of us chained to the whims of one who is unworthy even to speak the name of the Serene Oneness. Should your champion be successful, it will mean naught save that *he* is worthy!''

"Heresy!" choked the portly male, frothing as his face reddened with rage. "Those words will see you immured in my dungeons for the rest of your miserable life, fool! Which, I promise you, will not be as short as you will pray it to be! Mark my words! Mark my words!''

The portly male trembled with his fury, eyes glaring madly, soft hands folded to fists in the manacles, body twisted as though to hurl his venom with main strength. The male Relidose stood silently afrown, seeing, perhaps for the first time, the madness which filled the male called High Seat. Rogon, now close beside me, thoughtfully fingered the hilt of her sword, no doubt considering the manner in which those afflicted with madness are seen to among the Midanna. A sharp edge quickly puts an end to the suffering madness brings, both for the warrior involved and for those about her. No other than males would put such a one in a position of supreme power.

"I have returned, Blessed One!" called the male Thierlan, hurrying to the foot of the steps. So intent upon what he was about was the male, that he failed to note the state of his High Seat. Quickly did his eyes come to me, and a smirk showed with the sweep of his arm. "If you will accompany me to the grass, lady, our champion will be pleased to face you.''

The male of leather and metal, he named Hanitor by Relidose, indeed stood upon the grass beyond the stoned area, arms afold upon his chest, eyes moving slowly about me, a faint grin playing across his face. Many males stood about him at a respectful distance, others streaming up to join those already in attendance, each of them filled full with confidence in him who would stand for their High Seat. With a nod I began to move toward the steps, yet found the hand of Relidose upon my arm.

"There is yet time to reconsider," said he, strangely sober. "Give yourself as slave to Hanitor, else allow me to stand for you. In no other way will life be left to you."

"All is as Mida wishes," said I, gently removing my arm from his grasp. "Should it be her wish that I fall, I will fall. The sacrifice you propose on behalf of your city does you credit, male, yet is it contrary to the will of the gods. Another's blood will be spilled this fey, and that blood will decide the outcome."

Then I turned and walked from him, down the steps and toward the male of leather and metal. A frown had grown upon the face of the male Relidose, as though he lacked understanding of some matter, yet was the frown easily forgotten in the face of the smirk still visible upon the male Thierlan as I passed him at the bottom of the steps. Another would have been angered or put out that I failed to allow him to lead me to the confrontation he had arranged, yet the small male was capable of no such indication of pride. Hurriedly did he move to keep to my left as I walked, hopping about much like a child in playtime, largely ignored by all those who so eagerly awaited the coming battle. Across the stones I walked, disregarding their presence, my right hand reaching across to loosen my sword in its scabbard, and those males between me and the male Hanitor moved spritely to remove themselves from my path.

"And here we are at last," chattered the male Thierlan as I halted upon the grass, perhaps three paces from the male who awaited me. "This, lady, is Hanitor, guard Captain to the High Seat and his chosen champion, he whom you have indicated you are willing to face."

"Lady?" rumbled this Hanitor, grinning widely. Large indeed was the male, wide of shoulder and thick of arm, tall and broad, yet trim beneath the leather and metal, a plain, well-worn scabbard at his side, showing a hilt which had seen much handling. "I see you mistake her, little man. I see before me no more than a varaina, a pavillion—she, a cuddling slave let free of her chains. A man would be a fool to address this one as lady."

A muted gasp ran around those within hearing, for surely was I expected to fall to fury over the words of the male. Hanitor sought to give me deliberate insult, undoubtedly in an effort to blind me with rage, yet was I no newly blooded warrior to be done so. A faint smile touched me as I rested my left hand upon the hilt of my sword, and glanced briefly toward Thierlan.

"This champion you have chosen speaks well and boldly,"

said I, my gaze held to the male of leather and metal. "Should his sword prove to be as bold, it may take some small effort to best him."

Again a flurry of sound arose, many fearful glances bent upon the male Hanitor, yet the male's grin had widened rather than faltered. He, too, knew the folly of entering battle gripped in anger, and would no sooner fall to it than I.

"Ah, I believe we are now prepared to begin," said Thierlan, his tone hesitant yet his words spilling over each other in his haste to speak them. "I ask all of you here to back a bit and allow them the freedom of movement they will require to. . . ."

"Hold," said Hanitor, his calm rumble immediately halting the flow of instruction from Thierlan. The small, weak-featured male looked upon the larger with a good deal of anxiety, yet awaited in silence what words the other would speak; when they came, however, the words were addressed to me.

"Should you wish this farce to continue, girl," said Hanitor, "go you now and fetch what armor you have. It will not keep the life within that well-rounded body of yours, yet will I await the fetching of it. I will have no man say afterward that undue advantage was taken."

"I have no knowledge of this—armor of which you speak," said I, ignoring the new murmurs which flowed about us. "Do you seek to delay our meeting, male? I had thought you prepared and willing."

"This is armor, girl," said he, striking himself upon the metal which covered his chest, amusement no longer with him. "And indeed am I prepared and willing, far more so than you. You cannot face an armored man bare-breasted."

"I grow weary of being told what I may and may not do," said I, allowing a sharpness to enter my tone. "As you find a need for that leather and metal which covers you, you may keep it; I find no similar need. Now: Are we to continue, or have you further objections?"

The male growled low in his throat, a sound of vexation and anger echoed in the dark of his eyes, then did he turn and walk from me, his hands at the leather and metal which covered his side. Another male came from the midst of the gapers to assist him, and quickly was the covering removed, leaving him in naught save light blue cloth body covering, leather foot coverings, and swordbelt. In such a manner did the male return to where he had stood, and still was there annoyance within him.

"I will not have men say undue advantage was taken," he repeated, flexing arms and shoulders against the absence of accustomed weight. "I will not spare you, girl, of that you may be sure, yet was the choice to face me yours. We may now begin."

The male Thierlan again prepared to speak, yet did I step to my right and draw my blade as Hanitor drew his, the double action sending Thierlan scurrying to those who backed from reach of our swords. Many had seemed surprised that the thing might be begun so quickly, which showed them as the fools they were. To fight to the death was no play for children, to be begun at a word or gesture from another. To begin the thing one need only bare a blade, and that had already been done.

As ever in single combat, the presence of others was immediately ejected from my awareness. Well did I know that I gripped the silver and black hilt of the sword given me by Mida, and well aware was I of the grass beneath my feet, yet my eyes saw naught save the male Hanitor, the manner in which he stood, the manner in which he held his blade. The male moved quickly, seeking victory in immediate attack, his blade glinting in Mida's light as he struck at me strongly, attempting to knock my sword aside, and such was the beginning of his downfall. To meet the blow would have been foolishness, therefore did I slide it and immediately slash in counterattack, opening his arm before he was able to turn his blade to defense. So quickly did the thing occur, a brief meeting and then we had parted, yet the edge of my blade now shone red in the early light, drawing a grimace of pain from the male and a gasp of shock from those who watched.

Ah, Mida! Ever shall the sight of blood upon my blade stir me to burning life, take all reason from my mind, and fill me with the joy that battle brings. The sound of the hadat's capture croon escaped from my throat, the hissing growl telling the male before me that he was mine, and then did I begin my advance upon him, seeing naught of the paleness which began to take his features, the lack of understanding beginning to fill his eyes. A quick leap brought me within reach of him, and then did my blade begin the dance of death, a twisting and cavorting the male was hard-pressed to parry. Slash and cut, stab and slice, foot by foot was the male pressed backward, his arm working frenziedly to protect him from harm, his bewilderment so thick it nearly took my notice. How do these males face one another, one wonders, if not with eagerness to pierce flesh and spill blood? At that time I was able to wonder at naught, for the battle lust had taken me so deeply I was able to do no more than swing at the male, slashing here and there and adding to the first wound he had gotten. Each time he was touched his blade defense faltered; each time he was touched the hadat crooning grew stronger.

The battle was ended far sooner than I would have wished. Surely had I thought the male one to stand firmly before me, his sword a true challenge to mine, yet did he prove himself no more than the others. Panting, covered in sweat and blood, his backing across the grass was halted by a loss of footing, sending him sprawling to his back with arms flung up above his head. Quick as thought was I upon him, my sword raised high above his throat, and then was his head no longer a part of his body, the scream he had begun abruptly ended. The male had promised me no quarter in the battle, which was as it should have been, and yet did I believe he had expected quarter to be given to him, there just before the end. The thought touched me only lightly, however, for in victory there was an obligation to be met. Fiercely, proudly, did I stand above the body of he who had challenged me, and raised my arms and sword to the skies.

"For your chains, Mida!" I called in triumph. "Accept this worthless male from your Hosta war leader! Ever shall I spill blood to your glory!"

A deep and heavy silence greeted this dedication, strange in light of the number of gawping males who had witnessed the meeting, unexplained till I had taken my gaze from the skies and looked about me. Each male stood frozen in place, staring with shocked horror, taken by the sight of a victorious Midanna. Each seemed to shrink back as my gaze touched him, each save for the weak-featured Thierlan, who stood with back turned as he silently emptied himself of that which had been within. Once before had my battle prowess been received so, with shock rather than acclamation, and yet those who had done so had also been male. No warriors were about, no more than males, and what other thing might a warrior expect from a male than the look which named her savage?

"This meeting of blades has decided the fate of your city," I called to those about me, my bloody sword yet grasped in my fist. "Those who follow Mida stand supreme above him who once was called blessed and chosen. Are there any others who would deny this contention?" Slowly did I look about me, allowing sufficient time for a response, unsurprisingly finding none save the shuffling of feet and a looking away. "Very well," said I. "I would now have it known that we have not taken your city for all time. Strangers come, enemies who would do for all of us, those who would place the chains of slaves upon each and every one of us. It is we who shall face and best these enemies of all, my warriors and I, and then will your city be returned to you, to do with as you please. We have no desire for your city, yet must we have it till the strangers come. Should any of you attempt to force our departure before then, those fools will not live to see the end of battle. Go about what business you have, and do not again come before us bearing weapons. Those who do will go the way of this one."

My sword indicated him who lay at my feet, him who in life had been known as Hanitor, and the gesture proved sufficient. The males turned numbly and began moving off, not yet to the point of speaking one to the other, not yet to the point of ceasing their trembling. Our time of difficulty with the males was not yet over, yet would there be some measure of quiet before they again bedeviled us. During this time of quiet, our position would be consolidated.

The male Thierlan trembled heavily when I approached him, calming only somewhat when he heard my command that he gather those who stood high in the city, and present himself and them to me in the overlarge dwelling as soon as possible. This he quickly agreed to, then scurried off amongst the others, losing himself in their midst in the blink of an eye. After that was I able to cleanse my sword in the sweet ground of Mida, resheathe it, and turn to the dwelling known as palace, taking a straight path through what covertly staring males yet remained. The screams from the dwelling had fallen on deaf ears, yet, as I approached, the sounds resolved themselves into words.

"Fools! Cowards! Blasphemers!" shrieked the portly male, he who had been the High Seat, struggling in his chains and the grips of my warriors. "Do not abandon me to these sluttish females! I demand that you return and free me! I, your High Seat, command you! Return and free me!"

Shocked fear spoke in the male's screams, a forced realization that what had been no longer was. None would heed him, the male knew, yet was it necessary to what remained of his sanity that he make the attempt. Had I not known of the misery and agony he had caused to so many others, well might I have been moved to pity for him.

"Jalav, an excellent exercise!" called Rogon in high spirits, awaiting me beside the male Relidose as I climbed the steps. "You may now understand, male, why I spoke of your fears as foolishness. Jalav stands behind the shield of Mida, smiled upon as no other."

"Indeed," said Relidose, his tone even yet his gaze locked to my face. "And yet, from what I have seen, Jalav has little need of shielding from your Mida. I must admit, wench, that never have I seen the equal of your sword work. The sheer savagery of it overwhelmed Hanitor completely, sending him down to death by the unexpected ferocity of the attack. He, like me, undoubtedly anticipated a more feminine showing. We both were fools, yet is he now a dead fool.''

"And twice a fool for having removed his covering," said I, at last standing with them at the top of the stairs. "In battle one must fight as one is accustomed to fighting, with or without trappings, else does one find oneself without balance and timing. The male would still have found himself bested, yet not quite so soon.''

Then did I turn to the hand of warriors about the portly male, and instruct them to return him to his enclosure within the chamber of slaves. This they accomplished with small difficulty though the male continued his ranting, and as I moved to follow, a hand was suddenly upon my arm.

"Wench—Jalav—I would ask a thing of you," said this Relidose, the words coming to him with difficulty. "I—wish to accompany you.''

Though the male appeared to wish to speak further, no other words left his lips. He stood, broad and ruddy-cheeked, his dark gaze holding to mine with difficulty, a numbed surprise about him at what he had done, yet accompanied by an unwillingness to call back the words already spoken. Rogon, behind his shoulder, grinned knowingly, for what war leader of Midanna has not had a male trailing after her of his own volition, seeking to serve her both without and within her sleeping leather? I had no desire for the male Relidose, yet might his presence, properly used, prove beneficial to my efforts.

"For now you may accompany me," I allowed, staring into the depth of his eyes with a soberness which caused him to remove his hand from my arm. "What the future may bring remains to be seen. Stay close and do not attempt insolence with any of the warriors who follow me. If you should be slain by one of them, the loss will be entirely yours.''

"I believe I understand," said he, a small frown of pain coming to his large, dark eyes. "I am not the first man to follow you about, waiting and hoping for your notice. Before that notice is received, I must earn it.''

"The position has not been forced upon you," I shrugged, again seeing the manner in which his eyes moved about me. "Should you choose to follow, first remove that blade.''

With a gesture to Rogon, I strode off toward the entrance to the dwelling, making no effort to see whether the male followed. Were he to be of use to me, his presence must be entirely his own choice. Once within I paused to detail a strong guard for the entrance before dismissing the other warriors; when I turned from this task the male was there, unsure of the commitment he had made, yet silent and disarmed. Rogon, continuing to show her amusement, indicated that he was to follow behind me as I moved farther into the dwelling, yet I, myself, made no such acknowledgment of his presence. A male who accompanies a war leader must learn to efface himself, a lesson best learned when taught immediately.

Rediscovering the place of the chamber of slaves without guidance and without difficulty gave me a good deal of pleasure, nearly as much pleasure as speaking words of approval to those warriors I saw as I made my way through the dwelling. I had had each set of entrance guards replaced with other, fresher warriors, then had ordered that those without posts seek sustenance and sleep. The city males should by then have been thoroughly cowed, and yet how is one to know the minds of males? Best to be prepared should they take it in their heads to attack again, yet the clamor raised by those warriors who considered themselves denied the captures they had made nearly set the dwelling atremble. There was no refusal to obey among those warriors, of course, but their outraged moanings truly had me chuckling as I left them. They would obey my word, and completely, then once the unimportant matter of sleep was attended to, those males made captive would be used and well.

Within the chamber of slaves a bustle of activity had begun, showing that those occupants of the chamber were now fully awake. Slave females scurried about the enclosures in bright torchlight, bringing pots of heated grain to those who had not been allowed their limited freedom, carefully avoiding the warriors who stood about the chamber regarding them. All males who had been used the darkness before now sat chained about the walls of the chamber, all having been carefully served their sustenance before any of the others. Most knew well what this care portended, and few, if any, seemed pleased with the prospect. The portly male had been returned to his enclosure, and there he sat, upon the metal of the flooring, his body slumped and his eyes cast downward, aware of naught about him.

"Jalav, I am pleased you have returned," called Palar as she spied me, crossing the floor of the chamber in lazy strides. "With all battle done for the while, we too have returned here—to see to our captives."

The laughter of her warriors about the chamber was heavy with anticipation, causing a stirring of chain among the males in reaction. I, too, grinned with anticipation, yet not upon the selfsame point.

"Your dedication to lowly slaves is most gratifying, Palar," said I, folding my arms beneath my life sign as she approached. "As you and your warriors must now seek sustenance and sleep as the other clans do, your dedication also proves itself selfless."

"Sleep?" yelped Palar, halting abruptly with a stricken look, her Hunda mirroring her upset. "War leader—Jalav—there are males here as yet unused, and those who more than merit a second using—Sleep may be had at any time!"

"Palar, you speak truly," I nodded, unable to shed the laughter brought me. "And this, war leader, is the time it may be had. I will require a small number of your warriors for a short time, and then you may indicate those who will stand first watch."

"Ah, Jalav, I despair of you," said she, her head ashake, a deliberate surliness to her tone. "I had not known that the spilling of blood would bring such a viciousness to your naturally sweet nature. What number of my warriors will you have?"

"Four," said I with a laugh, "and a male of leather and metal as well. And see that the four are well rested enough to find themselves able to exhibit some small amount of sword skill. There is yet one portion of this dwelling untaken."

Prepared to indicate further displeasure with my commands, Palar halted the foolishness upon hearing my words, indicated four warriors to attend me, then accompanied them to hear what instructions I would speak. They knew naught of the area below the dwelling called dungeons, yet were they able to quickly grasp the necessary means of entry to the area. Two warriors would be first to descend below the ground, moving silently and taking care that those who stood guard within the confines of the metal door saw and heard naught of their approach. Next to descend would be a third warrior and a male of leather and metal, she struggling as though captive to him, he armed as she was not. Those males within the metal door would surely see it open to admit their brother and his captive, and then would they discover the presence of others. The fourth warrior would remain unseen as she followed the path of the male and his supposed captive, to insure the proper behavior of the male. Such a manner of entry had been effective on a previous occasion; there was little reason to believe it would not be so again.

"And yet, should the males have learned to be more cautious, do not attempt to force an entry," I ended. "Return here and inform me of the fact, and I shall seek other means."

"As you command, war leader," said the warriors, immediately taking themselves off to choose a male from among the captives. Palar stood silently, fingering the hilt of her sword, most likely considering the notion of accompanying her warriors to the area below. I, however, already being fully conversant with the damp and stink of the area called dungeons, had no interest in approaching them any sooner than need be. When they were taken would be time enough, time for doing what must be done, that which had long needed doing. The present would better be served by finding that which might be fed upon, as the short to-do with the male Hanitor had returned a small portion of the hunger which had earlier gripped me.

Farther within the chamber, not far from the midst of the chained males, stood a wide platform of carved wood, dark and rubbed with oils. Upon this platform had been placed a number of tall pots which were called goblets by city folk, a larger pot which often contained renth, and several metal boards of a golden color filled with that which was obviously meant to be fed upon. To this platform did I walk where, after filling a goblet with renth, I was able to choose a bevlin which was less shrunken than its fellows. The bevlin trees of the forests, most often found growing in small stands near glades, bear bevlind of great size; large, round and firm are they, of a deep and glowing orange color, sweet and refreshing to one who either hungers or thirsts. These bevlind of the cities were small, scrawny things by comparison, nearly shriveled and beyond the point where one might feed upon them, yet were their juices adequate for the oiling of my sword in the absence of proper oil. The leg of a forest paslat, too well cooked by far, as is the way of city males with meat and fowl, began to see to the hunger I had, and the dagger from my leg bands opened the bevlin as I perched myself upon the edge of the platform to observe the doings of Palar's warriors as they chose a male to accompany them below-ground. The four had some small difficulty in choosing a male, for none wished to choose a male with proven ability in giving pleasure, lest the male attempt escape or duplicity and force them to end him. At length an untried male was chosen, yet did I believe from the shaken expression he wore that he would make no effort toward escape or betrayal. The warriors who accompanied him had made clear their intentions, and no other than a fool would doubt their sincerity.

I had done no more than spread the bevlin oil upon my sword

when it came to me that I had no cloth to properly complete the doing. I looked about upon the platform and spied a length of yellow silk, encumbered in some manner about its edging with stitching which formed the images of small field flowers, those called lancillead. For what reason one would wish lancillead upon silk I knew not, yet was it also true that I cared not. The length of silk would do nicely to rid my sword of the last vestiges of male blood. I reached it to me and set it to the oil, and then did a voice speak from not far distant.

"Never have I seen wenches so filled with concern over the proper care of weapons," said the voice, a deep male voice I seemed to recall. "The others, too, did the same when first they returned to this chamber, though none with the draping of a wine slave, as you do. I would wager that sword has seen recent use."

I raised my eyes to find the gaze of the red-haired Sigurri upon me, he who had spoken the fey previous, he who spoke now. Easily did he lean upon the wall to which he had been chained, his broad, muscled body asprawl in seeming comfort, his right knee raised to support a wide forearm. The black loincloth which had been his had not been returned, yet did he seem less disturbed at the loss than his brothers, who sat, with thunder upon their brows, to his right. Well made indeed were these males, and again did it irk me that I had once more forgotten to attend to their disposition.

"Indeed has this sword seen recent use," said I, attempting to rid my tone of the impatience self-anger sought to fill it with. "As I understand it, you and your males may also be spoken of in such a manner. Should it be your desire to avoid the same again, I am able to see it so."

"Do you seek to lure me to your own side, wench?" laughed the male, abrupt and surprised delight upon him. "Should that be your intention, you need not ask. You need only remove that leather breech and replace it with that draping you have nearly ruined with blood and oil. The color suits you well."

"Lure you?" I asked, understanding naught of what amused the male. "For what reason would I attempt to lure a sthuvad already set to use? Had it been my desire to use you, there are none who might deny me. Am I to understand you have no desire to be released from sthuvad use?"

"Each of you will regret having done us so to begin with!" growled a second Sigurri, he of the darker hair, he who sat immediately beside the first. "To use warriors as though they were temple slaves is an insult which will not soon be forgotten! Should we ever escape these chains, Sigurr will see us avenged!"

The dark eyes of the male blazed with anger, a clank of chain underscoring his words as his fists tightened above the manacles. Indeed was the same to be seen in the eyes of each of them, perhaps not as strongly, yet indisputably there in the blaze of the torches. They would not beg for release, I saw, these males of Sigurr, and by that observation did I warm to them in some small measure.

"The oversight was mine," said I to the dark-haired male, with a shrug. "What was done cannot be undone, therefore is it foolish to consider regret. Should it be your wish to face me with swords when you are released, I shall, of course, meet you. To allow you the challenge is the least I may do."

The four Sigurri sat the straighter in frowning surprise, the looks exchanged between them as empty of understanding as the stares they sent to me. He of the dark hair was about to speak in answer, yet the red-haired male spoke before him.

"What oversight do you mean, wench?" he demanded, his air of ease completely gone. "Much does it seem as though we were meant to be other than captives and slaves, yet such makes no sense. Never have we seen you before your attack upon this place."

"And what of this release you speak of?" added the dark-haired male, his fist now closed about the length of chain between his wrists. "To be released and allowed the right of challenge is a thing unknown in these parts!"

"We are no more native to these parts than are you," said I, seeing it would be best if the entire tale were told. My sword was now clear of all traces of blood and dirt, therefore did I throw the bit of yellow silk from me, rise from the platform and resheathe the sword, then take what remained of the paslat leg and approach the males.

"I come from Mida and Sigurr," said I, speaking softly as I crouched perhaps a pace before them. "I have visited their domain upon this world, and there was told of their desires concerning the Midanna and the Sigurri. We, the Midanna, have taken this city in anticipation of the arrival of powerful strangers, those who are enemy to both Mida and Sigurr. We, with the assistance of the Sigurri, are to defeat these strangers when they appear, for it is here they will first show themselves. I am to see to the release of the four of you, and then return with you to your city, where I may raise the host of Sigurr to stand with the warriors of Mida. In such a manner shall the coming strangers be vanquished."

I took a further taste of the paslat as the Sigurri regarded me, bewilderment and confusion strong upon them. Each stirred in his place, their struggle with my words an inner thing, their desire to disbelieve evident in the silent protest in their eyes. Strongly would they have voiced that protest, and yet, were they to do so, well might they find themselves remaining as slave and sthuvad to armed conquerors. The face of the dark-haired male worked in indecision, his outrage wishing him to speak, his desire to be free cautioning him to silence, and I grinned at sight of his difficulty. Much as all males were these Sigurri, yet had they learned a measure of discretion with Midanna.

"You are amused," said the red-haired male, a touch of annoyance to his tone, his light eyes regarding me steadily. "This tale you tell us is fantastic indeed, yet our disbelief does no more than amuse you. I know not whether it be true or not, and yet— What if we refuse to guide you to our city?"

"Then I shall remain here and greet the strangers with none save my warriors," I shrugged, biting again at the paslat. "It is not I who demands the presence of the Sigurri, but the dark god himself who would have it so. Should there be one to whom you must answer, it will be he."

"Indeed do you speak as though well acquainted with the dark god," scoffed the dark-haired male, an additional affront seeking to claim him. "We are loyal warriors of his creed, loyal to his temple and loyal to his presence. Should he seek in our hearts, he will not find us wanting."

"Perhaps not," I agreed, purposely thoughtful. "And yet was it his desire for the presence of his warriors which caused Mida to call me to her, so that he might accept or reject me as his envoy. That I am here and aware of you must stand as proof of my acceptance, proof that I ride in his name as well as in the name of Mida. That I am able to force you to my will has no bearing; such a thing I shall not do. Should you refuse to guide me, so be it. I shall release you to go your way as I go mine."

"And keep all battle glory to your wenches alone," growled a third male, one of those two with light hair. "Should it be the truth you speak, girl, our forces are meant to stand beside yours, spilling the blood of the enemies of Sigurr the mighty. Should you seek to keep the glory from us, it is you who shall find the need to answer to the dark god."

"As to the truth of her words," said the red-haired male, "I believe I now see a thing which supports the contention even beyond her knowledge of our origins. Upon the darkness previous was there a deep wound in her shoulder, accompanied by those other, lesser wounds; this I saw with my own eyes, yet is that deep wound now healed beyond all memory of it. Is it possible for such a thing to be, save at the intervention of Sigurr himself?''

"Indeed not," said the dark-haired male, the thoughtful tone of the red-haired one touching him as well. "I, too, saw the wound she had, and yet now am I able to see naught save a faint line in its place. What are we to do, Mehrayn?"

"It seems clear we have little choice," said the red-haired male, stirring his chains as he moved his large body. "And yet would it be well for us to discuss the matter alone, among ourselves. Have us removed from this wall, wench, and provide us with a place of privacy."

Much did the male seem prepared for my immediate obedience, but that was scarcely forthcoming. Silently did I remain in my crouch before him, feeding upon the paslat I held, curious as to how long a time must pass before understanding reached him. As it happened, no more than a moment was necessary.

"Very well," said he, nearly at once, the annoyance once more with him. "You are leader to these others, and must be properly coaxed and tickled. To deny the need would be idle. May we impose upon your generosity, great war leader, and ask to be allowed some moments of privacy? We are mere men, and must consult with one another."

The grins the others grew at the red-haired male's insolence had no power to anger me, for these were indeed no more than males with whom I spoke. That they thought themselves untouchable was clear, a notion they had best be disabused of.

"Of a certainty you may have the privacy you require," I replied, smiling as I rose from my crouch. "My warriors will see to it immediately."

I turned from them and walked to the platform, tossed the paslat bone upon it and again took up my goblet of renth, then gestured Palar to my side.

"Those four males with black strokes upon their shoulders," said I to her, tasting of the renth. "Though it grieves me to deprive you, Palar, they are not again to be put to sthuvad use. They must soon be set free to go where they will, and yet I would see them discomforted in a small way before the time of their release. Have your warriors place them in an enclosure, their chains upon them, and then have the enclosure covered over, with drapings from the walls if need be. Proper provender is to be given them later, when your warriors have awakened from their rest; for now let that cooked grain called gruel suffice them."

"It shall be as you say, Jalav," acknowledged Palar, a faint grin touching her. "The males now examine their chains as though expecting to be quickly freed of them. Such a belief, of course, could not have been fostered by you."

"Most certainly not," I agreed, matching her grin. "Privacy was requested, and privacy did I agree to grant them. That they assume unchaining is also to be their lot is totally unwarranted. I leave you to see to their rude awakening."

"Where do you go now, Jalav?" asked Palar, no more than a glance for the goblet I emptied and returned to the platform. "Do you send us all to our rest and intend none for yourself?"

"I will rest when I have tended to the last of the city males," said I, finding the need to stretch widely. "In the interim, what rest I had during the darkness will suffice. It was, my excellent war leader, a good deal more than you, yourself, may boast of."

"Your point is well taken, war leader," laughed Palar, shaking her head. "Your rest would have been more had you had no more than a hin of sleep. I shall now see to your males."

She turned from me to choose among her warriors in the chamber, therefore was I able to take myself off toward the doors of the place. As I approached them I spied Rogon taking her ease among a number of her warriors, the male Relidose seated upon the flags not far from them. In some manner had I forgotten the presence of the male, and a glance at the quickly covered misery to be seen in his eyes showed he was well aware of my lapse of memory. Slowly did the male rise to his feet at my approach, yet was it Rogon to whom I gave my attention, for the diminutive war leader clearly had news.

"Two hands of males await you, Jalav," said she, stepping forward as I neared. "They are led by the male who spoke with you earlier, he who brought the male you bested. The male insisted that I apprise you of his presence at once, yet did it seem to me that you had no wish to be disturbed. Was my estimation in error?"

"Not in the least, Rogon," I smiled, placing my hand upon her shoulder. "It will do the males little harm to await my pleasure. What is your estimation of their overall attitude?"

"They seem much like those who anticipate their ending, Jalav," said she, a puzzled look to her as she gazed up at me. "The thought has come that they intend setting upon you when you appear, throwing their lives away in an effort to take our leader from us. They none of them appear the least familiar with weapons, and yet what other thing might there be to so take the spirit from them?"

"I fear these city folk have little in the way of spirit to begin with,'' I sighed, withdrawing my hand from her. "I shall go now to speak with them, yet am I to be informed immediately upon the return of Palar's warriors, who see to an errand for me. Keep your warriors close, for there shall soon be a further thing to be seen to.''

"We shall indeed be close," nodded Rogon, her tone even despite the strong resolve to be seen in her eyes. "You seem to anticipate no attack from these males, Jalav, yet shall we be near enough to insure their peaceful intent."

She then gestured to her warriors, bringing them closer, allowing me no further say in the matter. Again I sighed, for dealing with war leaders was not the same as dealing with warriors. To command war leaders was at times to be commanded by them, it seemed, a state I was not overly familiar with. Perhaps wisest would have been to allow no such commands from those I commanded, and yet did it seem wiser still to say naught concerning their resolve to see to my protection. I would not rest easy till I had begun the journey south, and first seeing to the city would require the assistance of all those with me.

The males awaited me in a corridor not far distant from the chamber of slaves, the weak-featured Thierlan leading two hands of those who seemed much like him. Some few were of a greater stature, one of a lesser, and yet, great or small, each seemed pursued by invisible worry and fear. They stood in their drab city coverings in the center of the corridor, each beside another, each taking comfort from the presence of the others, for none bore weapons from which they might take comfort. Their eyes came to me as I approached them, and much did it seem that they shrank back rather than gathered what dignity remained to them, to face what demands I would make. Truly did they seem captives to conquerors, their mien bringing disgust to the faces of those warriors who guarded them.

"We have come as you commanded, lady," said Thierlan as I halted before him, sending my gaze about those who accompanied him. "Our entire Council now stands before you, each man personally approved of by the High Seat—by him who was called High Seat."

The manner in which the male stumbled in his speech brought my attention to him, and a grimace of pain crossed his features as he nodded.

"Yes, it has finally been proven to us without doubt that we have paid homage to one unworthy of such homage," said he, nearly choking upon the words. "Had he truly been chosen by the Serene Oneness, his champion would have emerged victorious from the meeting of blades. The disaster which has fallen upon our city is clearly due to his presumption in taking to himself the office of High Seat.''

Those other males about Thierlan immediately muttered complete agreement with his words, some seeming outraged by the deceit perpetrated upon them. Much did I wish to point out that any with eyes would have known the portly male for what he was, yet were these males before me without eyes for the truth. It had been they and their ilk who had allowed the portly male his will in all things, just as they now sought to place all guilt upon shoulders other than their own. These city males were like the leaves upon the trees, which bent in new directions each time the wind blew differently; just then they would bend to my urging, and that right eagerly.

That which I required of these males was simple in the asking, yet not so simple in the doing. I wished the city folk to return to their usual manner of doing as quickly as possible, yet was it necessary to demand safeguards against further attack upon my warriors. The suggestion of specific hostages to bind those within the city was immediately rejected by me, as even males might well be capable of sacrificing themselves for their brothers. Instead did I make it plain to the wide-eyed males before me that should another attack occur, the entire city would be razed to the ground and those who survived sent possessionless into the forests. To have the city remain intact was unnecessary to my needs, therefore was the choice of its survival or destruction given over to those who dwelt within its confines. Should they wish to do without it, they need only attack again.

With the understanding of my intent clear to all, I then spoke again of the coming strangers. With nine full clans of Midanna warriors, I scarcely needed untried males to swell their ranks, yet did I inform these Council males that any of their city who wished to join us in battle might apply for training under the eyes of my warriors. Even should the Sigurri refuse to join us, it was not my intent to allow those who trained with us to stand in battle; the offer was made to mark out those city folk who would be most apt to raise sword against the warriors who had taken their city. In such a manner would they be known to us and before our eyes, rather than skulking about in discontent. My offer was accepted by the males with a pathetic eagerness that suggested they thought themselves offered an equality with those who had conquered them. Such a belief was absurd, of course, for none would wish to greet a vanquished people as equals, and yet such was the belief of these males. Truly are males strange creatures, taking unto themselves that which they deny to others, though their strangeness is at times of use to warriors.

There were many topics to be discussed between us, the males then insisted, far too many for the small amount of patience I felt; nevertheless did I have a wooden seat and a large pot of renth brought and grimly attempted to listen. Thierlan was greatly concerned over the need to hunt for the city and trade for foodstuffs, the need for guarding the city from those both without and within, the need to direct the city folk in their daily doing, and such like matters. Thoughtfully did I sip from my flagon of renth, understanding no more than a part of that which I was told. To protect the city from attack from without was clear enough, yet what of the matter of attack from within? For what reason would a people suffer the presence amongst them of those who would offer them harm? And for what reason need one keep watch over those of whom chores are required? Should the necessary remain undone, she—or, as these were males, he—need only be expelled from the group as a useless hanger-on. My thoughts upon these subjects undoubtedly would not have been to the liking of the males, yet a timely interruption was brought by Rogon which forestalled disagreement. The warriors who had been sent to take that area called dungeons had returned with two further captives to add to those already within the chamber of slaves. Surely had I thought the males would have learned from what had previously been done to them, yet it seemed they learned slowly in matters of self-defense. Rather than accept this news and return to the previous discussion I had been swallowed up in, I put my flagon aside and rose to my feet.

"These matters of the city shall be seen to in due time," said I to the males, reflecting that it was now possible to fetch Rilas from our camp and draw upon her wisdom to see to those matters. "For now there is another thing of more immediate need to concern us, and I would have you all accompany us in the doing of it. Perhaps it will assist you in understanding more fully the male you once regarded as blessed."

The males looked upon one another in lack of understanding and faint trepidation, yet were they quick to follow once I led off, Rogon beside me, her warriors arrayed about the males. The walk through the floor-clothed corridors was not long, for the area which led to the dungeons was no more than bare stone floors and walls, uncovered and undecorated. A now-open doorway gave access to the steps to be descended, and as my feet trod the rough stone made smooth by many previous feet, I became aware of the slowly lessening warmth which I had noted upon the first instance of my descent. The walls, so close about the rough-hewn steps, glistened more and more with damp the deeper we went, accompanied by feebly flickering torches which were not quite near enough one to the other to entirely dispel the shadows all about. A silence broken only by breathing hung upon the sound of descending footsteps, a sound which lessened as those who followed attempted to quiet their intrusion upon the silence of the depths. I knew well the disturbance brought home to one who had never before descended that distance into the ground, yet was I more concerned with the memories borne in upon me as the stink of the depths grew to overwhelm the clean, fresh air we had left. Death was a hovering member of that stink, as was pain and fear and horror; I continued to lead the spiral way down, and breathed as little as I might.

The final step into the depth found Rogon as reluctant as I to touch the cold, clammy stone with bare feet, yet did she go forward as I did, even more reluctant to halt. Before us, a scant few paces ahead, stood the door of metal which normally shut off that area called dungeons; it now stood ajar as it had been left when the males behind it had been taken. Those males in my wake trod the stones lightly, lightly, as though in fear of awakening some ravening beast, yet they knew not the true nature of the beast, he who had now been chained. Soon would they learn, soon would they know that which they had been serving, and soon would they be given the opportunity of redeeming that service.

"Follow closely and do not stray," said I to the males, my voice sounding flat and lifeless in those depths. "Rogon, there are torches to be found within this doorway. We will require a hand of them."

"Immediately, war leader," replied Rogon, disallowing a shudder to touch her as she gestured a hand of warriors forward. Within the metal doorway burned two torches, from which the others might be lit, yet the darkness pressed closer despite their presence. The males also pressed close, too fearful even to look about themselves, pressed down by the weight of the ground above us and the thickness of the stench all about. No sound was raised in protest from the warriors with us, yet did they loosen their blades as they raised the torches high, suspicious not so much of the darkness and the stench as that which produced it.

The task I had set to my own hand was one I did not relish, yet was it a task which badly needed seeing to. With all the torches lit I led the way into the darkness, farther away from the doorway by which we had entered, farther into the stench and an awareness of low, flesh-tearing sound. The males and warriors behind me stirred uneasily when the sound made itself felt, unaware of its source, unaware of that which awaited us. I spoke no word in explanation, merely continued forward, and eventually, after many reckid of walking, reached the blank wall which marked the far end of the area where the search might be begun.

The first four rows of cells, on either side of the central corridor, all proved themselves unoccupied. It was not till we had reached a cell in the fifth row upon the right that we found the first evidence of that which I sought. The metal door swung wide and the torch flared upon the picked-clean bones of what had once been a living being, forever still in the five chains that held it at throat, wrists and ankles. Three dark shapes fled the torchlight with squeals, shapes which preferred to inhabit the darkness, shapes I knew well from my time in those dungeons. Scarm they were called, and their movement close upon the sight of the one long gone caused the males to gasp and Rogon's warriors to reach for their swords. I, however, did no more than gesture the door closed again, for there was naught which might be done for the cell's occupant. There were others who undoubtedly waited farther on, and those were the ones I felt the need to seek out.

Perhaps three corridors farther on was the first of those who awaited assistance. The stench about the cell was so strong that it made itself known even above the general stench, and once the cell door had been opened more than one male and warrior turned away to gag and empty themselves upon the stone of the floor. He who had once been a male was revealed in the torchlight, scrabbling about upon the floor of the cell, held by no more than the chain about his neck. Empty sockets gaped where once eyes had been, both feet were gone to the ankles, and two skeletal arms flapped from a stick-thin, nearly naked body. Scraps of faded, filthy cloth clung to that body, doing naught to cover the festering sores and gaping wounds which stood out even among the patches of filth. A low, continuous mewling moan came from the thing as it dragged itself through piles of defecation and scarm bones to reach the trickle of water in the corner of the cell, the sound ceasing only when a hand with too few fingers reached a palmful of water to the gap-toothed mouth. There was no indication in its movements that it was aware of those who stood and regarded it, yet Thierlan, when he came hesitantly forward to grip my arm, moved and spoke in the softest of whispers.

"I believe—it is possible—I know that man," he gasped, skin pale in the torchlight, illness clearly all through him. "Perhaps half a kalod ago, the High Seat demanded the gift of a female slave from one Ostrion, a blacksmith of the city. The wench he wished had not been declared slave, for she was a distant relative of this Ostrion and therefore beneath his protection. Ostrion was to disavow the girl, allowing her to be declared slave, in return for which he was to receive the smile of the Blessed One, which would greatly enhance his standing in the city. Ostrion refused to disavow the pretty little thing, saying her mother had been dear to him when they both were children, and many considered him foolish for so refusing the desires of the High Seat. When, one fey not long after the refusal, the guard of the High Seat came and took up the wench, Ostrion was not to be found. No man in the city has seen him since—till now. We must release him immediately."

"To what purpose?" I asked, forcing myself to look upon the wreck which crawled and mewled upon the floor. "Are you able to return that of which he has been bereft of—including his reason? There is naught left of that which was, no more than pain unending and the agony of insanity. Are you able to look upon him and deny him the final favor?"

Slowly, with great reluctance, Thierlan's eyes turned from the crawling thing to regard me with pleading, yet was my sense of decision too strong for the male to deny. The truth could not be refused in that place, and though he shivered with the necessity, he also nodded acquiescence.

"I am a man," said he, speaking more for himself as he attempted to straighten himself. "As it must be done, I shall do it."

A dagger from the legbands of one of Rogon's warriors was placed in Thierlan's hands, and with a short hesitation and a great shudder, the male saw to him who had once been Ostrion the smith, opening the thing's throat above the collar and allowing the final rest. The balance of the males looked on in silence, no scorn to be seen in any of them even when Thierlan turned from the kindness he had performed and covered the filthy floor with his illness. Rogon and her warriors stood by in a matching silence, and they, too, failed to evince disapproval. The doing had not been one even warriors were well used to, and the male, despite his illness, had acquitted himself with honor.

The balance of our search was conducted in grim silence, and each victim found was dispatched by a male. In one cell was a female discovered, her face and body cut cruelly into horror, the life nearly fled from her, the thin metal collar above the neck chain proclaiming her slave. What her trespass had been was not discovered, for even the teeth of the scarm had failed to rouse her from her stupor. The male who dispatched her turned away with tears in his eyes, matched by the same in the eyes of some few of the others. The rest seemed filled with a poorly controlled fury, and none retained the look of fear they had worn when first they had come to that place. The males had been deeply touched, it was clear, as deeply touched as I had wished them to be.

The nearer we came to the doorway by which we had entered, the greater grew the number of cells which were tenanted. Some few of these were in need of the final favor, yet by far the largest number were in suitable condition to be released. Many and many of these captives were known to the males who accompa- nied me, each of them proving to be those who had, in one manner or another, displeased the former High Seat. Some were travelers from other cities, who had been accused of that which was termed crime before being sent to the dungeons, eventually to be declared slave. All these did we release and assist toward the outer corridor, in the company of warriors, emptying one cell after the other till there were no further cells to be emptied. Only then did we take ourselves after those we had released, through the doorway and into the area beyond.

"In the name of the Serene Oneness, I swear this is the first full breath I have taken since we descended," said one of the males, mopping at his brow with a cloth. Nearly as portly as the former High Seat was this male, yet his fury at what he had seen made him far from the same ilk.

"I had thought the air here fetid," said Thierlan in answer, wiping his palms upon the covering he wore. "In comparison to that which is found within, it is the purest of summer breezes. What are we to do with those we have released, lady? Are they to continue being considered as prisoners?"

"Has any of them done anything detrimental to your city?" I asked in turn, regarding the male. "Much does it seem that their sole trespass was upon the whims of him who was called blessed. This city, though in our capture, remains yours. Do with them as you please."

"Then we shall release them completely," replied Thierlan, a pleased look to him. "Their families will be eager to see to their wounds and sores and hunger. Let us attend to the matter at once."

With the decision made, we were able to continue upon our way to the surface, far from the horror and stench from below ground. The males climbed eagerly but steadily, fully aware of what lay behind them and no longer fearing it. They had exercised an honor long kept dormant, and now felt themselves as more for the doing of it; the males knew it not, yet would there be further matters which would allow them to feel so. Warriors have little liking for associating with cravens, and see the matter done differently whenever it is within their power to do so.

Upon reaching the surface once more, the males assisted their fellow city folk in departing the dwelling. All moved slowly with the pain of chains but recently removed, a tremble to their hands, a squint to their eyes. Much did they seem like those returned from death, disbelieving yet deeply grateful, eager to be on yet fearful that their newfound freedom might prove to be a dream sent to torment them. Those who were not of the city were placed in the care of those warriors who had freed them, warriors who were incensed that any might be done as these males had been done. To face an enemy in battle and slay him was no more than a doing filled with glory; to take an enemy and place him away from Mida's light, to deny him the right of self-defense, was an act too scurrilous to think upon. The once-captive males would be tended by the newly captured males beneath the eye of warriors; should the service be less than satisfactory, the new captives would be speedily informed.

"Jalav, I give thanks to Mida that we have returned to her light," said Rogon, watching as her warriors assisted the males we had freed to an untenanted chamber in the dwelling. "Should it be her will that I need never return to that place, I will be forever grateful."

"I think, Rogon," said I, "that we must return there but one time further. We have released all those unjustly placed there; we have not as yet brought down the one who most deserves the place."

Slowly did she turn to stare at me, as slowly the meaning of my words came to her. Where once she would have been full eager to assist me, now she did no more than shake her head.

"I know not whether I have the stomach for the thing," she quietly informed me, a great disturbance to be seen in the dark of her eyes. "Does not honor demand that even the portly one be given the opportunity of defending his life or losing it?"

"How may one deal honorably with a male who knows no honor?" I shrugged. "To do so would be a slap at the very meaning of honor. The horror he has meted out to others must be his, else are all things just and honorable spat upon and trampled into the dirt. How easily would your soul rest if you had found death in those dungeons, the while he was allowed a clean death in battle?"

"Not easily at all," muttered Rogon, her eyes continuing to hold to mine, and then a faint smile touched her. "You have made your decision clear in my eyes as well as your own, war leader, and for this I thank you. I shall, of course, follow as always."

"And, as always, you are welcome, Rogon," I smiled. "Come. I would have the thing done with and behind me as soon as possible."

Her fervent nod of agreement brought a wider smile to my lips, though there was little to smile at thereafter. The male was taken easily enough from his enclosure, yet were daggers necessary when he learned of our destination. Bringing him to a cell and placing him therein without taking his life proved a difficult matter; he, fearing the horrors he had so lightly sent others to, fought his chains and our daggers till our strength was nearly spent. When once his soft, fatty throat had been placed in a neck chain, Rogon and I quitted the place, bearing with us the torch we had brought, closing and bolting the cell door upon the male's screams of terror. Truly would slaying him out of hand have proven easier, yet that which is easily done is not always just. The male had earned his terror many times over; the length of that terror would be left to the discretion of his god.

I returned with Rogon to the chamber of slaves, directed her to the rest the others had already begun to take, then looked briefly upon the enclosure which had been covered over with blue wall silk, providing the occupants of the enclosure with complete privacy. Once my warriors had taken their rest, it would be necessary to release the Sigurri males. Their decision would likely be the one which I desired, yet must I consider what action to take should they turn to the stubbornness most males seemed prone to. To attempt forcing the location of their city from them would undoubtedly prove futile; wisest would be to follow at a distance, remaining undiscovered. . . .

"Jalav." The single word, in the voice of a male, snatched my attention from the far reaches and sent my hand toward my sword. Relidose, who had spoken, backed a step in surprise, then saw the reason for the abruptness of my actions.

"It was not my intention to intrude upon your thoughts," said he, an odd look about him as he attempted a smile. "I thank the Serene Oneness I did not place a hand upon your shoulder. I am unused to wenches who reach so quickly for a sword." The attempted smile then returned from whence it had come, and he retook the step he had earlier given up. "Those men—the four in the cage covered with silk," he said, his voice now heavy. "I saw the manner in which you spoke with them, as though they were your equals despite their chains. I would know if you mean to—take up with them."

The dark eyes of the male clung to my face, his hands tightened to fists. Males are filled with great strangeness, a truth I had learned when Fideran had been my male. Ever had Fideran sought to keep me as his alone, a foolishness no other than a male would attempt, for what male would be allowed a say in the doings of a war leader? This Relidose now seemed about to attempt the same, an annoyance I saw no reason to tolerate.

"The intentions of a war leader are rarely discussed with the male who follows her," said I, making no attempt to soften the sting of the words. "He who follows Jalav does so without question and without demand, asking for naught, taking no more than what is given. I had thought you understood this, male."

Relidose continued to stare a moment longer, then did a deep sigh take him.

"I had hoped—I might turn the matter about," said he, and then was he even closer. "I shall give you my love, and then will you know more of him who follows you, *he* who burns to bring you pleasure. That pleasure will be so great that you will then follow me, Jalav, to my house and to the life we will share. I knew from the moment I first saw you that I must have you, and I shall."

His brawny arms then rose to place themselves about me, to draw me closer, to hold me to his chest. This the male was intent upon doing, so intent that he failed to see the dagger in my hand till its point reached a short way into his throat.

"My life is the belonging of Mida, to do with as she wills," said I, taking no note of how still the male had become beneath my blade. "To see Jalav as a city slave-woman is to be without sight, for Jalav is destined to ride forever in the service of Mida. Go and find another to give pleasure to, male, and thank your god that Mida did not demand your service herself. I have seen those in her chains, and their screams are most unsettling."

I then stepped back from the male, withdrawing my dagger from his throat, yet retaining it in my grip. The male put a hand to his throat to touch the small trickle of red which the dagger had freed, vast confusion and hurt all through him, and then did he shake his head.

"I will not be refused," said he, his voice no more than a whisper. "I have prayed to the Serene Oneness that he grant you to me, and my prayers will be answered. This fey or the next, this kalod or the next, you will be mine."

With such words did he then turn and walk off, leaving n with a frown. I had little need of such additional foolishness with the tasks yet before me, and best would be to see the male barred from the dwelling. Quickly, then, did I follow to see the male well gone, paused to speak with those warriors who guarded the chamber of slaves, and then, at long last, was able to seek rest of my own.

4 Rilas—and dispositions are made

The fey was nearly gone when I once again descended from the chamber which had been that of the High Seat, trailed by two hands of silent warriors. I had intended to sleep no more than a few hind, merely to take the blinking from my eyes, yet had Mida—and perhaps Sigurr—visited me with a deep, dreamless sleep which had carried me through many hind, hind which were to have been spent differently. A crossness had taken me over the loss of that time, a crossness which I attempted to put away from me even as my temper flared beyond the bounds of my control. How foolish to rail at the doings of the gods, and yet how was a warrior to see to the tasks given her when those self-same gods plucked precious time from her hands? I paused at a wide, lightly curtained window to stare out at the lessening light, seeing naught without the dwelling save faintly browned grass and thin, poor trees beneath the blue of the skies. The males, it seemed, had not returned to harass us, which might or might not be an omen for the future. I disliked the thought of remaining within that city, yet how might I take myself off with the safety of my warriors no certain thing? And then the thought came that the turn of the spear might allow me no choice in the matter, for the gods were notorious in their impatience, and that, too, irked me. After another glance about at the weakening fey, I turned and strode off to seek what sustenance there might be in the dwelling. There were many decisions yet to be made, and for weighty decisions one required adequate sustenance.

I had thought to begin my search with the chamber of slaves and yet, upon passing another chamber whose doors stood closed, I heard the sound of many voices exchanging laughter. Thinking to find a chamber where males had been put to use—and, perhaps, where daru or renth had been brought—I threw open the doors to find surprise instead.

"Jalav! You have awakened at last!" laughed Tilim, rising to her feet in greeting, with Gidon and Rogon and Palar doing the same. In the midst of these war leaders, retaining her seat upon the floor cloth, was Rilas, Keeper of our clans, a sight indeed most welcome. Warmly did Rilas smile, the smile of greeting I knew so well, and I gave silent thanks that not all of the time I had spent in sleep had been wasted.

"Jalav, we attempted to awaken you when Rilas was at last brought to the dwelling," said Rogon, moving aside to allow me room beside the Keeper. "Though three of us made the attempt to say your orders had been carried out, nothing roused you. The Keeper felt your sleep was Mida-sent, therefore did we leave off our efforts and settle Rilas here."

"I, too, believe the same," said I with a grimace to Rilas, settling myself upon the floor cloth beside her. "Had I not had the foresight to leave instructions that you be guided here before I slept, your arrival would not yet have been accomplished. At times I wonder how seriously spoken are Mida's commands."

"The next task you have been given will be accomplished in its turn, Jalav," Rilas laughed, amused at my sourness. "That Mida prepares you for it in her own way is surely proof of this. You have located the proper males?"

"Aye." I nodded, looking toward those slave males who hovered about the edges of our talk, carrying pitchers and goblets. The one I looked upon blanched and hurried forward to serve me with trembling hands, and even learning that the pitcher contained daru failed to raise the deeper sourness settling upon me. Much do I dislike the look of slave males, those who bow and scrape and cringe in fear of that which might be done to them, and ever shall I feel so. These males, stripped of all covering and made to serve bare, were meant to please the eye of a warrior; none of those about me seemed quite pleased, and this I was able to understand.

"Do you speak of the males in the chamber of slaves, Jalav?" asked Palar as I sipped at my daru, she leaning forward in the place she had reclaimed. "The four who had been draped in cloth of black? What of them?"

"I must journey with them to their city," I replied with a glance toward Rilas, wondering as to her reason for having raised the question. I had not intended to speak of it till the time for departure had become more imminent. "It is the wish of Mida that I see to a thing there, and then shall I return."

"And the Happa shall, of course, accompany you," said Tilim, her tone having settled the matter.

"The Hirga follow me as I follow Jalav," said Rogon, her voice as cold as her eyes. "Should the Happa come as well, they will find themselves unneeded."

"The Homma stand before all others," said Gidon, looking about with a growl. "It is we who. . . ."

"The Hunda have first call!" snapped Palar, bristling immediately. "It was we who guarded these males, and we who. . . ."

The wrangling grew more and more heated, each war leader speaking upon the words of the others, and I turned my head to regard the Keeper.

"I see, Rilas, that you felt the need to partake in some part of the bloodshed so recently past," I observed, raising my goblet to sip again. "In future, I shall be sure to recall this need and send for you the sooner."

"Do not berate me, Jalav," laughed Rilas, stirring in amusement where she sat. "The matter is one best settled now, before your departure, when I may have your presence to soothe your decision. Do not forget that your sisters are war leaders all, beyond and above the required obedience to a Keeper."

Her words, though light, held a deep understanding of what I had done and what I intended doing. Never before had all our clans been combined in such a venture, to act as a single clan, to obey a single leader. Had I intended remaining to direct the doings of the following feyd, the matter would have been simplified; as I was unable to remain, the question of leadership must quickly be seen to.

"I bow to your wisdom, Rilas," I said, attempting a grin to ease her mind. "I will be pleased to settle the question at once. It is my decision that I shall go alone."

"Alone?" shouted those war leaders who, of a sudden, were full intent upon words not yet addressed to them, no longer enwrapped in wrangling. "Alone? Never! Impossible! Ridiculous!"

The growls of disagreement swept about the chamber to the warriors who stood a respectful distance back, each of them shaking their heads, many putting hands to sword hilts. Their war leader would not ride off with none to ride with her, said their displeasure, their scowls bringing a shadow to the face of Rilas. Her eyes came to me with a gaze which bid caution, yet the time for caution was not then. A long swallow emptied my goblet of daru, and then I rose to my feet.

"I hear words of council and support from my sister war leaders," said I, pleased at the silence which had fallen when I arose. "For your support and concern you have my thanks, and yet—I would know which of you speaks with the blessing of Mida."

The deep, attentive silence was broken by no more than the

faint turnings of heads as glances were exchanged, the slow removal of hands from sword hilts. All knew they had spoken at the urging of no more than their own hearts, a commendable source and yet in no wise to be considered on a par with Mida.

"It seems it is now clear to all that had I been bidden to take any of the Midanna with me, the matter would already have been seen to," I continued. "Another point I had not thought necessary to mention is the fact of the presence of Rilas. Has it not occurred to any to ask the reason for the presence of a Keeper among us when we rode to war? Is a Keeper not forbidden the glory of battle in the higher glory of service to Mida? For what reason, then, has Mida set her among us?"

A look of surprise had touched each war leader and warrior at my words, and a moment passed before Gidon nodded in sudden understanding.

"It was the will of Mida that she be among us," said Gidon, "therefore has a task been set to her hand. It is clear this task has to do with the journey of which Jalav speaks. Is she meant to accompany you, Jalav?"

"Her task has been made considerably more difficult, Gidon," I said with a headshake. "In the time our warriors must inhabit this city, it will also be necessary to deal with the males in a manner designed to avoid further bloodshed. As we are to stand against the strangers when they come, we will require every sword available to us, with none wasted in frivolous battle with males. This must Rilas see to, along with curbing the playfulness of our warriors. Who among us will not speak to her warriors on behalf of the Keeper?"

"Not I!" came from each of four voices, undoubtedly to be echoed by those five war leaders who were not then present. Fully outraged did the four appear at the suggestion that any would refuse support to the Keeper, and by those words was the obedience of the four committed to Rilas.

"Excellent," said I, smiling around at my sisters. "Mida is sure to be pleased—as shall I be, should I find that which may be fed upon in this place. Have we no hunters among us, that the Midanna must hunger?"

"That matter, too, has been seen to, Jalav," laughed Rogon, as amused as the others. "The provender has been prepared, and need only be fetched. The slaves will see to it."

Indeed did the males, at the growls of the warriors about them, jump to see to the fetching of the provender. One slave male, well made yet with hollow insides, found himself the last to remain—and the first to be detained. The warriors in the chamber wished to amuse themselves the while the provender was being fetched, therefore did two of them stand to block the male when he attempted to depart. In confusion and nervousness he turned from the two, only to find a third, a small yet excellent Hunda warrior, in his path of withdrawal. Slowly did she smile up at him as her small hands went first to his chest, then to the flat of his belly, and then below; his gasp as he looked down at her in shock was lost in the laughter of the balance of the warriors. Clearly was it the intention of the small Hunda warrior to do without the sthuvad drug, and as the attention of all those in the chamber turned to the amusement, Rilas leaned near to me.

"Clearly does Mida stand with you, Jalav," said she, a deal of annoyance to be seen in her eyes and heard in her softened tone. "To place a Keeper above war leaders—and have them pleased to have it so! What of the others, Jalav? If one should refuse as those here did not . . ."

"They will not refuse," I quickly assured her, feeling a strangeness in thus reassuring a Keeper. Always has it been the other way about, for myself as well as the others. "Should I attempt to choose among the war leaders for one who will stand for me, the blood will indeed run deep. You, Rilas, need do only that which you have ever done: advise those about you wisely and well. I must have a fighting force to return to."

"And shall have," said she, nodding slowly with the beginnings of a smile. "Indeed has Mida chosen wisely, taking the war leader of the Hosta to stand for her. Through you does her glory shine most strongly."

I drew a breath and forced a smile in thanks to Rilas, then made it seem that my attention was taken by the small Hunda who now coaxed the panting male slave to the floor cloth. In truth my thoughts had turned to Mida and the glory one received from her hand, as opposed to that which was received by actions in her name. The two were most damnably different, in some unknowable manner most distinctly unalike. It was a matter to be thought upon, perhaps when all tasks had already been seen to, when all other matters were done and over with. Till then the thought was idle.

In time was the provender brought by the slaves and served to all, and then were the slaves themselves served up to their captors. It had come to me that the sthuvad drug had been withheld from these males so that my warriors might test the depth of them, that they might see how deeply buried was the manhood in them. Truly were the males put to their knees and humiliated, and the sight recalled to me the fact that there were other males to see to, those who were called Sigurri. When I rose to my feet Palar also rose to hers, apparently aware of my intentions; I made no attempt to keep her from my side, for the warriors who stood over the chamber of slaves were hers without question.

Much laughter came from the chamber of slaves as we approached, much laughter and also much shouting. Many of the males within had not been slaves, taught to fear the lash and sword and those who wielded them. With such free, strong males does a warrior find true enjoyment, and such was that which the warriors of Palar had found. As we entered the chamber we found a hand of warriors whose attention was immediately upon us, yet this was naught less than to be expected when one is encamped among enemies. These guarding warriors nodded in greeting before returning an eye to the doings of the others, and softly did I direct Palar to join them before moving toward the silk-covered enclosure.

The flicker of torches jumped about upon the blue silk as I put a hand to it and lifted it from the flags so that I might approach a bit closer. Beneath was a darkness unrelieved by the torchglow, all shadows without that which casts them, and one of these shadows stirred and spoke.

"So you have at last seen fit to return," came the voice of the Sigurri male called Mehrayn, he of the hair of red. A thick calm was evident in his tone where another would surely have been annoyed or angered, and this I had not expected.

"Indeed have I returned," said I, holding high the drape of silk. "Has the privacy you required proven adequate?"

A stirring of shadows came in the dimness, accompanied by the clink of chain, and then was the male at the metal lines before me, his large fists curled tightly about two of the lines.

"Very well," said he, the calm in his voice unchanged, his face hidden in shadow. "My jest was at the expense of your dignity, your response to it at the expense of ours. May we now consider ourselves quits, and able to begin again? We shall find little accomplished in a back-and-forth of this sort."

"Certainly," I agreed in a matching calm, doing naught to hide the grin which touched me. Indeed was his request filled with wisdom, most especially as it came from one in the chains of a slave. "I would know if you are now prepared to voice your decision."

"Our decision is the obvious one," said he, moving very slightly where he stood. "We agree to guide you to our city, as

Sigurr demands. Where stands the light beyond these walls? We have not breathed of the outer air for many feyd."

"The dark is now upon us," said I, refusing the memory of my own time within such an enclosure. "I shall have you removed from your confinement at once."

"But another moment," said he as I began to turn away. "As I have said, we agree to guide you to our city in accordance with Sigurr's wishes; we, however, have been in captivity for so odious an amount of time that we shall not remain the longer within this city. We depart come the new light with your presence or without, and would have you know this before you release us. We will not have any man—or wench—say we spoke other than the truth in order to see ourselves free."

Having had his say the male then fell silent, an expectant air to the calm which remained with him. I, too, remained silent, for I knew not how I might see to all which was left undone with naught save the single darkness remaining to me. And yet— Ah, Mida! How the thought tempted me! To be free of that vile city, to return to the forests and the freedom therein, to begin at last the task set to my hand by the goddess and thereby be the sooner done with it! Indeed did I remain silent for a very long moment, a silence which was misread by the male.

"I believe I see a delay in our promised freedom," said this Mehrayn, and no longer was he able to keep the dryness from his tone. "Exactly how long a delay undoubtedly depends upon the amount of time required by you before you find yourself able to depart."

"A Midanna does not return ashes to one who speaks the truth," said I with sharpness, stung that these strangers would think Midanna so dishonorable. "We are warriors, not males nor city folk! As your freedom was promised you, so shall you have it!"

Before the male might reply, I allowed the blue cloth to fall again to the floor, and moved from the enclosure to gesture the guard warriors to me. Quickly were they before me to hear my instructions, and once those instructions had been given I left the area of the enclosure to join Palar where she stood laughingly watching the doings of her warriors. Pitchers of daru and empty goblets stood about; therefore did I pour a goblet for myself and attempt to divert my mind with amusement.

The males currently in use by Palar's Hunda were those who had been of the chamber of slaves, yet not themselves enslaved. Males of metal and leather were they, those who had taken pleasure in forcing obedience from slaves at the direction of the male Bariose and the female Karil. Now was it they from whom pleasure was taken, most especially the four who had been removed from the wall. These four males, stripped naked, had been bound wrist to ankle in the cleared space, two warriors about each of them, heating their blood. The broad bodies of the males writhed to each touch and caress, straining at the leather which held them, glistening in the torchlight as desire was put more and more strongly upon them. Their voices raised in shouts of protest above the laughter of the warriors, showing them entirely free of the sthuvad drug. No use was vouchsafed these males, merely arousal, and I knew not the why of it till Palar leaned to me with a chuckle.

"See these four, Jalav," said she, sipping from the goblet she held. "Those who were enclosed in this chamber informed us that among all the others, these four took the greatest pleasure in their cruelty. The males they lashed till they bled, the females they used till they wept, and they, secure in their freedom and position, laughed at the misery they caused. My warriors scorn their use, giving them no more than the agony they gave to others."

"Ever and again is the spear cast," said I, looking upon the four who writhed, knowing the face of one. The eyes of the male, he who had brought me great shame at the bidding of the female Karil, turned to regard me with fury and desperation, then widened and looked quickly away at sight of the smile I showed.

"And at each cast does one's lot in life undergo a change," agreed Palar, also smiling at the look upon the male. "A pity these four lacked understanding of that fact; they now pay for that which was done in ignorance."

"And yet not unwillingly," said I. "Had they been informed of this possibility, they would have done no more than laugh; had they believed, they would have refrained out of fear. To do as one must, knowing full well the possible consequences, accepting those consequences in the need of the moment to do that which must be done; such are the actions of a true warrior."

"Indeed," nodded Palar, turning more fully toward me, yet before she might speak again, an interruption came.

"I see you do indeed keep your word," came the deep voice of Mehrayn. I turned my head to see that he stood, unescorted and unchained, behind my left shoulder. And then his hand reached out, calmly and with full confidence, to take the goblet I held and bring it to his lips. "Ah, just the thing I lacked all these feyd of captivity," said he when the goblet was drained, his light

eyes sparkling. "Drink such as this sets a man's blood to thumping.
What have your wenches done with our breechclouts? It is
unseemly for a man without chains to walk about unclothed."

"I, for one, do not consider it unseemly," murmured Palar,
again sipping at her daru as her eyes moved about the male.
"For some, perhaps it would be; for you it is not."

The male returned her stare without also returning the faint
grin she sent him, in some manner disturbed over the observation
Palar had made. Males are strange in such things, deeming it
natural for them to find pleasure in looking upon females, yet
unnatural for warriors to find pleasure in looking upon them.
Indeed had Palar the right of it, for the male was broad and well
made, strongly muscled and a full head taller even than I, his
skin nicely tanned beneath his thatch of red hair. I, too, gazed
in appreciation, then voiced the thought which came.

"Should you find yourself too uncomfortable," said I, resting
my left hand upon my sword hilt, "you may feel free to request
that chains again be placed upon you. In such a manner shall the
unseemliness be seen to."

Immediately did the light eyes of the male flash with anger as
his skin darkened, yet his voice, when he spoke, retained the
calm which seemed so much a part of him.

"It gives me great pleasure that two such lovely wenches find
approval in my appearance," said he, putting aside the empty
goblet to fold thick arms across the broadness of his chest.
"Your gay, female laughter also gladdens me, yet would I have
a more direct answer from you. Are we or are we not to have the
return of our breechclouts?"

"Have the body cloths returned to them, Palar," said I,
holding the gaze of the male as he held mine. "We would not
wish our honored guests to feel that we mock them."

"Very well, Jalav," sighed Palar, also putting aside her goblet.
"Though mocking them is considerably less than that which we
wished to do with them. I shall see to the retrieval of the cloths."

With a last doleful look Palar took herself off, drawing the
male's gaze with her as a wide grin suddenly took possession
of him.

"Never have I seen such lusty wenches," said Mehrayn in
a soft voice, his eyes clapped to the roundness of Palar's thighs
as she strode away. "Had I been free when she used me, I would
easily have had her screaming with pleasure. A pity we must
depart so quickly."

"A pity indeed," I murmured, of a sudden understanding that
the haste of the males must surely be the doing of Mida. To have

them free among Midanna would undoubtedly cause much bloodshed, though little if any would be their doing. "You and your brothers will be given places where you may rest in comfort for this darkness, so that you will be well prepared to depart come the new light."

"And you?" said he, again bringing those light eyes to study me. "We have given you very little time in which to prepare, I know. Will you be accompanying us?"

"If it is Mida's will." I shrugged. "There are many things remaining to be seen to, yet might it be possible to see to them all. If it should not prove possible, I shall follow you as soon as may be."

"Follow us?" said the male, his brows drawn down into a frown. "You would ride the forests alone, unescorted and unprotected, attempting to follow the track of Sigurri warriors who are accustomed to leaving no track?"

"Of a certainty." I shrugged again, failing to see wherein his difficulty in understanding my intentions lay. "To ride the forests alone is a great pleasure, to follow the track of others the simplest of doings. Ah, here are your body cloths. Now I may show you to your accommodations."

A Hunda warrior appeared with the cloths, handing them out among the other three males who stood rubbing at unfettered wrists and looking about themselves. The male Mehrayn, after a short hesitation, took himself over for the cloth which was his and quickly wrapped it about himself, drawing the end up and tucking it in with a decisive gesture. I, indicating that the Hunda were to remain in the chamber, led the way from it and to the floor above, where guest chambers were to be found. Distasteful were those chambers to a warrior, filled as they were with city-folk contrivances, yet the Sigurri hummed with pleasure at sight of them. Also did they find much pleasure in the sight of the slave-females who had been unbound to kneel again at the corridor platform not far from their chambers, and swiftly was I informed of the fact.

"We will take these slaves for the darkness," said Mehrayn, looking down upon four females who trembled with fear and made no effort to meet his gaze. "They are pretty little bits of fluff who will warm our beds this darkness and our memories upon the long journey home."

"You may have them as long as they come to no harm," I said, also looking down upon the slave females. "I know not what may be done with such as these, and yet must their final disposition be decided upon. What is one to do with females who know naught of standing tall with dignity?''

"One makes slaves of them," said the dark-haired Sigurri, touching the throat of the female he stood above, causing her to shudder. "Just as you made a slave of that strutting female known as Karil."

"I made no slave of the she-sednet!" I snapped, annoyed that the male would see it so. "I merely gave her what she deserved. Sooner would I have faced her with swords, yet she refused!"

"I feel there are few females about who would not refuse to face you," said Mehrayn, a thoughtful look to him. "And as we speak of weapons, I would know when our own weapons are to be returned to us."

"Your weapons will be given you when you are prepared to depart," I replied, feeling a strangeness come over me. I did not hold with slaves nor the making of them, yet in the eyes of the males I had done that very thing. Never have I felt the need to explain what actions I take, and yet was I then filled full with the desire to make them see how wrongly they judged me. The beliefs of males mattered little to me, and yet had Mehrayn not spoken up, surely would I have continued in my efforts to sway the males! I looked from one to the other of them, meeting the gaze of each, then abruptly came to a decision. I knew not what ailed me, yet surely would I be best off leaving the males to their own devices.

"Should you wish provender," said I somewhat briskly, "send the slaves to my warriors. Perhaps we shall see one another again come the new light, before your departure. Should this not occur, we will undoubtedly meet upon the trail. I bid you a pleasant rest."

I turned then and walked from them all, intending an end to the talk, yet the male Mehrayn, in typical male fashion, felt the need to speak last.

"I do not wish to hear of perhaps, wench," he called after me, caring naught for the fact that I did not turn again to him. "Should you fail to be there when we are prepared to depart, I shall come seeking you!"

Acting as though I had not heard him, I continued up the corridor to the steps I wished to descend, silently calling down the curse of Mida upon his head. I knew not what humor rode the male, yet had I little need of so sudden a change of heart. Best would be to have the Sigurri quickly gone from the city which we had taken, yet now, despite his earlier words, their leader seemed intent upon vacillating. Ah, Mida! I know not the why of my being constantly thrust among males, yet would your warrior be grateful should they, at some time, be filled with reason rather than foolishness!

Though I spoke in my heart to Mida of reason, the following hind brought me little of the precious stuff. The five war leaders who had not yet sworn allegiance to Rilas did so without urging— then proceeded to insist upon accompanying me to the land of the Sigurri. Linol, war leader of the Hersa, tall and proud in her covering of orange, tossed her auburn-haired head and declared that Mida need not speak to her for her to know where lay her duty. Never before had Linol cared to follow another, yet had she seen me with sword in hand as we took the dwelling, and later, when I faced and bested that male chosen as champion to the High Seat, and now was Linol devoted to Jalav, war leader of all the Midanna. Softly did I speak with Linol, as one sister and war leader to another, yet were my words like feathers in a gale, lost as quickly as they came to sight. My well-being would be seen to by Linol and her Hersa, and no other thought would the Hersa war leader countenance.

In Mida's name, I knew not what to do! Linol and I had stepped from the dwelling so that we might speak without interruption, and well pleased was I that the darkness cloaked all vision of what expression I wore. As war leader of the Hosta had all my instructions been promptly obeyed, yet had there then been no other war leaders among my followers. My eyes found the faint points of light in the distance which marked the dwellings of those of the city, the points which were torches dancing gently in the slight breeze which tripped about the ends of my hair. Indeed did the chirping darkness smell sweet and free, unburdened with the scent of many males which the large dwelling reeked of, unburdened with the need to disencumber oneself from unwanted protection. I raised my face to the darkness of the skies, seeing the uncountable points of light shining above, and Linol stepped to my side, breathing deep of the sweetness about us.

"The new fey shall be as clear and bright as the one just past," she observed, scanning the skies as Midanna are wont to do. "Indeed does Mida smile upon us, sending us the glory of her light in which to obey her word."

"Were Mida to speak to you, Linol," said I of a sudden, "would you then obey her will rather than strut about doing as you please?"

"Jalav, I do not do as I please," returned Linol, a shadow of hurt hovering about her words. "I do as I feel I am commanded to do, and that is to see to the safety of our war leader."

"I have put a question to you, sister," said I, turning to face her in the darkness. "Should Mida speak to you of her wishes, would you then obey them?"

"With my last breath," she replied, turning her head to one side. "Yet I know not how I am to be spoken to. Never have I been blessed as you have been, Jalav."

"The matter may be seen to thusly," said I, refraining from dwelling upon the manner in which I had been blessed. "It is clear the new fey should be bright and sweet; you, yourself, have said so. Should it come to pass that the new fey arrives covered in the tears of Mida, you may know that Mida has spoken. How say you?"

"The matter seems reasonable," she allowed, a smile to be heard where it could not be seen. "Should the rains come with the new light when there is no sign of them now, it will surely be the doing of Mida. I do not think the rains will come, Jalav."

"The new light will show the truth of the matter," said I, agesture toward the large dwelling. "Let us now return within, for there are other matters which I must see to."

With a pleasant agreement Linol accompanied me, yet was her pleasure destined to be short-lived. It had not been my thought which had begun the matter of the rains, this I knew beyond all doubt. Upon previous occasions had Mida placed thoughts within my mind, and surely had she done so again. The new fey would bring her tears, whether I rode with the males or no.

The following hind were spent with Rilas, some alone, some with the presence of the war leaders who would see her word obeyed. The disposition of the captives taken was a point which saw long and stubborn argument, based as it was upon the release of certain males which each of the clans wished to retain the use of. The care of so large a number of captives would drain our strength in the midst of enemies, yet were the war leaders loath to release them. Again and again did I press the point, holding firm in the face of near rebellion, yet was it Rilas who found a stand of agreement all would accept. Each of the males would be examined by Rilas and the others, taking hunter from city male, slave from male of leather and metal. Those capable of wielding weapons would not be released, nor would those who felt a burning hatred for Midanna. All others would be examined and released if unwanted, or, in certain circumstances, held for the use of warriors. Those held who might be released would be given special standing, thereby lessening the sting of capture. The question of the female slaves was of lesser importance, yet did I carry the memory of a female who had gone from slave to sister by the strength of her will. Gladly did Rilas agree to examine the females held as slave, and free those who served only by cause of the lash; the others were a matter more difficult to settle, yet would Rilas think upon it.

The hind passed slowly as we moved to the deployment of warriors and the extent of freedom to be allowed the city folk, and of a sudden the daru I had swallowed began to weigh heavily upon my eyelids. I knew there was no time at all to be wasted in sleep, yet the voices of those who spoke about me slowed and slowly sunk to the depths, tugging at me to follow. Desperately did I attempt to struggle against the pull, calling to Mida to leave me be, yet the will of the goddess was firm. Down to the depths of sleep was I taken, raging at such treatment, yet powerless to deny it.

5 The Sigurri—and the strangeness of males

I awoke to find the chamber emptied, a single candle upon the wall remaining lit so that I might see about myself in the windowless place. I lay stretched out upon the floor cloth, my weapons remaining where I had left them, feeling as though I had not stirred once since Mida had sent me to the realm of dreams. Slowly did I raise myself to sitting upon the floor cloth, finding the need to stretch shoulders and neck before the cramp would leave them, again feeling that useless fury against being forced to the will of another as though I were a warrior-to-be rather than war leader of all Midanna. Certain was I that the new light had not yet come, for it seemed clear that Mida had done as she had to insure my readiness to depart with the males. Whether or not I willed it, whether or not the safety of my warriors was seen to, I would depart.

I rose to my feet with a growl of displeasure, then strode to a door and pulled it open. Without were warriors of the Hitta and Helda, clearly standing guard so that none might disturb my rest. Quickly did they step back from the expression I wore, speaking clearly of the need to gather in my temper, yet was the deciding far easier than the doing. A growl had I voiced and all growl did I feel, and let any who dared cross wills with Jalav of the Hosta. Silently did I stalk up the dim, empty corridor, trailing warriors who had been left to guard me, warriors who obviously wondered what being would be rash enough to attempt attack upon me. Had any dared, perhaps the dark mood would have somewhat been lightened.

Much of the dim corridor had I traversed before another Mida-forsaken fact came to light—or, rather, before the light. Beyond the windows the darkness continued, deep and unlit, yet with a pattering noise which forced its way to my attention. Fully afrown, I paused by a window to draw aside the thin cloth which covered it, immediately discovering the presence of thick, heavy raindrops covering the outside of the maglessa-weave panes. Without a word did I stand and stare at the evidence of

141

the will of Mida, my thoughts turning blacker than they had been, and a warrior appeared to stand at my side.

"Jalav, Mida has spoken, and I am the one to whom she has spoken," said Linol, her voice soft with awe and complete repentance. "All shall be as you say, now and forevermore. My Hersa will not accompany you."

"Indeed," said I, turning to look down upon the Hersa war leader. She, seeing my expression, paled somewhat, yet was she warrior enough to hold her ground. "I am pleased to learn that all is to be as I say, Linol. In that event, I say that there must be those who prepare mounts and weapons and provender for the journey which I and the males must undertake. All is to be fully prepared before the arrival of the new light, else shall there be those who are deeply in need of the blessing of Mida. Are my instructions clear to you, war leader?"

"Your instructions are most clear, war leader," muttered this Linol, she who had required a sign of the will of Mida. "I shall see to them immediately."

"And personally," said I, causing her eyes to widen farther. A stiff, repeated bob of her head, and then was she off up the corridor, hastening to where her warriors waited, no whit curious as to whether my gaze followed her. A warrior of renown was Linol of the Hersa, filled with justified pride in her skill at arms, yet was she now no more than a warrior-to-be, taken to task by the war leader of her clan. Foul indeed was the mood upon me, so foul that even Linol saw. I glanced again at the window covering, seeing traces of blood from the battle which had raged in the dwelling, and thought it a pity that all battle was over; much could I have used the spilling of blood just then.

A faint hunger continued to cling to me, one I found myself unused to at such a time of the fey. Midanna do not ordinarily partake of provender when they arise, for to remain within a camp when upon the hunt or in battle may cost more in lives than any such provender might be worth. Should it be necessary, provender might be had upon the trail, yet would it be foolish of me to wait till I was upon the trail. I gestured a hovering warrior to me, spoke of my hunger, then followed where the warrior led.

Once the provender was well within me, I prowled about till I found the area where the preparation for the journey was then taking place. Four kand had been brought by Linol and her Hersa, that soft-skinned riding beast favored by city males. Much would I have preferred being mounted upon a gando, yet that clawed and scaled mount of Midanna warriors rubbed along badly with, kand, and the males, unfamiliar with gandod, could not be mounted upon them. The lanthay I had brought from the north might well have served, yet that beast was not well suited to the greater warmth toward which we would ride. No, Linol had chosen wisely, both in mounts and in weapons to be taken; swords, daggers, spears and bows had been chosen for the males, as well as a spear and bow for my use. Small packs of provender and water skins adorned the necks of each of the mounts, hung in balance, matched to the presence of the skin-wrapped bows and arrows. When once the rains had ceased, the bows might then be unwrapped.

The tears of Mida fell steadily upon the kand and the grass, soaking all beneath it in the early, clinging dimness, yet was the wetness warm and pleasant, bringing a freshness to the air which the dwelling could not match. I stepped out upon a small covered area near which the kand were tied, gestured to the rain-soaked Hersa that they might return to the dwelling, then moved a short distance from the entrance to crouch down. The stone beneath my feet was damp from the mist which reached beneath the covering roof, yet was it insufficient to cool the impatience which had begun to build within me. I longed to be away and about my business, gone from the doing of city folk, shut of the need to direct the actions of obedient—yet disobedient—war leaders in a time of peace.

"Jalav." The single word, spoken softly, intruded upon my thoughts and moved me again to annoyance, yet did I hold my temper still and look to see who spoke. By the entrance stood Ilvin, the pale-haired Hitta warrior I had first seen when I had come upon the Midanna camp, in the woods beyond the city. Sober was the expression upon the face of Ilvin, and determined was the look in her light eyes.

"Jalav, I mean to accompany you," said she, quiet conviction to be heard in her voice, a single step bringing her within a pace of me. "No Midanna should find the need to travel among males alone."

"Such is not possible, Ilvin," said I, taking my gaze from her and returning it to the rain-soaked darkness which had begun, very faintly, to lighten. "Had I the wish to be accompanied, there are many among your sisters who would gladly see the wish fulfilled. The fact remains that I have no such wish."

"Perhaps by cause of the fact that we are not Hosta?" said she, though without rancor nor attempt at insult. "Though we fail to be of your clan, Jalav, yet do we remain your sisters and loyal warriors."

"You read me wrong, Ilvin," I sighed, concerned at the

possibility that she spoke the thoughts of others as well as her own. "Were the Hosta here, they, too, would be commanded to remain. It is the very fact that I ride with males, to a strange city of males, that I refuse to be accompanied by Midanna. In my service to Mida, I have been well taught the pain and shame which are the lot of a warrior among males. It is enough that I have learned this; I will not allow the lesson to be taught others, as it was taught to certain Hosta who once accompanied me. No, Ilvin, not again."

I realized then that the tears of Mida were more easily visible, yet the rain was not the sight which held the eyes of my mind. Again I saw those warriors who had ridden into Bellinard with me, Fayan and Larid and Binat and Comir, four fine, strong warriors who had been made slave with me. Before we had been struck from behind, Larid and I had sent three of our enemies to the chains of Mida, yet had the doing been of little comfort when we, ourselves, were placed in chains. No, I would not again take Midanna to a city of males, save that our purpose was to attack.

"So you seek to take the burden of shame upon your own shoulders, to keep it from those who follow you," said Ilvin, her voice odd after the moment of silence which had passed. "Now do I truly see the reason for your having been chosen by Mida to ride in her name. The breadth of your concern for her Midanna well matches the skill of your sword arm. And yet do I feel that our concern for you should not fall short of yours for us. It remains my desire to accompany you, Jalav, to share all that comes, even unto shame."

"And how would you share the protection given me by Mida, Ilvin?" I asked, at last turning my head to look up toward her. "Should it be battle wounds which come, how would it be possible for me to see to the wishes of Mida and a wounded sister as well? Would you place me in the position of needing to decide between disobeying Mida and abandoning a sister warrior?"

"Certainly not," said she, a sudden upset upon her, "and yet . . ." Her words stumbled to an end as she took a breath, searching for another gando upon which to mount her protests, yet was further argument impossible. This she saw after another moment and nodded her head slowly, in misery, acknowledging defeat in the manner of a true warrior. Seeing her unhappiness I would have spoken further, yet at that moment came a bustle which heralded the arrival of others.

"By the sacred loins of Sigurr the dark!" growled the voice of a male, hidden yet within the entrance. "The skies have opened upon us to bring interest to our journey, and the black-haired wench is not yet stirred from her bed! Should Sigurr continue to smile so upon us, we shall not live to ride home again!"

"We now stand unchained and uncaged, Bershyn," came another male voice, the voice of Mehrayn. "These weapons we now strap on were freely given, as are the kand which await us. The rains will eventually cease, and the black-haired wench may be roused from her bed. Those who discount such gifts from Sigurr soon find themselves without them."

"Mehrayn speaks truly," came a third voice, one filled with amusement. "Have you returned so soon to princely expectations, Bershyn? We have had no more than a single darkness of freedom."

"What more does a warrior of Sigurr require?" returned the voice of Bershyn, now also filled with amusement. "Though I would prefer to have sunshine pouring down upon me, Grandyn, I must admit I do indeed agree with Mehrayn. Freedom is worth such small inconvenience. Now: which of us is to fetch the black-haired wench?"

"The one who goes is likely to be called upon to—ah—impress the wench," said the one called Grandyn, causing laughter in the others. "After the darkness just past, we must first be sure the one chosen has the wherewithal to perform such an impression. With toothsome female slaves to divert him, a man often overextends himself."

"Sight of that black-haired wench is enough to restore any man," chuckled Mehrayn amidst the increased laughter of the others. "Should there be a need to impress, I doubt that any of us will fail—save, possibly, you, Grandyn. From the manner in which that slave clung to you when we gathered in the hall, I would say you were indeed tempted into overextension."

"Only in part, Mehrayn," laughed Grandyn. "When a need for impressing arises, I seldom find myself incapable. Shall we draw lots for the opportunity?"

Again the males fell to laughter, a thing which deepened the scowl upon the face of Ilvin. She, unused to the ways of males, felt prepared to defend me from insult, as the fist upon her sword hilt clearly showed. I, too well used to the foolishness of males, felt no insult, therefore did I rise to my feet and move to the entrance before Ilvin might do so.

"Indeed would I be impressed were I to find males prepared to depart at an appointed time," said I to the backs of the males, interrupting their laughter and causing them to turn toward me in startlement. The four stood in their black body cloths, swordbelts closed upon them, the black strokes upon their left shoulders clear even in the gloom. They stared upon me very briefly, and then the grins returned to them.

"It seems our opportunity is lost, Mehrayn," said the dark-haired male, showing himself to be the one called Grandyn. "A pity, for it is truly said that an opportunity wasted is an opportunity regretted."

"Long journeys provide their own opportunities," murmured Mehrayn, his light eyes upon me in an easy manner. "That the wench is already prepared to accompany us must be looked upon as an omen from Sigurr. Without her, the journey would be as empty as that which brought us here."

"War leader, you *must* allow me to accompany you!" blurted Ilvin in upset, astand to my left. "These males mean you harm of some sort, harm which you shall have to face alone!"

"Should it be the will of Mida that I come to harm, Ilvin," I said, "your presence will not avert the thing. You have my thanks for your concern on my behalf, yet must I continue to refuse you. Should these males ever bestir themselves, it is their company alone in which I shall ride."

"I believe the wench calls us laggard," said the smaller of the two light-haired males with a grin. His voice showed him to be the one called Bershyn, he who disliked the notion of riding beneath the tears of Mida. "Are we to accept such cavalier treatment, brothers?"

"In no manner," laughed Grandyn, briskly clapping the shoulder of Bershyn. "Let us be off, brothers, and we shall soon see who is to be the laggard. Are those spears meant for us?"

Lazily and with much laughter did the four males each take and examine a spear, finding little approval of the slim shafts of the city-male weapons, yet accepting them as the better bargain between their presence and no weapon at all. The swords and daggers they wore had also been taken from city males, yet were they deemed adequate to the needs of the Sigurri. Ilvin looked upon their frolicking darkly, totally displeased with the males, causing me to give silent thanks to Mida that the Hersa were not also about.

When the males had quit the entrance to examine the kand provided for them, I stepped within, took the spear which was mine, bid Ilvin a final farewell which was to be passed on to her sister warriors and Rilas, and then went to the kan which was mine. A fine, large beast was it, yellow and brown in color and eager to be off, and one jump saw me mounted with the spear in my right hand and the reins in my left. The tears of Mida beat down upon me in an unending stream, soaking my hair and the hide of the kan, yet was the wetness the blessing Midanna believed it to be, for it marked the end of my time in an accursed city of males. The Sigurri fussed about their kand, examining the provender packed for them, adjusting the wrapped bows on the necks of the kand, and abruptly I found myself without further patience. With a single movement I turned my kan, and trotted through the slowly brightening downpour toward the gate which stood not far distant.

At the gate stood a number of warriors, Harra and Helda by their soaken coverings, and quickly did they turn to open the gate when I rode up. The process, not being immediate, allowed time enough for a sudden flurry of hoofbeats to approach from behind me just as the gate swung wide enough for a rider to depart. Without turning to look at those who hastened behind me I rode through, paying no heed to the faintly heard laughter of the gate warriors. The Sigurri would not be pleased by such laughter, yet it mattered little. Males are rarely pleased with Jalav when she stands as a warrior, and the Sigurri were male.

Once Bellinard was well out of sight behind us, the rains began to ease. Within another hin the skies were clear, and Mida's light shone down warmly upon us, drying us and setting the country-side we rode through aglistening with gold and silver. The males laughed and gave thanks to Sigurr, and well tempted was I to call upon Mida to return the rains she had sent for a purpose. My mood, however, had lightened with the skies, and I, too, wished no more of Mida's tears. To allow the males to give thanks to their god was a small thing; to deny them the doing would ill befit the actions of a war leader.

We continued our ride till the first of the forests hove into view, then did we halt to rest the kand and take a meal. The Sigurri had addressed no word to me as we rode, yet once the nilno and cheese had been swallowed, the period of sweet silence was ended. As I stood contemplating the clean, rolling hills over which we had just ridden, wondering as to my wisdom in leaving Rilas and my warriors to deal alone with the males of Bellinard, the sound of footsteps came behind me.

"Do you contemplate a return to the city, wench?" came the voice of Grandyn, the dark-haired Sigurri. "Should that be your intention, there is a matter which first must be seen to."

"For what reason would I be prepared to depart—at the appointed time—and then consider return?" I asked, turning to regard the male. He stood close behind me, an amusement filling him which was increased by the first of my words. "And what matter is there between us that I have no recollection of?"

"You are wise in not recollecting the matter," said he, well agrin as he stood with left hand resting upon sword hilt. The others of the Sigurri lazed upon the grass, chuckling with the amusement they shared with the one before me. "I am no longer weaponless and held in chain, kept from acting as a warrior should," said this Grandyn.

"A true warrior acts as a warrior at all times," said I, folding my arms beneath my life sign. "The absence or presence of weapons and chain makes little difference to one who is truly acquainted with warriorhood."

"Well said!" called Mehrayn with a laugh, the others joining his laughter. Grandyn's grin grew rueful, and his head shook slowly from side to side.

"You are quick to take a man up on incautious words, wench," said he. "Perhaps I should have said I am now able to act as I wish in matters which involve swordplay. Should you cast your mind back to the first instance of your addressing us, you may perchance recall our discussion upon the point of challenge for insult given. Does the discussion begin to return to you?"

"Indeed do I now recall it," said I, nodding at the sudden rush of memory. "So hurried were my preparations for departure, all speech and doings prior to them are much of a blur. What of it?"

"It is now the time to discuss the matter further," said he, and again had his grin widened. "You no longer have your wenches about you upon whom you might call for assistance. Should I insist upon accepting the offer made then, you must face me alone. However, should we discuss the matter, we may perhaps find another alternative."

Again came the chuckling of the other Sigurri, showing they continued to share an amusement, yet was the nature of the amusement unclear to me. One either accepted or rejected a challenge, one did not discuss it; challenge was a matter of blood, not words. I looked upon the Sigurri I faced, tall and broad in his black body cloth, his sword-belt a familiar weight about his hips, his barefoot stance firm and unashamed. These Sigurri were warriors, I knew, yet were they male as well and strange as all males. Perhaps the male was unaware of that which the challenge entailed.

"I am unfamiliar with the manner in which Sigurri conduct a challenge, I know," said I, "yet do I know the manner in which Midanna see to it. The sole words spoken are those of challenge and acceptance, all else being seen to by swords. Should it be your wish to face me, I may not, in honor, deny you, which leaves little to be discussed. The Sigurri approach these matters differently?"

"In certain instances," nodded this Grandyn, untouched by the usual sobriety marking such occasions. "Were you male, there would be no call for discussion, yet are you far from male. You may, delicious wench, appease my insult with your body rather than your blood, for my desire to plunge deep may be sated by use of other than a metal sword. That it must be one or the other is unarguable; I trust to your wisdom to choose correctly."

The males, all agrin, awaited my response to this foolishness, mocking both myself and the concept of challenge alike. A warrior unfamiliar with the doings of males would certainly have grown exceedingly wroth, yet did I find it not worth the effort. Males are males, be they city male or Sigurri.

"There is but one choice to be made," I shrugged, holding his dark, amused gaze easily. "I, having no more than a single sword which may plunge deep, may choose no other. The need to spill the blood of one I was meant to liberate does not please me, yet the demands of honor may not be refused. Three may lead me to your city as easily as four."

"She already accounts you dead, Grandyn," called the male Bershyn, joining the laughter of the others. "Beware her edge, for she is a mighty warrior."

"And more stubborn than wise," growled this Grandyn, displeased with my words, his left fist tightening about his sword hilt. "It must be clear that I would prefer your use to your death, wench. Do you seek an end to existence, that you refuse me such use? Are you not aware that I might take such use without your let?"

"Not while I have sword to hand, male," I grinned, enjoying his dark humor. "Not for naught is Jalav the chosen of both Mida and Sigurr. My sword has already drunk deep of much male blood, yet has its thirst scarcely been slaked. Should you wish to add yours to that of the others', you need do no more than speak of it. Happily will I face you."

"And yet you were bidden by Sigurr to free us," said the red-haired Mehrayn, raising himself from the ground to approach as Grandyn stood and frowned. "It would undoubtedly displease the god were you to spill the blood of one of us."

"Then perhaps it would be my blood which was spilled." I shrugged, truly unconcerned. "As Mida wills it, so shall it be. One's fate cannot be escaped."

"Yet, one need not spend each fey of one's life seeking that fate," returned Mehrayn, a dryness to his tone. "That a choice was given you clearly shows that this need not be a matter of fate. Grandyn has no wish to harm you; he merely wishes your use, as do we all. You know well enough your use will be ours during this journey, for we are men and will not long be denied. You, a female alone, must sleep at some time, and then will you be ours no matter the keenness of your sword. Those others of your wenches took gladly the pleasure we were able to give; you shall be no different from them.''

''And yet I am indeed different,'' said I, looking up into his eyes, all amusement gone. ''No longer am I able to find pleasure in the use of males, as my sisters do. Best would be that one of you face me now, male, to decide the matter for all time. Should you attempt my use as you say you intend, all your lives would be forfeit.''

I turned from their silent stares and walked some paces across the grass, giving thanks to Mida in my heart that no other Midanna accompanied me. To find no pleasure in males was a crippling lack for a warrior to own to, one which would earn me the pity of my sisters. These males, however, were more likely to show me scorn, and scorn is more easily borne than pity. I stopped and stood in contemplation of the forest we rode toward, attempting to avoid bitterness in thought, yet were my steps dogged by another, who stood himself behind me.

''You may address me as Mehrayn, wench,'' came the voice of the male, again filled with calm. ''The term 'male' is not inaccurate, yet does it strike the ear with nearly the force of insult. And I assure you that you need not fear a lack of pleasure, for you will surely be well seen to. Warriors of Sigurr are sustained by the god himself.''

Chuckling agreement came from the others of the males, yet did I feel a shudder pass through me at thought of the dark god. The manner of his use of me had been unbelievable agony, a fouling of my soul I would never forget. Stiffly, in slow madness, I turned to Mehrayn, my right hand reaching for my sword hilt.

''Not again will I know the touch of Sigurr,'' I said, my voice part whisper, part growl. ''This did I vow to myself when I was again able to think, and know the extent of what he had done.'' My sword whispered from its scabbard, to point at the heart of the male. ''Sooner would I find the final death, and forfeit my soul to the darkness. Free your sword, male, for we are done with words.''

A frown sat clear upon the features of the male, disturbance strong in the light eyes of him, his hand making no move toward his sword hilt. He merely stood and stared a moment, then slowly shook his head.

"I find myself at a loss to understand your words, wench," said he, taking no note of the sword point at his chest. "Almost does it seem that your use has already been Sigurr's, though you continue to live and walk among us. Such a thing is not possible."

"Would that your belief were so," said I, my point held steady upon him. "In Mida's realm he was unable to take me, yet was it necessary that I strike a private bargain with him. His price was my use, freely given, and nearly did I fail to survive the doing. Perhaps it would have been best had I not survived, for I am no longer able to know pleasure from males. I have made the attempt, and much does it seem as though my soul were slain." I paused, now seeing pain in his eyes, then said, "Why do you not bare your blade?"

"There is no need for the baring of blades," said he, turning briefly to look upon the others of his males, each of whom nodded solemnly in agreement. "We are healthy men who much enjoy the use of toothsome wenches, yet are we also warriors with a knowledge of honor. There is no honor and little pleasure in taking a wench who feels her soul slain—and by the god whom we serve. Perhaps your soul merely slumbers deeply, girl. Should that be the case, we may discuss the matter again when it awakens. For now, I think it best that we continue on our way."

He turned and walked from me then, joining the others in gathering their weapons and mounts, leaving me to resheathe my sword in some slight confusion. Never before had I met males with a sense of honor which neared that of Midanna. Much had I believed that males had no honor, yet were these Sigurri oddly different. Were their actions to prove a match to their words, it would sadden me when the Midanna were called upon to strike them down. Silently, with much to think upon, I untied the reins of my kan from my spear, freed the spear from where I had driven it into the ground, mounted, and followed after the males.

The balance of the fey and those following were of necessity much the same, yet was the boredom of travel lightened by the presence of the Sigurri. They clearly joyed in the freedom of the forests quite as much as I, and seldom was there a time when their laughter did not ring out to the treetops about us. Not again did they speak of the matter of my use, yet my efforts to remain aloof from their set was not permitted. The hand of us rode together through the shining green and gold and warm, dark brown, and therefore did they insist that I be treated as one of them. Never before had males done such a thing; had they been unable to demand the use of Jalav, they were in no other manner concerned with her. These Sigurri, however, gave to me the same amused attention they gave one another, drawing me from the depths of thought and laughingly within their midst.

Easily might it be seen that these males were truly fond of one another, yet were they constantly raising doubts concerning the abilities each may have had. All were subject to this jocularity, save that Mehrayn was spoken of least. Famsyn, the fourth Sigurri, he who was light-haired and larger than Bershyn, spoke only rarely, yet was he also a full party to the amusement. Each of the males took his turn as hunter for the set, providing the meat which was fed upon each fey, yet none was able to find the full approval of his brothers in what catch he returned with. The nilno was aged, the paslat was tough, the deglin was all bone and gristle, and so on. Brightly did the males await my turn at the hunt, already commiserating with me should I return empty-handed, swearing most solemnly that they would not fault me should they find themselves without provender for the fey through my ill-luck and inexperience. In turn, I thanked them most solemnly for their understanding, thought upon the matter in amusement, then, at the proper time, took myself into the woods. When I returned with a handful of lellin the males took pains to exclaim in surprise, then spoke gently against taking the kill of a child of the wild. The meat was often tainted, they said, therefore was I, in future, to attempt a kill of my own. Much amusement did the males hide behind faces of gentle admonishment, yet did their amusement swiftly fly when I, with a shrug of perplexity, released the lellin to do the same. I had taken the trouble to capture the lellin rather than slay them; lellin are wont to hang limply from the hand when held caught by the feet, and when I released them, wildly did they fly in the faces of the males in their attempt to escape. With ragged cries did the males throw themselves to the ground to avoid the lellin flight, and then, rather than grow angry, rolled about in the throes of such strong laughter that tears came to their eyes. I, too, laughed well at the jest, and then fetched the lellin which were meant to be fed upon. Once roasted, not a single word was spoken against them, and this, too, caused laughter.

A further point of some amusement was the manner in which Mehrayn wished to be addressed. The male disliked the term "male," yet did he insist upon addressing me as "wench" and "girl" and "lovely one" and suchlike terms. The other Sigurri did I quickly come to call Grandyn and Bershyn and Famsyn, yet Mehrayn was "male" without apology or exception. His annoyance was clear enough when *I* addressed him so; when the others began joining me in the practice, his annoyance grew three-fold. The laughter at this was more hidden than overt, for the males held him in high respect, yet laughter was there aplenty, urged on by the stubbornness shown by Mehrayn. Had he called me Jalav, as did the others, he, too, would have been named.

The feyd fled one into the other, and quickly did we find ourselves at the banks of the Dennin river. The Dennin marked the beginning of the lands of Midanna, and this the males seemed to be aware of. Without hesitation was the lead of the march given over to me, so that I might see us safely through the area. Though the nine clans of warriors who were sister to the Hosta had been left behind in Bellinard, the nine remaining clans who were sister to the Silla and enemies to the Hosta, remained to hunt and rove unopposed. Laughter was given over into silence, sleepiness in the warmth and light of the fey was exchanged for caution and vigilance, fires remained unlit, and each of us took turn standing guard through the darkness. Had we come upon enemy Midanna the males would again have fallen captive, yet my fate would not have been as pleasant as theirs.

More than a hand of feyd passed in creeping through Midanna lands, and much did the need for such creeping come to rankle. I, a war leader of not one but ten clans of Midanna, should not have found it necessary to act so, yet was I forced, by the needs of the task given me by Mida, to skulk about as though in fear of a meeting of blades. My humor grew black and snarling, and the males, seemingly aware of the cause of such a humor, ringed me closely as we rode, as though to keep me from riding off in search of battle. This, too, brought a growling to my throat, yet was there little I might do for it. The males were of a mind to protect me from my temper, and naught save swords would have seen the matter done differently.

At last were the lands of Midanna behind us, and the males, although still vigilant, again returned to laughter. I, still held by the front teeth of the dark humor which had plagued me, was not of a mind to join with them, therefore did I take myself off when a halt was called for the mid-fey meal. I knew the area of wood we rode through, for I had hunted and explored it well when still a warrior. Not far from where the males had halted was a small glade beside a pond, a cool, lovely pond where one might bathe and swim with great delight. The heat of the feyd upon this side of the Dennin was most welcome after the cold of the north, yet did it bring one a great desire for cool waters within which to bathe.

I left my kan tied in the shade of a tree and approached the pond, smelling as well as seeing the cool blueness of the water, sparkling beneath the gold of Mida's light, in places rippling green from the trees which surrounded it. Had I intended merely looking upon it I would have been lost, for its call was so strong that I could not resist. Quickly did I drive my spear into the ground, remove my sword belt, dagger and leg bands, then undo the breech. About to step into the water, my life sign caught my eye, that life sign which had been transformed by Mida and Sigurr. Much effort had I put into forgetting the darkly roiling thing, yet would it be unwise to forget it to such an extent that it would be lost in the pond. No more than an instant did I ponder the question, and then was my dagger thrust into the ground not far from my spear, the leather of the life sign wound firmly about it. All would await my return in safety, for the dagger, given to me by Mida along with the matching sword, would surely be protected by the goddess herself.

Soft birdsong filled the golden air as I stepped into the cool, blue water, surrounding me as I lowered myself and began to stroke across the pond. How truly bereft were city folk, to know naught of the pleasures to be found without the walls of their cities, to live pent up as though they were slave, to bathe in narrow pots filled with water which was heated. To know no other thing than that would cause a warrior to sicken and die, yet were city folk pleased to have it so, calling warriors savages for not doing the same. I felt the caress of the water against my flesh as I moved through it, and knew beyond doubt that sooner would I be called savage a thousand times than lose the blessings which Mida has bestowed upon her warriors. To be savage is far superior to being city-pent.

I allowed myself no more than thrice a handful of reckid in the water, for no matter how lovely and compelling the pond was, the forest was scarcely a place to long remain unarmed in. Though only a few of the children of the wild would seek to enter the water to reach one, those few were enough to bid caution to a warrior. With regret did I once again stroke for the edge where I had left my weapons and kan, and only upon reaching it discovered another had found the pond after me. Mehrayn stood less than four paces from the pond's edge, his eyes on me as I climbed dripping from the water, his hands holding the breech I had removed.

"By Sigurr's blade, I believe I have found a water nymph," said he, well agrin as his eyes moved busily about me. "I believe I shall carry you off to my camp, little nymph, for my brothers, too, would take pleasure in seeing you so. It is not often a man finds a nymph in the wilderness."

"I do not know the meaning of 'nymph,' " said I, squeezing a deal of the water from my hair, "yet do I know, male, that I am scarcely little. The breech you hold is mine, and I would have the return of it."

"This breech?" said he, raising it with brows arched, then did he look at it again and nod with sudden agreement. "Ah, I see you speak the truth, wench, for the breech is indeed yours. So fine a piece of work could not be mistaken, even had I not seen it upon you these many feyd. The breech is indisputably yours."

"Then I would have the return of it," said I, stopping before him and looking up into his eyes. Indeed did I somehow feel "little" before this large, broad male, yet the feeling was one best kept from my thoughts—and tongue.

"Of a certainty you may have it," said he, holding the breech high so that I might see it more easily. "You need only reach for it to again have it in your possession."

I saw no difficulty in doing as he asked, yet as I reached for the breech his arm raised it higher and higher still, continually keeping it out of my reach. With a small sound of annoyance for his foolishness I stretched high upon my toes, determined to regain what was mine—and then was his free hand at the back of my neck, pressing my body to his and holding my lips still for his kiss. Warm and demanding were the lips of Mehrayn, his body as warm yet harder to the touch; so startled was I that no thought of struggle entered my mind. Deeply was I kissed and tightly was I held, so deeply and tightly that a weakness was forced upon me, the likes of which I had not felt in quite some time. With shock it came to me then that my body was about to move against the male I was held to, just as though I wished the use of him! I had no understanding of the reason for the feeling, yet do I know that it would have come—had not the keren appeared first.

My kan's scream of terror rent the air, silencing the birdsong and dragging Mehrayn's lips from mine. As he whirled to stare about him, I, too, was able to see the forest at his back, and from the forest loped a large, brown keren, still upon all fours. My kan had caught the scent of the beast, and had I not been preoccupied with foolishness, I, too, would have scented it. Mehrayn cursed in a low voice and quickly drew his blade, then stepped forward as though to bar the keren from reaching me. The keren slowed as it neared the Sigurri, then raised up on its hind legs with a growl, clearly intending to engage the male.

Raising up brought its height far above that of Mehrayn, and easily might it be seen that the outcome of a battle between the two was no predetermined victory for the male.

"Jalav, return quickly to the camp!" snapped Mehrayn, continuing to look only upon the keren. "I will hold it as long as I may, yet are you to go *now*!"

With another growl the keren swiped at the male, causing him to bend swiftly below the slashing claws and jump aside, swinging backhanded at the beast as he moved. The swing drew a scream of rage from the keren as a line of blood appeared on the brown fur, and no longer was the keren concerned with any save the Sigurri. It followed the male as though drawn on a leash, away from the wildly plunging kan—and away from Jalav.

No more than a small sound of annoyance did I allow myself before turning quickly and running the short distance to my weapons. To face an enraged keren with no more than a sword was a doing fit only for desperation—or a male. Swiftly was my spear drawn from the ground, and as swiftly did I return to the two engaged in battle. As I approached, the beast swiped again at Mehrayn, this time reaching the male who had been trapped by a tree at his back. The blow sent the Sigurri head over heels to the right, rolling to fetch up against another tree, his sword still firmly clasped in hand despite the thickening lines of red to be seen upon his shoulder and upper arm. In another moment the keren would be upon him; all time for waiting was at an end.

I took my stand perhaps four paces from the keren, then raised my voice in the cry of the zaran, a natural enemy to the keren. The screeing cry brought the beast around immediately with a snarl, thinking itself attacked by another child of the wild, presenting to me the target I required. Without thought did my arm go back and then forward, casting the slim-shafted spear of city males at the furious, advancing keren, sending the weapon hurtling into and through the throat of the beast. The keren choked upon its own blood and clawed at the spear, attempting to howl as it staggered in its forward rush, and then was it falling to the ground, its soul already sped. Fervent thanks did I offer up to Mida for having guided my arm, for the throw had been necessary, yet unwise. Keren have been known to lurch unexpectedly, throwing off the aim of any who were foolish enough to cast at any target other than its body, and had the Sigurri not been so close to it, I would not have attempted its throat. Mehrayn, beside the tree, lowered his sword at last, then breathed deeply of the sweet forest air about us.

"So much for that," said he, wincing somewhat with the pain

in his swordarm. "It is fortunate that you fetched your spear as I commanded, wench, else might there have been some small difficulty."

"I had thought," said I, approaching him where he sat, "that you had commanded me to run, male. Was I mistaken?"

"Certainly," said he with a large grin and a small laugh. "For what reason would I be so foolish as to send away so excellent a spear caster? Does it seem to you that I wish to join Sigurr's eternal legions before my appointed time?"

"Certainly not," said I, grinning down at his amusement. "Indeed must I have misheard you."

"Indeed," he nodded, his grin paling under the now-increasing pain of his wound. "And now, should you be so kind, I would appreciate assistance in seeing to this arm and shoulder. The wound is a mere scratch, yet should it be cleansed and dressed."

"I will fetch your brothers as soon as I have donned my sword and retrieved my spear," said I, turning immediately to the place where my breech had been dropped. "Or perhaps you would care to ride my kan rather than remaining here unguarded. With a wound such as that, you will not soon again swing a sword with ease."

Had I not glanced at him before bending to my breech, surely would I have missed his look of puzzlement.

"For what reason need you fetch the others?" he asked, staring at me. "Is your position among your wenches too exalted to allow you to offer assistance to a mere male? Or do you conceal a female-like squeamishness beneath that warrior-like exterior?"

His words caused me to straighten slowly with the breech in my hands, for surely was the wound affecting his reason.

"I do not understand," I said, knowing my face reflected the confusion I felt. "For what reason would you ask assistance of one who was not of your clan? Most especially as your brothers are near to hand? Your wound is not so serious that lack of immediate attention would slay you. Was that your concern?"

"It is now I who suffers from a lack of understanding," said the Sigurri, a frown creasing his broad face as he forced himself to his feet. "Among my people, a man asks assistance of those he trusts, those who have proven themselves brothers to him no matter their origins. Should I be foolish enough to keep my trust from one who has already saved my life, great Sigurr would turn his face from me in disgust. That you did not expect my trust after your actions disturbs me. Did you think me so boorish as to be ungrateful?"

Full serious was his face as he looked upon me, his left hand grasping his right arm near the wound, a faint hurt to be seen in the lightness of his eyes. I took my gaze from his and replaced my breech, then went to stand above the keren to retrieve my spear.

"In my travels, it has been my experience that few males feel other than horror and fear at being shown my ability with weapons," said I, pulling at the haft to free my spear. "As you are male, I expected little else. And as for gratitude, there is no call to feel such a thing. Had I not seen to the keren, it would undoubtedly have seen to me. You may tell yourself I acted only to save my own life."

A moment of silence passed as the spear finally allowed itself to be withdrawn from the carcass; when I turned with it, intending to clean it beside the pond, I found Mehrayn directly in my path.

"Running as I bid you to do would have seen to the saving of your life alone," said he, looking down at me from less than a pace away. "That you remained to face a beast which sought the life of another was an act of great courage, one I shall not ignore nor hold lightly, no matter your low opinion of those you term 'male.' I shall not forget I stand in your debt, wench—unless I succumb to these claw wounds through lack of attention. Am I to be forced to see to them alone?"

Once again his green eyes held to me, the lightness of his tone doing naught to alter the vow in his words. I understood little of the intentions of this male called Sigurri, yet was it becoming clear that he was not completely like other males.

"I cannot fault you for distrusting your own abilities, male," said I, leaning somewhat upon the shaft of the spear I held. "Are you able to make your way to the edge of the pond, or must this Midanna support you?"

"Oh, indeed must I be supported," said he, a wide grin appearing upon his face. "Bring yourself to my left side, wench, so that I may put my arm about you."

"Put your arm about this," said I, plunging my spear into the ground before him. "I must go and retrieve my weapons, lest another child of the wild appear and take both our lives."

His soft laughter followed me to the pond edge where I had left my belongings, yet did he make no attempt to prevent me from doing as I had said. He knew as well as I that the woods were not safe, especially for one who was unarmed. My swordbelt was quickly replaced, as were my life sign and leg bands and dagger, and then did I turn to Mehrayn, who had brought himself and my spear to the water's edge. The claw marks were painfully deep in his flesh, yet not so deep as they might have been had he not allowed himself to be thrown aside by the force of the blow. The Sigurri made no sound as I washed the wounds and then applied a packing of mud to halt the bleeding, yet when we both rose to our feet, his uninjured arm moved swiftly to draw me close to him.

"I thank you for assisting me," said he, looking down into my eyes. "Now that the scratches have been attended to, I would take up where we were interrupted."

Again his lips lowered to mine, yet where I had had difficulty in holding myself from him the first time, the second gave me no difficulty at all. The strength of his arm about me and the feel of his broad body against mine bred no sense of desire, and after a moment his head raised with puzzlement clear in his eyes.

"I feel no response from you," said he, releasing me so that I might step back from him. "Earlier I would have sworn I felt passion begin to rise in you, yet now— Am I mistaken?"

"You are mistaken only in believing other than that my soul is slain," I shrugged, turning from him. "Had it not been, I would surely have responded to your touch. Do you wish me to clean your sword for you after I have seen to my spear?"

"Indeed," said he in a weary voice, as he sat down on the ground. "I would indeed be grateful if you were to see to my sword."

No further words came from the male, and no further attempts to draw me close, and soon were we within the wood, seeking the place where the others were taking their meal. We found them asprawl upon the grass in the shade of a large tree, Bershyn and Grandyn dozing while Famsyn kept a casual watch. Surely did it seem that they had anticipated a lengthy halt, yet their amusement at our too-speedy return fled when they spied the wounds Mehrayn had taken. The male had refused the use of my kan, preferring to walk as I did, and the exertion of doing so after the loss of blood had paled his face beneath the bronzed tan of his skin. Quickly were lenga furs brought forth to lay him upon, and all plans for continuing our journey were abandoned for the fey. Even Mehrayn knew he could not sit a kan for long, yet did the male chafe at the delay he caused. The others turned their faces from the foulness of his temper, sent two of their number to cut large portions of the beast I had slain, then declared a feast. All partook of the feast save Mehrayn, who slept from an herb added without his knowledge to the water given him to drink. Other herbs had I also gathered, those which would draw any poisons from his wounds, yet were the other males most grateful for the herb of sleep. Without it would Mehrayn undoubtedly have insisted upon standing his share of the watch.

No more than four feyd passed before Mehrayn insisted upon resuming our journey. That his wounds were on the mend was clear to all, therefore did his brothers acquiesce and break camp. Nearly two further hands of feyd were behind us before the male was able to begin stretching the stiffness from his arm and shoulder, yet was his sword-arm as it had been before we neared the area of his city. At last a darkness came which was greeted by the males as the final darkness to be spent in the forests, and happily did they seek sleep after we all had fed. I, who had offered to stand first watch, moved about the camp in the heat of the darkness, glancing occasionally at patches of the brightness-filled sky which could be seen floating in gaps above black-colored trees. I knew not what sort of greeting I would find among the balance of the Sigurri, yet was I impatient to be done with the raising of them. I also knew not when the strangers would arrive near the city of Bellinard, therefore did I wish to rejoin my warriors as soon as might be. First would the strangers be seen to, and then the Sigurri—were they to come—and then would the Midanna ride to free the Hosta from Ranistard. With the Hosta free, Jalav would also be free, to seek an end to the involvement with gods which had so changed her life. I held the thought a number of moments, then sat myself before a large, dark tree, feeling a faint breeze stir the heat all about. The strong possibility existed that I would not be able to disassociate myself from Mida and Sigurr, yet was it necessary that I make the attempt. A great weariness lay asleep within me, one which would waken one fey to engulf me, and end the life of journeys which I had been forced to. Jalav sought an end to existence, yet must honor first be satisfied. I sat with the tree at my back and kept my watch, and then, when relieved, found sleep with no great difficulty.

6 Sigurr's city—and betrayal

Early upon the new fey the forests ended, much as they did about the cities of northern males. Occasional dwellings were spied in the distance, ones belonging to those who grew and raised provender for the consumption of their fellows. We rode on beneath the heat and glare of Mida's light, the males in high spirits, I remaining silent in an attempt to see what there was to see. More than once were there groups of males to be seen in the distance, many bending to that which grew all about them, some few merely standing and observing the rest. Smaller forms moved about among those who labored, yet was the distance too great to see what they were about. Herds of small beasts to be fed upon were tended in a similar manner, most laboring, some observing, and much did it seem that the lands and holdings were vaster than those in the north.

We made no halt to feed at mid-fey, instead partaking of our provender as we rode, for it was already possible to see the beginnings of the city in the far distance. High was the city, rising above the level of the road in wide, black terraces, a glittering, burning black which stood out sharply against the green of the surrounding countryside and the blue of the skies. No shielding wall was to be seen at that distance, and when, more than two hind later, we began to approach the first of the dwellings, it became clear there was no wall of any sort. The road we had followed suddenly became a way of the city, leading between all manner of dwellings, large and small. Many city folk rode and walked upon this way, choking and crowding it, and quickly were we taken up and smothered in their midst.

"As ever, I am pleased to be home," said dark-haired Grandyn, looking about himself, "and yet, as ever, it will be a while before I again accustom myself to the presence of so many others about me. The forests are fair and empty, yet they are not home."

"The forests are home to Midanna," said I, wrinkling my nose at the smells which now assailed us. So long had it been

161

since we had left Bellinard, I had nearly forgotten the stench to be found in cities.

"Which undoubtedly proves the wisdom of Midanna," chuckled Mehrayn, amused by the expression he saw upon me. "If it were necessary for me to dwell upon a lower terrace, I, too, would likely take to the forests. You will find the air cleaner in the higher reaches, wench."

"Perhaps," I shrugged, continuing to look about myself as we moved slowly through the din and press of the throng. The air might well be cleaner the higher we climbed, yet would it remain the air of a city. Jalav disliked cities, yet was it unnecessary to speak of the feeling; no longer was I covered with the happiness of freedom, and this the males could see.

All about us were old, badly-cared-for dwellings, of a black stone which contained much red in it. Sigurri city folk bustled all about these dwellings; entering, leaving, standing before them, both silently and in converse with others. Those upon the way had surged all about us in an uncaring manner, yet in no more than a moment were the hordes beginning to draw back out of our path, both male and female bowing with an awed look to them, gazing at the males I rode with and speaking excitedly to one another. I, too, was gazed upon with much excited chatter, but it bespoke curiosity rather than awe. It came to me then to examine the males upon the way more closely, and none did I see with the black stroke upon the shoulder possessed by the four I rode with. Cloth in many colors covered their bodies, yet none were to be seen with black. These four, then, were in some manner different from those about us, clearly higher and commanding the respect of those we rode through. If this were true, then I was well-enough pleased, for then might my task be more quickly seen to and accomplished. Already did I ache for the freedom of the forests; the sooner I returned there, the sooner would happiness return to me.

With the way cleared for our passage, it was not long before we had twisted and turned among dwellings to a gentle rise which became less gentle. Dwellings lowered as the way rose, and soon were we passing at the bases of larger dwellings, circling them and all about to at last find ourselves upon a leveling which now ran between these larger dwellings. Though the way was well peopled, less bustle and more calm was to be found than that which obtained upon the lower level. Males and females continued to bow and allow us our path, yet were there now a few males who strode about in black body cloths, though still without a shoulder stroke. Upon the lower level it had pleased me to see that these Sigurri females failed to cover their breasts, yet was the custom absent upon this higher level. Rather than the length of bright cloth wrapped about their waists and reaching to their ankles, these higher-level females wore lengths of cloth which covered them from armpits to ankles, cinched tight with leather about their waists. The doing seemed foolish to me, till we rode near to a very large dwelling which had more than a hand of females chained separately by the neck before its broad, undecorated entrance.

"Temple slaves," murmured Mehrayn from his place on my right, obviously following my gaze. "Their nipples are dyed red to make their status clear to all. The ladies of this level and those higher feel no need to prove their own status, yet the wenches below wish it clear to all that they are free. As temple slaves are for the use of all men, one can scarcely blame them."

"There have been incidents of confusion, and not only at the lowest level," chuckled Grandyn from my left. "Two or three kalod ago, a number of spirited young ladies of the highest level took it upon themselves to show their opinion of one of their number. The wench in question was one who continually looked down upon all the others, thereby earning their enmity. Consider her mortification when she awoke early one fey and found herself chained by the neck in a temple alcove, her breasts dyed a bright, accusing red, her body stripped naked to prepare her for use. Her wine had been drugged the darkness before, and all her protestations failed to free her from the chain which held her in the alcove. Her family found her at last, yet not before she had been taught humility through service."

"I recall the incident," laughed Bershyn, who rode to Grandyn's left. "The young ladies responsible for the prank were punished themselves in a similar manner, though not by the populace in general. Those of us who were called on for assistance found them delicious in their tears of repentance, eh, Famsyn? A pity you two were away about Sigurr's work."

Famsyn, who rode to the right of Mehrayn, joined Bershyn in high amusement at the sour expressions of the other two, yet I found little amusement in their talk. I dislike slaves and the entire concept of slavery, no matter the gender of the slaves in question.

The way we followed twisted less than the previous one, yet it, too, began to rise toward a higher level. Upon the third level were there a greater number of males in black body cloths and larger and finer dwellings, yet was it necessary to reach the fourth level before one found dwellings of glittering black among those of reddish black, and further males with black strokes upon their shoulders. There were not many of these latter males, yet did each raise a hand to the four I rode with, calling them by name and offering greetings. These greetings were heartily returned by Bershyn and Grandyn, and then did the dark-haired male turn to Mehrayn.

"If you are sure you will not require our presence, we will leave you here," said Grandyn, seeming more than eager to be away. "There is a little slave in the temple of this level of whom I have dreamt since we departed the city to the north. As the journey home was not as pleasant as I had anticipated it would be, I have great need of that little slave."

"More need than I have for your presence," said Mehrayn, with a chuckle. "It is my intention to take this wench here to Aysayn, and vouch for her when he has heard her tale. Should he also require the three of you, we will know where you may be found."

"Aye," laughed Bershyn, stirring upon his kan. "We may be found offering our devout prayers to Sigurr in his temple, as do all loyal followers. Be sure to mention that to Sigurr's Shadow Aysayn, Mehrayn."

"Unnecessary," laughed Mehrayn, shaking his head. "A Shadow of Sigurr knows well the doings of each of his followers. Come to my house at darkness, brothers, so that we may feast and drink till the new light. We have earned at least that much."

"Agreed!" laughed the others, and with final waves of their arms, took themselves off toward a large, undecorated dwelling of glittering black. Much did the dwelling appear to be a larger version of those to be found upon the lower levels, yet were there no chained and painted females to be seen before its entrance.

"The temple slaves of this level, the one beneath and the one above, are to be found in halls and alcoves," said Mehrayn, seemingly reading my thoughts. "Public displays, though occasionally indulged in, are not the norm. Sigurr will be pleased with the ardent devotions of my brothers, as will the slaves they choose. Slave females find great pleasure in strong use, and come to eagerly anticipate it."

I turned my head to regard the male, who sat quietly upon his kan, regarding me in turn, a faint grin lurking in his eyes. I had heard such statements made by males at other times, and felt no need to comment. The doings of slaves had little in common with the doings of warriors, save that both must at times endure the foolishness of males.

"Interesting," murmured the male after a moment, the amusement remaining in his eyes. "You make no attempt to denounce my comments, nor do you take them as personal insult. Do you agree with me, then, or do you think yourself too good to be compared with wenches chained in the service of men?"

"I do not care for slaves," I informed the male, allowing him to see there was no amusement to be found in the subject. "Jalav was declared slave by the High Seat of Bellinard, yet little pleasure did the males find in her enslavement. Had she been unchained and allowed a weapon in her hand, there would have been even less of pleasure. There is considerable difference between being enslaved and becoming a slave."

"I should have known better than to broach the subject," said Mehrayn, shaking his head in mock severity. "You would indeed make a willful and disobedient slave, wench, one who would require much training. I think it best that we continue on to the High Temple now, and leave further discussion of slaves for another time. Attempt to bear in mind that there are more sober matters before us."

With such words did the male turn his kan and continue along the way, leaving me to follow with no more than a small sigh. Always did the male act so, as though a subject he had broached had been first spoken of by me, and I failed to understand his purpose. The matter seemed pure foolishness, designed to cause anger and insult in others, and at times had the male seemed vexed that I failed to fall to anger. For what reason one would purposely seek to anger another I knew not; should their intent be battle, a simple challenge would see the matter done. Mehrayn's intent was far beyond me, as were many of the doings of males. Strange were males, and naught might a warrior do to plumb that strangeness.

The fifth level proved to be the highest of the city, save that one single dwelling, of very large size, perched above all at the very top of the small mountain against which the city had been built. All dwellings upon this highest level were of glittering black, large and imposing, and guarded by males in black yet without shoulder strokes. A number of females were to be seen strolling about, most of whom wore black cloth belted about their waists rather than leather. These females called laughingly to Mehrayn, who returned their greetings with high good humor, though making no attempt to halt and approach them as they requested he do. Instead he continued on toward the towering dwelling above us, urging on his weary kan with words of encouragement. Both our mounts were nearly done, and had we not been so close to our goal, I would surely have insisted that we stop to rest them.

When we arrived at last at the foot of the high, gleaming black dwelling, males in light-colored body clothes hurried over to take our kand and spears. Deep bows followed Mehrayn as he led me toward the broad, pillared entrance, yet did the male seem nearly unaware of them. More intent did he seem upon his thoughts, and once within the stark, bare dwelling, he halted and gestured me close.

"I feel I had best explain what we are about here," said he, looking down at me with sober calm. "I have brought you here to speak your tale to Aysayn, he who is the Shadow of Sigurr's will upon this world. When he is convinced of the truth of what you say, he will give his blessing for the warriors of Sigurr to ride forth. I am the one who will lead them."

"Then—you are war leader to your males?" I asked, no more than somewhat surprised at the revelation. The manner in which the others had treated with Mehrayn bespoke a status of no more than near equals.

"We do not call the position war leader," said he, folding his arms as he leaned a shoulder upon the smooth blackness of the wall. "There are twenty Princes of Sigurr's Blood, high born warriors who each lead more than a century of fighting men, and I am the leader of these warriors and fighting men, called the Prince of Sigurr's Sword. The Prince of Sigurr's Sword must defend his position against all challengers, most especially from Princes of Sigurr's Blood. Bershyn and Famsyn and Grandyn are such Princes, yet are they not of a mind to challenge me. Do you follow what I say?"

"Certainly." I nodded, looking about at the wide, clean, totally undecorated entrance area. "You are war leader of your males, yet must you add to the position as all males, with foolish-sounding titles which mean naught. This Aysayn you speak of is undoubtedly the Keeper of Sigurr's lore, as Rilas is Keeper of Mida's lore and Crystals. For what reason do you require the blessing of a Keeper when Midanna do not?"

"Without such a blessing, how are we to know whether our expeditions have Sigurr's approval?" asked Mehrayn, an annoyance having entered his eyes and tone. "Should we do without, we may well be acting counter to Sigurr's wishes."

"With Midanna, it is for the war leader to decide the merits of a particular action," said I. "Should she lead her clan into battle in error, Mida will not smile upon her cause, though she ever allows the glory of death in battle. It is through success or failure that we judge Mida's will. Our Keeper may do no more than offer advice and attempt to obtain Mida's approval of the doing.''

"We Sigurri prefer obtaining approval in advance of the doing,'' said Mehrayn, a deal of dryness having entered his tone. "We may then enter battle knowing we are in the right. And should the point have escaped you, wench, allow me to inform you that without the blessing of Aysayn, the Sigurri will not ride out as you wish. If you are wise, you will make an attempt to speak more civilly to him than you do to me. The Shadow has not the patience of the Sword.''

"Perhaps you may recall, male, that I care not whether the Sigurri ride out,'' I replied, amused at his growing annoyance. "I agreed to do no more than attempt to raise your force. Should the Sigurri refuse the will of Sigurr, I will merely return to my Midanna and inform them that the battle is to be ours alone.''

Upon hearing my words, the annoyance of the male turned in great part to anger, and he straightened himself from the wall to stare down upon me.

"I find little amusement in your lightness of heart, girl,'' said he, a disapproving severity clear in the green of his eyes. "Did I not know you are aware of how greatly I desire to join this battle, surely would I believe you meant to act in a manner which would ensure our remaining behind.''

"Jalav shall act as she ever acts.'' I shrugged, still amused. "As Mida and Sigurr are well aware of the manner in which I act, surely my actions are in accordance with their wishes, else would another have been sent in my stead. Does Mehrayn put his own wishes above those of Mida and Sigurr?''

A brief moment of silence ensued, during which high frustration took possession of the male, and then did he shake his head.

"I am unable to accustom myself to the familiar manner in which you speak of Sigurr,'' said he, straightening where he stood. "Despite this difficulty, it is clear that no matter what efforts I might attempt, matters will proceed as the great god wills them. I will therefore do no more than show you to Aysayn's precincts, and then retire to my house, from which I have been too long absent. Surely will your steps be guided from then on by Sigurr.''

"Such will undoubtedly be sufficient.'' I nodded, resting my left hand upon my sword hilt. "As Mida wills it, so shall it be.''

"You are insufferable,'' he growled, lowering his brows in vexation. "Had you requested my assistance, I would have remained with you, as originally intended. As you feel no smallest need for me, I shall be on my way. Take that doorway which stands before you, continue up the corridor to the fifth doorway on the right, take that corridor to the fourth doorway on the left, then ask further of the guards you will find. May Sigurr be with you.''

A small, stiff bow ended the words he spoke, and then was he striding toward the entrance through which we had come, to disappear into the fey beyond. I watched him till he was gone, puzzling over the new strangeness he evinced, then dismissed the matter with a shrug. Males are male, and foolish is the warrior who attempts to make sense of their actions.

The doorway Mehrayn had mentioned stood perhaps a hand of paces from me, a small opening in the unadorned black wall. There was little reason to remain where I was, therefore did I take myself to that doorway and through. Beyond was the corridor spoken of, sparkling black walls containing large candles in silver sconces, uncovered black floor, doorways appearing at long intervals to left and right. A hand of doorways to the right, Mehrayn had said, and easily was the direction followed, yet did I find myself puzzled once more. Those doorways one was able to look through contained naught save corridors beyond them; the rest, numbering more than half, were closed fast with wooden doors which disallowed sight of what lay beyond. Had I not been intent upon completing the task given me and returning quickly to my warriors, I would surely have taken the time to look behind each.

The second corridor proved less empty than the first, in that carvings appeared in the black of the walls between the heavy candles. The carvings showed males in their doings, in battle, in raising foodstuffs and herd beasts, all beneath the eye of one who rose large above them and smiled upon their efforts. He who watched was undoubtedly Sigurr, yet not the Sigurr I had met and treated with. No indication was there of the evil which emanated from the god, and this I could not understand. Were these not his followers, who knew him for what he was? The question, though disturbing, held short reign in my thoughts, for the fourth doorway was quickly reached, bringing sight of the three males who stood in the small area beyond. Well lit with candles was this area, with low, silver seats to either side of the doorway through which I entered, and a silver and black cloth covering the stone of the floor. The cloth felt odd to walk upon after the stone, and much did it detract from the pleasant coolness which the corridors had had. The three males, in black body cloths, swordbelts, and brief leather foot coverings, showed naught of shoulder strokes, yet were they large and well made and alert. Their eyes came to me the moment I appeared, and quickly did grins cover their faces.

"Greetings, wench," said one as I approached, his eyes busily taking me in. Light-haired was the male, as were the other two, also with light eyes. "Should you have lost your way, as seems evident, we shall be pleased to direct you."

"For a small fee," said a second with a large grin, causing laughter in the others. "Sigurr's blessing will be yours along with the directions."

"I have no need of directions," said I, halting before them. "I come to speak with the male Aysayn, he who is called Shadow of Sigurr, and was told he might be found here. Are you to fetch him, or am I to go where he is?"

"Rein in, girl, rein in," laughed the first of the males, folding his arms as he looked down upon me. "The Shadow does not grant audience to all who present themselves, else he would do naught else. Who are you, and what is your business with him?"

"I am Jalav, war leader of all the Midanna," said I, folding my arms in a like manner, though without a matching amusement. "I have journeyed far to speak with the male, entirely at the behest of another. What I come to speak of may be more fully discussed with Aysayn."

"Perhaps she comes to offer herself to the Shadow," suggested the second male to the first, also looking down upon me. "She would look well draped in silver chain, serving in his private apartments, would she not?"

"Perhaps more so than she who now serves there," murmured the first male, his light gaze unwavering. "Her hair is of the color of the great god, and with the rest of her makes her a fitting vessel for the attentions of Aysayn. The sole disturbing note is the sword she wears."

"And the dagger," agreed the second, also in a speculating tone. "She has named herself war leader of some group. Perhaps they have sent her as a gift to Aysayn, in advance of proposing a joint venture of sorts."

"Would she be sent so without an escort?" asked the first. "How might her people be assured of her arrival? What if she had decided against offering herself? What if some harm should have befallen her before she was able to reach our city?"

"Your speculations are idle as well as incorrect," I interrupted, beginning to feel impatience. "Should it be beyond the three of you to inform Aysayn of my presence, I shall seek him out through my own efforts."

"Indeed," said the first, less amusement now touching him. "And in which direction would your efforts take you, girl?"

"Through the doorway you stand before," said I, anod toward the portal they undoubtedly guarded. "I have not journeyed this far to be halted by words."

"Nor by swords?" asked the male, his tone now even. "We are three to your one, girl, and have been set here to keep intruders from entering. Though it seems you are familiar with the use of the blade you wear, you cannot hope to overcome warriors."

"I, too, am a warrior," said I, returning the even gaze sent toward me. "Should Mida and Sigurr have sent me here to fall in battle, so be it. Naught less will halt my intentions."

"You claim to be sent by Sigurr?" demanded the second male as the first frowned. The third, aloof till then, now joined the ring before me.

"I make no claims," said I, taking them all in with a sweeping glance. "I merely state what is. Am I to be given access to Aysayn, or is battle to be joined?"

"Perhaps it would be best to inform her of the Shadow's absence," said the newly come third, the disturbance of the others touching him as well. "Should she truly be from Sigurr, it would be sacrilege to raise a blade against her."

"Aysayn would determine the matter soon enough," said the first male, quickly mastering his upset. "As it is, we cannot make the judgment for him. The Shadow has gone into the mountains to commune with Sigurr, wench, and therefore cannot be reached. He will return when his soul is renewed, and may then decide whether he will receive you. To attempt battle with us now will avail you naught."

The three gazed directly upon me, an openness to their stares which put the face of truth upon their assertion. I stood a long moment considering the situation, annoyed yet unable to alter the thing, then nodded in decision.

"Very well," said I, accepting the chains of delay. "As Aysayn is not now available, I shall await his return."

I turned from the males, walked to the left-hand wall of the area, turned again, and sat myself cross-legged upon the floor cloth. The males watched silently as I did this, then exchanged looks of confusion.

"What do you do, wench?" asked the first, taking a short step toward me. "It may be feyd before Aysayn's return. You cannot await him *here!*"

"Should he indeed be communing with Sigurr," said I, "the dark god will undoubtedly inform him of my presence. As I have not been sent here with any purpose other than to speak with the male, I shall indeed remain here."

"Such foolishness!" began the male with heat, yet were further words denied him with the appearance of a female at the door before which he and the others stood guard. The door had been opened by one of further males clad in black who accompanied the female, and at sight of her, the three I spoke with turned quickly and bowed. Much did the female seem intent upon quitting the area from which she came, yet sight of Jalav halted her just beyond the doorway into the small area. Tall was the female, and clad in silks all of black, ones which covered her from left shoulder to ankles, and which were cinched tight about her small waist. Her golden-haired head was carried high and proud, that and the deference of the males contrasting oddly with the light silver chains in which she was enclosed. Both her wrists and ankles were enclosed so, the gleaming links meeting at her waist to encircle it, yet was she clearly no slave.

"What occurs here?" said she to the males of the area, her voice filled with the sound of authority. "Do you dare to sport with a wench of the first level while on duty?"

"High lady, this is no matter of sport," said the first male, the annoyance which set his shoulders unobservable in his tone. "This wench has come to speak with the Shadow, and insists upon awaiting his return on this very spot. We were about to remonstrate with her when you appeared."

"For what reason need you remonstrate with her?" demanded the female, her voice melodious even in impatience. "Remove her and be done with it!"

The first male stumbled upon hesitation, and into the gap fell the third of the three.

"High lady, we cannot!" said he, a pleading quality faint yet obvious in his tone. "The wench claims to have been sent here by Sigurr!"

A silence descended then, one which covered all those within hearing. The female turned light, thoughtful eyes to the task of studying me, and busy indeed did the thoughts behind those eyes seem. After a moment, the female drew herself up and nodded.

"I see," said she with interest. "Under the circumstances, I will interview her myself. Come with me, girl."

The female, though tall, was obviously far from being Midanna, and her tone, though brisk, had hardly been offensive; it was therefore odd that I felt an intense and almost immediate dislike for her. Slowly did I rise again to my feet, seeing the female's well-covered surprise that I was larger than she, and attempt to keep my tone as civil as hers had been.

"I grow weary of the fact that none of your city seem able to recall a name given thém," said I, resting my left hand upon my sword hilt. "I am Jalav, formerly war leader of the Hosta, now war leader of all the Midanna. The next who calls me other than that will regret the doing."

"Jalav," repeated the female, her eyes raised to my face reflecting a continued thoughtfulness. "I shall indeed remember your name. I am Ladayna, High Consort to Aysayn the Shadow and close confidante to him. If you will follow me to my apartments, I will hear your tale."

The female turned to retrace her steps through the doorway, the males stepping back to allow her her way; I hesitated only briefly before following, for though I had a somewhat uneasy feeling, I was anxious to be done with these city folk and on my way back to the warriors who awaited me. Perhaps speaking with this Ladayna would serve my purpose, and it would be unnecessary to await the return of Aysayn.

The males within the doorway numbered six, and each eyed me closely as I passed them, to where Ladayna had halted to await me. The female turned again as I reached her and continued up the corridor, seemingly unaware of that which she passed. The walls, no longer bare stone but hung in black and gold silks, sported gleaming golden candle sconces and many—drawings, city folk would call them—also in black and gold. Each drawing depicted no more than a single male and a single female, each male taking pleasure from an unwilling partner, each drawing depicting a different manner of doing so. Where the first set of drawings ended a second set began, the males continuing their doing, the females clearly less unwilling than they had been. The third and final set showed the females lost to the pleasures of that which was done to them, lost to the overwhelming desire to please the males who used them. I made no comment as I took these drawings in, yet was it obvious that they had been done by males. No other than they considered the simple taking of a female sufficient to give her pleasure; any female ever used knew the fallacy in that.

The female Ladayna followed the corridor to its end, then halted before a door in the wall to the left. To the right was a set of double doors, large and imposing, of black wood encrusted with gold, the sign of Sigurr clear upon each. Four further males in black body clothes stood before these doors, and one made his way to the smaller door opposite and opened it for Ladayna. The female spoke several soft words to the male, then turned to gesture me within.

"These apartments are mine," said she, "and we may take our ease as we converse. I have sent for refreshments to be brought, and we will not be disturbed in any other way."

The female led the way within and, once I had followed, the male who had opened the door closed it again. Within was a large room done in black and silver, wall silks, floor furs, deep, soft seats. Again was there less of a coolness to the air, and no windows were visible even behind the wall silks. Beyond a carving of a male figure all in black, no further adornments were to be seen in the room.

"Please seat yourself," said Ladayna, gesturing toward a seat as she, herself, took one perhaps a pace away. "I am curious to know what brings you here."

"The tale is simple." I shrugged, pleased to be able to lower myself into the seat with no difficulty. I was grateful that I had learned the use of city-folk devices such as seats for, despite her lack of enmity, I would not have wished to appear awkward before the female Ladayna. "I am the chosen of Mida," said I, "chosen to lead all of the Midanna in battle. By cause of having been chosen by Mida, I am also chosen by Sigurr to bring his word to his followers. Strangers come who are enemy to both Mida and Sigurr, and the goddess and god would have us do battle with them side by side. I am told this Aysayn is able to send the Sigurri to battle, therefore have I come to speak with him."

"I see," said Ladayna, her words accompanied by the clink of chain as she shifted somewhat in her seat. "And these others that you speak of—these Midanna. Are they male warriors such as the Sigurri—or females like yourself?"

"For what reason would I take the bother of leading males?" I asked, puzzled by her question. "The Midanna are true warriors, female warriors, and shall face the coming strangers alone should the Sigurri refuse to join them. You say you consort with the male Aysayn; are you able to raise the Sigurri in his place?"

"I fear I have no such power," said she, a faint smile touching her features. Bold were the looks of this female, with a face and body undoubtedly considered highly desirable by males. "I may do no more than speak to Aysayn on your behalf, explaining your request and asking that he consider it. You, yourself, may do no more, therefore are you free to return to your—warriors. We will share refreshment, then you may leave."

"I have not come the distance I have to leave word with another," I replied, gesturing a dismissal with one hand of the female's foolishness. "As it is Aysayn I must speak with, I shall await his return. And I shall not request his consideration of the matter. I shall inform him that I merely agreed to carry Sigurr's word to his warriors; should his warriors refuse his word, the Midanna are well able to carry on without them."

"Thereby insuring that the Sigurri will ride, through anger if naught else," said she, an annoyed clink to the sound of her silver chains. "And Aysayn. Aysayn will be charmed, by the barbaric nature of you, by the presumption of your insistence upon leadership, by the manner in which you speak familiarly of Sigurr—and by that which attracts all men who have seen you."

"Of what do you speak?" I asked, frowning. "Of what interest are the preferences of Aysayn to me—other than his directing the Sigurri to ride?"

"They should be of great interest to you!" she snapped, no longer pretending to indolent hospitality. "As they are to me! These chains I wear—do you think them mere decorations? I am high born, and was able to convince my father to refuse the petition of any man I disliked—save one. The Shadow of Sigurr upon this world did not petition. He merely had his warriors take me from my father's house, then placed me in the chains of a slave when I attempted to refuse him. He is a man who joys in taking unwilling women, in making them writhe beneath him. I had no wish to be his consort, yet the power of the position is considerably more than I would care to give up—and the freedom considerably less than that which would appeal to the likes of you. If you remain he will have you—and I will have nothing."

"Your fears are unfounded, woman," I snorted, somewhat amused by the city slave-woman thoughts of the female. "This Aysayn will have naught of me save the words I bring from Sigurr, for my presence is necessary to lead the Midanna into battle. Should he attempt otherwise, one or the other of us must fall."

"So you say," said the female, and I realized she watched as my hand stroked my life sign. Unconsciously, at the mention of battle, had I reached for that which had been the guardian of my soul, forgetting the sign of Mida and Sigurr it had become. I quickly withdrew my hand, yet the female's gaze remained a moment longer.

"So *you* say," said she, angered and patently disbelieving. "I say I have learned Aysayn well enough to be sure of what he will do. Will you leave, now, knowing I will relay your message, or do you insist upon remaining and provoking disaster?"

Flashing of eye was this female of the Sigurri, this female who no longer wished an end to the chains of a slave. Completely was she convinced of the harm my presence would bring her, yet I had not come to bring harm to any.

"The insistence that I remain is not mine." I shrugged as I rose to my feet. "I have pledged my word to attempt to raise the Sigurri, and so must I do. As my presence disturbs you, I shall await Aysayn elsewhere." I turned then and made for the door, yet halted when I had reached it to face the female again. "Do not fear that I shall take your place," I attempted to reassure her. "It has already been proven that Jalav does badly in chains—and worse to those who attempt to place her in them. Your slavery will be secure to you alone."

The female, angered further, made no reply, therefore did I open the door to the corridor and take myself through. Those males who had been there earlier remained in evidence, giving me no hint of their intentions till I had passed them. One moment I walked peaceably toward the far end of the corridor between them—and the next a large, heavy cloth had been thrown over me, it and many arms bearing me to the floor. I struggled and fought to reach my sword or dagger, yet the folds of cloth hampered my movements and large hands quickly removed my weapons. I continued to struggle as the cloth was drawn away from me, yet what may a warrior do against the strength of a hand of males? Though with snarls I attempted to attack with teeth, still was I held easily to the floor I lay upon, the males keeping their flesh safe through distance. It was then that the female Ladayna came close to stand above me.

"Somehow I find myself pleased that you refused to leave," said she, a smile again lighting her lovely features. "I despise women of your low sort, women who were born to be no more than temple slaves. Your foolish attempt to reach Aysayn and entice him with lies will not even be mentioned; the Shadow's time is too valuable to be wasted. It pleases me that I may see to this small matter for him." She then took my dagger from the hands of a guard male, bent to me, and cut the leather which held the life sign about my neck. "I will keep this little bauble as a memento of our meeting," said she, straightening again with the leather tight in her fist. "You may now take her to begin the life she was born for—the life of a temple slave."

Male laughter joined that of the female as I was forced amid struggles to my feet and taken up the corridor. Pleased was the female, and eager were the males—and Jalav was again to be made a slave.

7 Slavery—and the Prince of Sigurr's Sword

The chamber of shining black stone was large indeed, far larger than the slave chamber in the palace of the High Seat of Bellinard. Wailing cries and moans and screams were to be heard once the large double doors were thrown open, giving one the impression of entering a nether region for the lost spirits of females. Naught of males was to be heard save occasional shouts, and once within and able to see the lines and lines of metal enclosures, I also saw naught of males. No more than females did the chamber contain, all naked within their metal enclosures, some chained, some not, some weeping or screaming, some silent, some writhing with pain or need upon the metal of their enclosure's floor, all exuding so strong a stink of misery and fear that the air thickened with it. Again I struggled against the hands which held me, yet the struggle proved as useless as it had been till then.

The chamber was well lit by torches, and easily did I see the male who glanced up, saw the males who held me, and gestured them toward a door in the far end of the chamber. Quickly did the males follow the one who had gestured, a male in light green body cloth, and soon were we beyond the door in a second, smaller chamber, one which boasted enclosures of different size rather than the same. Once this smaller door had been closed, the silence which descended was akin to deafness.

"Ah, blessed quiet," sighed the male in green body cloth, turning to the two who held me between them. "I am well aware of the fact that occasionally allowing them their hysterics makes them more obedient slaves, yet I live for the fey when this batch need no longer be allowed the privilege. My ears ring longer than the hin they scream."

"And yet they learn that even screaming is a privilege which must be earned," laughed the male to my right. "When the privilege is taken from them, they at last know themselves as full slaves."

"And here we have another who begins the journey," said the male in green body cloth, looking closely upon me. "Larger than most and seemingly most wroth—yet clearly a vessel for the devout prayers of men. There will be many men who cry out the praises of Sigurr while deep within her, for there are few in chains—or without—to equal her."

"And chained she shall have to be," growled the male to my left, tightening his grip upon my arm most painfully as I struggled in anger. "A true she-devil is she, with teeth as sharp as any devil in the Caverns of the Doomed. She had undoubtedly been sent by the evil Oneness to plague us in our worship."

"Serain feels so only by cause of the fact that she bit him," laughed the male to my right when the male before me frowned. "She attempted escape two corridors from here, and Serain was the one to catch her. I arrived but a moment later, yet barely in time to take her teeth from his flesh before his flesh was taken from his bones. Have a care with her, Podelm; we do not wish to lose you."

"I shall not be lost," said the male called Podelm, his frown turning to laughter. "I have a special fondness for the wild ones, for they have ever proven to be the most passionate and most easily aroused. Once she has learned her place as a slave, I may even give her my attention."

"Which, as it includes sweets and privileges, all slaves are eager for," laughed the male to my right. "Podelm, your attraction for slaves outshines even Princes of the Blood. Where are we to put her?"

"Here," chuckled the male Podelm, moving toward two posts which stood to the side of the room, perhaps a pace from the wall. "Face her inward, toward the wall, and secure her well. Her lessons begin here, and they must be sharp ones."

Again was I forced to motion, in the wake of the green-clad male, and taken between the two posts. Despite the fact that I fought, my arms were raised and placed in thin metal cuffs which depended, one from each post, at the end of long, metal chains. To my ankles also were cuffs attached, their chains ending at the bottoms of the posts, and once the four cuffs were upon me, the slack in the chains was taken up so that I stood between the posts like the stroke called ecks by males. Well chained was the war leader Jalav, well secured by the metal of males, and safe would these males be only so long as she continued so.

The two black-clad males remained no more than a moment past my chaining, and once they had gone the male Podelm came to stand before me, his light eyes pleased as he took me in. The light-haired male stood no more than a finger-joint above me, yet were his shoulders and chest broader by far. A long moment he stood in contemplation, then did he move closer.

"You no longer have a need for this breech," said he, his hands going to the ties and removing it. "Temple slaves are allowed no coverings, and you are now a temple slave."

"Jalav is no slave of any sort," said I, gently testing the strength of the chains which held my wrists. "Jalav is a warrior, a fact you will learn, male, should I ever find myself free."

"A warrior?" said he, raising his brows in faint surprise. "There have been others through here, in kalod past, who called themselves warriors. Most were not properly cared for and sickened and died, those who did not attempt to do battle with our warriors, who slew them before they, themselves, were slain. I shall not allow you to die, wench, nor shall I allow you to throw your life away upon the blades of warriors. You are magnificent, too magnificent to waste."

He walked from my view then, taking my breech with him, and when he returned a moment later, he held a wooden pot in his hands, from which a slim bit of wood protruded.

"This is a dye made from the wild gembar plant," said he, stirring the contents of the pot with the bit of wood. "Its stain is long-lasting and easily visible, and will mark you clearly as a temple slave. This brush is necessary now to keep the dye from my fingers, yet does the dye dry quickly."

With a small laugh he withdrew the wood he called brush from the pot, bringing into view the end covered with bright red. As he neared me with it I moved as far as I might in the chains, yet was he expecting such movement and prepared for it. Not till I had backed as far as possible from the dye did the brush touch me, a cold, wet feel at the end of my breast. I shouted wordlessly and threw myself about, yet was the brush waiting each time I paused, to touch me firmly and with purpose till the deed was done. At last the male put the pot aside, then stood himself again to examine me.

"Most becoming," he chuckled, looking from one to the other of my breasts. "Such large nipples are a pleasure to paint, even more pleasant to touch. It is indeed fortunate that your lovely hair is so long, else would your struggles have thrown it upon the dye. Ah, I see the stain has already dried, therefore am I able to examine you further."

Again he closed with me, yet this time did his hand move to my thighs and between. I fully expected to feel naught from the touch, and gasped when the opposite occurred.

"Oh, excellent," crooned the male, touching me so deep I

could not keep from writhing. "I see the painting of your breasts did indeed heat you up, exactly as I expected. Move for me, sweet slave, move like the slave you are and will be."

The hateful croon of the male's voice ended, yet not so his touch. Fire flared through every part of me, burning me to ashes, forcing moans and whimpers from my lips as my body leaped and quivered and sought escape. I had no understanding of why my senses had again come alive; I knew only that they undeniably had. For long reckid the male stood and brought me anguish, then did he step back again with a large smile.

"You will be magnificent in use," said he, satisfaction filling him to overflowing. "As you will quickly come to beg that use, our men will be even more pleased."

"Sooner would I beg the final death," I panted, gasping air to cool the flames which continued to torment me, needs too long unseen to, yet were they far from the crippling needs forced upon me when in the capture of Ceralt. The pain was there in good measure, yet naught I could not best.

"Wild and unrepentant," laughed the male, shaking his head with mockery. "You think to resist till your final breath, yet resistance will not be allowed you. Naught will be allowed you save obedience to the will of men. You will learn—and you will rejoice."

"Jalav will rejoice when once again she stands free with a sword in her fist," said I, yet the male turned away with a final laugh, paying no heed to my words. Had he grown angered and given me pain, I would yet have had the satisfaction of knowing I had given him displeasure. Where was the satisfaction in giving the male no more than amusement? I stood spread in the grip of metal, having been made to squirm to the will of a male like the lowliest slave female, unable to free myself, unable to avenge myself, giving no more than amusement in return for intrusion. How great was the war leader Jalav, the chosen of both Mida and Sigurr!

My mood, none too light to begin with, grew darker with the passage of the hind. No more was I permitted to see than the wall before which I had been placed, yet were there sounds aplenty to take my attention. When next the door to the larger chamber opened, all screams and sobs had been silenced, save for the pleadings of the female brought within. I knew not what lack had brought her there, yet was she chained in some manner and then beaten, the sound of leather upon flesh nearly drowned in screams of pain and fear. With the beating done, there followed a long speech detailing that which was required of an obedient slave, a doing worse than the beating itself. I attempted to move restlessly in the chains which held me, yet was true movement utterly impossible. The voice of the male droned on, punctuated by sobs and sniffled responses from the female, all intruding, all infuriating.

At long last the voice of the male ceased, and there came the sounds of the removal of chain. I thought the female would then be taken again from the room, yet was I premature. A male suddenly appeared before me, tall with dark hair much like Grandyn's, his body cloth a bright blue. A length of leather hung at his belt, the sort of leather I had learned the touch of through Ceralt's displeasure. Gleaming of eye was this male as he looked upon me, and then did he cast a glance beyond my shoulder.

"A pleasing new addition, Podelm," said he, reaching forth to take my breast in his hand. "Is it the open floor for her, or an alcove?"

"An alcove," came the voice of Podelm from a distance behind me. "The high born must be allowed the having of her first, else will they have my heart and privates. Should they find her too willful, it will then be the open floor for her. A taste of that will soon have her begging to be returned to an alcove."

"Indeed," laughed the male before me, reaching to my thighs with his free hand. "This body will draw any man who sees it, leaving the other wenches to lie idle in their chains. She would ache and weep for feyd thereafter."

"Perhaps not," chuckled the voice of Podelm. "See how she moves to the quest of your fingers, seeking to ease the need I have given her. She will find no release from any save those who come to her alcove, and if I do not misjudge the depth of her passion, a brief use will be worse than none. She will learn more quickly than most that her needs will be seen to only through giving pleasure to those who use her."

"See how she struggles against her chains," laughed the male before me, slowly withdrawing his hand. "Your words touch her more deeply than I, for she begins to find she cannot deny them. I look forward to my own use of her."

The male then walked from my ken, leaving me to burn and seethe in the silence I thought it best to adopt. So certain were these males that Jalav would do as they wished, that they made no dire threats at which she might laugh and spit. Different indeed were these males from others I had known, and I liked it not.

Again and again were females brought to the room, some singly, some in groups, most to be punished, some to be taught.

I had long since passed from silent anger to silent pain, for I had ridden far that fey before being placed so openly and discomfortably in chains, with no opportunity for rest. Each new male who entered the room felt the need to explore me with hands and eyes, adding to the weariness and pain I already felt. After the last of them I found I could no longer remain upright, and merely hung limply from the wrist chains. After a moment there were further sounds from behind me, and the male Podelm strolled into view, accompanied by a second male.

"She is clearly done in, yet not a sound out of her," said the second male, one who wore a body cloth of gray and something of a frown. "Those before her unfailingly wept and begged to be released."

"I had scarcely expected the same from this one," said Podelm, a continuing satisfaction about him. "Had she wept and begged, I would have found myself disappointed. I shall require your assistance in removing her from there."

The male Podelm stepped to my right, then immediately returned with a snarl of chain. First were my ankles released so that I might again attempt to stand upright, yet as soon as the post cuffs were removed, a short length of chain with two slender cuffs were separated from the snarl and closed upon me. Standing and walking might be easily accomplished with such a chain, yet would fighting and running prove impossible. Despite my weariness I considered attempting resistance with the males, then dismissed the notion as being what was expected. I made no attempt to struggle as my wrists were released, yet was the satisfaction of Podelm as complete as it had been as he closed wide, short-chained cuffs about my wrists. It came to me then that I had perhaps been gulled out of an opportunity for freedom by attempting to disappoint the male, yet was the faint opportunity too long past to reclaim. A collar was put firmly about my throat by the second male, the long chain depending from it wound once about the short chain between my wrists, and then was I turned at last toward the balance of the chamber.

"That throat chain is incorrectly set," said Podelm to the second male as I looked about the room. "You give the slave permission to raise her head before she has earned it. Also, you allow her too defiant a stance. This is the manner in which it should be set."

The male's hand pulled sharply at the chain depending from my throat, pulling my head as sharply downward, then instantly took up the slack at my wrists by taking a second pull at the long chain's free end. In fury I attempted to raise my wrists to provide the slack I required to stand tall and proud, yet was the chain's end held firmly in the male's fist. Uselessly, I struggled against the metal which held me, and that, too, brought amusement to Podelm.

"The poor slave-child is weary," he chuckled, stroking my hair in a solicitous manner. "Her struggles are pale and feeble now, yet I confidently expect them to resume once she has rested. In point of fact I look forward to their resumption. Take her now, and be sure to hold the chain exactly as I have it."

"As you say, Podelm," agreed the second male, taking the chain so quickly and firmly that I was unable to move it so much as a finger's width. In such a manner was I led from the room, shambling slowly forward, seeing naught save the floor before my feet, my head bowed, my fury difficult to contain. Had Mida and Sigurr seen me then, the dark god's evil laughter would have whispered to the skies.

Fury is difficult to maintain when one has little enough strength to propel one. The unnamed male of gray body cloth moved through the large chamber and thence into a corridor at a speed which forced me to hurry somewhat in his wake, to keep from being pulled to the stone floor and dragged. The chain between my ankles was not quite long enough to allow a decent stride, therefore were short, quick, mincing steps my sole option. Much did I feel as though I were a slave-female indeed, prancing obediently in the wake of he who held my chain, yet the anger such a feeling gave was a strengthening one, keeping me erect and determined to break free. When once I stood with sword in hand again, these males would learn what sort of slave they treated with.

From corridor to corridor was I taken, yet no more than the first two were empty of life other than our own. I, who saw naught save the stone of the floor, also said naught, yet the male who led me was quick with greetings once others were in view. Once, in what seemed a wide, peopled hall, we paused so that the male might speak at more than greeting length. I, who had attempted to work the stiffness from my limbs despite the strange gait I had been forced to, gave silent thanks for the rest the halt provided and attempted to look about. No more than a short way to each side was I able to turn my head, yet was such turning necessary if I were to learn where I had been taken. Had I been released upon the moment, I would surely have stood like a hoodwinked kan, knowing not which direction to choose for escape.

To my left was a partial view of the hall we stood in, a wide, high-ceilinged hall filled with many pillars. Upon each pillar, black as the stone of the floor and walls, was a low perch with a candle upon it. Below these perches, tightly chained and tethered to the pillars, lay red-dyed slave females, each lying beautifully and temptingly, each as silent as the males were vociferous. Even as I watched, a male approached one of these, and no sooner had his body cloth been removed than the female's legs were thrown wide and he had entered her. Eager indeed was the male for her use, and tightly did she cling to the wide arms of the male, throwing her head back as she gasped at his onslaught. This, I thought, was undoubtedly the floor the males had discussed earlier, and my fists clenched beneath the wide cuffs at thought of being placed there. There would be little of the welcome these males preferred were Jalav to be placed there, no matter the pain she was given, no matter the cost. Jalav would not be slave, no matter the pleasure or lack thereof of the male Podelm.

"Were you given permission to look about you, little slave?" came a voice from my right, interrupting my thoughts. Quickly did my head turn of its own volition, and though I was not able to see the face of the male, the black of his body cloth was more than clear. This, then, was a male of importance who spoke to me, a fact which was to have impressed me more than it did. Slowly, deliberately, I returned my gaze to the left and made no answer.

"I hear no reply from you, wench," came the voice of the male a second time. "Have you not been taught to give proper answers to questions addressed to you?"

"You foolish slave!" came the voice of the male in gray, anger clear in his tone. He jerked so savagely upon the chain he held, that nearly was I thrown to the floor. "This slave is wild yet, warrior, unused and untrained in the proper manner. Should she displease the high ones, she will certainly be punished and set here for the use of all. You may then teach her the lessons she lacks."

"It would be my pleasure to do so," said the black-clad male, amusement now in his tone. "Yet do I feel that the high ones will not be so foolish as to send her from the alcoves. Were I a Prince of the Blood, I certainly would not do so."

"Indeed, indeed," said the gray-clad male nervously, and then was a tighter grip taken upon my chain. "I shall now take her to the alcoves as I was ordered to do. I wish you a joyful devotion, warrior."

"A moment," came the voice of the black-clad one, and a

large hand appeared upon the chain between my wrists and throat, halting the intended haste of the other male. "I would look more fully upon this slave before she is taken to the alcoves. It will undoubtedly be my sole opportunity."

With a single pull was the chain taken from the hands of the gray-clad male, and then was I able to raise my head once more, to look up into the eyes of the Sigurri warrior. Light-haired was the male, as many of the Sigurri were, yet were the eyes which regarded me as dark as mine.

"Wild indeed," grinned the Sigurri, holding to my throat chain, yet not as tightly as the other had done. "I had thought the demureness of her stance more a matter of chain than choice. A man would offer up to Sigurr great thanks indeed through a wench such as this."

"You may not use her!" fretted the male in gray, hopping about at my left. "She is to be kept as she is till the high ones have used her. Should you take her now, we will both stand in jeopardy!"

"I do believe you fear my use of her more than she does," laughed the Sigurri, untouched by the anxiety of the other. "Should I take you to lie with me, little slave, would I find great pleasure in your arms?"

"You would be more like to find a dagger in your throat," I replied, holding his eyes. "To remain among the living, one must learn the difference between a captive and a slave."

"And you are a captive," grinned the male, taken aback not at all. "Without a doubt, and most definitely—a captive. Very well, lovely captive. I shall leave you to the will of the Princes—save for this."

Upon the word was I drawn to his chest, and quickly were his lips upon mine. Strange were these Sigurri, for many things as well as for the great fondness they had for touching lips yet doing naught else. Briefly did I wonder at their ability to do other things, then did I recall the words of my warriors who had used the four we had found in Bellinard. They were, apparently, capable of giving pleasure; perhaps they had little experience in the taking of it. The Sigurri's kiss was deep indeed, his body hard against me, and then, as abruptly as I was taken, I was again released.

"You may have her now, slave handler," said the black-clad one, making no effort to touch me further. "The high ones allow small presumptions, therefore you need not fear."

"They do not allow presumptions from those who are not warriors," muttered the smaller, gray-clad male, though softly, so that the other might not hear him. Immediately did he pull upon the chain to take me with him, and again we traversed the hall, though this time with a difference. So anxious was the male to see us gone from the other, he had evidently forgotten to tighten the chain which depended from my throat. It was still necessary that I dance tiredly about, yet was I able to see.

The large hall, filled with females in use and males in converse, soon lay behind us. Through two further corridors did we go, then was I hurried through a doorway at the end of the second which led within a large, circular chamber. At the center of the chamber, beneath golden metal hangings bearing many candles, stood a large, circular wooden platform, laden with much provender and drink. About the outer edge of the chamber, two broad steps above the level of the platform, were hangings of heavy golden silk showing the stroke of Sigurr. At many intervals about the silk were indications of openings, and to one of these openings was I intemperately hastened.

"At last I am nearly done with you, slave," muttered the male in gray, reaching to my throat to remove the collar and chain, and then turning away to the silk. "This alcove should be empty, and as soon as I have arranged you within it, I shall—"

His words ended abruptly, for as his hand raised to the silk, my arms raised to bring the short chain of the wrist cuffs down before his face and then about his throat. Little strength was left to me after my time between the posts and the shambling trot through the corridors, yet was that little gladly spent in attempting to end the life of one who would see me slave. No more than small sounds came from the male as he clawed feverishly at the chain keeping breath from him; grimly did I retain my hold, for surely did the male stand between me and freedom. The flush of near death rose in him, and his body twisted about, almost taking me from my feet—and then were there hands upon me, forcing my arms and the chain from about the male, releasing him to fall to hands and knees, holding me in unbreakable grips. Two males were there, black-clad and bearing weapons, and they looked down upon the kneeling male who gasped as he held his throat.

"It was your good fortune we were here, slave handler," said the male to my left, speaking gravely yet exchanging an oddly amused glance with his companion. "Had we not been, your life rather than your duties would have been discharged."

"She is a savage!" croaked the gray-clad male, yet upon his knees, continuing to look down at the smooth, black stone floor. "She nearly took my life! Slay her, warriors, slay her!"

"And deprive the high ones?" asked the male, his amusement

now clear in his tone. "Has she not been sent to serve their pleasure?"

"Pleasure!" echoed the male upon the floor, shock turning him at last to look up at us, the track of the chain redly visible across his throat. "How is it possible to speak of pleasure with one who would as soon take your life as offer a caress? How might a man take pleasure from a savage?"

"A warrior finds no difficulty in taking pleasure from any female, civilized or savage," laughed the black-clad male, tightening his grip upon my arm. "Have you forgotten that the high ones are warriors all, fit to claim the blood of mighty Sigurr? There is little reason for a warrior to fear this wench, and much reason to find interest in her. Are you sufficiently recovered to place her in an alcove?"

The smaller male looked upon me, seeing the chains and weariness I wore, yet continuing to find fear in the sight his eyes gave. Indeed did I then stand the straighter between the males who held me, challenging with my eyes the one who slowly raised himself from the floor, yet had the challenge no hope of being accepted.

"As I am not a high one nor a warrior," he rasped, "I shall not approach her again. It is the place of you warriors to insure the safety of those who visit these alcoves, therefore shall I give you the task of securing her in place. Should she escape and cause harm, be it on your heads. I will await the chains you remove from her here."

"As you wish," shrugged the male to my left, his amusement most open and evident. "My brother and I will see to her placement, and you may await your chains here. If there is a small delay in our return, accept it with patience."

The gray-clad male began to open his mouth in the beginnings of protest, yet before he was able to find the proper words, the two males who held me had pushed the silk to one side and taken me past it, closing it again quickly behind themselves. The area we entered was small in relation to the over-all chamber, perhaps three paces by four, lit by three large candles in golden holders, one on each of the three walls of black wood. Upon the floor was a thick, soft floor cloth of a golden color, and in the center of the area was a contrivance longer than it was wide, knee-height from the floor, covered with the soft, thick cloth of the floor, yet in black. With the heavy silk hanging closed, I was immediately taken to the odd platform and forced down upon it on my back.

"A simple neck chain suffices for other wenches," said the

male who had been on my left, "yet you will require other restraints as well, little slave. The high ones will offer up fervent prayers to Sigurr through you, of that you may be sure, and yet their pleasure would decrease were they to find it necessary to fend off attack while doing so. It is therefore necessary that we insure their pleasure."

As the male spoke, he and the other stretched me flat upon the platform, removed the wrist cuffs, then raised my arms above my head. With the wrist chain gone I attempted to struggle, yet would the effort have been futile even had I not been weary. The strength of the two males overrode my struggles easily, the knee of the silent one in my middle holding me flat as my wrists were fastened with chain to the edge of the platform above my head. With my wrists seen to, a chain and collar was then brought to my throat, one which disallowed the raising of my head more than a fingerlength from the platform. I was sure I had then been secured as completely as necessary to the well-being of any mortal male, yet the two Sigurri were of a different mind.

"And, of course, the final touch," said the male who had seen to the speaking for the two, reaching for my ankle. He removed the one cuff and the other male the second, and then were slim platform cuffs set to replace those removed. At last was I secured to the satisfaction of the males, and they straightened from their task to look thoughtfully upon me.

"It is difficult to merely gaze upon her," said the second male in a husky voice, he who had kept silent now speaking with mouth and eyes alike. "And her hair should be spread all about, rather than being crushed beneath her."

"Her hair is easily attended to," said the first male, coming forward to pull hand-wide locks of hair from where it was trapped beneath me. "To do other than merely gaze upon her is a matter done with more difficulty. See how high and firm her breasts are, impudently beckoning a man's hands to them."

The hands he spoke of left my hair and came deliberately to my breasts, hovering just above them, about to touch yet just short of touching.

"It is the soft roundness of her thighs which calls to me most strongly," said the second, "that and the heat to be found between them. It is there my hands are most earnestly beckoned."

The second male moved so that his hands, too, were above me, poised to touch yet not yet touching. I had been moving about upon the platform as much as the chains would allow, yet so close were their hands that the heat of their flesh reached out to overwarm me. Had I moved again as I had been doing, surely would their hands have been upon me in full.

"How still she lies," murmured the first of the males, his eyes looking deep into mine, his body unmoving above me. "Do you think, brother, she fears the touch of men?"

"It is undoubtedly some fear which grips her," said the second, also unmoving. "Were she not fearful, she would joy in serving the high ones in their devotions. She is a fearful little slave, one who will fall to tears during her service, bringing disgust to the high ones."

Anger touched me upon hearing such foolishness, and nearly did I struggle against the chains in vast annoyance—till I saw the hidden amusement in the eyes of the male above me. Surely was he and his brother anticipating such movement from me, hoping to use anger and foolish speech to force me to foolishness of my own. My fists closed tight in the cuffs which held them above my head and my lips tightened in anger, yet no other motion did I allow myself.

"Alas, I see the wench is not to be gulled," said the first male, straightening away from me with something of a grin. "Perhaps she has been told that no other than the high ones may touch her here, and therefore takes care not to give others the touching of her even in anger."

"Perhaps so," said the second male, and then, surprisingly, his hands were firmly upon my thighs, stroking slowly and squeezing gently. "If so, she has surely been misled. I think it possible that this one is unbroached, brother, a fact that high ones would wish to be told of. We must investigate the possibility."

"Indeed," laughed the first, highly amused at the manner in which I snarled and struggled in vain. "Indeed must the possibility be investigated. I shall see to it personally."

The first male moved backward to stand opposite the second, and slowly, with much relish, did his hand approach me. As the other held strongly to my thighs he touched me more and more deeply, laughing softly as I failed to deny him entrance, continuing with the probe till my body attempted to rise against the restraining hands of the other. Then did he withdraw as slowly as he had entered, and turn to look upon the other male.

"By Sigurr's loins, I must admit to a great lack, brother," said he. "I find myself unable to determine whether or not the female is unbroached. I fear your greater expertise in such matters must ascertain the truth."

"I will be pleased to assist you, brother," answered the

second male, the sobriety of his tone belied by the sparkle in his eye. My breathing had increased in pace and sweat covered my body, and much did I wish to groan when the first male took possession of my thighs from the second, freeing the hands of the second male. The second toyed with me a moment before plunging within, and quickly did my eyes close as my throat pulled against the collar holding to it.

"Ah, see how she writhes and attempts to capture my hand, brother," came the voice of the second, huskier now than it had been. "Obviously this is no untouched vessel, new to the use she will be put to. The slave is new only to the chains of men, straining to deny the need raised in her only to find the doing beyond her. When the high ones arrive to see to their late-fey devotions, she will be open and helpless in their arms."

"Your wisdom is great indeed, brother," said the first male, his hands squeezing at my thighs as the other continued his efforts to bring me to insanity. "I am now able to see how deeply in need the slave is, so deeply that the high ones will surely be pleased. Whether she wills it or not, she will serve them eagerly when they arrive—and each time thereafter, else will we find the need to visit her again."

"Do you hear, slave?" asked the second, pinching painfully with his free hand to assure himself of my attention. "You will give pleasure to the high ones of your own volition, else will you please them because you must. Consider the point well in the hind before they arrive, and choose wisely. The choice will not be given you again."

Only then did the male withdraw from me, and the first release me as well. It made little difference that they no longer touched me, for the fire burned high from their efforts, causing me to strain terribly to keep a moan from escaping. Dimly I heard the sound of chains being gathered, and then the scuff of their receding footsteps, just before the flap of silk being brushed aside. The males then left the small room I had been chained in, leaving me to the contemplation of the point they had made.

"Mida choose them!" I snarled low, opening my eyes at last and attempting to slow my breathing. Indeed did I writhe and strain from their doings, the sweat glistening upon my flesh, my hair damp where it lay upon my arms. My ankles, chained to either side of the platform, were not permitted to close, though the accursed chains allowed the bending of my knees. Much did I feel the need for a male, yet would the Sigurri high ones find disappointment when they came to take my use. I was Jalav, war leader of all the Midanna, and would greet no male warmly while held in chains.

Perhaps four hands of reckid passed before Jalav, a fool of a warrior, ceased struggling against the chains which held her. It had been my intention to reach to the cuffs about my wrists and open them as easily as did the males, yet the difficulty had lain in reaching the accursed things. Though my wrists were held quite close to one another, the distance was wrong for the fingers of one hand to reach the cuff about the wrist of the other. Again and again I had tried, first one hand and then the other, till both wrists ached and burned from the clasp of the metal. The weariness I had felt earlier had greatly increased, yet I felt too filled with fury to rest as I should. I could do no more than lay spread upon the platform as the males had placed me, cursing feebly against the lack of vigilance which had brought me to such a pass.

Surely no less than another four hands of reckid went to naught before I was able to admit the true state of affairs to myself. I had found it utterly impossible to rest, and not through the presence of too great an anger. It was need that kept me from finding rest, a need which would not take its talons from my flesh till it was seen to. That I wished to struggle against whichever males came meant naught; the need brought forth from within me would not allow the struggle to long continue. The males would find their victory, and dark Sigurr would laugh long and hard.

So low were my spirits that the time passed unnoticed, my attention so far within that it took the sound of a voice to rouse me. From immediately beyond the silk to my area did the voice come, filled with amusement and eagerness and a good deal of respect.

"Indeed there is a new one worthy of prolonged attention, Prince," came the voice of he who had been the first of the two males to chain me in the area. "There is one here capable of rousing a man with the mere sight of her, and you shall be the first to have her. It is early yet, too early for any other to have come to his devotions."

As the silk was pushed to one side my body tensed, a foolish reaction for one chained as I was. The male would enter and have his use of me, and in no manner would I find myself able to avenge the doing till the chains which held me were gone and a sword was once more grasped in my fist. How I was to be freed of the chains and acquire a sword I knew not, yet was the accomplishment surely to be mine alone. Dark Sigurr would not act against those who paid him homage, and Mida would find it distasteful to assist a warrior foolish enough to allow males to enslave her. No, the doing was mine alone; I had only to conceive of the manner in which it might be done. As the silk was thrust even further aside, I pulled again at the wrist cuffs—then gasped aloud in surprise.

"Jalav, what do you do here?" demanded Mehrayn, allowing the silk to fall closed behind him. The red-haired male seemed much refreshed from our journey, and now wore a close-belted covering of black which reached to mid-thigh, rather than a simple body cloth. His now-leather-covered feet moved him quickly to stand above me, and the blaze in his eyes was easily seen.

"Mehrayn, release me at once!" I ground out harshly, suddenly filled with great, grim joy. "I shall have the lives of all of them, male and female alike! By Mida do I swear it!"

"Calm yourself, wench, and answer my question," said Mehrayn, making no effort toward doing as I had demanded. "How do you come to be here, chained and marked as a slave? If you have angered Aysayn after all my cautions, I will surely punish you as you have never before been punished!"

"Your Aysayn was not present to be angered!" I snapped, pulling again at the chains which held me. "It was the female Ladayna with whom I spoke, a foolish slave-female who demanded that I depart before the return of Aysayn, leaving the task given me by Mida and Sigurr undone."

"And, of course, you refused," nodded Mehrayn, folding his arms across his chest as he gazed down at me. "Your refusal was undoubtedly as abrasive as your nature seems to demand, and the Shadow's consort had you taken up as a slave."

"As sure as Mida's light appears anew each fey, I shall have her blood upon my sword," I vowed. "Should she refuse to face me with blades, I will open her throat with my dagger!"

"And thereby have Aysayn set every Sigurri warrior to the task of hunting you down," Mehrayn nodded again, an exasperation in his tone. "Can you not see how foolishly you speak, wench, to even consider such an action? What then of the task given you? What then of your very life?"

"All shall be seen to as Mida wishes," I informed him, moving again in the chains. "At the present, male, I am sure that it is within the bounds of Mida's wishes to unbind me. Why do you merely stand there?"

"I stand here regarding a dilemma," said he, his tone remaining exasperated, though having become distant. "I am sworn to the ranks of Sigurr's legions, yet do I owe the continuance of my life to you. I cannot in honor release you to cause bloodshed among my brethren, nor may I, in honor, leave you as you are. Will you give me your word to refrain from taking sword in hand till you have my permission to do so? In such a manner may I then release you immediately."

He stood to my right looking down upon me, his well-muscled arms afold across his broad chest, the wide male face of him serious beyond that which I had come to expect from the male. Much did I wish to be released from the chains which held me to the platform, yet thoughts of Ceralt and the vow he had stolen from me stood as a large stone in the path toward that desired end. How might I again pledge myself to weaponlessness, when memories of the previous instance continued to plague my sleep with pain? How was I to again bind myself to a male, when all knew what strange concepts of honor they held?

"I am a war leader of Midanna," said I at last, knowing it would be necessary to find another path from the chains. "No war leader may pledge herself to taking up weapons only at the bidding of another. Protect your brothers well, male, for they shall require such protection when I have freed myself from these chains."

I then turned my face from him, yet was sight unnecessary to know of the anger which took him.

"Of all the stubborn females I have ever encountered—!" he began in a rasp, chopping the words short with difficulty before beginning upon a new tack. "And not a hint of a demand from her to honor the debt I owe! Likely she believes I will not honor it, for I am—male! By the dripping sword of vengeance of Sigurr the Mighty! What am I to do?"

He turned then and strode from the platform, reached the hanging of silk and turned again, then strode back. Back and forth did the male go, from platform to hanging and back again, his anger great, yet not so great as his agitation. Truly did his thoughts seem in a turmoil, yet I understood none of his difficulty. Above all things save Mida did a warrior owe her loyalty to her clan and sisters; to accept personal dishonor was perferable to betraying them. To believe that I would demand—or expect— Mehrayn to betray his own merely because his life was saved through my efforts was foolishness. Had our positions been reversed, I certainly would not have freed him to cause havoc among my own. The male, it appeared, sought to satisfy all concerned, a matter more easily conceived of than executed. A number of reckid passed with deep thought upon him, then he returned once again to stand himself above me.

"Very well," said he, decision firm in his voice and eyes. "I cannot abandon you here, nor may I set you free. As you do not care to be parted from your word, we shall see if being parted from your freedom is preferable. I will take you into my own household as a slave."

"Jalav is no slave," I growled, discovering that I again pulled at the chains which held me. "Beware, male, lest you discover this to your sorrow."

"Indeed?" said he, raising a brow in annoyance. "Inasmuch as appearances are concerned, Jalav is much of a slave. If you are free, wench, close your ankles and hide from me the sight of your most delicate softness. I find the view most enjoyable, yet if you are free, you may take it from me."

In anger did I attempt to move my ankles, yet such a thing the chains would not allow. Amusement touched the features of Mehrayn, lightening the anger which had been upon him.

"And your breasts seem brightly painted for one who is free," he said, reaching a finger out toward me. "I seem to recall a much lighter red from the time of our—"

Again his words ended abruptly, yet this time the cause was not from anger within. His fingers had taken hold of the tip of my breast, and when his thumb had come to caress me, I could not halt the hardening and tightening of my flesh. A shiver ran through me to reignite the flame, not yet dead, caused by the other males, and this the male was immediately able to see.

"Your flesh responds," said he with a frown, reaching forward with his free hand to take my other breast. "I had not thought to see it so, and yet—there is no mistake."

"Mehrayn, no!" I whispered, beginning to writhe from the touch of his hands. "I am not a slave! You may not take me so!"

"Lovely Jalav," he murmured, a chuckle in his tone as one hand left my breast for my thighs. "A wench such as you need not be slave to be taken by men. I burned for your use from the moment I first laid eyes upon you, keeping from you only through the demands of honor. Honor no longer demands that I keep away."

Much did I wish to demand that he leave me be, yet his hand between my thighs had rendered me speechless. No more than the ability to gasp was left me, my head thrown back against the chain, and suddenly was Mehrayn above me, his face very near to mine.

"I give unending thanks to Sigurr for having restored you,

wench," he murmured, his manhood positioned so that it did no more than torment me. "As I offer up my prayers, accept my use without thought of that which holds you here before me, for I would have had you with or without them."

His lips came to me fiercely yet briefly, and then did his head raise so that he might look upon the candle which burned upon the wall behind me.

"Mighty Sigurr, hear me!" he called, his hands now stroking my sides. "I, Mehrayn, your loyal warrior, give thanks for your blessings and approval, and special thanks for the wench beneath me. Through her use do I fulfill my obligations of devotion, bringing forth the juices of her body to dedicate to your unequaled prowess. Come the fey I am unable to so dedicate a female to you, I will know I no longer have the privilege of such use and give over my position of favor to another. Till then I shall draw all I may from the vessels of my devotion, knowing I am sustained through your pleasure at the dedication. This one is Jalav, truly worthy of use, a wench you, yourself, may have tasted. Should this be so, I thank you for having sent her to me, and shall not fail you in your expectations."

The eyes of the male then came to me, fierce and bright as his hands covered my breasts.

"All females are desirable in the sight of Sigurr," said he, much as though he spoke words already spoken many times before. "Even more desirable is the sight of a female put to use, for in such a way does she serve Sigurr and his warriors. To writhe upon his altar is the highest service a female may perform for the great god, therefore are you to rejoice as I take your use in dedication to him. Rejoice wench, and exult in your blessed privilege, for no man may serve as you do, to the center of your very soul."

Perhaps I failed to rejoice as bidden, yet was it beyond me to keep from writhing. The hands at my breasts sent lightning all through me, causing me to wrench at the merciless cuffs of metal, the torment begun at the center of my being increased by no more than the introduction of his desire. Hoarsely I panted as I attempted to capture him to soothe my need, yet was I not so soon to be soothed.

"Ah, Sigurr, feel the warmth and heat of her!" cried the male, truly taken up in the act he performed. "The flow of moisture from her is so great, I find it nearly impossible to keep from plunging deep! Sustain me, great god, sustain me so that I may take her in accordance with your tenets!"

I knew not the meaning of the words he spoke, yet I knew

well enough the near-insanity he caused me to feel. So slowly did he enter me that I screamed with madness, the need I had felt earlier a mere nothing in comparison. His hands came to my thighs and hips, keeping me from frenzied movement, the strength in them more like metal than flesh. Again I screamed, madness encompassing all, and then he was fully within, filling me with torment rather than release.

"The wench is now mine, Sigurr!" cried the male, great strain evident in the hoarseness of his voice, the tensions of his body. "I restrain my desire a moment out of deference to your greatness, a bowing to your power. Now—I am able to restrain myself—no longer."

With a great gasp the hands of the male released me, and then came the storm, the avalanche, the torrent I had been seeking. My need, though great, was fully matched by the need of the male, and we continued on for an uncountable time before the torrent eased. I, so far beyond the end of my strength that I could do no more than moan, stirred feebly as the male above me chuckled.

"It seems I have found the one sure method of silencing that sharp tongue of yours, wench," said he, continuing the stroke of his desire with lazy movements of his hips. "Indeed must Sigurr be pleased, to have had such writhings from you. Even now, well used and much spent, you cannot deny the demands of my body. You are a wench made for much use by men, one of those who are helpless in their possession."

The flash of anger I felt was dulled by exhaustion, my effort toward struggle little more than the stirring I had accomplished a moment earlier. Even so, the movement amply acknowledged the presence of the male within me, bringing his laughter forth as he surged with strength.

"Your effort toward anger has become a moan of yielding, little one," he whispered, pressing his lips to my throat above the collar as his hands moved against my back where he had raised me somewhat from the platform. "You cannot deny the man who possesses you, and surely is that blessing sent by Sigurr. To match the blessing now comes the one I have withheld from you, merely to extend my own pleasure rather than through any fault of yours. The blessing is yours, for surely you have earned it."

Then was I filled with the seed of the male, a blessing to all Midanna save their war leaders. A war leader has no need of such, for the glory of bearing daughters to her clan is denied her so that she may be ever able to lead her clan to war. To this end does a war leader chew the leaves of the dabla bush, and to such an end had I chewed them more than once. No male had the ability to give me a child, and this despite the efforts of Ceralt.

"You are as delicious as I knew you would be," said Mehrayn, and then his lips came to mine for a long moment before he released me and withdrew. "From this time on, my devotions will be more fervent than ever before—and possibly more frequent than required. I shall speak to the guards about having you unchained."

He moved from the platform and straightened his covering, then made his way to the hanging of gold silk. I felt a great need to close my eyes and lose myself in the mists of sleep, yet such a doing was not possible just then. If the chains were to be removed from me, escape might somehow become possible. Surely did I expect Mehrayn to leave the alcove, yet rather than do so, he brushed the hanging aside and called the guard to him.

"How may I assist you, Prince?" asked the black-clad male of Mehrayn as soon as they both stood within the alcove. "Was the slave less than you wished her to be? Shall I have her beaten?"

"Beating her will not be necessary," laughed Mehrayn, clapping the other male upon the shoulder. "The slave was all you said she would be, and more to boot. She was able to deny me nothing, despite her initial unwillingness."

"I see the fight has been taken out of her," chuckled the male, turning to gaze down upon me. "It will undoubtedly be some time before she attempts the life of another slave handler."

"Before she what?" demanded Mehrayn, the amusement suddenly gone from him. "How could such a thing have come to be?"

"The man was a fool," said the guard, shaking his head in disgust. "Anyone with eyes could see that she is scarcely your usual slave, eager yet timid, frightened and confused. The fool turned his back on her, giving her the opportunity to put her shackles about his throat. Had my brother warrior and I not been present, she would have taken his life."

"I find myself scarcely surprised," sighed Mehrayn, joining the other in head shaking. "The incident does no more than firm the resolve I made earlier. Never before have I exercised my right to claim a temple slave for personal use, yet now I shall do so. I will have this slave unchained so that I might take her with me."

"This one, Prince?" asked the male, surprise and disapproval clearly upon him. "You would release her in your household, to do Sigurr knows what? Wisest would be to enjoy her here, where your safety need not be jeopardized."

"I thank you for your concern over my safety, warrior," said Mehrayn, his voice exceedingly soft as he folded his arms across his chest. "However, I feel I must ask a clarification of one point. Am I correct in believing you think I require protection from a wench? A wench who is stripped naked and who stands nearly a head below me?"

"That was not my meaning, Prince!" said the other male at once, a visible paling of his skin to be seen. "I merely meant that she was— That is, that you are— That she and you—"

"Enough," laughed Mehrayn, unfolding his arms so that he might strike the shoulder of the guard male a second time. "Despite all, your meaning is quite clear, and I shall indeed be wary. Let us now unchain her."

The second male, remaining quite skeptical, left the area briefly to return with two lengths of leather. I had hoped that the chains would be removed before any other restraints were considered, yet was the guard male too wary to act in so offhand a manner. On the moment he and Mehrayn released my ankles from the cuffs, the guard male immediately bound them together with one of the lengths of leather, knotting the strip tight. Mehrayn took no notice of this act, as he left my ankle as soon as it was uncuffed and moved to my throat. A brief moment saw the collar opened and removed, and then did he reach above my head for my wrists.

"By the black sand of the Caverns of the Doomed!" growled Mehrayn when he had gathered my hair from about my arms and hands. "See what she has done to herself from struggling against the bracelets! The bruises have already darkened, and it is Sigurr alone whom we must thank that she does not bleed!"

"Truly, the wench is a wild one," agreed the guard male, leaving my ankles to come toward my wrists. "I shall bind her tightly so that she does not escape or injure herself further. To use an injured wench detracts from a man's pleasure."

Mehrayn's face tightened and his eyes grew hard, yet the words he had been about to speak went unuttered. His lips closed briefly, as though he fought within himself, and then did he put a hand out toward the guard male.

"I shall bind her," said he, seemingly displeased with all about him. "It is true I have no wish to see her free at this moment, yet are there other considerations which I shall not speak of."

With surprise touching him, the guard male yielded up the

leather, then did both of the males free my wrists. I attempted to struggle free despite the leather about my ankles, yet was I turned face down and my arms forced behind me. Fully did I expect my wrists to be tied then, but only my hands were bound, the thumbs last and separately from the fingers. I had never before been bound in such a manner, yet did it prove most effective. Though my wrists were free, I could not separate my hands.

"I will take her now," said Mehrayn, turning me again so that I now sat upon the platform. "Do you by chance know what became of her breech?"

"She was brought here as you see her, Prince," shrugged the guard male, and then did curiosity touch him. "What gives you to know she wore a breech?"

"The Sword knows many things, my friend," said Mehrayn, his voice and expression uninflected as he gazed upon the other male. "Warriors would do well to understand this."

"Indeed, Prince," answered the guard male in a faint voice, his skin paling again as it had earlier. "Indeed do we understand this."

"Excellent," grunted Mehrayn, already bending to me, a twinkle hidden in his eye. No more than a brief instant had I to see him, for he took me about the waist, raised me from the platform, and slung me over his left shoulder. "I shall require your assistance in donning my sword at the portal," said he to the guard male as I foolishly attempted struggle. Had I succeeded in freeing myself from his arm about my legs, surely would I have fallen to the gold-colored floor cloth with a solid thump. "I shall be able to draw and wield the sword if necessary, yet donning it is another matter."

"It is my privilege to assist you, Prince," replied the guard male, no longer in a place where I might see him. Craning my neck about was idle, for all I was able to see was the great mass of my hair, falling before my face with no more than one or two small gaps. Mehrayn then began to move, to the hangings and through them, and we descended the two broad steps to the floor area, crossing it swiftly. At the entrance to the large area we halted, where an arm moved past beneath my hair after a moment, a broad leather belt held in the hand. When the hand withdrew, a plain, wide-hilted sword was visible upon Mehrayn's hip, near enough to reach easily—had I not been tied. Mehrayn shifted the sword hilt considerably forward, toward his right hand, just as the guard male spoke.

"It would be best, Prince, if you were to hold her hair as

well," said he, gathering my hair between both of his hands. "It sweeps the floor behind you, and may conceivably cause a misstep or fall."

"I had not realized that," said Mehrayn, taking the hair in his left hand before returning his arm to its position about my legs. "My thanks, warrior."

"It is an honor to serve you, Prince," returned the male as we moved through the entry into the outer corridor. "I wish you much pleasure with the slave."

"I wish myself no less," muttered Mehrayn, striding up the corridor I was barely able to see. "It is to be hoped that *Sigurr* wishes me no less."

The words of the male made little sense to me; filled with anger and annoyance as I was, the presence or lack of sense in the male made little difference. I hung head down over his shoulder, unable to free myself, unable to do more than feel the fury of insult when his free right hand came to my bottom and stroked gently. Had I been free, the caress would have made me smile; bound as a slave, I wished only to snarl.

One corridor led to another, and a third to a fourth, each traversed quickly and quietly. Just as quietly were we suddenly without the large dwelling into the outside darkness, treading steps and then a smooth path across the black stone. Those folk who had earlier lined the ways no longer seemed in evidence, and Mehrayn, too, spoke no words. To my great surprise my lids grew heavier and blinked slowly to the rhythm of the pace Mehrayn kept, even and steady yet unhurried. I attempted to rekindle anger to fend off the waves of sleep which pursued me, yet did I find that my anger was already asleep, first victim to the great weariness I felt. I stirred faintly where I hung, my gaze captured by the movement of Mehrayn's legs, stride and stride and stride and stride and stride . . .

Between one stride and another, the flight from sleep was done.

8 Captivity—and a tale is told

Awareness returned as quickly as ever, yet the comfort I felt urged me to remain as I was, stretched out at ease upon a smooth, thick cloth. I opened my eyes somewhat to gaze lazily about, seeing first one part of a strange room, and then, more rapidly and more open-eyed, the rest. I sat up and looked all about me, frowning at the thick, soft green cloth beneath me and all across the floor, at the white walls and ceiling, at the yellow curtains fluttering at the two long, open windows which stood in the wall to my right. Carved wooden platforms stood about the floor at various points, and upon the walls were hardwood candle sconces, the candles unlit in the brightening light of a new fey. In the wall to the left was a door, dark carved wood to match the platforms, and firmly closed. Directly across the room from where I sat, perhaps five paces away, stood a wide platform covered in black cloth, upon the wall above it a ledge holding a large, black candle. It was then that I recalled what had occurred before exhaustion had claimed me, and I turned my head to look down upon Mehrayn, who lay upon the floor cloth to my right, breathing slowly and evenly in sleep.

The male wore no more of coverings than I, a point of curiosity which drew my attention to a second: though I had been tightly bound the darkness previous, there was no longer leather upon ankles or hands. I knew not what the male intended, yet had he been foolish in the extreme. Now that I was free I would go where I willed, with none to keep me from it.

Tossing my hair back I rose quickly and quietly to my feet, then crossed first to the door. As I had expected, neither push nor pull would open the thing, therefore did I abandon my efforts and next stride to the windows. From floor to ceiling did they stand, much like those in the dwellings called palaces in the cities I had seen, yet was there a difference which might be seen once one reached them. Beyond the opened window I chose was a small standing area, it might perhaps be called, one large enough for no more than three males to stand shoulder to shoulder, wide enough for one long pace forward. The area floor was constructed of heavy wood, thin lines of metal bounding it in all about to a height of just above my waist. Beyond—beyond was a sight which took my notice from the sweet, fresh air of the new fey, from the glorious, just-beginning heat of Mida's brightening light.

Beyond the standing area was no more than air, sweeping away into the distance. Never had I seen Mida's skies looking so wide, never had I seen a deep valley from so far above it. Far, far away and below were slopes, clad in tiny, dark trees, marching down to a bright, curving sword of a river, all beginning to turn silver and gold and green as the new light advanced higher above the mountains not far beyond them. Surely had I thought the Sigurri had chosen to live among hills, yet was the far side of their hill a mountain in truth. Slowly I moved closer to the metal which kept me from slipping away to the wide, empty air and put my hands upon it, gazing all about at never-before-seen wonders.

"I would have wagered that the sight would captivate you," came a voice from a distance behind me, a chuckle clearly to be heard in it. "This guest room is the best in my house, one reserved for the most welcome of guests."

Clearly, Mehrayn was no longer asleep. I stood a moment longer and gazed out upon the vast openness, drinking in its beauty to take with me in memory, then turned and retraced my steps into the room.

"I am pleased to note you appear well rested," said the male, eyeing me from where he lazed upon the floor cloth, propped upon one elbow. "You slept so soundly when I brought you here, I had not the heart to wake you."

I folded my arms and gazed down upon the male, sharing naught of the pleasure and lightheartedness he seemed filled with. He had not been as foolish as I had thought in removing the leather from me, yet did he remain foolish to a great extent. Jalav was not one to be taken and kept as a slave.

"That flat-footed stance and cold-eyed scowl is undoubtedly meant for me," sighed Mehrayn, stirring briefly before rising reluctantly to his feet. "You are displeased with your treatment of the last darkness, I know, yet I had little choice in the matter. I could not free you to begin a war with my people which would end only after much blood had been spilled, some of it surely yours. Also, it would not be wise to let Ladayna know you have an ally here, and among the Princes of the Blood. Though she wears the chains of Aysayn, she is not without power, especially in his absence. We must either hide you among the slaves of my household till the Shadow returns, else must you retire to the forests beyond the city, there to await word of his return. The choice is, of course, yours."

"I choose to be set free," I said at once, looking up into the eyes of the male as he stopped before me. "Return my weapons and breech immediately."

"I do not fail to note the order of priority in your demands," Mehrayn replied with a wry grin taking him. "I cannot say it surprises me, for it does not. Give me your word now to refrain from seeking vengeance, and I shall arrange for your covert exit from the city—and, of course, for your weapons."

"Vengeance is my right as a warrior," said I, seeing the grin fade from the face of the male. "None save Mida might take the right from me—save at swordpoint. I repeat, male: free me and return my weapons."

"You stubborn she-zaran!" growled Mehrayn, fists cocked upon hips as he glared down at me. "Do you not see I seek to preserve your life? Certainly vengeance may be taken from you at swordpoint—yet at what cost to both my people and you? And what of your mission here, given by the hand of Sigurr himself? The great god will not be pleased should you give over this mission for the personal satisfaction of vengeance."

"Your great god finds little pleasure in Jalav save from her use," I returned, raising my chin at his glower. "Should he be so far displeased that he takes my life, and should Mida allow this, then I shall be no more. And yet, for as long as life is mine, I may do no other thing than I have ever done. Vengeance may not be denied me."

"Even at cost of your life," said Mehrayn, heavy disapproval in his tone and eyes. "You will do as you wish till the gods show their displeasure by striking you down. Very well, allow me to rephrase the choice which stands before you: you may give me your word to keep your sword sheathed, else you may continue as a slave, without a sword. Which will it be?"

I felt a growl scrape from my throat at the tone of the male, a tone showing he was well used to commanding and being obeyed. He knew full well that I would not be a slave, and therefore sought to command me to the choice he had decided upon. I, who was Jalav, war leader of all the Midanna, would not be commanded to such a choice, and this the male should have known.

"Should I allow myself to be forced to an oath, I truly would be a slave," I said, holding his eyes with my own. "Fetch your lash and chains, male, and then pray to your god that I do not escape them and win free. It will be your life I seek first should I do so, and I will not rest till I have it."

"Should this continue, it may be yours sooner than that," muttered Mehrayn, frustration filling the green of his eyes. "Look you, wench: I will readily admit that I would enjoy keeping you as slave in my household, even for so short a time as till the return of Aysayn, yet do I offer you your freedom in all things save one. Is that one thing of so overwhelming an importance that the rest must be suborned to it? Will you choose the loss of all freedom rather than the loss of one small part?"

"Unlike the warriors of Sigurr," said I, eyeing the male with a good deal of scorn, "the warriors of Mida are taught that the loss of a single freedom is but the first step toward the loss of all. One is either free or not, for there is no ground one may make a stand upon in between. Midanna warriors may be slain, yet their freedom may not be taken from them."

"A lovely philosophical thought," nodded Mehrayn, a judiciousness to his tone. "Were one to dwell in a matching world, all would be easily seen to. And yet, we do not dwell in such a world. In my world, men may make slaves of women, just as you have been made a slave, for the women hereabouts are far too few in number. Should a woman be unprotected, or displeasing to her family or mate, or taken for committing a crime—or gain the enmity of one with power—she will be declared slave and set to serving the needs of those without women of their own. Her approval will not be sought, nor will her wishes and philosophies be consulted; she will simply be declared slave, marked as such, and used as such. She may continue to think of herself as free—yet her state will be that of a slave. We Sigguri are well versed in the keeping of slaves; there will be little opportunity for escape."

So seriously did the male speak that I turned from him, walking a step or two as my thoughts whirled. Among the Midanna, as warrior and war leader both, I had at times been faced with matters which required deep consideration before a decision might be made, no matter the clarity of the law or custom which governed the point. These decisions, though ofttimes difficult despite their seeming simplicity, were each one seen to at last in a manner which satisfied honor. It had not been till I had begun moving among males that the concept of concession had been presented me, that concept which declared it honorable to compromise one's sense of right in order to gain a desired end. How was a warrior to tell these males that the sworn word of one who was willing to compromise honor was as useless as a sword without an edge? How was she to tell them that dishonorable compromise was not as easily reached by others as it was by them? They would hear the words, yet the meaning would be lost in incomprehension.

"Do not hesitate, wench," urged Mehrayn from behind me, his hand coming to stroke my arm. "Give me your word and you will be quickly gone from here, a slave no longer. Will you not be greatly pleased to be no longer a slave?"

"Jalav has never been a slave," said I, shrugging his hand from my arm. "To be taken as a slave and to be slave in truth are not one and the same. There is little need to give my word on any point; when I have escaped, all will be as *I* wish it."

"I see," said Mehrayn, coming about my right side to stand himself before me. "You will accept freedom on no one's terms save your own, and that is your final word. I admire your sense of purpose, girl, yet do I find it exceedingly foolish under these circumstances. Perhaps I erred in attempting to keep you from that which would surely change your mind, yet am I keenly aware of the debt I owe you. And yet, now that I come to think on it, perhaps this is best after all. Keeping you here will not only allow me to be certain of your safety, it will also allow me your use whenever I wish it. A slave may not deny her master."

The grin the male was taken by brought an immediate flare of anger to me, one which was destined to blossom into a full-blown conflagration. About to heatedly deny slavery once again, my words were cut short as the male reached forth to take my breast in his hand, the gesture clearly being one of master to slave. With a growl I knocked his hand away, yet did the gesture produce no more than a laugh from the male as he began to advance on me. Large and broad was this Mehrayn, the muscles moving easily beneath the bronze of his skin, the light hair of his body nearly invisible till one was close before him. Without a weapon I had little choice save to back away before his advance, a doing which filled the male with even greater amusement.

Around and about the room was I pursued, yet in no simple manner. Time and again was I caught with a wall at my back and Mehrayn directly before me, the bulk of the male impossible to dart past. At such a time was I pinned to the wall with the body of the male, his hands touching me all about, his lips seeking mine. In fury did I strike at him and attempt to sink my teeth into his lips, yet the strength of my blows was as nothing to the male, and my teeth were avoided with a laugh. Then would I be released by him, to back away once again and be pursued once again, on and on about the room.

The foolishness continued perhaps three hands of reckid and more, and then, as I kicked and beat at the male to break free once more, his arms suddenly went about me and I was taken down to the floor cloth with him. Roundly did I curse the strength given males above warriors, fighting all the while, yet did the second prove as useless as the first. With little difficulty was I forced to my back upon the floor cloth, Mehrayn kneeling above me, his hands to either side of my head, resting on my wildly flown hair. He chuckled softly as he looked down on my struggles, pleased with how well-caught I was, and then did he suddenly lean close.

"I see you already squirm in my embrace, slave," said he, unmindful of the manner in which my fists beat at him. "The feel of your brightly painted breasts against my flesh delights me, as does the touch of the rest of you. Are you prepared as yet to serve me?"

"I would gladly see Mida serve you," I panted, finding it impossible to reach the eyes of the male by cause of the manner in which he held me down. "You would be served up by her to a turn, I think, no matter the foul strength you brought to bear."

"And yet it is you I hold here beneath me," he laughed, increasing his weight as he leaned down even farther. "A man is able to take much pleasure from the slave female he holds in his arms, for her pleasure is not necessary to his own. Had I left you in the temple, you would have been made to serve many men; here, you must concern yourself with me."

"That I shall gladly do," I spat, "the moment I have sword or dagger in my fist! And that fey shall come, Mida take me if it does not!"

"Again you are mistaken," laughed the male, "for it is I, not your Mida, who will take you. Think well upon the matter of freedom as I do so, the freedom you spurned so easily. The choice has now been withdrawn from you, and will likely not be offered again."

Despite my efforts to halt him, the hands of the male then drew me to him as he threw himself to the floor cloth beside me, rolling us both onto our sides. A fist in my hair raised my lips as he wished them, and quickly did I set myself to bite, yet was a gasp forced from me instead, just as his lips took mine. His leg had forced its way between my ankles, preparing an unimpeded approach for his hand, a route he was quick to take. Between my thighs did he go with purpose, drawing a gasp from me as red-tinged heat flared, touching me so deeply and surely that the breath fled from my body.

Ah, Mida! Well did that male know the manner of reaching my soul! I fought his lips as I fought his hand at my thighs, yet with little strength and for no more than a moment. My need was so quickly called forth that the doing left me dizzy and weakened, beyond the ability to refuse, beyond the ability to struggle. Much dismayed was I at this turn of events, for surely had I thought myself freed from the chains of desire and need which had bound me to Ceralt. That this Mehrayn had great skill in taking pleasure from females was clear, and yet did the truth make little difference. I was bound to give use to this male of Sigurr's whether I wished it or no—and were he to continue as he then did, surely would I soon wish it in truth.

Knowing full well what he did, the accursed male gave me no rest. His hands and lips were everywhere, touching, kissing, caressing and nipping, drawing moans as easily as a lash draws screams, filling me more and more with the need to do as he did. At last I could bear it no longer and threw myself upon him, thinking I would surely be disallowed the touching of him, yet unable to control the demands of desire. Consider my surprise when my advances were not only not repulsed but welcomed! Our lips met fiercely and our tongues fenced in joy, then did I taste the flesh of his body as he tasted mine. From his chest to his belly to his loins did I go, trailing my tongue through the pale forest of his hair, finding his manhood prepared and awaiting me. Groans echoed from Mehrayn as I attempted to take the nectar from him, and soon he could bear it no longer. His hands at my waist pulled me from him and threw me to my back, and then was he thrusting within, so deep and hard that a cry was forced from me. His arms went about me, crushing me to him, and as our lips met, all rational thought fled from us both.

The end of the storm brought an end to motion, and I lay quietly in Mehrayn's arms, my cheek to the damp of his chest, still in his possession. Well spent were we both, and well used to boot. At least I felt well used, well and fully and happily used. The use of the male was like no other I had known, so fiercely demanding and yet so completely sharing. Was this the manner in which Sigurri used slaves, it was difficult understanding why each of their females had not long since declared herself slave.

"I swear my Sigurr that this was better than the first time," said Mehrayn with a sigh of satisfaction, his lips coming to my hair. "Should your performance improve each time I use you, I will surely soon fail to survive. Is this the manner in which you intend doing me in, wench? With pleasure?''

"A true warrior uses whatever weapon comes to hand—or elsewhere," I replied, slowly moving my cheek among the thick hairs of his chest. "And now do I understand the reason for your having been used by so many of my warriors. Your staying power is quite adequate, considering the limits of most males.''

"I thank you for so high a compliment," he chuckled, moving one hand down to my bottom. "Your wenches did indeed enjoy the time I took with each of them, yet was there another point which was equally favored. Are you not yet able to tell?''

At first was I puzzled by his comment, and then, as I attempted to move, was his meaning suddenly made clear. Though much had been done to drain the male, the presence I felt within me was not lacking in vigor; quite the contrary. So soon after having eased himself the male was again prepared, yet was I then the only warrior within reach. Again I attempted to move, this time in withdrawal, yet his hand on my bottom prevented such a thing.

"I see you are now aware of the point," said he, the amusement growing in him—just as he grew in me. "Had I not had the ability to do this, I could not have used you so close to the time of first devotions. The bell will ring soon, and then it is the altar for us, wench. Sigurr will not be denied.''

"I—I do not understand," I stumbled, closing my eyes against the slow, persistent movement he had begun. I had no true desire to be used again, and yet— "What is an altar, and what has Sigurr to do with this?''

"Sigurr has much to do with it, for it is he to whom we pray," responded the male, bringing his other hand to my bottom to join the first. With both hands then was I pushed upon him, allowed to draw somewhat away, then pushed forward again. The gentle movement was disconcerting to say the least, yet before I might jerk free, a deep bell began to toll from somewhere below. Over and over again did the bell sound, and with the first of it, Mehrayn released me and withdrew.

"Now we go to the altar," said he, rising to his feet then drawing me up to mine. With his arm about me, I was taken to the black, cloth-covered platform and allowed to sink down upon it, then watched as he went to light the black candle on the ledge above. He returned the flame-starter to the ledge beside the candle, then came to stand before me where I sat.

"The altar is where you now rest yourself," said he, "and is the place where I must make my devotions. Thrice each fey must

a man use a woman on the altar, giving Sigurr the thanks due
him for making such use possible. As I told you last darkness,
the privilege of service thus given you is great. Lie down and we
will begin.''

"I have no devotions to make to the dark god," I denied,
beginning to take myself from the platform. "You must seek
elsewhere, male, for I will have naught to do with. . . ."

My words were abruptly interrupted as the male took me about
the waist and threw me back upon the platform, following
quickly after so that I might not rise again.

"You have little in you which might be mistaken for gratitude,
wench," he growled, pressing me belly down upon the platform.
"Does the pleasure you felt mean so little that thanks are not due
Sigurr for allowing it? Is your soul so small that you begrudge
your use in honor of the mightiest of gods?"

"Mida is the mightiest!" I snapped over my shoulder, stung
into response by the accusation. "Sigurr is no more than a god
of males, fit to lead no others, fit to be followed by no others! I
will have no more to do with him than I must, for I am happily
not male!"

"Such a fact pleases me as well," said Mehrayn, his weight
bearing me down as his knees kept my legs apart. "I believe I
am now able to understand your refusal, yet you, also, must
understand that such refusal is not even permitted a free woman.
As a slave you will be taught to submit gladly, yet there is little
time now for such instruction. Sigurr, to you alone do I dedicate
the use of this foolish, stubborn wench, asking only that you
school her in the joys which may be hers upon your altar. She
will learn soon enough of that which awaits her in its place."

Then did the male raise my hips and slowly enter me once
more, forcing his strength past my attempts to bar his entry.
Where earlier I had been made to feel great desire yet no sense
of shame, this second use was more punishment than pleasure.
Slowly was my heat drawn forth once more, yet only to cause
my body to writhe upon the platform, held by the shoulders as
the male thoroughly pummeled me. Indeed was my use taken for
the pleasure of Sigurr, and when it was done, I was near to fury.

"It is clear there is anger all through you," said Mehrayn as
he withdrew and stood, freeing me at last. "It disturbs me that
you fail to feel a proper joy in serving Sigurr, as do other
wenches. I will pray that you are quickly allowed to know him
and follow him as you now do your Mida. It is your right as a
female."

I twisted quickly upon the platform to stare at the male, and saw that he had turned away and now walked toward the door of the room. Many angry words had risen to my lips in reply to his comments, yet did I swallow them again without voicing them. The male gave devotion to a god he knew no better than I had known Mida; were I to attempt speaking the truth to him, he would no more believe than I would have before my journey to the north. It was clear the male wished me well—in the odd manner of all males—and anger would be foolish and futile. Best would be to find my way free, take the vengeance that was due me, speak with the absent Aysayn, then return at once to my warriors, leaving Mehrayn and the Sigurri far behind.

"It is now time to break our fast," said Mehrayn over his shoulder, pausing before the closed door to rap twice upon it. Immediately there came a rattling at the door, and then was it opened by a young male, tall and thin and clad in a dark blue, thigh-length body covering, who had clearly not yet come into his manhood. The boy looked to me briefly with a grin writ plain, then turned his attention to Mehrayn.

"How may I serve you, Prince?" he asked in a voice not far removed from a girl's. "I have no more than a hin before my lessons begin, yet am I willing to delay their start should you require my assistance beyond that time."

"Your selflessness warms me, Kerlehn," laughed Mehrayn, clapping the boy gently upon the shoulder. "I shall, however, require your assistance only briefly, therefore are your lessons in small jeopardy. At the moment, I would have my loincloth which sits upon the table beside this door in the hall. Once that is done, you may go to the kitchen and have its master arrange for the meal I wish brought here. Should his devotions not be complete, you must await his arrival. Is that clear?"

"Indeed, Prince," nodded the boy, dispirited that his assistance would not be longer required, yet determined to show none of his dejection. "I shall await the kitchen master should he not yet have returned from his devotions, and I will fetch your loincloth immediately."

The boy stepped without the room and stretched his arm into the unseen hall, handed to the Sigurri his black body cloth, then took himself off. Mehrayn chuckled as he once again closed the door, then turned to me.

"The boy labors under my aegis to become a warrior of Sigurr," said he, wrapping himself in the black cloth. "He, along with the others I sponsor, must know his letters and numbers as well as the use of sword and shield and spear and bow. Though he grudges the time spent among his books, Kerlehn is a fine student as well as quick and deadly with his weapons. Once he has reached his manhood, he will surely win to the changing of his name."

"The changing of his name?" I asked, wondering if all males were so concerned with this thing called lessons. Ceralt had been more than insistent that I learn that which is called reading, and so I had, yet not as well as I would have liked. Had I not been Jalav, bound to serve Mida, it would have pleased me to continue what Lialt had begun.

"Aye," said Mehrayn, stepping closer before me. "When a Sigurri youth becomes a Sigurri warrior, he is permitted to change his name to show his pride in his new position. Kerlehn will become Kerlain, the ay-eye of a warrior replacing the ee-aitch of his birth name. Should he continue on and win the place of a Prince of the Blood, his name would then become Kerlyn, the ay sound being forsaken—save it is my place he wins. Then would he be called Kerlayn."

"The birth names of the Midanna do not change," said I, freeing my hair from beneath me as I stretched upon the platform. "As we are warriors all, we retain the names handed down to us by those who have gone before. She who wins a place as warrior wins a silver ring for her ear; she who wins the place of war leader wins the second silver ring from the body of she who *was* war leader. What name was yours before you became Mehrayn?"

"My birth name was Mehrdin," said he, his tone distracted as he looked down upon me. "Aysayn and I were boys together, and he was Varsan. How lovely you are, wench, lying so upon my altar. Surely does Sigurr smile broadly upon me, to have sent you to me."

"You would be wise to see the matter correctly, male," said I, sitting up quickly and then rising to my feet. "It is in Mida's name that I ride, no matter that I carry the word of Sigurr. I have been sent to no male, nor shall I ever be. To believe otherwise would be a well-proven folly."

"There are men who have attempted to claim you, then," said he, his light eyes continuing to gaze upon me as they had done. "Such a revelation is scarcely surprising, considering the look of you. That none have yet made you their own is equally unsurprising, for you are clearly not like other wenches. Which is not to say no man ever shall."

With a gentle laugh his hand touched my chin, and then did he turn away to walk to a small platform which held a low, wide bronze bowl and a tall silver pitcher. In the pitcher was water, and once the male had poured the water into the bowl, he began washing himself therein. I considered the matter even more foolish than the large, high pots used by other city folk to bathe in, yet once the male had dried himself upon a cloth from beneath the platform and had emptied the water he had used into the bright air beyond a window, fresh water was poured into the bowl and offered to me. Indeed did I carry the heavy scent of sweat and dirt and the use of a male, yet was I moved to laughter and scorn at the thought of bathing in so small a bowl. Mehrayn joined my laughter in his usual way, but then I was taken by the waist and quickly moved close to the platform, his free hand in the water then showering droplets at me. Indeed did I wish to find anger at such treatment, yet certain laughter, once begun, is difficult to halt. Though I attempted to return to Mehrayn the shower of droplets, I soon found that I was too strongly taken by mirth to do so; Mehrayn, though also in the grip of laughter, nevertheless was able to cover me well with water, in the process also covering himself. The struggle I accomplished before the platform, held by the waist against the male, was a sorry attempt indeed, weak and ineffectual and totally lacking in accomplishment. That the doing was much filled with the delightful foolishness of the forest journey came to me only when Mehrayn touched hand to my thighs, seeking to take the excess of his own spendings from me. Nearly did I gasp at the unexpected touch, at the cool of the water against my heated flesh, at the cleansing stroke which immediately became a caress. My face raised to his as the amusement fled from both of us, and then did it strike me how deeply I was aware of the broad, strong male against whom I was held. His flesh, too, was warm from the rising heat of the new fey, tan and firm and softening the thick cords of muscle which lay beneath. The arm about me tightened, drawing me more fully against him, and then were his lips on mine, just as they had been in the forest beside the pond. I still knew naught of the reason these Sigurri had for touching lips so often, yet was I beginning to find the practice extremely pleasant. I put my arms about Mehrayn and joined his kiss, pressing myself to his body and the touch of his hand as his tongue sought mine. Our murmurs of pleasure mingled, the heat beginning to rise all about—just as the door to the room was flung open.

"Prince, I have brought your meal," panted the young male Kerlehn, entering bent over by the large, laden board he carried, hurrying to place it upon a wide platform. Mehrayn's lips had left mine the instant the door had opened, his large body immediately tensing in readiness for whatever occurred, relaxing again only when none save the boy entered.

"Excellent, Kerlehn," said he, his voice husky yet filled with amusement. "We will partake of the meal in due course. You may now return to your room till the time for your lessons."

"I shall, Prince," said the boy, turning from the board to see that Mehrayn had wrapped his arms about me from behind, his cloth-clad body pressed firmly against me. "I must, however, first relay the message sent you by the Arms Master. In honor of your return a review has been prepared by those who train within your household, one which now awaits your presence. When may I tell the Arms Master to expect you?"

The young male stood and mopped his brow, attempting to swallow the smile which threatened to take him. A low-voiced groan came from Mehrayn as he released me, and then was he standing beside me rather than behind.

"You, young Kerlehn, should know better than to smirk at the discomfort of your elders," said the Sigurri, the sternness of his tone taking all amusement from the boy. "You may tell the Arms Master that I will attend the review as soon as I have finished with my meal. And you I will deal with as soon as you have become a man. A taste of forced abstinence will remove all humor for you from a situation such as this. Now, take yourself off!"

The boy, bowing in agitation, quickly did as he was told, pulling the door to behind him. Mehrayn saw him gone then turned to me, sighing at the look I gave him.

"There is naught I may do, lovely wench," said he, reaching out to stroke my hair. "Duty calls, and I may not refuse to answer. We shall have our meal, and then I must leave you."

"Clearly, I should somehow have retained my spear," said I, turning from the male in displeasure, yet also too well aware of the truth he spoke. When there are duties one must perform, foolish little pleasures must be forsaken.

"For the sake of Kerlehn, I give thanks you did not," chuckled Mehrayn, taking himself toward the board of provender the boy had brought. "I do not doubt you would cast at a boy as willingly as you cast at the keren. Come and choose what you will have to break your fast."

Though it was not provender I had begun to feel a need for, I followed after Mehrayn to see what was to be had. As a Midanna, I was not in the habit of taking sustenance so early in the fey, yet was I quickly reminded by the sight and aroma of the provender that I had not fed later than mid-fey the fey previous. Indeed did my insides echo hollowly when presented with roast lellin, grilled nilno, wrettan eggs, dark baked grain, yellow fellin tubers and short stalks of rich, green valk. As I took a cut of valk to chew, I also noted the presence of a tall pot of steaming, golden liquid, the aroma of which was totally unfamiliar to me.

"That is thrai," said Mehrayn, seeing my curious examination of the golden liquid. "When sweetened with halus resin, it makes an excellent beverage to take the sleep from one's eyes. I will pour you a cup."

The male did so, pouring a short pot—cup—for himself as well, yet I made no attempt to taste it before I had swallowed a bit of the lellin and nilno and one of the wrettan eggs. Drink does badly upon empty insides, leaving one lightheaded and somewhat ill, therefore did I provide that which the drink might lie upon. My surprise was considerable, however, when I raised it at last to my lips: the drink was naught save heated and sweetened water, a soft tang hovering in its taste. Drink such as that was fit for none save very young warriors-to-be, who would find comfort in its warmth and joy in its sweetness. For full-grown warriors there was far better drink to be had, yet Mehrayn drained his pot with relish, scarcely noticing that I returned mine to the board with no more than the single taste taken. He did, however, notice a considerably different matter.

"Your wrist," said he with a frown, turning from the board to take my hands. "It failed to take my attention sooner, yet both of your wrists remain as bruised as they were the last darkness. Why have you not been healed of the bruises as you were healed of the wound in your shoulder?"

I, too, looked at my wrists, yet was the answer to his question easily understood.

"Clearly, Mida is displeased with my efforts," I shrugged, taking my hands from his grip, recalling only distantly that slight wounds had been overlooked on previous occasions. "I have not been sent here to dawdle and sport, yet no other thing have I accomplished since my arrival. I must see this Aysayn of yours and return to my warriors."

I turned from the board and walked to the center of the room, reflecting that Mida—and Sigurr as well—must also be displeased that I had allowed their sign to be taken from me. It now lay in the possession of the female Ladayna, who had been marked as mine as soon as her challenge had been given. That her challenge had been through the use of armed males mattered little; challenge had been given and would be accepted as soon as weapons were again mine.

"The Shadow's return cannot be hastened by any save himself," came the voice of Mehrayn from behind me, he having remained at the board. "There is naught you may do save await him, here in my house."

"I have not the time to await the pleasure of a male!" I snapped, turning again to look upon Mehrayn. "Should the strangers arrive before my return, my warriors will find the need to enter battle without a war leader! I will go in search of this Aysayn, and then I will return to my warriors. Where are my breech and weapons?"

"A slave has no need of a breech and weapons!" Mehrayn snapped in return, anger putting his fists to his hips. "You cannot disturb the Shadow in his meditations, you cannot take the lives of his woman and her guard, and you cannot leave here without my permission! Sigurr does not demand the performance of your task while such performance is patently impossible! When Aysayn returns I will take you before him, and then will you be free to return to your wenches. You would not have been sent here to raise the Sigurri, were the strangers destined to arrive before our host might ride to meet them."

"With Midanna warriors already there, there is little need for haste among the Sigurri," said I, folding my arms and straightening my stance. "Surely Sigurr hopes to have his followers in at the kill—a kill performed by Midanna—and thereby allow them the reflection of glory they would by themselves be unable to take. You may safely bide your time in waiting, male, yet I face the loss of true glory, personal glory! And Jalav is no slave!"

"Jalav has not the wit to know what she *should* be," growled the male, moving forward till he stood directly before me, the anger burning in the green of his eyes. "Had Jalav given me her word, she would now be free in the forests about the city. Had she accepted the need to wait as an adult, she would have been a guest in my house. Rather than that, she behaves as an ill-mannered, ill-disciplined child, giving me insult and making demands to be freed of a state her own unbridled tongue brought her to! You will not be released, my girl, nor will you be accorded the privileges of a guest! A slave you have been declared, and a slave you will remain—till *I* decree otherwise!"

"How like a male," I sneered, looking him up and down in scorn, to his greater anger. "I have met many males who spoke to Jalav of slavery, yet none who spoke so when Jalav had sword to hand. Why did you not attempt to name me slave in the forests, male? Why did you never accept what offers for challenge I gave you? Possibly it was my weapons which deterred you, whose absence you now celebrate by speaking of that which I have been declared, and that which I shall remain. Return to me my weapons, male, and then speak to me of slavery—if you dare!"

"Ah, I see you have found me out," said Mehrayn, a false heartiness above the growl of his anger. "Indeed do I fear you and your weapons, wench, so greatly that I shall endeavor to keep them from you as long as I may. And during the time you grace my household with your presence and service, I shall also endeavor to have you taught a proper regret for the insult you so casually give others. One who stands armed may give insult; one who stands unarmed may not."

It was my intention to point out that I gave challenge, not insult, yet the words were not destined to be spoken. With the last of his own words, Mehrayn's fist was in my hair, bending me forward and forcing me toward the door. With a snarl of fury I struggled against the painful, humiliating grip, yet when has the strength of a warrior, unarmed, equalled the strength of a male? To the door was I pulled, and through it once it had been opened, and into the hall which lay beyond the room.

The hall was a long one, the stone of its floor covered with a dark gray cloth, its walls dressed in silver and black silk where doors did not interrupt them. Here and there against the walls stood small wooden platforms, some empty, some holding sprays of wildflowers in tall pots, candles in silver sconces lighting all beneath them. Through this hall was I taken, then to the right up another, and then to the left up a third. Some males did we pass, and some few slave females as well, yet none halted Mehrayn in his ever-forward stride, though they, themselves, halted and stared after us in puzzlement. Stumbling, wrapped in rage, I was taken up the balance of the hall and thence to an outer door, which opened on a wide courtyard full in Mida's light, filled with many males. At sight of Mehrayn each of these males bowed, yet Mehrayn made no acknowledgment of the salutes, halting, instead, before one of the males.

"Greetings, Hesain," said the Sigurri to this new, black-clothed male who bowed a second time. "I am told there is be a review given for me, and I am eager to have you begin. I have been too long away from those who strive for the honor of my house."

"Sooner would we consign ourselves to the Caverns of the Doomed than disappoint you, Prince," said this male called Hesain, a large, square, darkish male, yet not so large as Mehrayn. His brown eyes came to rest on me where I stood attempting to loosen Mehrayn's hold upon my hair, and Mehrayn chuckled in amusement.

"A new slave for our house, Hesain," said he, his fist tightening as he forced me straight and over-straight, so that I might be presented to the gaze of the second male. "Would a man not be consigned to the Caverns for the crime of covering such a body? Have you ever seen a more toothsome morsel?"

"Never, Prince," said the second male, his eyes moving slowly about me as a smile appeared upon his face. "May I touch her?"

"Certainly," agreed Mehrayn, no more than pleasantness to be heard in his voice. "She is a slave, is she not? Slaves may be touched by any man, whether they will it or not."

Well did I know that the male spoke largely to me, though he seemingly spoke to the other. I growled wordlessly and swiped at Mehrayn, catching him in the middle with my elbow and the weight of my body, then immediately kicked at the second male. The kick narrowly missed the male's privates, striking instead on his thigh as he twisted desperately aside, more fortunate than Mehrayn. The larger Sigurri had given me pain with his hand in my hair, yet had my blow to his middle taken his breath with an aching grunt, bending him forward as he had bent me. With the loosening of his grip I would surely have been quickly free had his fingers not been deeply tangled in my hair from the struggle. I, too, went down, forced to my knees, and then was Mehrayn recovered enough to retighten his grip. A sound of laughter came from those males who stood in the walled-in area, yet the male who held me firmly before him seemed unshamed.

"As I said, Hesain," panted Mehrayn, "no slave may say what man will touch her. However, due to my—ah—eagerness to have the review begun, perhaps it would be best to delay the touching for another time. What say you?"

"As ever, Prince, your wisdom transcends all," replied the second male with a laugh. He now stood back from us, his hand rubbing at his thigh, the others holding their places behind him, though every eye was upon us. Those others behind Hesain were clad in every color save black and were young, yet not so young as the boy Kerlehn. It seemed odd that Mehrayn showed no anger for their laughter, yet I had little time to think upon the point. Quickly was I raised to my feet by the pull on my hair, and guided again toward the dwelling.

"I will return in a moment," Mehrayn called back to those we left before entering the dwelling. "I will find more pleasure in the review if this one is deposited elsewhere, where I will not need to keep watch upon her."

Hesain's acknowledgment reached us as we entered and turned

right up the hall, going to a stair which led downward. Though cloth-covered, the stair clearly had been cut from rock, and led to a lower hall which we merely trod briefly before entering a large, bright, windowed chamber in which the odor of provender and cooking was strong. A number of slave females hurried about or saw to tasks in the chamber, and a larger number of males tended their own tasks, one or two directing the slave females. One single male, golden-haired and older than the others, stood about directing all, and to this male was I taken.

"Sadrin, a moment of your time," said Mehrayn as the golden-haired male bowed with a smile. "I will explain what aid I must have from you, yet first I would see this she-keren caged. Do you have one to spare?"

"Certainly, Prince," said the male Sadrin, turning and leading the way to the far side of the chamber with a gesture which Mehrayn followed. "I see we have a new slave for the house. Is she to be mine?"

"Her duties will be diverse," said Mehrayn, "and are a matter which must be discussed between us later. For now I wish merely to see her caged and kept from causing further—distractions. An excellent one for distractions, this one."

"A thing a man may easily see," chuckled Sadrin, halting before a low, small enclosure of metal, one far smaller than any I had yet come across. "It is a punishment cage you are seeking, is it not, my Prince?"

"Exactly," said Mehrayn, looking down upon the enclosure with a good deal of satisfaction. "Certain slaves require punishment, to assist them in recalling that they are, indeed, slaves. In with you, wench."

It was difficult to credit that one of my size was to be put within an enclosure of such meager dimensions, yet Mehrayn showed no hesitation. Again was I bent low to the floor, in this room an uncovered stone block, and then was one end of the enclosure opened by Mehrayn so that I might be forced toward it. Halfway within was my hair released, therefore did I quickly twist about to attempt exit once again, yet to no avail. A push on my legs from the Sigurri warrior sent me farther within, and then was the metal closed and barred behind my feet, locking me within. I could not turn to shake the metal which held me prisoner, and the growl which came to my throat was stronger by cause of that.

"Indeed like a keren," muttered the male Sadrin, looking thoughtfully down upon me. "Had she more room within, I feel sure she would crouch rather than sit, perhaps even baring her fangs.''

"She is not an animal!" said Mehrayn sharply, turning to look upon the other male. "She is a—*was* a warrior, just as I am! No warrior is pleased to be caged!"

"My Prince, I meant no insult," replied the other male, his voice calm and quiet. "I merely spoke what seemed an observable truth." And then did he hesitate before adding, "In view of your opinion of the cage, I fail to comprehend why you place her there. The experience will be neither comfortable nor dignified, most especially for one who is—*was* a warrior."

The hesitation then touched Mehrayn, taking the sharpness from his gaze and tone before turning him to gaze down upon me.

"She must be taught," said he, again speaking to another with words meant for me. "Even a warrior must learn to walk softly in captivity, else there is little chance he will ever again walk free. To learn such a thing is to retain one's life so that it may be given properly, in battle, dedicated to the god one serves. All other action is folly."

"One may not die as a warrior if one does not live as a warrior," said I, looking up through the lines of metal at the male. "To live as any other thing is less than life, and fit only for males. Jalav is no slave, nor will she ever be."

"More growl than voice," remarked the male Sadrin, a murmur behind the silence of Mehrayn. A long moment did the two stand regarding me, then did Mehrayn turn and walk off, gesturing the other with him. They two paused for conversation, discussing various matters beyond my hearing, then did Mehrayn depart the chamber, leaving all to the tasks they had been attending to before our arrival. Sadrin did no more than glance toward me before he, too, turned his attention elsewhere.

Few words were spoken in the large chamber, perhaps by cause of the greater heat therein, which brought sweat to one's body as it lay heavily all about. I stirred within the metal enclosure, attempting to ease the cramped position which had been forced upon me, yet it was as the male Sadrin had said: comfort was not possible within such close confines. Stretching out full length was disallowed one of my size, as was taking a seated position. Lying on my left side upon the bare metal floor of the enclosure, my knees drawn up, the metal lines close above my head, before my eyes, and all about; this was all I was able to do, lie there curled, beneath the weight of the growing heat, feeling the lines of metal move closer and closer still. The desire was great to throw myself against the metal as I had done when enclosed so by those in Bellinard; the effort required to keep from doing so was greater still. Only the knowledge that such struggle would be futile, as well as strong aversion to showing these Sigurri how deeply the confinement touched me, enabled me to lower my head to my left arm and remain unmoving. So would the hadat have lain in the trap, luring the hunter into believing it was bested. Not for naught was the hadat the living symbol of the life sign of Jalav.

With the slow passage of the reckid and hind, even the hadat would have grown restless and impatient. Those Sigurri in the chamber continued their doings, some concerned with filling large metal pots and setting them upon fire, some seeing to mixtures of various sorts, some seeing to the sectioning of large cuts of meat or opening large sacks of vegetables. Those who saw to these doings were largely male, each in a body cloth of a color other than black, the females among them also wearing many colors, their breasts well covered by the selfsame cloth. Those females who were clearly marked as slave were not as bare as the captive who watched them. Though their red-painted breasts were clear to the sight of all, long cloths of red were wrapped about their waists and tied at their left hips, the opening thusly made running the full length of their legs to their ankles, where the cloth itself ended. Sight of such red brought unreasoning anger to me with the thought of Silla, yet the tasks set to the hands of these slaves did much to allay that anger. Though few in number, these female slaves were set to the constant cleaning of the chamber and its contents, floors, walls, platforms, pots, peelings from vegetables, fat from meat, spillings from platforms and pots. Directing them was a large free female, nearly of a size with me, who stood and watched their efforts with a frown. Upon occasion did the efforts of the slaves fail to meet the approval of the female, and then was the switch hanging at her belt put to use.

After perhaps two hind of watching, it had become clear that one female slave was most often singled out by the free female as she who would feel the switch. The others seemed well accustomed to their lot, seeing to their tasks quickly, quietly, and to the best of their ability; this lone slave, with hair as pale as that of Ilvin the Hitta warrior, worked with little enthusiasm, little skill, and many indignant screams when struck with the switch. Her hair hung longer than that of the others, reaching to the middle of her back above the red covering, therefore was the covering itself the area which was most often struck. Much did it seem indignation rather than pain which touched the light-haired female so deeply, and at long last she became willing to accept no more.

"Sadrin!" she cried when the switch rose to strike her again, darting out from beneath the arm of the free female and running to the male. "I cannot bear any more of this, do you hear? No more!"

The male Sadrin turned slowly from the pot he had been inspecting to look upon the angry, indignant female. His look contained little friendliness and no approval, and he folded his arms as he looked coldly down upon her.

"In what manner do you address me, slave?" he demanded, making no direct answer to her protests. "Have you been given permission to leave your work and approach me?"

"I need no permission to speak as I will!" The female bristled, indignation growing truly high. "I have had all I care to of this—this—ridiculous farce, and I will have no more! I am going to the home of my aunt, and will never speak to my father or Mehrayn again! When they come seeking me, you may tell them that!"

With a firm nod of her head, the small, light-haired female turned from Sadrin, her evident intention to leave the chamber at once. Her high-chinned stride took her all of four paces before the male signaled to by Sadrin put his fist in her hair, halting her abruptly with a cry of pain. Her next stumbling steps returned her to the golden-haired male, who continued to look down upon her with great disapproval. No longer was the female indignant, and she returned the look given her with uncertainty.

"How dare you do this to me?" she quavered, her voice taking on the trembling her body was not allowed. "Have him release me at once!"

"Your memory seems to be extremely faulty, Cynena," said Sadrin, his voice remaining cold. "Your father, having grown weary of your constant, wilfull refusal of all suitors, has allowed you to be declared slave despite your high station. The Prince Mehrayn, out of friendship to your father, has agreed to have your slavery taught you here. Neither of them will seek you out, for they do not concern themselves with the disposition of slaves."

"What you say is untrue!" cried the female, painfully aware of how openly her body was held by the large hand twisting in her hair. "My father thinks to force me to his wishes by this charade, and Mehrayn assists him! I have not truly been declared a slave! I could not be!"

"No?" asked the male Sadrin, raising his brows. "You think

not? Perhaps, then, this is for the best after all, for you need to learn your true condition. The beating for insolence should teach it you.''

"No!" screamed the female Cynena, struggling against the grip of the male who held her. "You may not beat me! I am free and you may not beat me!"

No answer was vouchsafed the female in words; instead did Sadrin gesture, indicating that the male who held the slave was to proceed with the instructions given him. With shrieks was the female pulled away from before the golden-haired male, and taken across the floor to the wall to my left. Perhaps a pace before the wall stood a low, wooden contrivance, much like that to which city males tied their kand, two upright posts joined by a crosspiece at their tops. The female struggled as she was bent forward over this crosspiece, yet the chains which came from the wall and were attached to her wrists by another male served to hold her as she was put. The first male then released her hair, reached to her hip to open and remove the half-covering she wore, dropped the covering to the floor, then went toward a switch which hung upon the wall near to the wooden contrivance.

Truly frantic was the female Cynena, yet her shouts and shrieks were ignored by all in the chamber, including those who were also marked as slave. They, beneath the eye of the free female, worked more eagerly than they had earlier, barely pausing to flinch when Cynena's shouts became screams of pain. The male with the switch struck her sharply and with strength, tearing cries of humiliation and hurt from her twisting body. The doing was far from the lashings I had had at the hands of males, little more than a punishment fit for a child, yet memory rose of those lashings and I gritted my teeth, fighting against the illness which threatened to rise up and engulf me. I moved as far as I might upon the metal floor of the enclosure, and fought to let my mind know the difference between the two actions.

The female Cynena was soundly switched, well past the point where screams became true weeping. Having been punished as a child she wept as a child, offering no least resistance when the chains were removed from her wrists and she was raised from the post. The male Sadrin had taken himself over to witness the last of her beating, and when she was stood before him, she could not raise her head to meet his gaze.

"Much more acceptable," said he, looking down upon the small, shaking, weeping form before him. "Your punishment, slave, was for insolence rather than for attempted escape, a leniency you may thank me for. For a slave to attempt escape is a serious matter, and one more harshly punished. How say you?"

"Thank you, master," whispered the female, her ragged words so faint they barely reached me. "Please, tell my father that I beg his forgiveness. I will do anything he asks, if only he will. . . ."

"Silence," rumbled the male, his face expressionless. "A slave has no kin. Return yourself to your duties now, and do not give me further reason to punish you. Should you cause another incident, I will remember that you attempted escape."

The female, pale and shivering, threw one pleading look at the male before reaching a trembling hand out toward her covering which lay upon the floor to the left of the male. Her foolishness was made clear to her when the male placed his leather-covered foot upon the cloth, denying it to her, returning the tears to her eyes. A strangled sob came from her throat at this further punishment, and then she had turned and fled back to the area of the free female, who awaited her with the task she had left unfinished with her initial outburst. The satisfaction was so strong in the eyes of Sadrin, I could do naught save close my own eyes to erase the sight of him. Had he looked at me as he had looked upon the slave Cynena, I would surely have thrown myself upon the lines of metal in an effort to reach him.

Forced inactivity often brings a greater weariness than strenuous labor. Closing my eyes took my attention from those around me, and in such a manner did sleep find me without difficulty. How long a time I spent in sleep I know not, yet when I awoke, attempting to stretch the ache from my cramped body, I immediately became aware of the greater heat within the room—and the greater silence. No longer was there the sound of folk moving about seeing to various tasks, and when I looked out into the chamber, the reason became clear. All of the female slaves, eight in number with the female Cynena, knelt in a straight line before the male of the chamber, each of them under examination by the males. Even as I watched, the males stepped forward one by one, took a slave by the hair, then hurried her from the room by the door which had provided my own entry. In a very short time none save Cynena remained, even the free female having departed in the company of a male. The light-haired slave trembled where she knelt, her head down, for Sadrin stood above her, studying her without words. A moment or two passed in the thickened silence, and then did Sadrin bend to the female.

"It seems you have not been chosen, slave," said he, taking

her by the hair and raising her to her feet. "The men of the house obviously have no desire to perform their mid-fey devotions through you. Even I have chosen another."

"Please, do not beat me!" whispered the female, fear and satisfaction doing battle in her eyes. "It was no doing of mine that I am to be left untouched during devotions! I did not refuse!"

"You were not given the choice of refusing," said Sadrin, his voice even. "Refusal is not allowed to a female, slave or free. And you will not be left completely untouched, slave, not as you were in your father's house. Sigurr will yet have squirmings from you."

With a cry of dismay the female was taken a number of paces to the right of my enclosure, where a small door stood in the wall. As the two disappeared a heavy silence descended, broken only when Sadrin reappeared alone a hand of reckid later and came to stand before my enclosure.

"And here is another who has not been chosen," said the male, his tone and look different from that given to the slave female. "In your case it was instructions from the Prince which kept you from an altar, for surely would I have chosen you myself had I not been told you were to be taught the alternative to sharing a man's devotions. From the look of you, I think the lesson will not need to be taught a second time."

The male's words made little sense, yet was I not to be left to ponder them. He bent and opened the enclosure beyond my head, the opposite side from which I had entered, then reached within and took me by the hair as he had done with the slave female. It was surely my intention to struggle against being done so, yet was it all I was able to do to crawl from the enclosure at the urging of the pull upon my hair. The stiffness and ache in my body was greater than I had thought it would be, greater than that brought one from lying in wait upon the hunt. I held my breath as I crawled beyond the enclosure, refusing to give voice to the pain, and he who held my hair made a strange sound in his throat.

"No screams of pain?" he asked, in some manner pleased. "No begging for mercy? Indeed do you seem to be the warrior the Prince named you, and such is a great pity. The true warrior does badly in prolonged slavery, a state you have little hope of escaping. Should the Prince fail to claim you as a mate, as now seems likely, you will serve men as long as you breed desire in them, which will undoubtedly be for some time yet. Let us see if you are able to walk."

The prattling of the male was of little interest to me, all save the last of it. Indeed was I full eager to regain the ability of walking without pain, yet regaining the ability proved of little value. My steps, directed by the male, took me to the doorway the slave female had been taken through, and sudden struggle did not prove sufficient to loosen the hold the male had upon me. Without surprise or protest the male tightened his grip, and then I was through the doorway and into the small room beyond.

The room itself was bare save for three strange devices of wood, one of which already held the slave female Cynena. The devices seemed no more than sheets of wood with narrow circles held upon four short legs of the same wood, the entire thing clear in the light streaming through two wide-flung windows. The male Sadrin forced me to one of the devices, raised the top of the circle with his free hand, then pushed me within the remaining half of the circle, closing the top before I might straighten up again. In such a manner was I then placed as the slave female had been, belly down within the now close circle, held in place and unable to squirm free. Turning my head to the left showed me half of the slave female, the nether half; as she faced the door, I faced one of the bright, open windows.

"The time grows short before I must be at my devotions," said Sadrin from behind me, his hand suddenly about my left ankle. Having been put within the device had taken my feet from the floor, and now was there the claps of metal about my ankle, quickly followed by the same about my second ankle. The slave female, too, had been done so, and I knew not the necessity for such. I could not have taken myself from the tight circle of wood about my waist even without the chain.

"Now are you both prepared," said the male, the sound of his steps taking him farther away. "When the bell signals the time for devotions, there will be others here to see to you. Do not forget what was done—or the reason for it—lest you find yourself done so again. I am told that once is quite enough."

Again the sound of footsteps came, signaling his departure, and silence closed all about us like the folds of a heavy cloth. The slave female to my left stirred with the sound of chain, and I, too, felt the discomfort of the position we had been left in. Though the circle of wood had been padded to near softness, the bottom length of wood separating my arms from my legs was rough and splintered in places, as though the claws of some child of the wild had torn at it. Raising my head showed me naught save an open window I could not reach and a slave bottom I had no interest in, therefore did I allow my head to hang to keep the strain from my neck as I waited.

I had little notion of what it was I awaited, yet the tolling of the bell I had heard earlier in the fey was surely a part of it. The slave female stirred again as the sound rang clearly in the confines of the strange prison we shared, and then, above the tolling, came the sound of a number of hurrying footsteps. The footsteps approached and entered, and the sound of breathless laughter entered with them.

"You see, there is indeed one for each of us," said a voice, a young, high voice, that of a boy. "We were not given two for the same slave."

"I have never seen two being done at once," said a second voice, also young, also male. "Are we to do them together?"

"Certainly," replied the first boy, smugly confident. "There is scarcely time to do one after the other. Do you need to be shown how?"

"No more than you!" snapped the second boy, anger and affronted dignity clear in his tone. "This is not the first time I have done a slave!"

"Well, then, get on with it," laughed the first boy, and with an indignant huff the one who was obviously the second appeared by the back of the slave female, a large something held carefully wrapped in a cloth of black.

"What do you children do here?" demanded the slave female in a trembling voice, a growing fear draining the snap of command she had attempted. "Leave here at once, do you hear me? At once!"

"Silence, slave," grumbled the boy behind her, young yet not too young to have commanded slaves. "What we do here will soon become quite apparent. I see you have need of some oil."

The slave female gasped as the boy put a hand to her, yet I merely stiffened as the same was done to me. The indignation the female was taken with touched me not at all, yet the struggle I attempted was as fruitless as her action. We were to be done in some manner by these boys, and there was no escaping it.

"There is always a need for oil," laughed the boy behind me, a faint sound of cloth being unwrapped accompanying his words. "I was told by a warrior that they would be upon an altar rather than here if there was no such need."

"I shall do with only a touch of it," sniffed the second boy, not to be made to feel less experienced and knowledgeable. "Here, just within her, and then she must provide her own."

"What do you do?" screamed the slave female as the boy

touched her again, causing her to pull against the ankle chains. "How dare you touch me so? How dare you— No!"

The last word was a scream indeed, for the boy had unwrapped his burden and presented it to her inner thighs. Large was the instrument, far longer than anything she might be able to take, wood at its base, skin-covered where it would touch her. With little feeling for what he did, the boy twisted the instrument about, forcing it within the slave female despite her screams and struggles. To the very end of the skin covering it went, and suddenly the slave female moved not at all.

"You have not told them what we were instructed to tell them," said the boy behind me, and then did I feel the touch of something other than fingers. "All females save those who are ill, aged, infirm or with child must be filled during the time of devotions to blessed Sigurr. Should you prefer to be filled with something other than wood, you must strive to be pleasing to the men of this house. When we have become men, we, too, will insist that you be pleasing."

"I will be pleasing!" whispered the slave female, her body remaining as rigid as it had been. "I swear I will be pleasing! I will be anything you wish, only take that monstrous thing from within me!"

"We are not yet done," chided the boy behind her, annoyed with her words, his pettish tone covering the small gasp forced from me as the instrument was worked as quickly and deeply within me as it had been put within the slave female. Indeed was the feel of it beyond description, more painful and paralyzing than pleasurable. A male of size and strength brings great joy to a warrior, yet the Instrument was of covered wood, too large and unyielding for joy, wielded by a boy who knew naught of what he did. I closed my eyes and scraped at the wood beneath my hands, unable to reach the place of torment to force the terrible thing from me.

The screams of the slave female quickly began filling the air of the room, fear and pain and humiliation striking ear and nerves alike. Well did I know the reason for her screams, for the boy who tormented me had begun to move the instrument he held as though he used me, in and out, harshly and with strength, performing a task he had no true knowledge of. Despite the pain, I could not keep from moving with the thrust, a small reaction compared with that of the slave female. She, treated more harshly by the boy who did her, kicked and writhed and wept as though taken by madness. My claws did not quite tear at the wood beneath my hands, yet was it a near thing. For a warrior to be treated so and unable to claim vengeance brought on a madness of its own.

It seemed the doing would never cease, and when it did it did not cease entirely. The boy withdrew the monstrous instrument after a final thrust, yet a brief moment later another thing was slid within to replace it, a thing of cold wetness, considerably smaller than the instrument, which brought a shudder to me. The slave female moaned low, evidently having the same done to her, and then was there the feel of leather being tied, first at my left hip, then at my right, last about my waist just above the hips. With the tying done the hands removed themselves from me, leaving the cold wetness within, held in place by the leather which had been tied to me. I hung with head down from the circle of wood, some of my hair tumbled to the stone floor before me, finding little gratitude for the soothing which was beginning from the presence of the cold wetness. The shame I felt was not as deep as it would have been had I not known the ways of city males, yet was there shame enough to bow my head and fill my heart with bitterness. The true shame was the foolishness of Jalav, who had not the wisdom to keep far from males and their doings. Should she ever again find the freedom of the forests, the error would not be repeated.

Their task seen to, the boys who had tormented the slave female and myself took themselves off, laughing between themselves over the successful performance of their duties. For a number of long reckid we were left to ourselves in the warm, fresh-aired silence, and then came the sounds of many folk returning to that which they had abandoned a short while ago. Well pleased was the laughter of the males, the shrill, higher pitched laughter of the females matching it, and then was there the sound of further steps within the room which held me. A male appeared as he approached the slave female, and at the same time there came the touch of hands at my ankles, releasing the chains. I stirred as the chains fell away, desperately anxious to reach and remove that which had been placed within me, yet such a thing was not in accordance with the will of the males. Two there were who removed me from the wooden circle, they catching at my hands when I immediately reached for the leather at my waist, holding me tight as I thoughtlessly began to struggle, then laughing as I froze with a gasp. The thing within was not to be ignored, sending added flashes of weakness through my body as the males forced motion upon me, taking me toward the wall beneath one of the wide windows. Once there, I was put to my knees below the bottom of the window, my arms were forced behind me, and slim, rounded cuffs were closed about my wrists. A single pull showed that the chain between the cuffs was held in some manner at the wall, tying my arms and disallowing the rising from my heels. The two males who had put me there straightened with grins of satisfaction, then one crouched before me.

"The loss of your use was a great loss indeed, lovely slave," said he, raising his hands to touch the tips of my breasts. "You must see to it that such a loss does not occur again. It gives a man little pleasure to see a wench writhe to the urgings of a device rather than his own doings. Are you not eager now to give men the pleasure due them?"

That I did not gasp again was due only to great effort, for the touch of hands upon my breasts had caused me to move, again awakening the thing within me to motion. It was then that the second male reached toward me with a laugh, touching the thing held close with leather and pushing it farther within. Where the boys, in their ignorance, had caused naught save pain, the elder male knew well what he was about; his touch caused me to bend low with a moan, again bringing laughter to him and his companion.

"This packing is meant to take the pain from you," said the second, moving the thing gently about with his fingers, driving me near to insanity. "It will remain with you till all your pain is gone, and you are again prepared to serve men. Are men not preferable to a thing such as this?"

Had I been able to speak, I would undoubtedly have brought further punishment and pain upon myself, therefore was it fortunate that I was unable to speak of what manner in which I most wished to serve males. The two before me amused themselves a bit longer; then did they straighten and walk from me, chuckling as they quitted the room. I remained as they had placed me, on my knees, wrists held tight behind, head hung low against the flame which raced through my blood, at first unaware of the sound which came from the slave female. She, as I, had been placed beneath a window by a male, one who had undoubtedly done to her that which the other two had done to me. Only slowly did her weeping penetrate the thick wall of shame and fury and need which surrounded me, bringing my head up to see how pitifully hopeless she appeared where she knelt, her head as low to her thighs as the chain upon her wrists allowed, her slender body shaking to the sobs which wracked her. Much did her weeping seem that of a small child, now filled with pain and fear and deep hurt from that which she had never before been subjected to. Mighty indeed were these males, to so quickly diminish so terrible a thing as a city female such as Cynena. I moved my wrists within the circles of metal which held them, then returned to my own thoughts.

Nearly a hin passed before those from the outer room again took note of the slave female and myself. Two rosy-breasted slave females entered carrying good-sized wooden pots, the aroma arising from those pots saying they held a meat stew of some sort. Behind them walked Sadrin, his presence causing the two slaves to move with care and extreme nervousness. The first of the slave females was directed to crouch before the female Cynena, who did no more than raise her head very slightly till she became aware of Sadrin. Once the golden-haired male's presence was known to her, she began trembling as a leaf trembles in a wind, then quickly accepted the provender brought to her lips by the wooden device males called spoon. In such a manner was one slave fed by another, their doings briefly watched by the male. When he had satisfied himself that all was as he wished it, he then turned his attention to me.

The second slave had crouched before me, her offensive red covering spreading to bare her leg to the left, her hand raising the filled wooden spoon to my lips. There was little room for movement as I was, yet was I able to straighten myself away from the offering, refusing the provender without words. The slave before me grew greatly upset, far more so than her master, who had observed the by-play. Sadrin moved closer so that he might stand above me, his face again wearing that same odd expression.

"Do you wish to be beaten, slave?" he asked, looking down upon me. "You have been ordered to eat, and will do so immediately!"

I made answer by meeting his eyes, and spoke no words to add to what was quickly understood by the male. No captive willingly partakes of the provender insultingly granted by her enemies; sooner would she accept what pain was offered. Little dignity was allowed me in the position I had been forced to, yet was my meaning made clear to the male.

"How foolish you are, slave," said Sadrin, straightening where he stood and folding his arms. "You think to accept punishment rather than sustenance, the former being more palatable to one such as yourself, yet you will not be allowed such a choice. After the punishment you will be made to accept the sustenance as well, and all the pain will be for naught. Should there be the least amount of wisdom within you, wench, you will accept your new lot rather than struggle to deny it. Take the food *now*, and prepare yourself for pleasure rather than pain."

Again I spoke no words in answer, yet the scorn I felt was surely clear in my eyes. To capture a war leader was not to conquer her, and to speak of pain was not to frighten her. I had made the acquaintance of true fear and deep pain, and though I would not willingly face them again, neither would I cringe from them like a craven. There was time enough to consider defeat when I was no longer able to hold myself with dignity.

"So you continue to refuse," said Sadrin, his voice uninflected. "I find myself touched with a strange sadness, for it will not be pleasant to see you succumb at the end of your strength. Sooner would I have you bend than break; a pity bending is disallowed by your nature. I will now fetch those who will see to you."

Unfolding his arms, the male turned away to the doorway, yet did he halt no more than two paces toward it. Coming through the doorway were Mehrayn and Famsyn, the black of their body cloths and shoulder strokes a sobering note among the bright colors of the others. The two Sigurri looked only toward Sadrin, yet the slave female Cynena gasped low and paled, then attempted to hide herself. A second gasp followed to color her cheeks as the device within her shifted to her movement, and deep misery took her completely. The last of the stew was then being given her, and though she clearly wished no more of it, she found herself unable to refuse. Head bent low, eyes closed, she continued to do as she had been commanded, as one who approached the end of life; all she possessed had been taken from Cynena, and therefore was there naught left to be lost save life itself.

"Sadrin, how goes it?" called Mehrayn, his spirits clearly high as he approached the golden-haired male. "The meal you provided for us was as perfect as ever, greatly satisfying after strenuous devotions."

"Your satisfaction is mine, my Prince," answered Sadrin with a bow, obviously pleased with Mehrayn's words. "May I do a further service for you or the Prince Bersyn?"

Mehrayn's lips parted to reply, yet an exclamation from Bersyn halted his words. The second Sigurri had looked upon me with amusement as Mehrayn and Sadrin spoke, and then his gaze had drifted lazily to the female Cynena. Clearly had Bersyn expected to see me in the room, yet equally as clearly was the sight of Cynena unexpected. The male left Mehrayn's side to stride quickly to the female, then put the other slave female aside so that he might crouch before her who knelt chained with head down.

"Cynena, what do you do here, marked as a slave?" he demanded, putting his two large hands to the female's face so that he might raise it to his own. "What has happened to your father and your suitors, that such a thing might come to be?"

"Bersyn, I beg you, do not look upon me in my shame," whispered Cynena, silent tears rolling from her still-closed eyes. "I am no more than a slave now, to be beaten and humiliated at the bidding of men. Offer me no kindness, for I will surely have naught of kindness from others."

"I do not understand!" protested Bersyn, releasing the female and straightening to glare at Mehrayn and Sadrin. "For what reason was Cynena declared slave?"

"The choice was her father's," answered Mehrayn, his voice a calm which was meant to calm Bersyn. "Not only did she continue to refuse all suitors, she even began to insist that she be left untouched during devotions. The altered slaves sent to fill her to Sigurr's glory were refused admittance to her apartment, shocking all who heard of the sacrilege. Her father found himself with little choice, therefore did he allow her to be declared slave."

"Is this true, Cynena?" Bersyn asked, turning again to send a frown to the slave at his feet. "For what reason would you commit such sacrilege?"

"I loathe the use of slaves," the female whispered, her head as low as her voice. "Never have I received true pleasure from one, therefore did I seek to avoid the use of all men. You are all alike, each of you, and I would run from you if I could, yet will I obey my father should he appear, for I loathe even more the life of a slave."

"So all men are alike, are they?" mused Bersyn, continuing to stare down at the slave. "Free men and male slaves have little in common save their beginnings, yet no sheltered female would know this. As you had knowingly and willingly descended to sacrilege, it is clearly for the best that you were declared slave. As such, you will quickly be shown the power of a free man."

No more than an instant passed before Cynena understood the meaning of the words Bersyn spoke, and her head snapped up to allow her to stare at him wide-eyed.

"Bersyn, no!" she begged, kept from writhing in distress only by cause of the device within her. "I could not bear to be used as a slave by a man I knew when free! I would die of humiliation! Have I not been humiliated enough?"

"Apparently not," said Sadrin from where he stood beside Mehrayn, a coldness in his voice. "How have you been taught to address a free man, wench? Do you require further punishment to remind you?"

"No, master!" gasped the female Cynena, fear clearly touching her as she again looked up at Bersyn. "I beg you, master, choose another to vent your need upon! I would give you little pleasure, even though I were punished for the lack! I have little of the desire granted other women, and therefore little passion to give!"

"All women are filled with an equal amount of passion, wench," said Bersyn, crouching again before the female. "With some, such passion is easily released, with others, a greater effort is necessary. I do not believe too great an effort will be necessary with you."

With the last of his words, the male's hand moved to the body of the female, bringing her a horrified gasp as she attempted in vain to rise from her heels. Escaping the touch was more than impossible, and quickly did her eyes close as her body shuddered to a moan.

"Scarcely my concept of cold and unwilling," chuckled Bersyn, closely observing the helpless writhings of the female beneath his hand. "Mehrayn: I ask the favor of the use of this slave. What say you?"

"How may I deny you, brother?" returned the larger Sigurri, obviously amused. "Are you not a guest in my house? Take her when you will, and keep her as long as you wish."

"My thanks, brother," laughed Bersyn, taking no note of the renewed weeping and head shaking of the female before him. Quickly did he lean behind her to release the cuffs at her wrists, and just as quickly did he throw her to his shoulder once she was free. The female gurgled and choked at the sensations forced upon her by such brisk handling, then began a wailing cry when Bersyn's hand went to the round bottom so easily reached upon his shoulder. Her small fists beat at his back as he paused for a final word with Mehrayn, and then another distress came to her.

"Bersyn, I am uncovered!" she cried, her misery clearly to be heard. "I will die of shame if I am carried through the halls uncovered—and with that—that—*thing* in me! You must remove it and give me my draping!"

"Perhaps I will not carry you through the halls so," said Bersyn, his hand stroking her bottom. "Perhaps I will walk about all of the level instead, seeking out old friends. By what name did you call me, slave?"

"Master!" shrieked the female, clutching at his back as his hand saw to her again. "Master, do not shame your slave!"

"A slave cannot be shamed," said Bersyn, working her so deeply that all save mewling was beyond her. In such a manner did he bear her from the room, beyond all protests, and the two remaining males turned their deep amusement to me.

"And what of that one, Sadrin?" asked Mehrayn, slowly coming forward with the other to stand before me. "Has she, too, been taught to call men master?"

"Scarcely, my Prince," snorted Sadrin, his gaze unwaveringly upon me. "She has even refused to take sustenance. I was about to have her beaten when you arrived."

"Beaten," echoed Mehrayn, staring down upon me with no further evidence of amusement. "I much doubt that it would be the first time. Why do you refuse to bow to necessity, wench? Are you one who craves pain as others crave pleasure?"

"I am a warrior," I informed him, speaking the words though I knew them useless. "A warrior may be bested by the edge of a sword and in no other manner. A pity your fear is too great to face me, male."

Sadrin drew himself up in anger, preparing to speak, yet Mehrayn gestured him to silence, then crouched before me.

"Do you believe I have never stood in battle against another?" he asked, his deep voice calm and somewhat saddened. "A true warrior faces all who challenge him, whether or not he is filled with fear. The point which seems beyond you, warrior, is that I have no need to face you, for you are female. There are other things a man may do with a female, things a female may not refuse him. What sense is there for you to cause men to give you pain, when you may not deny them? A captured male warrior is of little use to men; a captured female warrior may be put to the same use as other females. Whether or not she is a warrior—she remains a female."

So intent was his expression, so grave the look in his light eyes; in Mida's name, I knew not how I might reply to him. The male spoke what he saw as truth, from a view I had no understanding of.

"I am a warrior born as well as by choice," I groped at last, held by his sober green gaze. "Of a certainty I am female, for how else might I be Midanna? The doings of males are less than nothing to me, for they are the enemies of Midanna. I care naught for what they do with their females, for I am not one of them. Why, then, would I concern myself with any thought other than escape from them? To consider their wishes and desires would be more than foolish.''

"You believe yourself female in no more than form?" scoffed Sadrin when Mehrayn did not reply. "Do you fail to realize that you need be female in no other way? That should you refuse to bow to the will of men, they will break you?''

"Sooner broken than bowed!" I snapped, sending my anger toward the golden-haired male. "And I believe myself female in all ways save as a slave-female! I am a warrior and war leader, male, and would be no other thing even at the cost of my freedom! Were I to give over being what I am merely by cause of chains and a lash, surely I would not have been that thing to begin with!"

"And from us you expect a lash as well as chains, for we are your enemy," Mehrayn suddenly put in, a strange anger upon him. "Were we to stand aside and allow you to do as you pleased, we would be weak; as we protect the lives and well-being of our people by restraining you, we are your enemy! The outlook is one more suited to a savage than a warrior, yet I shall not attempt to take it from you! Enemy you have named me, and enemy I will remain!"

Quickly, then, did he lean past me to release the chains which held me to the wall, immediately thereafter throwing me to his shoulder as Bersyn had done with the female Cynena. Great fury flared within me that I might be done the same as a slave female, yet another thing also flared within me, bringing forth a gasp I could not withhold. Frantically I attempted to reach the leather about my waist which held the device in place, yet Mehrayn took hold of my wrist and then strode from the room, his large fingers clamped tight about my wrist, his arm about my legs. My hair hung free and brushed the floor, yet he took no note of it.

The long, angry stride of the male quickly ate the distance between the chamber of my capture and another chamber, one of greater size than that in which I had awakened. Once within, I discovered that Mehrayn had also taken the shackle which had held me, for I was placed upon a low, wide pile of furs upon my back, my wrists then being taken above my head and in some manner again fixed to the wall. With teeth gritted I sought to turn about and move forward so that I might reach myself, yet this the male would not allow. He sat himself facing me, his hand grasping my thigh, his eyes showing full awareness of my desperation.

"For one who will not allow capture to affect her, you seem quite discomforted, wench," he observed. "Were I a friend and comrade to you, I would surely have offered my assistance; as an enemy, I shall do no more than enjoy your difficulty. And this magnificent body of yours."

His free hand then came to touch and stroke me, firing my blood, yet I dared not writhe. The furs which held me were very soft and thick, yet I dared not think of the manner in which they caressed my flesh. I wished to throw my head about, yet found myself unable to do so; my hair lay trapped beneath me, held by a weight I could not move. The desperation I had felt increased more than I would have believed possible, and yet, through it all, I felt the disturbance which had come to touch me with the rest.

How angered Mehrayn had become when I had named males as enemies to Midanna! Surely did it seem that the male felt betrayed, yet in what manner I could not imagine. With all that males had done to myself and my warriors, were we to name them friend? I gazed upon the male who now raised himself from the fur as he looked upon me, who spread my knees with his hands so that he might kneel between them. Was it a friend who had kept me slave in his household, a comrade who now placed his hands to either side of my body so that his lips might reach me more easily? It was clear he would not use me, for his body cloth had not been removed. He meant to do no more than fire me with need and humiliation, and this was not an enemy? His lips lowered to my throat, drawing a moan with the touch and his nearness, and I found I must fight to speak.

"The Sigurri, too, were kept from taking vengeance among the Midanna," I gasped, my head awhirl with the smell of him. "They, too, were stripped of dignity in the process, as well as denied all chance to regain their honor. To do others as he was done is surely the right of a Sigurri."

Mehrayn raised his head to look upon me with startlement, then sat back upon his heels to stare. A long moment passed in such contemplation, and then his hand came to my side.

"I had forgotten," said he, his tone quieter and without anger. "My brothers did indeed wish for vengeance for what was done to them, and were promised that vengeance and then allowed the opportunity to take it. You have not been accorded the same honorable treatment, and therefore do you see us as rogues and enemies. You are not wrong in feeling as you do—yet, at the same time, you are very wrong."

The sigh which took him was deep and deeply felt, and he seemed much concerned with searching for further words. Though I wished otherwise, he had not removed himself from between my knees, nor did he seem prepared to do so. I began to shift with extreme care, and again he leaned down toward me.

"Wench, I do not wish to face you with swords!" said he, an earnestness strongly upon him. "I have met and bested every challenger to face me, yet I would not find myself able to plunge a sword deep within this body of yours! The right of challenge is surely a thing due you, yet I could not face you myself, nor allow another to do so."

"For the reason that I am a slave?" I rasped, looking up at the green eyes so close above me. "For the reason that I am no more than merely female to you and those about you?"

"For the reason that I find myself in love with you!" he snapped, placing his hands to either side of my body again. "Do you think me blind to the warrior you are, the warrior who would surely best any number of those who faced her? It matters little which of us is most skilled with a sword, wench. Should I find the need to face you, you will surely have my life, for I could not strike at you, nor allow another to do so while I lived! No matter the right or the wrong of it, I shall not allow you the challenge till the fey I wish an end to life!"

Surely must I have appeared most foolish then, my eyes wide, my voice silenced in shock, my body held rigidly still. The words of the male had set my thoughts whirling even faster than his nearness, confusion covering me and taking the breath from my throat. This concept of "love" had been presented me before, by other males, yet never in the manner of this Sigurri. I well understood the thought he had voiced, the concept of being unable to harm another for whom one felt a strangeness, and yet—never had a male spoken so, at the same time praising my skill as a warrior. I knew not what words to speak in reply—save that I remained a warrior of Mida, pledged to her service.

"Above that, you have little cause for complaint," continued Mehrayn, a faint amusement taking the sharpness from his eyes and voice. "As you, yourself, pointed out, my brothers and I were held as slaves by you and your wenches. Is the fact that I now hold you as slave not an equitable reversal? I, personally, find it highly enjoyable as well as equitable, for I could not see a free woman done the same as a slave. I could not touch her—nor taste her—nor use her—as I do a slave. Have I a right to my slave—or have I not?"

Those green eyes now gazed upon me in amusement, yet they also awaited a response. My lips parted to supply that response, yet no words came forth to fill the silence which had been mine since the discussion took on its strangeness. Mida! Of a certainty a warrior was entitled to repay slavery with slavery, yet how might I condone such a thing done to me? To deny Mehrayn a right I had myself indulged in would be dishonorable, yet wherein lay the honor in declaring myself his? Without thought I began to move in upset, then drew my breath in sharply as Mehrayn chuckled. The male knew well what I had caused myself to feel, and anger at his amusement at last brought me words.

"The slavery of the Sigurri beneath the sway of Midanna was brief!" I snapped, taking care to remain still. "As they were released, so must this Midanna be released, and that right quickly!"

"More quickly than my brothers and myself?" laughed Mehrayn, sliding his hands beneath my back as he leaned the closer. "No, wench, no more quickly than we were done, for I have not yet had all the pleasure I wish from you. I doubt I shall ever have all the pleasure I wish, yet do I fully intend to make an effort toward that end." His lips then lowered to mine, briefly, gently, a touch meant to do no more than caress. "Come the new light you will again be free, yet for the balance of this fey and the darkness following, are you my slave," said he. "You must obey me, and give me much pleasure and amusement, for that is the lot of a slave. Let us begin immediately."

Again his lips took mine, disallowing the indignant response I had begun, his tongue attempting to reach mine. In my annoyance I refused to allow this, then immediately regretted the refusal. The body of the male suddenly thrust at mine, driving deep the device which had me, forcing my lips wide in a gasp. Instantly then, was the male in possession of that which he wished, and I left moaning and pulling at the chains which held my wrists.

During the following hind I was much used, yet not as quickly as I would have wished. The male Mehrayn, insistent upon the point that he must do me as a slave for the short while I remained a slave, continued with me as he had begun. That I was able to remain unmoving while his hands and lips touched everywhere was not to his liking, therefore did his hands raise my bottom while his tongue sought my soul. The scream forced from me echoed again and again to his great delight, each gentle caress causing frenzied movement and further screams. The doing went on and on till I wept like the slave he had named me, ending at last when his hands went to the leather about my waist. I clearly recall the great joy I felt that I was soon to be free of the maddening device, and also the great horror upon realizing that freeing me was not Mehrayn's intention. The male spoke gently of the insult I had given him after having been declared a slave, and then proceeded to punish his slave for the great insolence. Indeed was I then made to weep, for Mehrayn was a male who knew well the needs and vulnerabilities which are a warrior's, using them to take vengeance for insult given. When I had howled out an incoherent apology he ceased, yet still took care not to remove the device. The hip leather remained to hold it somewhat in place as he took me in his arms, then allowed me the privilege of attempting to convince him to remove the hip leather as well. Through heavy tears I saw to the need that had become great necessity, greater than the shame brought about by such an act.

Deep pleasure was thoroughly enjoyed by Mehrayn before his slave was at last allowed her relief, before the device was slowly withdrawn from her body. The glimpse of the life of a true slave was highly dismaying, for I had found that courage and determination were not sufficient to keep one from acts which would be despised by all who witnessed them. Far better to keep oneself from slavery even at the price of one's life, I thought as I moved with some comfort upon the furs. To be given the choice between life and death was to be given all, yet Mehrayn had given me no such choice. The slaves of these Sigurri were made to obey, without choice, without dignity, without volition. I thought perhaps it was that that Mehrayn had wished to show me, that and the necessity he had spoken of, yet I had little time to consider the point. Again was I taken in the male's arms, and this time it was clear that his body cloth was no longer with him.

When the need was gone from both of us, Mehrayn stretched out beside me upon the furs, his hand slowly stroking my middle. I stirred in the chains which held me at his side, his for the taking, yet continued to fail to find the means of releasing myself. The chains would not be released, I had been told, till I regained my freedom, and though I found their presence a heavy burden, there was naught I might do to remove them. Mehrayn stretched hard, causing his muscles to crack, then moved nearer so that he might look down upon me.

"Come the new light, you will be taken to the forests where your weapons will be returned," said he, beginning to trace the bones of my face with one finger. "Aysayn may not return for feyd yet, for this is not a time when the Golden Mask need be filled."

"What mask do you speak of?" I asked, unconsciously pulling at the chains once more. To be free again with a sword at my side!

"The Mask of the Shadow is worn whenever the Shadow appears in public," said Mehrayn. "It is solid gold, cast in the features of immortal Sigurr, meant to show that he who is Shadow speaks not for himself but for the god. The people have never seen Aysayn in his true self, and never shall. No Shadow would put himself above Sigurr."

"No one has seen him?" I asked, failing to comprehend his words. To attempt to be any other than oneself is a foolishness which should be beyond even males. "How, then, do the Sigurri know it is Aysayn upon whom they look?"

"What other would be behind the Golden Mask?" Mehrayn smiled, seemingly amused. "And of course there are those who have seen him. His woman Ladayna knows him, as do the members of his personal guard, and I, myself, grew to manhood with him."

"Exceedingly strange," I pronounced, wondering at the doings of these Sigurri. "And for what reason do I now await Aysayn in the woods with my weapons rather than here and without them?"

"For the reason that I have recently received unexpected word," said he, bringing a second hand to my face. "Ten feyd farther south lies a small city of those who long ago turned their backs upon blessed Sigurr to follow the twisted Oneness. From time to time they march out to harass us, stealing wenches and girl children when they are able, and I have just learned that they now prepare to march. This time we will march first, catching them at their own city, perhaps taking back what has previously been stolen from us. Considering the time I shall be gone, I cannot leave you here, and as a slave. The forest will be best for you, even should you turn about and immediately seek vengeance."

His final words were spoken with no question in them, making it clear that he no longer sought a vow from me on the matter. I considered him in silence for a brief moment, then asked, "And how am I to learn of Aysayn's return? Should I be in the forest and he in the city, my task will remain unseen to."

"I will have one of my men bring you word of his return," smiled Mehrayn, seemingly greatly pleased with some matter. Perhaps he thought that my presence in the woods would preclude my taking vengeance, yet such was not so. One may take vengeance first and then retire to the woods. Filled then with pleasure, the male again touched his lips to mine and continued, "As for the love I spoke of, I could not but note that you failed to reply in a like manner. Perhaps you are wiser than I, for we yet have the strangers to face. Afterward, should we both fail to find the final glory, I will press you for the lesser glory we may find together.''

His lips then came to me for a longer time, making it unnecessary that I attempt a reply. In truth, I knew not what such a response should be, and for many reasons. Had I been in search of a male for my home tent among the Hosta, surely would Mehrayn have been acceptable. His strength and humor and ability to give pleasure were great indeed, and more than that he knew me as a warrior and found no disapproval in the state. He, however, was not alone in consideration, for there was another who brought thoughts of strangeness to this warrior. That this other was one who found little approval in warriorhood seemed unimportant to that within me which desired him, yet was that desire, and any other of the same sort, destined to be idle. Jalav rode in Mida's cause which did not, in any pleasant manner, concern males.

The kiss given by Mehrayn was of no short duration, nor were his hands idle during the time. He made free with me as I lay chained, just as though I were truly a slave. My body gave him the response my mind would have chosen to withhold, and he laughed at that which he called slave-eagerness even as he caused me to jump and writhe. He toyed with me a considerable time before granting me use, a slow, agonizing, drawn-out use which saw to my needs only after I had been reduced to begging. Such begging was good for a female's soul, the male maintained with a laugh as he slid lazily about within me, then did he suddenly begin to seek his pleasure in earnest. I drowned beneath that which he forced upon me, gasping at the change, and barely had the strength, when it was done, to sink my teeth into his shoulder as he lay upon me. He shouted in pain and pulled loose from the feeble grip my teeth had taken, throwing himself to the furs beside me where he sat to stare at my grim satisfaction.

"Jalav is no slave," I said, my fists pulling at the chains which bound me. "Perhaps this fact has escaped your memory, male."

"Male, is it?" said he, rubbing at his shoulder as his stare hardened. "Perhaps it is you who has forgotten, wench. I am master in this house, and it is not I who wears chains."

He turned then and rose to his feet, striding at once toward the door of the room. Throwing it open he shouted for a slave, waited impatiently for the hurried appearance of a red-clad, rosy-breasted female, then spoke rapid commands. The female bowed in acknowledgment and departed as rapidly as she had come, and Mehrayn swung the door to once more, strode to a small platform, and began to fill a tall, metal goblet from a larger pot. Once his drink had filled the goblet, he carried it to a window and stood silently staring out.

For the first time since I had been brought there, I was able to look about the room. It was immediately clear that it was not like the one I had awakened in, for it was considerably larger and contained many more items than the other had had. Rather than two windows this room had four, two in the wall directly opposite where I lay, two in the wall to the right. All four stood opened wide, allowing in a pleasant movement of air which cooled the area more than two would have done. Upon the rock of the floor was a black floor cloth, thick and soft, touched here and there about its edges by long, golden cloth hangings. In and about the hangings upon the walls were shields and weapons, some well-used and clearly old, some equally well-used yet newer and in condition to be used again. Candle sconces also lined the walls, some black, some gold, all unlit candles within them white save for the one above the black altar, which stood between the windows to my right. Between the windows directly ahead was a round platform surrounded by four leather covered seats, naught to be seen upon the platform which would speak of its purpose. Other, smaller platforms stood about the room, one with goblets and drink upon it, one with large pot and water holder upon it, one with flowers, two others empty. A hand of low, leather-covered seats also stood in a circle in the center of the room, and in the corner to my right stood a large, metal bound wooden chest. I thought the room most likely Mehrayn's, and not only by cause of the presence of weapons. The black altar was larger than the others I had seen, a wide, well-made sword hanging point down and unsheathed above it and below the black candle. She who was taken upon that altar would be twice beneath Sigurr's Sword, two equally undesirable conditions to my humor at that time.

Mehrayn continued to stand unspeaking by the window a number of reckid, drinking now and then from the goblet he held, and then a thought came to him. He turned and retraced his steps near to where I lay, retrieved his body cloth and donned it, then returned to the window. The late-fey light continued to be bright and pleasant, far more pleasant than my position in that city of males. The Sigurri had ignored my presence as though I were a platform or a seat—or perhaps the slave he had named me. I felt a great impatience to be done with the foolishness of being chained, and to be on my way again to freedom. I stirred upon the over-warm furs and pulled at the metal upon my wrists, yet the metal took as small note of my displeasures as had the male.

A moment after Mehrayn had returned to the window, the door to the room opened a small way to admit, one after the other, four of the slave females. Each of the females carried a wooden pot containing small and varied bits of provender, and after each female had slipped within, the last of them reclosed the door. The four, in a body, then approached where Mehrayn stood, halted perhaps two paces from him and slipped to their knees, then bowed with heads to the floor while their hands held the pots up toward the male as far as they were able. Not a word had been spoken by the four, yet they knew as well as I that Mehrayn was aware of their presence. That he chose to refrain from acknowledging them was his right, said their slavish poses, an attitude which again set me pulling at the chain which bound me.

A full hand of reckid passed before the male turned from the window, walked to refill his goblet, then returned to look down upon those who knelt to him. Little pleasure was to be seen in his eyes for the space of three heartbeats, and then a deep breath took the silence of dark thought from him.

"A tempting variety," said the male, looking upon both the provender and the females. "You four may rise and follow me now, for there are a number of tasks to be seen to."

The females scrambled quickly and carefully to their feet, yet Mehrayn had not awaited their rising. He strode past them to where I lay, stepped onto the fur, then crouched beside me.

"You appear displeased with the very proper actions of your sisters, little slave," said he to me, sipping at the drink he held. "It seems difficult for you to grasp the true nature of the position you now occupy which, under other circumstances, could well cost your life. One must learn to walk softly when one is in chains, else is it often difficult to find one's way out of them. For the time you remain my slave, this lesson will be taught you."

I gazed up at him where he crouched drinking his drink, lacking understanding of why he spoke as he did. Had he been treated as I had been, would he not have done as I had?

"I believe I know what thought now occupies your mind," he said of a sudden, studying me through narrowed eyes. "You feel that should I be made to take your place, I, too, would behave as you have. A pity you are entirely mistaken."

He abandoned his crouch to sit upon the fur beside me, then gestured the slave females to their knees about us. One, bearing a pot of mixed meat and vegetable bits, was near enough for Mehrayn to reach to easily; he did so, then ate in silence for a moment before continuing.

"My brothers and I had not been in captivity long in Bellinard when you arrived," said he, "yet the captivity had not been an easy one. We had gone to the city to learn what we might of it against a possible time of conflict with its inhabitants, an excellent suggestion made by the Shadow's woman, Ladayna. Once there, we quickly discovered that we had made an error in believing we had brought enough trade goods to obtain a sufficient amount of city coin to see us through the visit. Fully half of our furs and jewels were taken when we first set foot in the city, the High Seat's just portion, it was called; scarcely just *or* fair, yet what were we to do? We paid the levy, then rode within to sell what was left to us, only to find that all those who bought furs and jewels offered the same price, one considerably below the true value of the goods. After the same insulting offer was made us for the sixth time, my brothers and I grew angry at such dealings and resolved to leave the city again without selling what we had brought. We spent a hin or two in looking about, seeing how few of those who dwelt there were warriors, then rode for the gate by which we had entered. It was there that we were arrested by the guard."

Mehrayn paused to swallow at his drink, then continued, "After our swords were taken by the nearly thirty guardsmen who were awaiting us, we were told that it was against Bellinard law to fail to sell what goods were brought within the city. The livelihood of the merchants was otherwise in jeopardy, said they, and their citizens were to be protected from the depredations of wandering strangers. Our goods were this time confiscated entirely, and then we were taken before the guard commander, a sharp-faced, sharp-tongued individual who pronounced us guilty of the accused crime. When we were told we must pay a fine of twenty silver pieces each in consequence of this guilt, my brothers and I laughed. How were we to pay such a fine, we asked, with all of our trade goods taken? Surely did we believe that our goods must be returned or the fine revoked, yet was there a third alternative which we had not anticipated. Our goods were not returned, yet was the fine paid—by the coin obtained from selling us as slaves."

The four slave females stirred and sighed where they knelt in their red clothes, pained by the tale they heard, yet Mehrayn was too deep in his narrative to take note of them. His free hand came to my middle to trace the birth-groove there, but his eyes saw naught of what his hand did.

"We were placed in chains and taken to the slave quarters at the back of the Palace," said he, his voice faintly angry from the memory. "Once there, we were stripped naked, given a taste of the whip to silence our cursing, then thrown in a cage. We fully expected to be dragged into the fields or worked in the mines the High Seat possessed, yet after no more than half a fey in the cage, we were taken before the High Seat himself.

"The fat fool sat among half a dozen of his hangers-on, all of them jovially amused by our nakedness when we were dragged before them. With one of the hangers-on was a young free female, disdainful of the female slaves who tended the free men, condescending to the men themselves. Her lips were full and pouting, her eyes spiteful and displeased, her red hair too short for the roundness of her face. It was she we had been brought there for, we discovered, for her father intended giving her the gift of a male slave, to celebrate her overly late arrival into womanhood. She inspected each of us before her, noted that the color of my hair matched hers, and chose me.

"When my brothers had again been taken from the room, the guardsmen holding my chains forced me to my knees, then gestured closer the first of the female slaves. I was touched by every slave in the room, heated so by their fingers and lips and tongues that I was convinced my flesh would soon part from the strain. To the amusement of the free men I was allowed no release, no more than screams and shouts and cursing. I fought the chains and the men who held them, straining to break free, yet the effort proved impossible. I knelt covered in sweat, my body in agony, my mind wild and savage, and that was when the free woman herself approached me.

"Hold him close," she commanded the guardsmen about me, stepping nearer as one hand held back the costly white gown she wore. The other small hand came to trail a finger down my chest, and when I snarled and fought the chains she laughed a malicious laugh. 'Your weapon seems quite extended,' she observed, looking down upon me. 'Are you in great need?'

"I had no wish to answer the insolent wench, yet even in my pain and madness I understood the needs of chain. The daggers worn by the guardsmen could easily have opened my throat—or worse—and I, a captive, would have been unable to defend myself. I swallowed the rage thundering through my blood, and looked up at the free woman.

" 'Yes, I am in need,' I growled, attempting to frighten her back to her place beside her father. Instead of feeling fright she laughed a second time, and spoke to the others without turning to them.

" 'As he is now mine, I demand that he be left with the need put upon him,' she said, the maliciousness increasing in her eyes. 'I will use him in my own good time, which is as it should be with all impudent, demanding men. Male slaves, that is.'

"Nearly all of those listening laughed in amusement, all save he who was called High Seat. The man frowned in immediate insult, seeing the truth behind the wench's words, and abruptly he gestured. The gesture was to the guardsmen holding me, and just that quickly was I released."

Mehrayn paused to sigh and sip at his drink, then shook his head.

"No matter how great my need, I would not normally have touched the girl," said he, "if for no other reason than that it was demanded of me. I was repelled by her and would sooner have gone without, yet was I a captive to men with chains and weapons. My hesitation was so brief that the wench had not yet realized I was no longer held when I reached up and seized her, pulling her down to the carpeting before me. Her screams rang out with her father's shouts, yet neither had the power to halt what the High Seat had decreed. I had the girl's skirts up above her waist and had straddled her before it occurred to her to struggle, and by then struggle was useless. My chains covered her nearly as well as I did, and forcing her knees open was the work of no more than a moment. The laughter of the men watching nearly overcame her shrieks and screams, especially when I forced my need within her. It had not occurred to me that she would be untouched—no similar girl of our city would be left so—and when I discovered the fact it was too late. The burning of my body could no longer be denied, and the wench was well punished for her insolence. She had no pleasure from the use made of her, and was at last assisted from the room in tears, no longer interested in possessing a male slave. I was returned to the cage with my brothers, our loincloths were sneeringly thrown to us as slave-payment, and the next fey's darkness brought you and your wenches."

Again he paused to look down upon me, and the sobriety of his regard was truly deep.

"Do you understand my meaning, wench?" he demanded. "Do you understand that a captive is not like a free warrior? That in order to continue with life and unmaimed, a captive must at times be wise enough to act the slave? Time enough to act the warrior when the chains are gone and weapons are again to hand.''

"One does not 'act' the warrior," I said, stirring in the chains which continued to hold me. "One is either a warrior or not, at all times a warrior or not even once. It is not possible for a true warrior to fail to be a warrior."

"Not even when necessity dictates otherwise," said he, nodding in a manner which indicated that he expected no other response. "You will be a warrior even in the chains of a slave, for that is the choice your nature forces upon you. One must be taught to counter one's own nature, and not in words. Perhaps the lesson which is to follow will some fey assist in saving your life."

He then handed his goblet to the slave beside him, and immediately began that which he termed a "lesson." With the chains twisting about my wrists I was turned to my belly in the fur, Mehrayn kneeling between my legs to keep me as he had placed me.

"I now have here beneath my hands a disobedient and insolent slave," said Mehrayn, the lightness of his tone causing high-pitched laughter in the slave females who watched. I struggled in humiliation, wishing I might sink my teeth into his flesh once more, yet belly-down I was unable to reach him.

"Tell me what is done to a displeasing slave, slaves," said Mehrayn, gathering my hair together in his hands so that he might throw it to one side.

"A displeasing slave is punished, master," said one of the females, the others softly echoing her words. "A displeasing slave is not allowed to remain displeasing."

"And is the slave allowed her choice in the matter?" asked Mehrayn, sliding his hands about upon my bottom. "Is she given the choice between obedience and death?"

"No, master," laughed the same slave. "What man would be foolish enough to throw away that which he might use? The slave is forced to obey, whether she wills it or no."

"Which is scarcely difficult," said Mehrayn, his tone dry. "We will now punish a slave, and show her how obedience may be forced upon her."

I considered his words no more than an attempt to anger me, yet it quickly became clear that such was not his intention. As I gazed upon the metal ring above the furs to which I was chained, I became aware of Mehrayn's hands and what they did. The Mida-forsaken device which had so tormented me was again being presented to the place from where it had so short a time

ago been withdrawn. I gasped and attempted to deny the now
dried and hardened object, yet the male would not be refused.
With strength he forced it within mé to the accompaniment of
laughter from the slave females, then tied its leather about my
hips and waist. Where the waist leather had at first been tied in
front, the knot now rested at my back where my chained wrists
might not reach it. Much did I wish to moan at the terrible feel
of it within me, yet was I able to keep silent by remaining rigidly
still.

"I see a slave no longer struggles," said Mehrayn, amusement in his voice. "Why do you not throw yourself about in
defiance of me, slave? Why do you not continue your disobedience?"

His taunting voice again brought laughter to the slaves who
watched, yet in Mida's name I was unable to defy him. Though I
wished with every part of me to pull angrily at the chains which
held me, I could not move myself about so and increase the
feelings already begun by the device. Mehrayn chuckled, fully
aware of that which I felt, and then his arm moved itself about
my waist.

"I will see you upon your knees for a time, wench," said he,
immediately forcing me up from the furs. I gasped again at the
movement, my eyes widening, and then was I directly before the
wall to which I was chained, attempting to rise off my heels to
relieve the position of the device which used me too eagerly.
Mehrayn's arm, however, remained about my waist, disallowing
the movement. "You will kneel in this manner," said he, moving his free hand around to cup my breast. "Should you attempt
to disobey me, you will be punished further. One of your sister
slaves will now comb your hair, for I dislike seeing it as tangled
as it is. A slave must be presentable for her master."

He released me with a chuckle and lay himself upon the fur to
my right, stretching out in comfort and gesturing the slaves to
him. Three attended him immediately and began feeding him the
provender they had brought, and the fourth came to kneel behind
me.

"Master, she has risen from her heels," announced the one
behind me at once, an eagerness in her tone. "Will you now
punish her further?"

"No, I will not punish her," said Mehrayn, unmoving where
he lay. "You will punish your sister, slave, with the switch
which hangs upon the wall there. Fetch it down and return to
your place with it."

The slave quickly rose to her feet and ran to the wall, took the thin switch from it, then returned to her place behind me. The others laughed in anticipation as the hair was thrown from my back, yet the slave did not strike at once. After a moment of silence, she stirred where she knelt.

"Master, this slave has been lashed," said she, her voice touched by trembling as her hand lightly touched my back. "I have seen the scars before and know them, and these are they beyond any doubt. How is she able to act as she does if she has felt a lash?"

Mehrayn made no immediate response, yet his chuckling had ceased and the weight of his eyes was heavy upon me. Then he left his place to rise to his knees, and it was his hand upon my back.

"Marks of the lash, to be sure," he muttered, a deeply angry sound to him. "And more than a few, if I do not mistake it. When were these given you, wench?"

"This is scarcely the first time I was taken as slave or captive," I replied, continuing to stare upon the wall ring. "Never had such occurred till I began moving through the lands of males. Should Mida see me through the coming battle with the strangers, never again shall I seek those lands."

Again a silence, and then Mehrayn said low, "And for what reason were you lashed?"

"For the reason that I am a warrior," I replied at once. "Had I been a slave, I would merely have been sold or used or handed about among my enemies. I am, however, a warrior, a thing males have difficulty seeing in the form I wear. The lash was painful, yet far less painful than submission would have been. You, as a captive, were not forced to submit as a slave-female. In the eyes of males, I am no other thing."

Again a silence fell, one encompassing the slave-females as well as the male, one in which I attempted to maintain the calm dignity I had pretended to. Even to speak of the lash was pain, to bring it to memory more than difficult. The sole thing worse had been my time with Sigurr, yet memory of the dark god was no assistance. Best to recall only that Jalav was a warrior, and send the rest to whatever oblivion I might manage.

"It is indeed difficult seeing beyond your form," sighed Mehrayn at last, stirring where he knelt or crouched behind me. "My mind knows you for a warrior, yet my body sees you only as a woman. Due to this, I punish you as a disobedient wench rather than a captive warrior; were you male, you would already have felt the lash. Perhaps it was those others who saw you as you truely are, and I who am blinded by flesh. Would you prefer the lash to the switch?''

The ring I gazed upon was a blackish silver, dull rather than bright, heavy and firmly set in the rock of the wall. My inner being had begun to throb to the presence within me and the nearness of Mehrayn, and my fists clenched and unclenched in the shackles below them. The thought of again facing the lash sickened me, yet what else was I to do?

"I—cannot choose humiliation over pain," I replied at last, taking myself into the darkness of closed eyes. "As the others did, so may you do as well, male, and leave your mark beside theirs."

"Woman, you tremble!" said Mehrayn, his hands coming to my upper arms, upset clear in his tone. "Never before have I seen you tremble, not even when facing the keren in the forests! There is no longer amusement in this thing." His hands left my arms as he rose to his feet, and his voice was harsh as he said, "Slaves, you may leave your burdens and go! Now!"

The slaves moved more than quickly in their hurry, and in a moment were gone from the chamber. With the door closed behind them, the male was again beside me, his hands at the leather about my waist. Another moment and the device was gone, taken even more quickly than it had been placed. Though I felt puzzlement that the male would do such a thing, consider my surprise when his hands next went to my wrists. The chain released me more reluctantly than the leather, yet when I was also free from the shackles, Mehrayn's arms went immediately about me.

"There will be no more of this foolishness," said he, stroking my hair as he held me tightly against him. "Though I have now more than earned your poor opinion of me, never would I see a lash taken to you. I had wondered where your fear lay, and now I know: just where mine is to be found, and for a similar reason. You are more a true warrior than am I, wench, for your bravery is deeper than mine. I could not defy my captors as you have done yours."

"The matter of bravery is no longer as clear as once I saw it," said I after a brief hesitation, keenly aware of the broad body against which I was then being held. "To face great pain rather than discomfort of the pride is not a thing I do willingly. Perhaps I would be more fortunate as well as wiser were I able to do as you do."

"Do I comfort you, or do you comfort me?" he asked with a sudden chuckle, holding me somewhat away from him so that he might look down upon me. Then, though he attempted to sustain the humor, it quickly fled. "I sought to teach you a thing concerning captivity, and was taught a thing myself, instead," said he with great sobriety. "It is the spirit which dictates our actions in captivity, the more flexible the spirit, the greater the range of choices in action. For one whose spirit is indomitably strong and set to a single path, flexibility is not possible. Sooner would such a spirit break than bend, and a man must be a colossal fool to set his mind on attempting a bending instead. Now that I have succeeded in placing myself with every other man who has ever given you pain and humiliation, I am able to see the truth. Had I been able to see it sooner, my land might well have been blessed with seeing you again. And I with my land. Now I no longer even have the heart to pursue you."

With a deep sadness the male rose to his feet and walked from me, returning to the window he had stood at earlier. His sadness and self-inflicted pain were clear, yet did it seem that he walked where he did and as he did in the hopes of being followed. Once I had had a male in the home tents of the Hosta who had acted so, a male who would be brash and intrusive, and then who would fill himself with great self-condemnation when censured. His purpose had been to lure me into giving approval to his annoyances, which I had done before understanding of that purpose had come to me. I had no wish to act the fool again, therefore did I seat myself upon the fur beneath my knees and rub briefly at my wrists, then reach for the heavy wooden comb which the slave female had left. My hair did indeed need seeing to, and it was best done before I continued upon my way.

Perhaps two hands of reckid passed in silence before Mehrayn sighed and turned from the window. He stood a moment gazing upon me, a faint smile coming to his face, then he left the window to move nearer.

"I have just made a strange observation," said he, halting perhaps two paces from the fur. "I had thought that seeing you bound as a slave upon my bed gave me great pleasure. I now find that seeing you there of your own free will and entirely free is an even greater pleasure. Will you spend the darkness with me, or do you insist upon leaving immediately?"

I looked up at the calm patience he showed, continuing to comb my hair in an effort to keep from frowning. Why he failed to press the point of his remorse as had the male I had had I knew not, nor did I understand the question he had put to me. Surely I had expected to find the need to battle my way from his house, not merely express my preference. Perhaps the male sought to put me off my guard, and would not honor the decision I made. If that were the case, best would be to find out quickly.

"For what reason would I wish to remain?" I asked, drawing the comb through the very end of my hair.

"For what reason, indeed," he sighed, smiling quickly to mask the brief flash of hurt in his green eyes. "You have scarcely found such joy and happiness under my roof that you would wish to remain. I will have a meal prepared for you, and you may partake of it when you reach the forest."

He turned away to walk to the door, called a slave female to him, spoke to her briefly, then closed the door again. I had expected him to return to where he had stood earlier, yet he walked instead to the large, metal-bound wooden chest which stood to the right of the furs. A quick movement of his hand raised the top of the thing, and then he was turning to me with a length of green cloth in his hand.

"I had meant to keep this as a gift for you, to be given with the new light," said he, the same quiet smile upon him. "As you will not be here with the new light, I give it to you now. I spoke with one of your wenches in Bellinard, asking what color you would have worn had you worn a color as the others did, and was told that your clan color was green. As I cannot retrieve your breech without raising questions as to why I would wish it, it would please me if you would accept this in its place."

He then held out the length of green cloth to me, watching as I put the comb aside, rose slowly to my feet, and walked to him. The cloth was much like that which he wore in black, meant to wrap about one's body as did his. Though the green was not Hosta green, I found it difficult taking my eyes from the cloth so that I might look upon his face again. Once had the male Nidisar attempted to give me the gift of a silver metal comb, yet the gift was one designed to give more pleasure to the giver than to the receiver. The male had enjoyed the thought of seeing the comb in my hair, caring naught for whether the comb gave *me* joy. Ceralt, upon seeing that my life stood in jeopardy, had given me the gift of freedom from my vow, yet even he had never given such a gift as the green cloth. That the gift would truly have been mine with the new light was clear, as clear as the fact that the male's sadness and self-condemnation were no ploy. I gazed into the green of his eyes, making no attempt to touch the cloth, making no attempt to return his smile.

"You were mistaken earlier," said I at last, feeling a strange tightness in my throat. "Those others were not able to see me as a warrior, for had they done so they would not have attempted to cow me with a punishment a warrior might expect. The pain they gave was designed to drive me from my stand, to fill me so with terror that I cringed and shook at their feet, the place they felt I belonged. You—you gave me the treatment of a slave, to humiliate and anger the warrior you saw before you into heeding the words you spoke. I will some fey demand a reckoning for those actions, yet I am not ignorant of their purpose. A pity my—spirit—rendered your effort useless."

I then took my gaze from him and reached a hand out toward the cloth; he released it immediately, and then it was I who was held in his arms. His kiss was strong and demanding, reawakening the need he had produced within me earlier, and when his lips left mine, I saw that the twinkle had returned to his eye.

"So there will some fey be a reckoning for my treatment of you, eh, wench?" he chuckled, spreading his hands upon my back. "I will not find myself able to counter such a reckoning, therefore will you have little difficulty in attaining satisfaction. Should you consent to remain here for the darkness, you may even find your opportunity within the next few hind. Is it my life you mean to take, or merely some portion of my blood?"

Though his amusement was clear enough, it was also clear that he did not speak to make sport of me. He knew I would not fail to take the revenge I had promised, yet he had no fear of what would come. Foolishly, I felt a sudden sharing of his amusement, a sudden urge to join his game.

"Perhaps it will be neither life nor blood that I seek," I replied, moving my hand about till it rested upon him properly. "Perhaps it will be some portion of flesh that I take, a portion so little used that it will hardly be missed."

"Now you malign me as well as threaten horribly," he laughed, pulling me closer so that my hand was trapped between us. "Despite your insults, that portion would indeed be missed, by others as well as myself. And as for how little it has been used, that may be remedied throughout the coming darkness. I promise it as yours alone, and more fully than if you took it with a sword. You had best burn for me, wench, for I mean to quench your very soul."

With a single movement he had lifted me in his arms, taking me toward the furs I had so recently left. Both green and black body cloths were soon forgotten, as were all other things about us. At some time a slave must have come with provender, yet neither of us was aware of it at the time. My intention had been to leave before the light had gone; so much for the intentions of a fool of a warrior.

9 The Caverns of the Doomed— and the fruits of attempted escape

I lay upon the furs clutching at Mehrayn and moaning, no longer able to bear the need he had produced in me. The male held me to him and spoke soothingly, his eyes filled with compassion for what he had done, yet also filled with knowledge of the need for it. His hands continued to keep me in a state of deep excitement, yet his body, though well prepared, made no effort to use that excitement.

"Just a few reckid longer, lovely wench," said he, kissing my face as I writhed against him. "The new light grows brighter and brighter, and soon the bell will surely ring."

"Mehrayn, now!" I wept, reduced to begging and caring naught for the shame of it. "I cannot bear it a moment longer! You must use me *now*!"

"Jalav, you know I cannot!" he begged in return, keeping me from slipping away from his merciless, probing hand. "If your need grows less than it now is, you will not allow me to use you upon my altar during devotions! You must recall that the suggestion of this course of action was yours, and that I burn with you! Be brave, my love, and you will soon have that which you crave."

Be brave! I moaned again and attempted to fight the strength of his arms, yet there was no escape, no release. Faintly, through the waves of flashing, weakening heat racing about my body, I did indeed recall that the agony I now faced was my own doing. The darkness before, I had attempted to refuse Mehrayn my use during his devotions, only to find myself forced to the service of his god. Afterward I had been furious enough to demand that he release me and face me with blades, yet the male would not release me till he had explained the reason for what he had done. I impatiently listened to all I had been told previously, caring not a whit for it, and then I had heard a point never before mentioned. The male believed that any warrior who failed to participate in devotions when he was able was thereafter in danger of his life and soul in any battles he next found himself embroiled in.

254

Though Mehrayn spoke only of my life and his refusal to allow me to throw it away, I was suddenly minded of the battle he intended marching to once I had left. It was clear the male held deep beliefs concerning his devotions, and I had wished to give him a gift before his journey, one which would equal his gift of the green cloth. How else was I to gift him save with my willing use, and how else was I to provide willingness in the face of that which I loathed? The answer was simple, the results not as easily accepted.

"Mehrayn, allow me to pleasure you," I panted, touching his chest with my tongue in a hand of places. "You need only release me so that I might reach you properly. Release me and I will bring a glow to your soul!"

"My soul is too well occupied with imminent bursting," he moaned, pulling my head away from him by a fistful of hair. "Perhaps we would be well advised to begin making our way to the altar in anticipation of the bell. Should we remain here any longer, Sigurr will turn his face from me in disgust."

"No," I moaned as he forced me from him and to my knees, he following along in the same manner. "I cannot move from here without being used! Mehrayn, I am in agony!"

"Then let us hasten to the altar," said he, returning his hand to its place between my thighs. I cried out in fury and threw myself from him, turned to my back, then kicked with all the strength in my legs. The blow caught him on the chest and threw him backward to the floor cloth, and with another cry I was upon him. If he would not have my use, I would have his!

Nearly did I have him within me before his hands came to my arms, attempting to force me from him. I snarled and pounded at his chest with both fists, glaring down upon him, and an answering growl came from him before he suddenly pulled me close. His fist buried in my hair crushed my lips to his, and then he released me with a howl as both of my fists pulled at *his* hair. His red mane was thick enough to fill many hands, and we rolled about upon the floor cloth, anger filling our minds, till it came to us that the fresh, new air of the fey was now filled with sound.

"The bell!" said he, looking down upon me where I lay between his knees. "Jalav, the bell! Now we go *quickly* to the altar!"

He jumped to his feet and pulled me to mine, and together we ran laughing to his altar. As quickly as the black candle was lit, that quickly was he within me, taking the pleasure he knew so well how to take, giving the pleasure he was so well able to give. Had the dark god been observing us, he would surely have been pleased with my cries and Mehrayn's grunts, yet not nearly as pleased as were we. When the storm had finally passed, Mehrayn did not withdraw till our lips had had enough of touching and being touched. It had been so throughout much of the darkness, his presence within me adding to the sweetness of his kiss. I felt a great reluctance to release him, a reluctance he apparently shared, as he continued to remain in possession of me. Our lips met and our tongues joined, and the hands of each touched the flesh of the other.

"For one who so dislikes this altar," said he in a murmur between lip-touching, "you seem oddly content to remain where you were placed. Should we continue to lie here so, I will soon be prepared to praise Sigurr a second time."

"It need not be done here," I murmured in return, gently moving my hips. "And this time I might perhaps use you."

"I believe I have decided to take you with me when I march," said he, taking my face in both of his hands. "I will have a long, covered litter prepared to be carried by four kand, and I will spend the entire march in the depth of your warmth. When we have arrived at our destination, neither of us will be able to walk."

"Are we not two excellent warriors?" I sighed, smiling as I touched the face so close above me. "Our sworn duties await, and here we be, pleasuring our bodies and befogging our minds."

"Our sworn duties," he said with a sigh to equal mine. "We have much before us of that sort, do we not, lovely wench? When I return, the balance of my warriors will surely be prepared to march against the strangers. I would be pleased if I found you here awaiting me, so that we might take the return journey to Bellinard together. Will I find you awaiting me, my love?"

"I am already awaited," I answered with a good deal of difficulty, strangely finding myself unable to meet his eyes. "Without me my warriors are crippled, for I am their war leader. Their need, Mehrayn, is greater than yours, I think."

"Not so, and yet unarguable," he sighed again, a heaviness to his tone. "You must see to your responsibilities as leader just as I must see to mine, and yet what of our own, personal needs? Must we deny them forever?"

"Those of us who ride for the gods are not permitted personal needs," I said, this time meeting the rebellion in the green eyes which gazed upon me. "The gods are jealous of their service, and those who attempt to deny the call are terribly punished. What call then from personal needs?"

"I see you speak from personal experience," said he, the rebellion having faded, yet not entirely disappeared. "Let us see to our duties, then, and speak again of ourselves when the duties are done. Go where you must, my lovely Jalav. Sigurr's Sword will follow and find you."

His lips then came to mine a final time, a last touching of length before he withdrew and arose. The desire we had felt but moments earlier was no longer with us, and we went together without words to the platform where we might wash the spendings from ourselves. During that time I noticed that the red dye upon my breasts was considerably faded, due in great part to the efforts of Mehrayn, yet found no opportunity to mention the observation. Two slaves arrived with boards of provender, and these Mehrayn and I saw to with more determination than appetite.

With the provender gone, we covered our bodies, Mehrayn in black, I in green. The cloth was soft yet serviceable, and then I was given an additional gift. My swordbelt and weapons were farther out of reach than was my breech, and therefore did Mehrayn produce ones of his own to take their place. I donned the swordbelt with a good deal of pleasure, put the dagger aside till I might fashion leg bands to replace those taken from me, then joined Mehrayn in a final touching of lips. The reluctance to release him continued to pull at me as it seemed to do him, yet the need for parting was inevitable. This male would be denied me as thoroughly as any other while I rode in Mida's name; I spent no thought on what would occur afterward, for I did not believe there would be an afterward. In one manner or another, the time would never come.

A length of leather secured the dagger to my right leg, and then we quitted the chamber to find a small door which led from the dwelling to a quiet side court. Awaiting us there were two kand and the black-clad male called Hesain, he who had nearly felt the full strength of my kick when Mehrayn had attempted to name me slave. The young males he trained were nowhere in evidence, and he bowed to Mehrayn—and myself as well.

"All is prepared as you directed, Prince," said he, agesture toward the kand. "As you depart publicly with your warriors from the front of the house, the wench and I will depart quietly from the rear."

"I see you have the spear I returned with," said Mehrayn with a nod of approval. "The weapon will be of greater use to the wench than one of ours, for the balances are not the same. See her safely to the forests, Hesain, and then return here immediately. As soon as Aysayn has resumed residence, she must be told."

"I will see to it with the utmost dispatch, Prince," said the male with a look of curiosity. "And yet, would it not be wiser to appoint another to bring word the while I remain with the wench in the forests? The dangers there are not to be dismissed due to the forest's nearness to our city."

"I am well aware of the dangers," grinned Mehrayn, "and it is for that reason you are to return. There is no need to give Jalav the chore of seeing to the safety of more than herself."

Mehrayn's hand had gone to rub at the now-healed scars upon his right shoulder, causing me to laugh with him at the jest he had made. The male Hesain, rather than finding insult at our laughter, smiled quietly with the knowledge that Mehrayn and I shared a private amusement which did not reflect upon him.

"You had best go now, Prince," said Hesain after another moment. "Your warriors and many citizens await your appearance."

"Indeed," said Mehrayn, a quiet smile taking him. "When one is awaited, one must go. Care for yourself, my Jalav, and recall my words."

His hand came to touch my face gently, and then he turned and strode back into the dwelling, disappearing behind the door. I stood a moment with hand resting upon sword hilt, resisting the desire to consider the concept of afterward, then returned my attention to Hesain.

"I see the Prince has chosen his mate," said the male, allowing his eyes to move about me as he grinned. "A pity the Shadow is not present to bestow Sigurr's blessings upon the union. I now understand why you must be informed so quickly of his return."

"Your understanding is as complete as that of all males," said I, folding my arms as I looked upon him. "You may remove that leather seat from my kan, for I shall not be using it. A Midanna warrior has no need of such artificial aid."

The brows of the male rose in surprise, yet he did as I bid him. I took the bow and quiver which had been tied to the seat and hung them about me, then jumped to the back of my now-seatless kan. From what seemed a long distance off came the sound of many voices raised in shouts of approval, and the male Hesain nodded as he mounted his own kan.

"The Prince departs, and now we may do the same," said he, drawing from the ground the spear which was to be mine. "Come, let us traverse the streets before the people return to them."

He turned his mount and led the way to a wide door, and a moment later we were without the court and riding between the large, glittering-black dwellings of the level. The heat and light of the fey were rising, yet not so the brightness. High clouds rode the air a distance above the city, speaking of the possibility of coming rain. The ways we traversed were empty of all folk, as though they hid from the clouds high above, yet were they in reality occupied with bidding farewell to Mehrayn and his males. The male had spoken jestingly of my accompanying him, and yet had I not had other commitments pressing me, the journey would have been one I would have joined with pleasure. This the turn of my thoughts as I rode, and the sight of the dwellings about me faded from my inner eye.

There was scarcely time enough to see that we were about to begin the descent to the level below when the attack came. Males in black cloth were suddenly all about us, most carrying oddly shaped spears. My sword flashed from its scabbard as the males closed, Hesain first ridding himself of my spear before doing the same. In truth, I could not fault the male for his actions, for the added reach my spear would have given would have done little against the sharp, curved metal heads of the spears of our adversaries. I slashed at a male who foolishly came too near, opening a gaping wound between neck and shoulder, and thereafter the males used their spears to defend against my blade, slashing at me to keep my sword constantly moving in defense. Hesain, too, was done so, our kand being held closely by our enemies to keep us from freeing ourselves of blade confinement, and then was the male done for all time. One of the odd spears thrust from my right, penetrating the body of Mehrayn's male, sending his blood flowing free as he fell from his kan. A fury rose up in me and I beat at the forest of wood and metal before me then jumped snarling to the ground, intent upon taking many lives before mine was taken as Hesain's had been. I swung my blade more in attack than defense, forcing the enemy males to back or die, knowing naught of the coward's stroke before it fell on me. From behind came the haft of a spear against my head, taking my senses and sending me to blackness.

Surely I must have thought that I had been done the same as Hesain, for I recall a sense of surprise when voices penetrated the dark in which I was wrapped, bringing me a short distance toward the light.

". . . see no reason for her having been permitted to slay a warrior," said a female voice, annoyance and anger hardening it. "Was the fool so taken with the low-born look of her that he mistook what he was about?"

"I was not present, high lady," came a different male reply, stiff yet restrained. "I am told, however, that. . . ."

"Enough!" snapped the female voice, rude in its awareness of power. "How this slave gained her freedom is clear enough, Mehrayn being the fool he is, yet he is not alone in his folly. What was done once may be done a second time, and I will not have her running about free and interfering with the plans!"

"Then you wish her slain," said the male voice, a touch of regret to be heard. "A great pity, that, for there are few to equal her."

"You may wipe away your tears of disappointment, man," sneered the female, anger increasing. "Should I order her slain, her trials would then be over, no further punishment to be given her. She merits punishment, this one, for daring to set her will against mine, and she shall have it. Her slavery will continue as I originally commanded, and the place she serves will be the Caverns of the Doomed."

"There?" demanded the male, a sound of shock to him. "High lady, that would be more than punishment, more than simple slavery! The survivors of the trials are feral beasts, uncaring of what they do to those about them! A wench in their hands would be. . . ."

"Used as she should be used!" snarled the female, nearly choking with rage. "Should your concern for her be so deep that you cannot accept my command, perhaps you would care to accompany her farther than the first portal! Well?"

"I cannot find concern that deep for any person save myself, high lady," returned the male, his tone having gone dry. "I had merely wished to point out that the wench would be wasted, ruined for those of us who might otherwise enjoy her. I would not enter the Caverns of the Doomed, as one condemned, for the use of any female living, nor would any man not bereft of his senses."

"Your practical nature is a great comfort to me, Pinain," said the female, her voice now a purr. "You and your men may take this slave to the Caverns now, and when the deed is done you may return here. That slave may attract the baser side of you; I will show you how superior a true woman is."

"The reckid will be kalod, high lady," said the male, a huskiness evident in his tone. "I will return as quickly as she is secured in the outer Cavern."

I attempted to move then, discovered that my ankles and wrists were bound, and discovered also that consciousness was not a permanent thing. A humming darkness took me for a time,

and when it left I found I rode the shoulder of a male, belly
down, wrists and ankles as tightly bound as they had been. The
feet below the shoulder strode a corridor, the sound of other feet
accompanying them, and then the feet passed through a doorway
and began a descent. So far down into the ground did we go that
surely did I believe I would again be placed in a dungeon, yet
the end of the descent found us in a long, torch-lit stone corridor.
Up this corridor I was carried to its very end, down another long
flight of steps, across into a second corridor, and then downward
again. The deeper we went the cooler it became, and at last the
corridor opened out to an area hidden in shadows, the trail we
trod only faintly lit by the torches two of the others had taken
from a wall. Though I had been aware of the journey to that
point, it was only then that a sense of urgency made its way
through the faint mist my mind had been surrounded by. These
males took me I knew not where, yet was it surely a place I had
no wish to be. I stirred where I hung upon the shoulder of
the male, testing the strength of the leather which held my wrists
behind me, and the male who carried me grunted.

"The slave has awakened, Pinain," said the male, placing a
hand on my thigh to hold me still. "Shall I untie her ankles and
have her walk?"

"Not yet," came the voice of the male I had heard earlier, in
converse with the female I now knew was Ladayna. "There is a
stretch of large boulders just ahead, and a place in the midst of
them where her ankles may be untied. Yet not to allow her to
walk."

The males all joined in coarse laughter, and I struggled again
to part the leather which bound me. The fury I felt added to my
returning strength, yet not nearly enough. The boulders the male
had spoken of were reached, our party stepped well among them,
and then I was thrown to the dark sand which covered the
ground. A hand of them stood looking hungrily upon me, and
then the first among them, undoubtedly he called Pinain, stepped
forward. His hands slowly undid the green cloth from about my
loins, threw it away into the shadows, then reached for his own
body cloth. His intent was strong and easily seen, and when the
leather was removed from my ankles I kicked at him, hoping to
ruin his intent and manhood together. The kick, however, was
not unexpected, and with laughter the two who held no torches
took my ankles and spread them wide for their grinning leader,
who quickly put himself between my thighs. As I had no desire
for him his first thrusts were pain, as were his squeezing hands
upon my breasts, and then my body saw to its own salvation,

accepting what was forced upon it. The male took his pleasure quickly, withdrew immediately, then stepped away to allow the second his place. One by one each of them used me, none caring for giving pleasure, each intent only upon taking it. I had no need to do other than endure, yet my mind seethed with near-madness the while. The single thought which kept my sanity was the determination that one fey I would again be free with a sword in my hand. Come that fey, these males would pay in blood for that which they did.

When the sport of the males was done, I was pulled to my feet and returned to the path we had left with a sharp thrust. The path was stone with a light covering of sand, the same dark sand which now covered me and snarled my hair. All about was deep shadow whispering of far, unseen reaches, yet the males kept me from losing myself in that darkness by the simple expedient of holding to my sand-twisted hair. At first the males took amusement from coming close and touching me insultingly, yet the farther we went, the less amusement was to be found in them. They grew increasingly ill at ease, and then the torches they carried shone upon the mouth of a cavern, ending the path we approached it upon. In silence was I hurried to the cavern entrance, and then inside.

Inside was a high cavern of no great width, the walls before and behind us perhaps four paces apart. Directly across from the entrance stood a large, heavy, metal door, ominous in the faint flickerings of the cavern torches. The males did no more than glance at this metal door before hurrying past it to the left, to where perhaps three females and more than twice that number of males sat or lay chained to the walls to either side. The females wept and the males moaned, and some few began to beg freedom of the males who had brought me. The males, however, paid them no mind as I was taken beyond the last of the chained males and thrown to the cavern floor before a heavy shackle let into the rock, which ended in a thick metal collar. The collar was quickly put about my throat and closed, the chain pulled upon to be sure it remained secure, and then the males took hasty leave of the place, returning with their wildly dancing torches to the darkness without.

The doing took a number of reckid, yet was I at last able to squirm about so that I was seated rather than lying down, my back and bound arms leaning upon the wall behind me. The moans and weeping had continued the while, none speaking, none cursing and shouting. The females, I discovered, were held in place only by the collars about their throats, as were a surprising number of males. For the most part these males were thin and weakly, if not in body then certainly in spirit. No less than four of them wept openly, the others curled up in an attempt to hide their nakedness. It was clear that the place I had been brought held great terror for these folk, a thing which brought a frown to my face. What manner of terror was it which awaited, and how might it be fought?

A number of hind passed without bringing answers to my questions. No others entered the cavern to be chained by the neck to the wall, and above this, none came with sustenance. I felt no hunger after having shared provender with Mehrayn, yet my throat could have done with a few generous swallows. My body, too, would have done well with wetness, if not to cleanse it of sand, then to remove the stink of the males who had used me. The presence of that stink continued to bring me fury, there in the dim cavern so far below the ground.

And then there came the sound of footsteps approaching from without, many feet which were leather-shod. The whimpering all about suddenly ceased as though silenced by Mida, and a held-breath sense of expectation filled the cavern. Into this silence came many males, all black-clad, all wearing weapons, none seeming moved by their surroundings save the lone, unclad male in their midst. Large was the male and light-haired, and no more might be seen of his face by cause of the black cloth covering his mouth. He struggled in the heavy chains which bound him, yet the males who brought him paid no mind to his struggles. They halted before the dark metal door, one drew his sword and pounded upon the door with its hilt, then all stood in silence and waited. No more than a few reckid passed before rattling and scraping came at the door, and then it opened outward to reveal four burly males.

"Greetings," said one of the black-clad males to the four who had appeared. These four wore white, yet was it a dirty, stained, and sweat-soaked white. "We bring you a new addition to your flock, one well deserving of whatever tender mercies are shown him. He committed the sacrilege of attempting to pass himself off as Sigurr's Shadow, ignorant of the fact that the Shadow had already returned from communion with Sigurr. So insistent was he that the lady Ladayna was disturbed, yet did she clarify the difficulty for the guardsmen who were new to their post. This one is not the Shadow despite his rantings, and he will not be permitted to disturb the Shadow and his woman again. You may remove his gag if having your ears assaulted with shouts does not disturb you."

"He will not shout," rumbled one as two others stepped forward to take the male and force him within the doorway. "At least, he will not shout at his own urging. Few here do."

The black-clad males watched the chained one gone within the doorway, then did they nod to those who remained at the door and turn away, leaving as they had come. The burly males stood within the doorway till the sound of sandaled feet had faded, then did their eyes come to those who lay chained about the walls.

"Let us also take this dross within," said the one who had spoken to the black-clad males, his eyes moving over what the neck-chains held. "There is garbage to haul and weapons to be cleaned, and bodies to be thrown in the abyss. This scum has lazed about long enough."

"There are females," observed the other, licking his lips as the two moved forward. "Undoubtedly the worst to be had, yet female none the less."

"Perhaps not quite the worst," returned the first male, pausing to look down at me. He was large and thick in the shoulders and chest, covered all over with dark, curly hair, even his brows thick over dark eyes. "This one, I think, we will keep a longer while than usual."

"In Sigurr's name, how does one such as she come to be *here*?" demanded the second, stopping beside the first. He, too, was thick in the shoulders and chest and dark-haired, yet, unlike the first, his middle was less trim than thick. Heavy bands of leather were to be seen upon his wrists as he put his fists to his hips, bands which seemed something other than restraints.

"In Sigurr's name, I know not," replied the first, a faint smile upon his lips. "Shall we return her with a note stating a mistake has been made?"

"Certainly," laughed the second, clapping the other upon the shoulder. "In due course, we should do no other thing. We would not wish to be condemned for taking what was not ours."

The two males laughed together over the jest they shared, then did they begin taking the waiting males from their collars. Most whimpered, many begged, and some cried, only one attempting to regain his freedom through struggle. The male was well made yet small in stature, and though he had little hope of besting the two larger males, still did he make the attempt. Two strong blows were delivered by him to the middle of the second male, he who had seemed merely thicker than the first, yet to my surprise and the small male's, the thicker male seemed to feel naught of the blows. He caught the arm of the small male before

a third blow might be struck, twisted the arm with little effort,
then turned the small male from him, producing a gasp of pain in
he who was held. The two large males exchanged looks of
interest and approval, and the first male came to take the captive
by the hair.

"This one may do for the trials, brother," said he, inspecting
the small male who seemed incapable of moving from the position he had been twisted to. "It will likely be necessary to train
him first, yet does he seem to have the required drive. What
think you?"

"That he is the best of the dross does not mean he will survive
elimination to continue in the trials," said the second, his tone
dubious yet reserved. "We will perhaps try him and then we
shall see."

The second male then took his captive within the still-open
metal door, leaving the last of the begging males for the first.
He, too, herded his captives within, and when the two reappeared they began to uncollar the females. These had seemed too
frightened to weep aloud in the presence of the white-clad males,
the two slaves as well as she who was not marked as a slave.
The first male now paused before she who had been free, and
gazed down upon her.

"And for what thing have *you* been sent here, hey, wench?"
he asked, inspecting her slight, light-haired, trembling form.
"Surely not coldness, else would you already have been declared
slave. Were I asked to speculate upon the matter, I would wager
heavily upon theft. Is this not so?"

"No, no, you are mistaken!" the female wept, sending up a
terrified glance to the male, and surely did it seem that his
speculation had hit the mark. The female had paled visibly in the
torchlight, and her trembling had increased.

"It matters little whether I am mistaken or speak the truth,"
said the male, continuing to look down upon the frightened
female. "Should you attempt to practice such a trade within these
precincts, you will not merely be given to the victors of the
trials; you will be declared live prey for those who train for the
trials, with a bounty placed first upon your hands, then your feet,
and lastly upon your head. There will be no second chances. Do
you understand?"

Rather than reply, the shuddering female choked and turned to
the wall, then emptied herself of all within her. Again and again
the spasms struck, twisting her to helplessness, the slave females
watching with disgust mingled with a strange sort of calm. The

male above her watched with silent approval a brief moment, then moved two paces to stand above me.

"And here we have the one who should surely have been kept to warm the high ones," said he, inspecting me slowly and deliberately with his eyes. "What crime have you been found guilty of, wench? For what reason have you been brought here?"

"I know naught of this thing you term crime," I replied with as much of a shrug as my bound arms allowed. "I am here due to the number of males who faced me. Had there been fewer of them, or had they not come at me from behind, I would surely have won free."

"What nonsense do you speak, slave?" frowned the male, folding his arms. "No man or wench is sent here save that they are condemned for a crime against the city, for there is no return from these precincts. Who brought you here, that you consider yourself unjustly served?"

"She was brought here by members of the personal guard of the lady Ladayna," spoke up one of the slave females, an eagerness in her tone. "I recalled them from having seen them about the temple during my service there."

"So that was your crime," said the male with a slow nod, his dark eyes unmoving from me. "Offending the high lady is a crime most wenches take care to refrain from, yet would the very sight of you be an offense to her. You were condemned and lost the first moment you came to her attention, wench."

"The spear has not been cast for the final time," said I, my hands fists below the leather which bound them. "As long as life remains to me, I shall continue to look forward to the fey my sword finds her throat. The fey that will surely come."

"I fear you delude yourself, girl," said the male, unfolding his arms and bending to the collar about my throat. "None of the condemned who enter here are ever permitted to leave again, not with the breath of life remaining in them. Were you male and able to compete in the trials, your life would be prolonged by the skill of your arm, yet even then no more than life might be won. Freedom is now permanently beyond your reach, as it is beyond the reach of those others within. Best you reconcile yourself to the fact, and strive to serve your masters well. Only through our approval will you find some bit of ease and comfort in your slavery."

He threw the collar from me and pulled me to my feet by an arm, and I felt a constriction within me that the leather would be left upon my wrists. With wrists bound, I had little hope of attempting escape before being taken through the doorway, yet were my fears unfounded. The collared males had been taken within unbound, therefore was I also turned with my back to the male, my hair thrown aside, and the leather touched by his hands.

"She is larger than any female I have ever seen," said the second male, coming close to look down upon me as the first worked at my wrists. "She will have the strength to serve many of us before she must be allowed to rest."

"Do not clench your fists so," said the first male to me, his voice distracted. "This leather is not as tight as it might have been, yet are the ends knotted. Had I brought a blade with me. . . ."

His voice trailed off as his efforts continued, and though I found it difficult, I forced the anger from my hands and arms. I had no wish to cause the male to abandon his efforts, yet the words of the second had rekindled the fury I had earlier felt. Large enough to serve many, indeed! Much would I have enjoyed serving them with sharpened metal, yet not so much as serving them with my absence.

Had the doing taken much longer, surely would the male have left the leather to be parted by a blade edge within the doorway. A muttered curse came to speak of the frustration he felt, building the anxiety within me, yet a moment later came an "Ah!" of satisfaction achieved, followed immediately by the leather falling away from my wrists. I quickly moved my arms before me to rub at my wrists, and the male, too, came from behind me.

"Now we may take them within," said he to the second, coiling the leather he held. "A bit of a taste, perhaps, and then we may return to coaxing skill from our nestlings. Should they be sent to face the victors as they are, they will make longer acquaintance with the abyss than with the trials."

"They will most of them make the acquaintance of the abyss," said the second, stepping backward and turning to gesture at the slave females, who had not stirred from their places despite their having been uncollared. "It merely remains to be seen how long they will keep themselves from it."

The first male grunted agreement with the second, then walked forward toward the female who had come there free. She lay upon the floor of the cavern in seeming exhaustion, at last beyond the spasms which had emptied her, her slight form holding the attention of the first male as the two slaves held the attention of the second. That I caused as little concern within the two males as did the other females pleased me, for that very unconcern would be their undoing.

The cavern floor contained fewer stones than had the wider area beyond it, yet was it necessary that I do no more than bend to find two to my liking. I straightened again with the stones in my hands and moved immediately toward the cavern entrance, willing to grant the males safety from harm so long as they granted me the same. They, however, whirled as quickly as I had thought they might, and started toward me with annoyance clear upon them; had I allowed them to continue as they had begun, they would surely have had me before I was able to reach the entrance.

In one motion I turned and threw the two stones I held, the second following immediately after the first, both flying true toward the faces of the males. It would have been foolish to pause and survey what damage I caused, therefore did I turn and race toward the entrance again, hearing a shout and a curse before I had passed through. At least one of the males had been struck, a matter of small surprise to one who had so often won at the stone-throwing game played by warriors-to-be. Had I not been bound so long and so tightly, surely would I have expected both stones to find their mark.

Once without the cavern, I ran no farther than a double hand of strides before halting with a curse. No torches burned in the darkness I stood wrapped in, therefore was I at a loss to find the area with large boulders which I had planned on losing myself among. So deep was the darkness that even the trail I stood upon was lost to all senses save the bottoms of my feet. I had regained the freedom to go where I would, yet was I unable to see where that freedom would take me.

I moved a bit farther into the darkness, then turned at the sound of footsteps some distance behind me. From the entrance to the cavern came two large forms, breaking the feeble glow of torches as they passed through into the darkness, the sound of their leather foot coverings ceasing as they halted where the glow did not outline them. Neither of the two had seemed badly injured, and then the sound of their steps came again, this time toward me. Silently calling down the wrath of Mida upon them, I began again to move farther into the darkness.

The dark and stillness was flat and empty, holding me in the cool of its clasp, urging me to move more and more slowly. I continued on with what speed I could manage, sinking into unseen patches of sand, stumbling upon stones and pebbles, keeping my arms stretched out wide before me. Each time I looked back to take a bearing upon the light from the cavern the light was less, and then I turned to see that it was gone entirely.

Had I merely passed from it with distance I would not have been disturbed, yet did my hearing tell me that footsteps approached with greater rapidity. The males came toward me with a speed I found incredible, blocking what light there was as they neared. I turned again into the darkness, this time toward my left, and broke into a slow, hesitant run.

As unbelievable as it seemed, the sound of males in pursuit continued behind me, following rather than ranging on in the direction I had turned from. Though I moved as silently as a light breeze across a plains, still were the males able to follow me! Were they able to see in what was to my eyes total darkness? Were they able to see me as I groped my way through the unfamiliar, unknown terrain? Did they laugh softly as they closed with me, ridiculing my feeble attempts at escape? Anger took me then, adding to the wildly raging frustration I had been gripped by, sending me hurtling even faster into the nothingness—till I tripped upon the half-buried boulder and went flying and sprawling across dark, clinging sand.

Surely was the darkness filled for me then with bright spots of light, twirling and jumping all about as I lay belly down in the sand. Well did I know that I must be up and off again before those behind me came even nearer, yet was I able to do no more than rise to my hands and knees before those in pursuit arrived. Big hands wrapped themselves about my arms after an instant of groping touches, and then was I pulled to my feet and held there.

"If you continue to struggle so, I will tie you in your own hair," came the voice of the first male, no sign of breathlessness upon him. "I have no pity for slave wenches who attempt to run off, and less for those who make it necessary for me to hie after them. Your punishment will be keen once we have you within the doorway."

"Given by me," came the voice of the second, his hand tightening about my left arm. "Were you not female, I would surely set you to training at throwing daggers, for few of the dross sent us have so excellent an eye. Yet you are indisputably female, and therefore barred from the trials where death would put an end to your use. It is punishment alone which you face, wench—if we are able to find our way back to the entrance cavern."

"A thing more easily decided than done," muttered the first, stirring to my right as though he searched the darkness. "Now that we have her, we must attempt to find the direction from whence we came."

"If you cannot see in this blackness, how is it you were able to pursue me so easily?" I demanded, more furious with myself than with them. A war leader of the Hosta, to trip and fall like the veriest child!

"Moderate your tone, slave," growled the second male, again tightening his grip. "We are to be addressed as 'master' when you speak to us, and then only when you have been commanded to speak. As you have not been so commanded, you will remain silent. Let us attempt to retrace our steps, brother, and see if we might catch a glimpse of the cavern."

The first male grunted, evidently an often-used manner of indicating agreement, and the two moved off, forcing me with them. The care they used as they stepped forward showed that the darkness held them as closely as it held me, and this I could not understand. If they could not see, how had they been able to follow me? The question vexed me as I stumbled along between the two, yet no solution was forthcoming. What appeared instead, after perhaps two dozen steps, was a faint glow off to our right, the sight of which caused the males to chuckle.

"Sigurr protects his own in the darkness which is his," said the first male, his tone openly relieved. "I would not care to join the spirits of those foolish enough to send themselves into this eternal blackness in search of escape. A swift swordthrust would be considerably more merciful."

"As any save this witless female knows," grumbled the second male, stumbling somewhat over an unseen obstacle. "To rush out into the blackness which none have emerged from alone as though it were the entrance to Sigurr's Blessed Realm!"

"In a manner of speaking, it is exactly that," chuckled the first male. "Not so much to the Blessed Realm as to its deep caverns, yet still a road to Sigurr's Domain. And if we are to consider the wench witless for nearly losing herself in the darkness, what are we to consider ourselves for having followed her?"

"Men with unthinned blood," snorted the second before chuckling took him as well. "There are few enough slave wenches to see to our needs, and those the least which might be sent. To have one such as she for use was worth the small risk taken, especially as she could not have escaped us. Had we become lost, we would simply have awaited the search party which would be sent, amusing ourselves the while with our quarry. She, having run, was witless; we, having followed, were not."

"An excellent summation," laughed the first. "I agree completely, and will not mention my own point again. Most especially as we have no need to await a search party."

The two shared their laughter as they took me along between them, disallowing me further opportunity for escape. Though they considered it witless to once more enter the darkness, I would have done so immediately had I been able to free myself. It had been my intention to prowl about the vicinity of the boulders, awaiting the next group to bring a male or female for the collars, and then follow them and their torches when they departed. The plan would have done well taking me from the darkness and returning me to where Ladayna might be found, yet was I taken in another direction, to the cavern, and with the other females, within the doorway of metal. Once within, the two males released me, yet only to close and bar the door behind us. I was now within the place which caused the other females to tremble and moan again, and there was naught I might do for it.

The inner cavern was well lit by torches, and well-filled also with a strong, odd odor. I had detected the same odor in the outer caverns, considerably fainter, and had not known what it might be. Now, as I leaned one shoulder upon the black stone of the wall, I could not find any curiosity within me over the matter. Twice had freedom been put into my hands, and twice had I managed to make naught of the opportunity. Ancient lore spoke of one being given three opportunities for success before one was forever condemned, yet which of the gods would have the patience to offer a third chance for freedom to one who had already thrown away two? This time my captivity would not be brief, nor would I find Mida awaiting me with smiles at the end of it. Were escape from that place possible, the finding of the third opportunity would be my task alone.

I looked up at the sound of footsteps, and saw four white-clad males making their way toward the metal door. The area before the door was wide enough for all four to stand abreast, yet the corridor of rough stone leading from it became so quickly narrow that there was not room enough for two to walk or stand so. In single file, then, the males came toward us, and suddenly the first male halted with an incredulous laugh.

"Chaldrin, what has happened to your eye?" the male demanded, staring agrin toward the two who yet stood by the door. "Has a true champion been left for us in a collar? Never, in all the kalod I have been here, has a nestling found it possible to reach you, and now. . . ."

"Silence, fool," came the growl of he who was the second male, he who was thicker in the middle and who wore bands of leather about his wrists. "The one who reached me was not you, yet am I of a mind to offer you the opportunity to do the same. Do you care to face me in the exercise cages?"

"Not I, Chaldrin!" laughed the male, his hands held high before him, palms toward the other. "I have already faced you, and learned then that I am no match for you. And yet I would still know how you came by so livid an injury. The one who gave it you will surely be a victor in the trials."

"The one who gave it to me will not even enter the trials," said the male, and then he was beside me, his fist in my hair pulling my head back so that I must look up at him. I had known that one of the stones I had hurled had struck its mark, and now was I able to see the results of that throw. The left eye of the male was livid with color, bruised and puffed and swollen half shut. "The one who did me this way will simply be punished for the doing," said the male, "for she is a wench and a slave, and threw more with Sigurr's aid than with skill. Had I thought her capable of skill, I would not have grown lax in her presence."

"Jalav is no slave," said I, dismissing the pain of his grip as I met the steadiness of his gaze. "There was skill aplenty in the throw, male, and more to be found beside. Offer to me that which you offered to that other, and you will not be refused. Never have I been bested with blades."

"So, you are skilled with a sword, are you?" said he, this male called Chaldrin who looked down upon me with no more than a single eye. "And yet, the trials are filled with more than sword use. To survive, a man must be skilled in dagger throwing and spear fighting as well as sword use—and to reach the first weapon, he must be capable of besting his opponents with bare hands. Force me to release you, wench, stand free of my hold, and *then* I will face you with weapons."

The male made no attempt to tighten his grip; he did no more than stand as he had been, honoring the offer he had made in words. Though I felt vast surprise that such an offer would be forthcoming, I nevertheless attempted to free myself, using the desperation of my need for a sword as a spur to my strength. The pain I felt pulling at his grip added to my anger, yet even raining blows and kicks upon him failed to free me. The male was like the stone of the walls and floor, unmoving and unfeeling even when struck. I continued beating at him a short while and then ceased in disgust, understanding that his offer of freedom had been no such thing. It was not possible to free myself from his grip, and I had been a fool to believe otherwise. As soon as I had ceased completely, the male forced me to my knees and bent me well backward, then crouched beside me.

"Your efforts were worthy of a child of no more than three kalod," said he, his tone even despite the biting of his words. "You have some small concept of the use of body weight, yet not nearly enough to accomplish a movement worthy of note. I had no need to defend myself from you, for you failed to threaten me seriously even a single time. You ignored the pain given you rather than attempting to end it, making no effort to gain greater freedom prior to attacking. You are a helpless little slave wench, filled with unjustified pride."

"Should I ever find a blade in my hand," I gasped, aching from the position in which he held me, "you will find that my pride is well justified, male. You now find yourself free to do with me as you wish; come the fey, I shall then do with you as *I* wish!"

"Spirited," said another male voice, that of the first, as he came to look down upon me. "Few of our nestlings are that eager to face you again after having been bested by you, Chaldrin."

"Spirited is not enough," returned the second male, continuing to hold my gaze. "A nestling must earn the privilege of facing me with more than his hands. This one lacks the ability to learn what must be learned, and is female to boot. She will never earn the privilege of facing me. Let us be about our business, Treglin."

The first male signaled his agreement with a grunt, and I was pulled to my feet by the male Chaldrin. So filled with fury was I that I again attempted to escape his grip, yet to no avail. The male forced me ahead of him up the corridor of stone, past the grinning males who had so recently arrived, to the end of the corridor which then turned right. This second corridor was shorter than the first, boasting two further white-clad males at its end. Beyond the males was a small, wider area of stone, a second short corridor with two males at its end, and then a broad area at last, a chamber with furs and platforms and seats and a number of doorways. Within this chamber were more than a hand of males, some taking drink or feeding, some doing no more than taking their ease. Two slave females knelt by one wall, an unclad, kneeling male beside them, laughter touching only those in white. At sight of us, the white-clad ones rose to their feet and came quickly forward, their voices raised in a babble of exclamation.

"Hold!" called Chaldrin, halting me as he, himself, halted. "What do you all do here at this time of the fey, squawking about like so many lellin? Why are you not about your tasks?"

"We heard there were females," said one of the males, shame-faced yet speaking for them all. "We have set the new slavies about their chores, and chained the blasphemer for whipping; now do we await sight of the females. Is this truly one of them? Are the others as compelling as she? Are they truly for the use of all?"

"The others, as you are now able to see, are here," said Chaldrin, stepping aside to allow the one called Treglin to herd the three frightened females within the chamber. "They are not of the same cut as this one, yet are they all, as ever, for the use of all. This one will bear her share of use, no less—and no more. To waste her would be utmost folly, yet is she soon to be punished. Those who have completed what tasks they have may assist in her punishment."

"For what reason do those three kneel at the wall of judgment?" asked the male Treglin, looking upon the male and two females. The babble had begun to grow again among the white-clad males, yet did the question silence it.

"An accusation has been made by one of the females," replied the same male who had spoken earlier, turning to look upon the three. "The slave wench insists that the slavey attempted to use her, and brings the other wench forward as one who was used by him before his attempt upon her. We have set them there so that you may hear the accusations and hand down a decision."

"We will do so now," said Treglin, gesturing Chaldrin to him. The male took me forward with him to one of two seats, pushed me to the rock floor at his feet, then sat as Treglin sat beside him. I attempted to rise again, yet the male had put one great foot upon the mass of my hair, holding me as he had placed me. I snarled in fury at such treatment, yet the males ignored my anger and gave their attention to those who knelt at the wall.

"Which of you wenches first accuses this slavey?" said Treglin, settling back in his seat. The two females started nervously, then she who knelt in the center rose to her feet.

"I accuse him, master," said the female, her voice sharp and thin. She seemed taller than many other Sigurri females I had seen, tall and thin and stiff in her carriage. Light-haired was the female, as was the other, and clad in the same pale-red cloth from waist to ankles. "It was in a storage chamber where he attempted to use me," said she, "yet I escaped from him. My dear friend was not as fortunate."

"It is true, master," said the other from where she knelt, her voice trembling. This one appeared smaller than the first, her pale hair somewhat longer than that of the other, her features softer. "The slavey took me despite the rules to the contrary," said she, "and I too frightened to speak of it. When my dear sister told me of her own narrow escape, we resolved to speak of it together."

"I see," said Treglin, his tone contemplative. "And you, slavey. What have you to say concerning these accusations?"

"I am innocent, master," whispered the kneeling male, his eyes unmoving from the stone of the floor before him. "I cannot deny thoughts of desire, yet am I innocent of such attempts. I have not had a woman since the fey I was condemned."

"Um," muttered Treglin, his hand to his face. The slave male appeared totally without hope, as though guilt had already been pronounced his. A moment of silence passed, and then did Chaldrin stir behind me.

"Rise to your feet, slave," said he, speaking to the male. The slave looked up in surprise and, when no further commands were forthcoming, rose quickly to his feet. A brief silence ensued, and then Treglin glanced toward Chaldrin.

"I believe I see your point," said he to the second male. "You are undoubtedly correct in your assumption. Would you care to continue?"

"Only if we may settle the matter quickly," said Chaldrin. "There are tasks of greater consequence awaiting us both. Turn about and face the slave you accuse, wench."

The male had addressed the standing female, and after a brief hesitation during which a flicker of suspicion crossed her face, the female turned to face the now standing male slave. The two were no more than a single pace apart, and it was immediately clear that though the male's body was thin and not as well muscled as it might be, the female was not of a size with him. The male was both broader and taller than the female, even with rounded shoulders and bowed head.

"You now look upon the man you claim to have escaped from, slave," said Chaldrin, his voice uncompromising. "Explain to us in what manner he attempted you, that you were able to avoid his use."

The slave female stood stiffly in silence, staring upon the frown the male before her had grown. It had come to the male that those who listened to the accusation of the female did not necessarily believe the matter as truth. The silence continued another moment, and then the female's head jerked about.

"He awaited me in hiding in the storage chamber," she rasped, smoothing the fists her hands had become. "I was surprised when he appeared before me and stretched a hand out, yet was I able to turn and run from him."

"Indeed," said Chaldrin, his voice continuing unmoved. "What was done once may be done again. Run, slave!"

Shock touched the features of the female, yet did she turn immediately and attempt to run from the slave male. He, however, had risen far from the depths of hopelessness and despair, and moved as quickly as did she. Within three or four strides were his hands upon her arms, halting her roughly before she might reach a door leading from the chamber.

"And the storage chamber is more than twice the size of this one," said Chaldrin as the female was pulled about and thrust back toward him. "Was the slavey fool enough to attempt you before you entered the doorway?"

"Yes!" shouted the female, standing at bay, her eyes wild. "He attempted me and I escaped him!"

"For what reason does this slave accuse you?" said Chaldrin to the male, who no longer stood with head down. "Did she attempt to raise interest in you and fail? Did you express distaste for her in her hearing?"

"Neither, master," said the male, looking upon the female with disgust. "No slavey would refuse the use of any female if it were offered to him. This one attempted to silence me, to discredit that which I would say of her."

"He lies!" shrieked the female, throwing herself to the stone of the floor not far from me. "He attempted me and now seeks to escape punishment! I have done nothing! Nothing!"

Chaldrin shifted about behind me, undoubtedly looking upon the second slave female where she knelt by the wall. This second female had gone pale and trembling, and now bent forward with head toward knees.

"Speak of the nothing this female has done," said he to the slave male, his voice far colder than it had been. "A nothing Treglin or I should undoubtedly have been informed of considerably sooner."

"Master, I did not know of it sooner!" pleaded the slave male, again falling to his knees. "Nor did I know that the doing was against your laws! I merely came upon the two of them by happenstance. Before I might consider reporting what I had seen, I found myself accused!"

"Speak of what you saw, slave!" snapped Treglin, annoyed. "There are other things to be done this fey!"

"The two females lay together!" quavered the male, again beaten down. "As though they were man and woman! Never before have I seen such a thing, therefore was I at a loss as to what to do! I beg you not to punish me!"

"There will be no punishment," growled Chaldrin into the sudden silence. "Return to your work and do not bring yourself to our attention again."

"Yes, master!" babbled the male, tottering to his feet and backing quickly from the chamber. "Thank you, master! At once, master!"

Once without, the male turned and ran from sight, to the left of the chamber door. The silence which had fallen was broken only by the near-soundless sobbing of the slave female by the wall; the other, near to me, merely knelt where she had thrown herself, her head down, her arms wrapped about her thin body. After a long moment, Treglin stirred and then stood.

"You, girl, look at me," said he to the sobbing female, she who knelt by the wall. Her head raised slowly, the despair of the slave male now filling her, misery clear in her eyes. "For what reason did you lie with this slave?" he asked, his tone uninflected and unaccusing. "Were you forced to the act by word or deed?"

"No, master," she whispered, her voice nearly choked to naught. "I was no longer able to bear the burden without comfort, a comfort unknown in this place. My sister offered that comfort, and I accepted. Am I now to be slain?"

"The females in this domain are too few in number for one to be slain for such a reason," said Treglin with a sigh. "Return to your work now, and we will speak further of this at another time."

The female hesitated, more disturbed than relieved, then rose to her feet and ran lightly from the chamber. It seemed from the set of her shoulders that she wished to look back, yet did she disappear from view without doing so.

"Good fortune smiles upon you, wench," Treglin then said to the remaining female, she who continued to kneel with head down. "The reason for your having been sent here is now clear, though there were suspicions of it sooner. Your private preferences may be your own affair, yet only insofar as the tasks assigned to you and those about you are unaffected. We are none of us free here, yet some are more slave than others, and you are one such. Had you in any manner coerced that wench, your life would have been forfeit. Walk softly, slave, and do not forget what you have been told."

"Yes, master," whispered the female, her eyes remaining down even as she rose to her feet and ran from the chamber. Those remaining within stirred and drew breaths, yet I had no true understanding of that which had occurred. What had the female done such that Treglin had spoken of her life as having been in danger of being forfeit?

"And now we may get on with what we were about when we entered," said Chaldrin, rising from the seat and removing his foot from my hair. "You will see to having the two females beaten, Treglin? We cannot permit lies and false accusations to go unpunished, else there will be no peace for us."

"I will see to the beatings," agreed Treglin, watching as I rose quickly to my feet and shook some of the ever-present sand from my hair. "As you are to concern yourself with this one, I will also see to the disposition of the other new wenches."

"Excellent," said Chaldrin with a nod, and then was his hand wrapped about my left wrist. The male stood quietly observing as I attempted to pull free, then shook his head in disgust at my failure. "Totally inept," said he in a mutter, then did he turn and stride from the chamber, taking me with him. An odd fury had risen in me at his scorn, yet was I as helpless as I had been to revenge myself. None of the males had worn a sword which might have been taken as my own, and barehanded a warrior was no match for them.

Without the chamber was a long corridor leading right, which took one to a wide, torch-lit area with many doorways and many slaves to be seen. The male slaves far outnumbered the females, and none did more than pass through the area without pausing. Some carried various items, cloth, sacks, wood, and the like, and some were empty-handed, yet all hurried as a matter of course, increasing their pace even further when the gaze of a white-clad male fell upon them. Chaldrin strode to the third doorway to the right and entered it, taking me into a half-corridor which passed four empty chambers of moderate size, undecorated and undoored. The fifth chamber, also undoored, stood at the end of the corridor and was not as empty as the others had appeared. Once I had been taken within, I was able to see ropes suspended from the stone ceiling, chains set into the floor and walls, wood-braced wooden punishment forms of the sort the female Cynena had been bent over in Mehrayn's house, a low pile of thick furs—and various whips hung upon the wall to the right of the doorway. It braced me somewhat to see that no lash hung among them, yet were those items which did appear scarcely constructed to give pleasure.

"This is the punishment room for female slaves," said Chaldrin, moving to the center of the chamber before halting. "Stubbornness, pride, and false beliefs are all left here to fade and die upon the stone of the floor, leaving naught behind save obedient female slaves. You, too, will be taught your proper condition here, a lesson which will aid you in surviving in our domain. If you are wise, you will heed that lesson."

"Wisdom is seldom looked upon the same by any of those who claim to know it best." I shrugged, meeting the calm of his dark gaze. "Jalav is no slave, nor shall she ever be. She will survive your domain continuing in her own beliefs, and escape her captivity in the same manner."

"Bravely spoken—by one who has not yet faced the punishment for disobedience and attempted escape," said he, his calm undisturbed. "I will see you punished more and more sternly each time it becomes necessary, this time being the least for you are newly come here. The next time I have you under the whip, I will not be as lenient."

With such words did he then turn and look about him, considering each of the devices at his disposal. His gaze rested upon the leather ceiling rope suspended not far from us, appearing to contemplate the possibility, yet did he shake his head slightly before turning to the wooden form.

"To suspend one such as you would be to allow too great a sense of dignity to be kept," said he, speaking almost to himself as he pulled me nearer to the form. "You must be punished with as much humiliation as possible, to give you further reason for avoiding repetitions. That you are able to withstand a great deal of pain was clear from the first; we will see how you fare with deep shaming."

Though I again attempted struggle, I could not prevent the male from placing me as Cynena had been placed, belly down over the top wooden bar, my wrists clasped in unyielding leather, the same holding my ankles. Fury set me to pulling madly at the leather, the humiliation the male had spoken of sharper than I had thought it would be, yet all that was accomplished was the resettling of my hair, which had been thrown forward along with the upper half of my body.

"This whip will be the best for you," said the male from my left, taking down one from the wall which seemed to have many leather blades. "It imparts a true sense of having been punished, yet does it do no more than leave the skin of the wench brighter than her hip wrap. No blood will be drawn from you, girl, therefore will you have naught to feed your pride upon."

He approached with the whip and stood to my left, shaking out its leather blades as I twisted upon the form I had been tied over, attempting to pull loose. The top bar of the wooden form was hard in my belly, my hair surrounded my face and fell to the stone of the floor, my wrists and ankles were held close by the leather, none of which aided me in freeing myself. I pulled and struggled—and then the first stroke reached me, assaulting my ears with a sharp crack! even as the leather struck at my back. My head came up at the deep sting of the blow, yet was it light when compared with the touch of the lash. After the first instant the sting grew to heat and greater pain, and then the second blow came, enhancing the first and beginning its own path in my flesh. The third and fourth came at similar intervals, calm and unhurried yet timed to bring a maximum amount of anguish. The male knew what he was about with the whip, and my struggles took on a new tone.

"What, still no screams and beggings to be released?" mocked Chaldrin, well aware of what hurt he had given. "Your silence tempts me to strike harder, wench, in an effort to give proper punishment. Bravery is not always the best and wisest course of action."

He immediately swung the whip again, allowing no opportunity for reply even had I wished to make one. Again the question of wisdom had come forth, and even as the pain resumed and mounted, I could not see the wisdom in abandoning my stand. Pain is much the easier to bear in silence, not to speak of less damaging to the pride. It was a lesson I had learned many kalod ago, and one I was not prepared to abandon.

Before the thing was done, all of the back of me had felt the touch of the whip. I ached and burned from neck to ankles, filled with humiliation as well as with pain. The accursed male had beaten me all about, and then had he announced that he would then punish me for having thrown the stone which had struck him in the eye. The blades of the whip gently moved over my bottom the once, and then was its touch no longer gentle. Again and again was I struck, with greater strength than previous, till I truly wished to scream out my fury and pain. As he struck, the male chided me with stern comments of, "Bad girl!" and "Naughty child!" and "Disobedient little wench!" till I pulled furiously at the wrist leather and threw myself about in a frenzy of rage. It was ever so with a male, to punish with humiliation rather than demand the right of challenge. The beating continued a short while longer, yet silent tears of frustration had already come to my eyes.

The male replaced the whip upon the wall before coming to free me of the leather. Once free, I raised myself painfully from the form, finding that movement added its own throb to the beating. There was indeed little in the situation for pride to feed upon, for the beating I had withstood in silence had not been a warrior's beating. I had been done as a miserable, lowly slave, punished by one who was free, struck even on the bottoms of my feet in consequence of my having run. The cool, uneven stone of the floor broke roughly through the burning ache of my soles, making me shift from foot to foot, and finally sending me off balance. I would surely have fallen, had Chaldrin not suddenly grasped my arm.

"Having the bottoms of one's feet beaten is worse with a heavy reed switch," said he as he took me to the right of the wooden form, toward a wide fur he had placed at the foot of the wall opposite to that of the whips. "The men here are subject to such a punishment, slaves and nestlings and trial survivors alike. It does well in teaching them the consequences of attempted escape. Give thanks that you are female, and not to be so harshly treated."

The comment might perhaps have evoked bitter amusement within me, had it not felt as though I walked upon broken twigs and sharp stones. For those like Chaldrin and the others, who habitually wore leather foot coverings, the punishment would undoubtedly be much sharper. With uneven and painful tread then was I taken to the spread fur, thrust down upon it, and immediately put within the metal collar which depended from the chain let into the wall above the fur. Wide was the collar, and of a tightness to make itself fully known to the wearer, the sort to make me snarl and pull at the chain—had I not been aching so.

"The wenches in this domain are commonly used carefully, so as not to overuse them," said Chaldrin, rising to his feet and undoubtedly looking down at me where I lay upon my side on the fur with eyes closed. I had been in greater pain on other occasions, yet the beating Chaldrin had given was not one to give him shame for the effort. I would have found much joy in spilling his blood, yet even had I been set free upon the moment, I could not have properly wielded a sword to insure victory.

"Under normal circumstances," continued the male, "there will be a set number of men for you to serve, the exact number depending upon the number of females available. When you earn punishment, however, the limits upon your service are removed, and you may be used by any man who completes his work in time to do you so. This, of course, does not include slavies, who are allowed no females, nor nestlings nor trial survivors who must earn the use of a wench. Should one of these attempt you without permission, you are to inform Treglin or myself, or one of our men."

"And who may I inform if you and your males attempt me?" I asked, greatly aware of the throbbing red behind my closed lids. "Is it Sigurr himself I must then speak to?"

My words had been filled with bitterness and irony, for surely the dark god would do no more than approve the efforts of these males of his. Rather than make immediate answer Chaldrin was silent for a moment, and then the bitterness entered his own voice.

"That this domain is Sigurr's is true," said he, "and yet is it far different from the city above it. Those who dwell above us are privileged to worship Sigurr as the great god demands; those who dwell in this domain have been turned from by Sigurr, and forever denied his worship. Call to him if you wish, wench, yet he will not heed you any more than he heeds the rest of us. Truly doomed are those of us in these caverns, and most grown used to it."

The oddness of his words brought a frown to me and reopened my eyes, yet the sight of Chaldrin halted any words I might have spoken. The male had removed the white covering from about his loins, and was then kneeling to join me upon the fur. Never before had there been an attempt to use me after I had been beaten so, except by the male Nolthis, who had found his own pleasure only in the absence of mine. Were Chaldrin one such as that, his pleasure would be full; were he not, he would drink deep of the cup of frustration, which I had so often drained of late.

"Your eyes discount my presence," remarked the male, settling himself beside me. "A wench fresh from a whipping should be anxious to please he who gave her that whipping—lest he decide to give her another."

"A warrior fresh from a beating is too greatly concerned with thoughts of vengeance to be taken by anxiety, male," said I, lying unmoving upon my right side. "You are now free to do with me as you will, yet the situation shall not continue so forever."

"The situation has no choice save to continue so forever," said he, putting his hand to my face. "We will none of us ever leave this domain with life remaining in our bodies, and you had best accustom yourself to that truth. To believe otherwise leads to insanity."

The sobriety of the male disturbed me, for I had surely expected him to fall to anger. That no anger had built within him meant there was none to overcome as he bent toward me, raising my face for his lips. As I could not easily struggle, I merely gave him no response, a thing he refused to accept. His hand came to my body despite my sudden attempt to halt him, and to my shock immediately succeeded in beginning to raise my heat. With the pain so clearly present I had not thought it possible, and the male chuckled at the expression he saw upon me.

"All wenches are eager to serve those whom they recognize as their masters," said he, bringing forth the gasp I had not wished freed. "Your body will give me the pleasure I demand, to save itself from further pain at my hands. A wench's body is often wiser than her will."

I snarled an oath on the subject of wisdom, yet was the attempt at defiance fruitless. The male, holding to my collar chain, forced me to squirm and writhe as he willed, his hands and tongue firing me as deeply as his whip had reddened my flesh. When I was put to my belly in the furs and my thighs were spread, I was already sunk so deep in the pit of need that I welcomed the humiliating posture.

"Never have I seen so hot a slave," murmured Chaldrin where he knelt between my knees, his hands below my thighs raising me higher. "My flesh finds no need to penetrate yours, for I am eagerly taken within the moment I approach you. And the heat within! Attempt to deny me, slave, attempt to keep me from my pleasure."

The taunting of the male stung me, yet when his hands circled me to touch my breasts, I could no more deny them than his presence within me. With a laugh he began to use me, and easily was I as well used as I had been well whipped. The male knew what he was about in both areas, and rage though I might in my innermost thoughts, my body rejoiced in the pleasure given me. That more was taken than given mattered little, for what was given was enough to please a warrior's soul. When, after a long while, the need had passed from the male, he touched my breasts one last time and withdrew.

"More than acceptable," said he as he rose to his feet, his voice heavy with satisfaction. "I had never thought to have one such as you again, and yet you were sent to my domain and are now a part of it. When I put you up as prize, the nestlings and victors will outdo themselves to win you."

"Prize?" I echoed, twisting gently about to look up at him.

The heaviness of great need fulfilled had entered my mind, and I understood little of what he said.

"My fighters and would-be fighters do contest in the trials," said he, retrieving his white body cloth and beginning to don it. "In the trials they contest for life, yet there must be other prizes to lure them to effort after a time. I often tie a slave wench to the prize post in the practice area, allowing my fighters to see what it is they contest for. The ploy is even more effective than angering them. When you are done with your punishment, I will have one of the other slave females show you your duties."

With body cloth in place, he knelt briefly to put his lips to mine one final time, then did he rise again and quit the chamber. It had not disturbed him that he had found it necessary to put his fist in my hair before he might take my lips, no more than my evident displeasure had disturbed him. It was not my intention to be put up as prize for males, yet Chaldrin cared little for my intentions. It was his intentions which prevailed, proclaimed by the metal collar closed about my throat. I struck the soft fur I lay upon with a fist, grasped the collar chain near the wall in both hands and pulled hard despite the pain, then slowly sank down to my side again. Despair is ever an enemy to the purposes of a warrior, yet are there times when it may not be denied. I required a weapon, and the strength and lack of pain to wield it, yet I knew not where these were to come from. I lay unmoving upon the fur, battling despair, yet knew not where the answer to my needs was to come from.

10 The blasphemer—and bound as a prize

There was some pain in movement, especially in walking, yet I had little choice save to follow the male. The leather knotted about my throat stretched to his hand, and in such a way was I taken through the corridors and chambers. The white-clad male before me did the bidding of Chaldrin, and it was his wish that the new slave see to a task.

I had lain upon the fur in the room of punishment no more than a short while before others entered to intrude upon the solitude. The first to be brought was the female who had falsely accused the male slave, she who was tall and thin and sharp-voiced. The male who brought her tied her wrists to the leather suspended from the ceiling, pulled upon the leather to raise her from the floor and then tied it off, then proceeded to beat her with one of the whips from the wall. It was not the whip Chaldrin had used, and despite her efforts to remain silent, the female had soon fallen to screaming wildly and twisting about in the air. The male beat her till his arm grew tired, then did he leave her hanging in the leather, replace the whip, and bring himself over to me. His use was not as lengthy as Chaldrin's had been, nor was it filled with pleasure for the slave beneath him. The male found a good deal of pleasure, and chuckled softly as he replaced his body cloth. That I lay curled in pain was of no moment to him; punishment had been decreed for me, and it pleased him to assist with it.

The next to be brought to the chamber, some reckid later, was the second female who had accused the male slave, she who had remained kneeling by the wall. She stopped in upset before the first where she hung in the leather, and the first stirred in pain.

"Later we must comfort each other, sister," whispered the first, looking down upon the second. "Though they give us pain, they cannot deny us the comfort we find together."

"Not again," said the second with a head shake, stepping back from the first. "We have earned the pain, and have not earned the comfort. What we did together was no more than our right; the false accusation we swore to was not within our rights. Had we not been ashamed of what we did, we would not have sought to hide it with lies.''

"You know not what you say!" protested the first, pain crossing her face when she attempted movement. "They would not have allowed us to be together if they had known! It was necessary that we lie!''

"Then why are we to be punished for the lying rather than for having been together?'' demanded the second, looking up at the first with fists clenched. "It is clear to me that you, yourself, consider the act wrong, and for that reason I will have naught further to do with you. With so few things allowed to me in this place, I will not waste opportunities with one who feels shame for that which she does.''

The first female, again taken by tears, attempted to plead with the second, yet was the second allowed no further time to talk. The male who had brought the first took her roughly by the arm to the wooden form, yet her punishment, filled with weeping though it was, was not witnessed by me. He who had brought the second female concerned himself with punishing another slave, one who had been left chained by the neck for his use. Suffice it to say that the time was not pleasant, though the male attempted to make it so. There had been too many that fey, and the kiss of the whip as well, and I knew not how much more I could bear.

More than a hin passed before another came, and though I knew the effort useless and foolish, I fought him when he came to me. Rather than growing angry the male was delighted, and was deep in his pleasure when Chaldrin returned. The brawny male stood silently watching as the other pummeled me, a faint frown touching his brow, even his bruised eye seeing clearly the pain and fury I would not voice. When the one who had me finally spent his desire and rose to his feet, Chaldrin stepped nearer and crouched down beside me.

"One of the wenches brought within with you has told me that five men brought you to the Caverns," said he, smoothing the sweat-dampened hair back from my face. "She also believes that those men used you before leaving you chained, this despite the lack of tears she, herself, would have shown. Is this so?''

I lay flat upon the now badly used fur, seeking to gather enough strength to sit, nearly ill from pain and the odor of spendings, and the confinement of the collar. At mention of those who had brought me, my lips moved back from my teeth and a growl escaped my throat; were all of these males not the death of me, I would surely be the death of them.

"Not the answer I had envisioned, yet an answer leaving no doubt," muttered the male, faint anger touching him. He straightened and walked to the male who had last used me, spoke quietly for a moment, then watched the male hurry from the chamber even as he replaced his body cloth. With the other male gone, Chaldrin returned to crouch beside me in silence.

Perhaps four hands of reckid passed before the male returned with three slave females, yet in that brief time four other males had been turned away by Chaldrin. I had not known that the punishment was at an end till Chaldrin had spoken of it to the first who came, a thing which surprised me. The slave had been used too far, he said, and should we continue, we may well lose her. The male acquiesced with disappointment, as did the second and fourth, yet the third seemed disposed toward disputing the decision till Chaldrin rose from his crouch to face him. Truly did it seem that the male would have fought on my behalf, yet memory returned the knowledge that he wished me for another purpose. A prize which was unusable was no prize at all, and this I knew as well as did the male.

The three slave females came to me at Chaldrin's command, and despite the fact that I would sooner have been left to my own devices, a great deal of the pain was quickly and quietly taken from me. Naught was done for the beating I had been given, yet the use of males was washed and salved from me, chalky water was given me to drink, and a good wooden comb was produced to see briefly to my hair. When I was able to sit and move about, green leaves were handed me which made me laugh without mirth. Leaves of the dabla bush were they, used by war leaders of the Midanna to keep them childless. That the same was given to these slave females of the Caverns was something of an affront, yet there was no denying the necessity. Was one to bring a daughter into a world such as that, where her sire had not been carefully chosen? Though I had no need of them I took the leaves to chew, again dedicating my battle prowess, life, and soul to the service of Mida as I had done among the Midanna. The dedication heartened me in the midst of my enemies, so much so that I struggled only a short time when Chaldrin freed me of the collar, only to tie a pale red cloth about my hips of the sort worn by the slave females. Had the red been Silla red I would have spent my life sooner than wear it, yet the shade was nearer to that worn by the Happa, sister Midanna who now followed my leadership. There was little reason to waste my strength upon the point, yet Chaldrin had grown annoyed at my initial resistance, therefore was a length of leather tied about my throat. The male who had brought the slave females had been given his instructions, and I was quickly led from the chamber.

The caverns and corridors spread all about, many torches to be found upon the walls, the same strange, elusive odor penetrating chamber and corridor alike. The cloth knotted about my hips felt strange to move about in, yet the thought soon fled from my mind when we reached the area of lined metal. A long corridor had brought us to a circular hall, the entrance we had used and two others being the only ones without lines of metal closing them off. Beyond the various barred entranceways there were males to be seen, unclad males of good size who either grappled with others like them, stretched their muscles alone, or swung odd-looking swords about, again either alone or with others. White-clad males stood about both beyond the metal and within the hall, and I was allowed no time to halt and look more completely about. The male who held the leather hurried me toward one of the two remaining unbarred entrances, leaving the hall behind us.

The corridor we then entered led past metal enclosed areas to both sides, small areas separated one from the other by thick sections of stone wall. Within each cell was naught save a thin fur and heavy shackles let into the walls, a single torch lighting each space. The corridor stretched on a goodly distance, yet naught living was to be seen within the cells till we came to the one, to the left, which was our destination. There, lying face-down upon his thin, torn fur, chained by the neck and wrist-shackled, was a large, unclad male, his back beneath his light hair well touched by a lash. The small streams of blood running from the deep welts brought such strong memory to me that the leather was gone from my throat and the cell door opened before I knew aught was occurring. The white-clad male pushed me within by one arm, then reclosed the door and shot the bolt before I was able to even consider protest.

"Chaldrin orders you to tend that one, slave," said the male, assuring himself that the door would not open again by pulling upon it. "Wash his wounds and salve them, and then feed him as much as he is able to take. And mind you! Do not eat his food yourself, nor fail to tend him properly, else will you be punished again, and this time more harshly! Chaldrin has great hopes for that one in the trials, and will not look kindly upon you if his hopes are dashed through your negligence!"

With a final glare the male took himself off, leaving me to

look about the small area. On the floor, to the left of the door and within the lines of metal, were two piles of objects I had not seen sooner. One was a wide board with three wooden bowls, and the other was a wide clay basin filled with water which rested upon a pile of cloths, with a smaller clay pot standing beside them. I looked upon these items for a moment, curious as to what gave the male Chaldrin reason to believe I would obey him. That he wished use of some sort from the whipped male was clear; less clear was the reason I had been chosen to tend him. Were Chaldrin foolish enough to believe I feared his punishments, he would soon learn better; Jalav was no slave, to be sent about and commanded to his bidding.

And then I looked again upon the whipped male, recalling the agony of the lash, the fire of the soul brought by its touch. Naught save pain had I had from these males about me, yet the one who lay awash in his own blood had had the same. It was scarcely likely that I would have other at his hands than I had had from those about me, and yet—the lash—

It was foolish to continue insisting to myself that I would not aid him. Had it been anything other than the lash, I would have turned my back and allowed him to find his own way through the darkness; as it was indeed the lash, I took the basin and cloth and salve and knelt upon the edge of the old, thinning fur beside him. The shadow of pain continued to plague me with movement, yet was movement necessary to wash away the dried blood and halt the bleeding where it had not yet stopped. I had thought the male gone to that nether realm awaiting one whose pain grows too great, yet the first touch of a dampened cloth to his broad back drew a muted moan, one quickly swallowed and not repeated. Thereafter I used greater care, and refused to allow the trembling to touch me.

The water in the basin had long since turned deep red before the task was done. Applying the salve was more difficult than removing the blood, for each welt and cut had need of a coating, yet the male made no protest, nor did his flesh do more than twinge. When the coating was complete and I took a cloth to wipe my hands upon, a deep sigh came from the male, and he turned his face toward me for the first time. Eyes as dark as mine regarded me carefully, and a faint smile touched his lips.

"It is more than a pleasure to see you again, wench, yet I had not expected our second meeting to be here," he said, his voice heavy with effort. "For what crime could you possibly have been condemned?"

I gazed upon the male with some surprise, for I now saw him

to be the black-clad male of the hall of slaves, he who had taken a kiss from me before I was placed in the alcove where Mehrayn had found me. His words made little sense, and I shook my head.

"I do not know the meaning of 'crime,' " said I, throwing the cloth from me. "I am here for a reason I do not clearly understand, yet do I understand full well whom I must thank for the doing. When I have escaped, my thanks will be given with a sword."

"Ah, yes, you are a captive rather than a slave," said he, his faint smile strengthening. "The last I heard, Mehrayn had claimed you from an alcove and carried you off to his house. As he has never before claimed a wench, from an alcove or otherwise, I had hoped he had finally found one to his taste. Did you attempt escape, and thereby earn condemnation? I cannot imagine Mehrayn allowing such a charge to be placed against one such as you, yet times have turned strange with unexpected events."

"There was no need to attempt escape, for Mehrayn himself saw me off," said I, wondering at the odd expression which had taken him. "The male understood that I could not await the return of Aysayn under his roof during his absence, therefore did he arrange my temporary withdrawal to the forests. I would then have. . . ."

"Hold, wench, hold," interrupted the male, attempting to move about upon the well-used fur. A clank of chain accompanied a quickly swallowed groan, those being the only fruits of the male's efforts. The lash drains the strength from one, as the male had learned, and he lay with eyes closed and breathing heavy as he strove to push the flaring agony back to where he was able to bear it. I rose clumsily to my feet and fetched the pot filled with water, then knelt again and awaited his return from the land of blazing red. When his eyes opened again I offered the water, then aided him in drinking some small bit of it. Once I had withdrawn the pot, he rested his cheek upon the fur, and looked at me with weary determination.

"So much for freedom of movement," said he, a sort of anger belying his attempt at lightness. "I had not thought a lashing would constrain me to a greater degree than chains, yet I have never before been lashed—nor chained. For what reason were you awaiting—Aysayn, and where has Mehrayn gone?"

"Mehrayn has gone to do battle in the south," I replied. "He has learned that this city's enemies plan an attack, and has gone to see to them before they are able to accomplish mischief. As to my reasons for wishing to see Aysayn, Mehrayn is aware of them and will speak to the male himself upon his return if I have not succeeded in freeing myself."

"There is much here I do not understand," muttered the male, nearly to himself. "Mehrayn returns sooner than he was expected, then leaves again almost immediately. You wish to speak with the Shadow, and end condemned to the Caverns. And I—I am told the Shadow has returned to his residence when such a thing is patently impossible."

"For what reason is it impossible?" I asked, only then recalling the announced contention for the male having been brought to those precincts.

"It is impossible for the reason that I am Aysayn," said he, moving very slowly to pull one manacled arm beneath his chest and then raise himself to lean upon it. "As I am Sigurr's Shadow and not yet returned to my residence, how may I be already there?"

"An interesting question," said I, regarding the male with no expression. "How is it you went unrecognized when you attempted to return?"

"The thought has been plaguing me," said he with a short breath of vexation. "The guards before my apartments were new to their post—which should not have been. When Ladayna appeared and denied my identity, I thought the wench angered with me again and merely set upon spitefulness which would slightly disaccommodate me. When I promised her punishment for such childish behavior, the guardsmen fell upon me and brought me here."

"And none other know the face behind the Golden Mask," I mused, of a sudden feeling great suspicion.

"Sigurr's Sword knows well the face behind the Golden Mask," began the male who called himself Aysayn, and then his broad face opened with revelation and anger. "Indeed does Mehrayn know the face of Aysayn, and Mehrayn is no longer within the city, sent off once again while I lie festering in these Caverns! By Sigurr's thundering blade, I have been snared as though I were the most innocent of children!"

"So it seems," I said, paying no heed to his anger. "And by what other name does Sigurr's Sword know you?"

The male's flashing gaze snapped to me and then a bark of laughter escaped him. "The other name he knows me by is Varsan," said he, "and you are a canny wench indeed for having asked. I, too, have great interest in a name, and that is the name of the man who set this trap!" Again his dark eyes flared, and he looked upon me with metal in his gaze. "And now, wench, I will hear the reason you sought to speak with me.''

"To speak of the thing now is idle, yet it is, after all, the reason for my having come here." I shrugged, then regretted the shrug. The whip is not the lash, yet is it scarcely a thing to be overlooked. I spoke to the male Aysayn of my charge from Sigurr, of my finding Mehrayn and the others in Bellinard, of our journey to the city of the Sigurri, and of my meeting with the female Ladayna—which I still understood only imperfectly.

"The female insisted that if I were to meet with you, I would be taken as slave by you," said I, looking upon the pensive cast Aysayn now wore. "I gave the thought the small consideration it merited, then naturally refused to agree. As I attempted to leave the area, I was taken captive."

"For a reason which is now quite clear," said the male. "Had you remained about and attempted to speak to the Aysayn who appeared, the supposed Shadow would have faced great dilemma. To invoke our host in the name of Sigurr, the Shadow must perform solemn and dangerous ritual, a good deal of which only I and the consecrated judges of the temple are familiar with. To refuse to invoke the host would bring Sigurr's wrath down upon his head, not to speak of the wrath of the Princes of the Blood. It is certain that you were taken the second time for the selfsame reason; Mehrayn had freed you, and you would soon be about and under foot again.''

The male sighed, shifted his position slightly yet carefully, then closed his fists upon the linked metal which stretched between his wrists.

"As I gather it," said he, "the chain of events went as follows: when I first spoke to Ladayna of my intention to soon go off and commune with Sigurr, he who stands in the darkness began to put his plan into effect. Mehrayn, the one man in the city who not only knows me well but who also has the power to demand an accounting of me, is sent off on the pretext of his examining an enemy city. His return is not expected for some time, therefore does the delay in my departure fail to distress the unknown foe. He has only to wait till the unexpected demand upon the Shadow's time is done with, and then the Shadow will take himself off.''

The male paused to reach painfully to the pot of water, raised it in a shaking hand, then drained it quickly.

"Perhaps he even sent traitors about, searching for me in the woods and upon the mountain," he then growled, wiping his mouth with the back of his hand as he allowed the pot to drop from his fingers. "Should that be so, I find great joy in the thought of his deep frustration. Sigurr's Shadow did indeed go to commune with Sigurr—and where more clearly does one find Sigurr than among the great god's people? To move about as a simple warrior allows me to gauge the benefits and deficiencies of the policies I have instituted in Sigurr's name—and also allows me to joy in life a short while without the burdens I otherwise carry so gladly.

"In any event," he continued with a short though deep breath, "the Shadow has disappeared and cannot be found. The foe must cool his impatience and bide his time till the Shadow's return, and then disaster strikes! Sigurr's Sword returns considerably sooner than his originally announced intention, and a strange female arrives, demanding to speak with the Shadow! Ladayna attempts to send the female away, and when that proves impossible, has her enslaved. The wench should then be permanently out of the way, yet is it Mehrayn who takes her from the alcove to his house, a place she cannot be retrieved from. It becomes necessary to await Mehrayn's next departure, which has hastily been arranged for, and therefore is the foe prepared to recapture her when she attempts to depart. The Shadow makes an appearance at last, is neatly snagged by guardsmen who think him a deranged blasphemer, and he and the strange female are sent at last upon the journey of no return—with not a single drop of their blood having been spilled. Should Sigurr seek vengeance against those who ultimately take the lives of his Shadow and his messenger, the foe will not stand among them."

"Should the vengeance be mine rather than Sigurr's, the foe *will* stand among them," I assured the male. "Do you think yourself able to survive in these trials spoken of till Mehrayn's return? I do not yet know what they entail."

"I am all too well aware of what they entail," said the male, his voice again filled with anger. "The trials have been a tradition among us for untold numbers of kalod, and though the practice offended me, I made no attempt to end it and put another in its place. I now reap the fruits of my reluctance to tamper with tradition."

The male's self-anger attempted to grow stronger, yet did he throw off the useless emotion with a small shake of his head, and again met my eyes.

"Among other displays of prowess, the trials are held each and every fey, with victor trials held each fifth fey," said he. "Upon the first fey fight the newest and most inexperienced men, upon the second fey the next most able and so on, through the fourth fey and the best. Upon the fifth fey stand the victors of the previous four feyd, the lowest facing the next highest victor, the victor of that match facing the next highest, and so on. This is done till but one victor stands for each of five sets of five feyd and then, two feyd later, the five must contend among themselves for the ultimate winner. Twice each kalod the ultimate winners contend, and once each kalod the two winners of those contests face one another. As there is no release from the Caverns of the Doomed, each man, no matter his position or skill, fights to the best of his ability, for there is naught further for him to lose save his life, which he finds most precious even in this place."

"The male Chaldrin spoke of training," said I, considering his words to that point. "For what reason must these males be trained? Are they not capable of wielding a sword in these trials?"

"For the most part, these—males are not warriors," said he with something of a smile. "A warrior will most often be given the opportunity of fighting to the death rather than being condemned to the Caverns. And the trials consist of more than simple swordplay. In the elimination trials, three contestants are sent forth unarmed into the deep cavern where only two sets of arms await. They contend unarmed for the weapons, the first of which are daggers. Should there be two survivors once the daggers have been reached, the next weapon they attempt to keep each other from is swords. Beyond the swords are crescent spears, and he who obtains one first is usually the victor."

"Crescent spears," said I, recalling the look of the strange spears the attackers had used upon Mehrayn's male Hesain and myself. Taller than the large males would the spears have stood from the ground, one end of the thick, dark, wooden shaft knobbed, the other surmounted by slim, sharp, slightly curved metal joined to the shaft by a flat, wide circle of metal. The males had swung the weapons in double circles, the sharp blades flashing in to slash with a passing stroke, the knobbed end blocking sword thrusts and riposting with solid blows. "I would enjoy learning the full use of these crescent spears of yours," said I.

"Such an eventuality is scarcely likely, here," said Aysayn with a grimace. "Here, one learns weapons for survival, not sport. And to reply to an earlier question you put, only Sigurr knows the length of time I shall survive once I enter the trials. I count myself an able warrior, yet one accidental misstep may end all. And it is not the time of Mehrayn's return with which we must concern ourselves. How is Sigurr's Sword to know where we have been sent—or that we are any place other than where we are supposed to be? And what if he speaks with the foe behind the Golden Mask and tells of your mission from Sigurr? Will he not merely join us here, to stand his turn in the trials? Or perhaps, as he is fully known to our warriors, might he not be struck down without warning? The foe is ruthless, and he will not cavil at Mehrayn's death."

"You undoubtedly speak the truth," said I, shifting where I knelt upon his fur to the urging of a growing anger. "Mehrayn will likely lose his life to this foe of yours, knowing naught of the reason for his having been done so. Mida take me for not having spilled her blood when she first stood before me!"

"She?" frowned Aysayn, looking upon me with a great lack of understanding. "What she do you speak of? The foe behind the Golden Mask *cannot* be female!"

"Yet Ladayna is female, and Ladayna is without doubt the primary foe," I retorted, gesturing an angry dismissal of his foolishness. "Was it not Ladayna who suggested Mehrayn's visit to Bellinard? Was it not Ladayna who was told of your intention to commune with Sigurr? Was it not Ladayna who had me declared slave without hesitation, who stood able to order new guards to the place before your chambers, who swore she knew you not? Was it not she before whom I was taken when I was recaptured by her males? What does it matter upon whom she has put the Golden Mask? It is her will alone which directs it!"

"Sigurr take me for the fool that I am," breathed the male, enlightenment reaching him at last. "Ladayna was ever the sulking, petulant, badly raised child of an indulgent father, yet did I believe her slowly maturing to true adult outlooks beneath the firm hand I saw to her with. Rather than maturing, she was indulging in plots which would allow full rein to her willfulness! Should I ever find my way from these caverns, she will rue the fey she first conceived of them!"

Aysayn now shared the anger I felt, yet did his anger seem to stem from a source other than mine. He shifted about carefully in his fury, enraged even more that he might not move with accustomed freedom, then became aware of the look I sent toward him.

"You think me more than a fool for having loved her," said he, a great deal of bitterness in his voice and eyes. "To love an overindulged child who has the form of a woman is the act of a king of fools, yet did I believe I might teach her to love me in return. You are not a man, and therefore know naught of the feelings of a man, wench. Perhaps I indulged her also, more than I intended, yet I now pay for my folly—with more than an aching back.''

"The price of her willfulness has been taken from others in addition to you, male," said I, rising to my feet to ease the stiffness brought about by kneeling. "There are those who await me in another place, those who may wait in vain should I fail to escape this place. The male Hesain has given his life, and Mehrayn may well do the same. Rather than cast about for one to blame, you would be wiser to cast about for an avenue of escape—as I shall be doing."

"It is said that there *is* no escape from these caverns," said he, the difficulty he found in looking up at me without pain taking his mind from the bitterness. "I will not see a wench risk the penalties of recapture under conditions such as these. Once the soreness is gone from me, it is I who will find release from this place—for both of us. Till then, you need only obey what commands are given you to continue in safety. I have no wish to be held accountable by Sigurr for the lack of well-being of his messenger."

"Your dark god cares naught for what befalls this message bearer, now that his word has been brought," said I, looking down upon the male with as little expression as was possible. "Should I fail to find my own escape, there will be no other to aid me. When you have healed, you may do as you wish, male; I shall seek release from capture long before then."

"Such a seeking will have you find no more than punishment, slave," came another voice, interrupting the words Aysayn would have spoken. I turned to see the arrival of Chaldrin, who was accompanied by two other white-clad males. Chaldrin's first words had been for me, yet as soon as he stood directly before the lines of metal, his gaze went to where Aysayn lay.

"I trust you now understand who is in command and who must obey in these precincts, nestling," said he to Aysayn, looking upon the male much as he had looked upon me. "Should my eye for trialflesh not be failing me, you will surely stand for many encounters upon the glowing sands. I will begin your training as soon as you are able to move without pain, and will have you in the trials as soon thereafter as I deem you fit for them. You will not be lashed again, save that you forget your place a second time."

"Forget my place," growled Aysayn, anger hardening the dark of his eyes. It was clear he wished to raise himself from the fur and meet the eye of the other as an equal, yet the lash would not permit him such dignity. He lay belly down in the fur, his wide fists clenched against the manacles upon his wrists, his light, pain-dampened hair reaching for his eyes. "I am all too well aware of my place in these precincts," said he, attempting to sound as though he stood with head high. "And if I should refuse to train for and enter your trials? What then of the place you think to put me in?"

"It will merely be changed to the place of a slavey," shrugged the brawny male, folding his massive arms across his chest. "With the large number of trial fighters ever to be found here, we require nearly as large a number of slaveys to see to their needs. Should you wish to serve, held in the chains you now wear, so be it. Should you wish to be denied all save the sight of slave wenches, so be it. A victor in the trials is given a slave female for the entire darkness after the fey of his victory. A victor of the fives might confidently look forward to the use of this slave who now stands before you. Can you not feel the pull of her, even through the pain of the lash? Will you find yourself able to look upon her as a slavey, knowing yourself forever forbidden to touch her?"

The voice of Chaldrin had grown persuasive, and I turned in the silence to find Aysayn's eyes upon me, his determination to give Chaldrin no satisfaction wavering. Without thought, my body straightened and my chin rose higher in anger, and a sudden spark showed in Aysayn's eyes before he returned his gaze to Chaldrin.

"You seem to be well aware of the price a man will pay for certain objects of value," said Sigurr's Shadow, his tone having lost much of its previous stiffness and anger. "I will consider your offer during the time I rid myself of your gift of immobility. Once that has been accomplished, I will require a loincloth and the services of this slave."

"You may have neither," replied Chaldrin, nodding to one of his males, who began to open the bolt which held the cell door shut. "Neither nestling nor fighter is permitted to cover his body, therefore will you remain as you are. The services of this slave are required elsewhere, therefore will you be attended by a slavey, learning of his duties so that you may be aided in your decision. At no time will you be given a slave female for your own—save that you win her for a darkness."

A measure of anger returned to Aysayn, yet he made no comment as the white-clad male entered the cell, walked beyond me to the bowls of provender and looked into them, then shook his head toward Chaldrin. At Chaldrin's nod he returned to wrap his hand about my arm and pull me from the cell, and Chaldrin again looked upon Aysayn.

"You will be wise to eat as soon as you are able," said he to Aysayn, glancing at the male who reshot the bolt upon the cell door. "The preparations for the trials take nearly as much strength from a man as the trials themselves, which may be replaced only with food and rest. A slavey, too, requires his strength, the better to serve those who fight. Consider well, nestling."

With such words did Chaldrin himself take my arm, and then was I pulled from the area of Aysayn's cell. No words were spoken as we traversed the corridor between cells, yet when we entered the chamber area of barred doors, Chaldrin halted and looked down upon me.

"So, you continue to think of escape, eh, wench?" said he, amusement rather than anger touching him. "Has it not yet occurred to you that as impossible as escape is for all, it is yet more possible for any other above you?"

"You speak foolishness, male," I scoffed, dismissing the near-painful strength of his hand about my arm. "I much doubt that there is one among your set of slaves who is my equal, not to speak of my superior. How, then, might they escape more easily than I?"

"Woman, the reason is the very truth you spoke!" He laughed, joined by the others of his males. "There is indeed none here to equal you, therefore will you be watched and guarded like no other. Neither my men nor the fighters will countenance the idea of losing your use, therefore will you be given no opportunity for escape. And I! I, too, will not lose the use of you, though my use will not be as theirs! With you, I will surely have the means to save the best, rather than lose them to the final despair of the sands! When a man fights too often for his life, knowing there is naught before him save further battle for that very life, too often he will grow morose and begin brooding. From the brooding comes despair, and then the man finds that he has no further interest in victories, no matter that his life hinges upon them. With you, I will find it possible to offer interest as well as life, and bring many through the dark time back into the light. No, my girl, you will not find escape an avenue open to you, no matter your own beliefs on the subject."

He then turned and pulled me toward the last of the unbarred entranceways, an empty corridor running for some distance behind it. Beyond the corridor was a farther chamber of barred doorways, with a greater number of white-clad males standing at what seemed guardposts. Chaldrin took me to the first barred door upon the left, waited as the lines of metal were drawn back from the opening, then hurried me within.

The area was a good deal larger than it had seemed from without, containing perhaps ten hands of males, all bare of covering. Some had been in the midst of bare-handed strength play, some with dagger-sized carvings of wood, others with wooden sword or spear shapes. Nearly a third of the males sat or lay about the large, well-lit yet nearly bare chamber, seemingly lost in their own thoughts, and Chaldrin paused near the entrance till even these had looked up and seen him. When a silence had fallen and then been replaced by growing murmurs of surprise, the burly male took me to the left of where we had stood, to an area where a large, male-shaped stuffing of cloth hung suspended from the ceiling by a length of leather tied off at the wall behind it. The white-clad males accompanying Chaldrin quickly removed the cloth stuffing from the leather, and then was I pushed forward and my wrists as quickly entangled in the leather. A single pull raised me to my toes with my arms high above my head, and Chaldrin turned to the males of the chamber as the leather holding me was tied off.

"I was not pleased when I entered this exercise area," said he into the silence which had resumed. "Those of you with swords and spears stood and moved as though gut-stabbed; you who practiced with daggers seemed about to drop them, and those half dozen engaged in hand-to-hand would have fallen to a single twist administered by a tiny girl child. I had thought I entered the exercise area of victors; perhaps I mistook my direction and now stand before nestlings instead."

A low mutter began as Chaldrin looked about himself, yet the mutter receded before the gaze of the male, and none spoke aloud in insult at his words. I pulled at the leather which held me so easily in place, and Chaldrin turned to regard me where I hung suspended on my toes.

"Had I truly found myself before victors," said he, "I would have shown them the newest slave female sent to our domain. The wench attempted escape and was punished for it, yet does she continue to contemplate the possibility. Perhaps she is filled with a truly great fear, for she has been told that her use will be given to victors of the fives. Perhaps her fear is well-founded, for it is said among slave wenches that to be taken by a victor—of even a lesser encounter—is to be conquered to the soul."

A wide sprinkling of laughter rippled through the listening males, increasing when I again fought the leather. To say that I feared any male was to offer deadly insult, yet Chaldrin cared not. He merely moved closer to where I hung, and took my face in his hand.

"Is there none among you who would fight to have this wench?" he demanded, again looking about at the males. "Do you all find solitary comfort, or joy in no more than the screams of slaveys? Look at her!" Hands groped at my left hip, and in a moment the pale red cloth had been untied and allowed to fall about my feet.

"Merely gaze upon her!" said Chaldrin, releasing my face so that his hands might move together down my body. "The wench cries out for taming by a victor! Which of you will fight for her use in the victor trials?"

"I!" shouted many voices together, the large group moving slowly yet surely closer. "She will be mine!" "No, mine!" "It is I who will claim her!" said many voices at once, and Chaldrin held his hand up. When silence returned at last, he nodded toward the eager, hungry horde.

"Spoken like victors to be," said he. "It now requires no more than your survival to see the matter so. Is your use of the practice area done for the fey?"

Again something of a silence came, yet one which lasted a very short time indeed. By twos and threes the males turned away to resume their play fighting, till none were left about me save the two white-clad males and Chaldrin. The latter nodded very slightly to his two males, then turned away and began to move among the uncovered males. As soon as he no longer looked upon me, the male to my left approached with a length of dark cloth and, to my deep surprise, wound it about my eyes. For a time had sight been denied me, yet I needed it not to see that the gesture boded no good.

The reckid passing were few indeed before the truth of my thoughts was proven. I had not heard the white-clad males leave their places to either side of me, yet suddenly there was the heavy breathing of more than one male to my left, and a hand came to the back of my thigh to stroke it. I attempted to move away from the sting of the touch, yet the hand followed without pause.

"Your attack was lacking in the necessary speed, man," came a low, short-winded voice which somehow seemed to belong to the hand. "Your blood will blot out the Shining Sand, and you will never taste the sweetness of this slave."

"I rarely waste my speed in practice," came the equally low, short-winded reply from a point slightly before me. "I use my speed only upon the Sands—and never in a place such as this."

My low gasp set both the males to chuckling, for the second had touched my thighs in front. I stood poised between the two unseen males, touched by both, able to escape neither. To kick out blindly was to find naught save the air reached, and also caused a greater amusement between the males. They and their touches remained only a short time before they presumably returned to that which they had been about, yet they were not the last who came. Others brushed past and lingered, all discussing the needs of the trials, all seeking a knowledge of Jalav through touch. Two went so far as to bring their mock battle to me, grunting and grappling briskly to my right and then, without warning, before and behind me. Around me did they attempt to reach one another, yet not as seriously as they attempted to reach me. Pinned between their sweating bodies, their hands and desires touching all about, I was unable even to struggle to any degree. These two proved to be the last, however, for a hand of reckid after they had left me, hands replaced the cloth about my waist as other hands removed the cloth from my eyes; Chaldrin himself stood and awaited the lowering of the leather and the release of my wrists, and when it was done he again took my arm and pulled me from the area.

I knew not how many practice areas we visited in just such a manner, nor the number of hind passed in the doing. I knew only the growing pain in my body and the weakness of my limbs, the emptiness in my middle and the despair in my heart. I had attempted to disbelieve the words of Chaldrin concerning my escaping that place, yet the pleasure he showed when his males looked upon me with interest was undeniable. I would not be allowed even limited freedom in that place; my lot would be to give service to males as long as I was able. I hung in the leather of the latest of the practice areas, my sight closed away behind darkening cloth, attempting to deny the urgings of despair, yet the truth it spoke could not be gainsaid. My task had been to carry Sigurr's word to his Sigurri, and this I had done. The standing task of any warrior to escape capture had been shown to be impossible. Was I, a war leader of Hosta, war leader to all Midanna, to meekly serve my enemies in whatever manner they wished? Had I not thought with pleasure of the end to all service, to Midanna and males and the gods alike? Perhaps the end to all service was not as far as I had thought, and these males were destined to aid in the attaining of it. It would be more easily done than escape and perhaps more pleasant, for the absence of my life sign would put me beyond even the reach of the gods. A part of me still denied such an action as despicable surrender, yet the rest of me was too filled with pain and weariness to agree.

"Chaldrin, I think you had best see to the slave," came a soft voice from my right. "She has not fought the leather nor the touching in too long a time, and seems more lifeless than listless. What ails her?"

With the sound of footsteps came a groping at the cloth about my eyes, and then did the cloth fall away to reveal Chaldrin peering at me with a frown. I blinked away the immediate brightness of the torches, and paid the male no mind.

"What ails you, slave?" asked he, taking my face in his hand and raising it toward his own. "The fire has gone from those dark eyes of yours, and pain has entered in its place. If you were in pain, why did you not speak of it?"

He waited only a moment, then made a sound of annoyance.

"For the same reason, no doubt, that you refused to cry out during your punishment," he muttered, displeased to a large degree. "Sooner would one such as you see herself senseless than admit to discomfort or pain. It is apparently beyond you to understand that the last thing I wish is for true harm to come to you. Should this occur again, speak to me of it."

He then gestured for the leather to be released, yet not, as I had thought, to find another area of males. My faltering steps were directed instead toward a corridor which returned us to the area leading to the punishment area for female slaves. Rather than return me to that end chamber, however, I was taken within one of the nearer chambers, a fur was thrown to the stone floor, and Chaldrin pushed me down upon it.

"There will soon be slaves here to tend you," said he, crouching down beside me where I lay, without strength, upon the fur. "Salves and herbs will take the pain from you, washing and combing the sweat and dirt, food the beginnings of gauntness, and sleep the weight of weariness. I will allow you to serve the needs of none save Treglin this darkness, for the recovery of your strength is of paramount importance. A wench may be used many times by many men, if she is well cared for during the times between that use."

He looked upon me with narrowed eyes, perhaps awaiting what words I would speak, yet I closed my own eyes without wasting breath in useless words. To spend an eternity in service to males was not a thing I would accept; the final darkness was an end to all pain and weariness, an end to the need for bravery and bitter choice. The fur beneath me held my aching body with a softness and comfort I found laughable, there in the midst of my enemies. The war leader Jalav had been captured and penned, yet would she find an escape these others had not the courage to seek.

The male stirred with what seemed to be annoyance, yet the silence which was apparently the source of his annoyance remained undisturbed till the arrival of three slave females. These females sought my cooperation in their ministrations, but I cared too little to make the effort. My body was washed and their salves were spread, yet their herb-mixture went unswallowed, and they found it necessary to comb my hair as I lay unmoving upon my side. The male Chaldrin had gone elsewhere at their arrival, therefore were they helpless to counter my refusals. Their upset was strong as they toiled over my well-being, and I misunderstood their concern till a fourth female arrived, bearing a wide wooden board with many pots and platters upon it. The aroma of fresh-cooked provender assailed me as the board was lowered to a place not far from my fur, and the fourth female turned to me with a smile clear upon her.

"I wish you a hearty appetite, sister," she whispered as she knelt to smooth my hair. "You must eat all that I have brought and grow strong again, so that the masters who seek the rest of us will be fewer in number. Surely has Sigurr answered our prayers with your appearance, and will answer them again with your return to health."

"You think me one who will lighten your burdens?" I rasped, shaking her hand from my hair as I straightened to sitting. "Seek, instead, to lighten your own burdens, and do not welcome me so gladly, slave. I am not the answer you have prayed for."

"You think to refuse your use to the masters?" she laughed, regarding me without fear. "How well did you deny them earlier, sister? Were you able to keep them from entering deep within you then? No more than we are you able to deny them, and word has it that you are also meant for the victors. They are far worse than the masters, for they will use a slave through all of the darkness they possess her, taking all they might against their time without. When you are returned weeping from their cells, we will tend you gently and lovingly, knowing you bear the burden you have freed others of us of. Sigurr's blessings upon you, sister, and know that you have our compassion."

The others murmured wordless agreement as all four rose to their feet, smiled a final farewell, then hurried lightly from the chamber. I stared after them, knowing them mad, then lay down again upon the fur. How might they not be mad, so few females, and slaves, among so many males? Had they been wise, they would have taken the direction I, myself, would take. The aroma of provender wafted to me, yet it tempted me not; my eyes closed slowly, and sleep soon found me so.

The approach of another woke me, yet not as quickly as it normally did. My eyes opened to the sight of Chaldrin, who stood frowning above the board of pots and platters, and who then moved his frown to me. When he saw my gaze upon him, he walked to take a fur from the pile in the corner beyond the provender board, returned to drop it beside mine, then sat himself upon it.

"Not a single dish upon that tray has been tasted," he informed me, clearly displeased with such a state. "Should it be your intention to demand better fare, you would be wise to understand that that is the best to be had. For most feyd, our slaves are given no more than gruel; they must work long and hard to earn a taste of meat. Never are they given such an array as that."

It seemed he intended continuing his description of my good fortune, therefore did I close my eyes again, to avoid the flow if not to halt it. My doing did indeed halt the flow, yet only temporarily, and only upon the original topic. A sound of annoyance came, and then his fist in my hair pulled me closer to him and raised my head.

"Speak to me, slave," said he, his gaze and tone calm even with anger lurking behind. "Why have you not eaten from the tray?"

"I have no interest in your provender," I gasped, trying uselessly to loosen the metal of his grip. "You may send the worst in place of the best. I care not."

His hand brought me even closer to his face, and his eyes stared into mine for a moment before he nodded with his anger now most obvious.

"Indeed does Sigurr continue to turn his face from me," he growled, more, perhaps, to himself than to me. "Our wenches are all touched with hopelessness, yet never have I seen one who could not be commanded to her duties with the threat of punishment. For some reason, yours is the hopelessness that touches my fighters, the sort which drains interest in all things, including life. Wench, I will not accept it."

"You may do naught else save accept it," said I, still held painfully in his grip. "I have labored long and hard, and now I am weary and wish to rest. I shall not be put at service to your males."

"Ah, I see," said he with a slow nod. "Being put to the

service of men offends you, and you think to escape from such service into death. This fey has seen you condemned to lifelong slavery, used harshly by many men, well whipped in punishment, and displayed before those who will fight to win your use. You feel the weight of these things pressing down upon you, pain and weariness defeating even anger, and think to embrace death rather than continue with the humiliation of life. What will you do, slave, when the pain and weariness are gone, and the vital life force you are so filled with refuses to allow a passive death? How will you deny its demand that you continue living?''

"Such a thing will not occur," I said, unable to shake my head as I wished to. "The final darkness is mine by right, and I will not be denied!''

"Aha, anger already takes the place of lethargy," he grinned. "You cannot refuse the urgings of your spirit. Should it be necessary, I will have the slave gruel force-fed to you, giving you the nutrition of better fare without its flavor. My men and fighters will enjoy your use no matter if you are free and willing, or chained and savage. Truth to tell, they will prefer finding it necessary to chain you, for Sigurr smiles upon the taking of unwilling wenches.''

"I will not be used!" I shouted, a sudden madness filling me. Ignoring the strength of his grip upon my hair, my claws flashed toward his eyes, my teeth thirsting for his throat. Though I moved in a blur of speed, his movement was faster yet; his free arm came up to block my hands and keep them from him, though he made no attempt to capture them. He allowed me a few moments in futile attempt to battle my way through his defense, and then I was thrown to my back upon the fur, with the impossible male kneeling across me.

"You will be used as often as I allow it," said he, looking down upon me with calm fully restored. "I will not allow your death, for your death would mean the death of too many others. You are a slave and I may do with you as I please, yet do I prefer your willing cooperation. If I should receive it, I will strike a bargain with you: you will eat as well as do my men and I, and I will teach you that which I teach to every awkward, unschooled nestling. Your hands and feet are weapons which are ever with you, and ones which, when properly used, are capable of defeating opponents much larger than yourself. Do you agree to this?''

"I agree to naught!" I spat, struggling to free myself of the grip of his thighs. "Do you think me so foolish as to believe you would school me in a thing which would allow resistance to your commands? The sole weapon I wish to face you with is swords, to show how much slave there is in Jalav! Face me in that way, male, and we may indeed strike a bargain!''

"You have not earned the right to face me with swords," said he, a litany I wearied of. "And as to your belief that my teaching would enable you to disobey me, you are entirely mistaken. There is a deal of difference between learning a thing and mastering it. I teach my skills to all fighters who come here, yet none has mastered them to such an extent that he has been able to defeat me. Should it be your wish to make the attempt, you must first begin the learning. Will you begin with the new light?''

"No," I denied, my fury blazing up at the immovable bulk of him. "I will not give my use to one and all in return for some fatuous male teaching—and one which, by your own words, would not allow me to defeat you. As you continue to fear to allow me to face you with swords, I shall not face you in any manner. It will be the final darkness which I shall face, a thing more pleasant-visaged than you!''

"You sadden me, wench, yet the choice was allowed you," he shrugged, continuing to look down upon me. "You must learn, I think, that you are subject to the commands of men, not the other way about. You will be force-fed, and chained for use, and looked after as though you were a kan broodmare, all of which will be a great humiliation for you. Do not cease to recall that the choice was yours. And Treglin will not visit you this darkness.''

His hands went to the soiled white covering about his loins, speaking of his intention more clearly than words. I increased my struggles, attempting to escape him, and had nearly squirmed to freedom when his big hands took me by the waist.

"Treglin felt the need to use a slave to exhaustion," said Chaldrin, putting himself beside me upon the fur, and rolling me easily against his broad, hair-covered body. "He agreed that you could not now be used so, therefore was I to take his place and reward you with pleasure for the doings you will so obediently perform for us in the coming feyd.''

"As there will be no obedience, there need be no reward," I grunted, held too closely to him for struggle. The flesh of the male was cooler than mine, and his hands moved all about the back of me.

"On the contrary," said he, a chuckle in his voice. "There will be complete obedience from you, therefore do you merit what you will receive. It will be my pleasure to give what a wench such as you requires.''

His hands moved further than my back then, and though I strained with all my will to resist him, it was as it had been earlier. The male well knew the paths to heating my blood, and heat it he did till I could not deny my desire for him. Pleasure he had spoken of and pleasure he gave, in full measure and only that which was asked for. The male did not force himself upon me, entering me only when the desire was mine, seeing to my needs as though he were the supposed slave. When he withdrew and left the chamber so that I might seek sleep again, the memory of pleasure did not befog my understanding of what had occurred. Were I to give the male Chaldrin that which he desired, I would know such pleasure again whenever I wished. Should I continue in my opposition to him, the harshness of forced use would be my only lot. I lay flat upon the sweat-stained fur and closed my eyes, banishing the flicker of the chamber's single torch. Had I been foolish enough to expect aught save pain from males, Chaldrin's ploy might perhaps have succeeded. Pleasure was a thing Jalav the captive had learned to do without—and would continue to do without till the pleasure of final darkness came.

11 A victor—and a bargain is struck

I knew not how the males of those nether regions knew the time of the fey without seeing the new light, yet know they did—and acted accordingly. True to Chaldrin's word, the first who came after I had awakened from sleep bore chains with them, thick, ponderous links into which I was placed with a solemn air of finality. I fought the closing of the cuffs about my wrists, yet the three males who had forced me face down upon the fur had little difficulty in completing their task. My arms were shackled behind me, and then the new fey was allowed to begin.

Thrice that fey was the gruel of slaves forced down my throat, each time with much difficulty, yet each time successfully. With the spilled gruel washed from me by slave females and my hair twisted about itself to keep it from knotting, I was then taken to a large chamber already filled with other females and white-clad males. The males removed the pale red hip cloths from the females and the white loin coverings from themselves, and then were we used by the males, turn and turn about, till all had been satisfied. I made no effort to count the number of males who took me, and felt no gratitude that each took care to be somewhat gentle in his use. Though I attempted to recall the despair which would carry me to the final darkness, I was able to find no more than the blaze of fury which lit the burning blood-lust within me. Had I had a sword to hand, I would have slain without stop till all of them lay dead in their own blood.

Thrice, also, was I taken to serve the white-clad males, and between these times was I taken before the bare-bodied fighting males and promised as a gift to him who found victory over the others. Once only did Chaldrin attempt to put his hand to my face with his eyes elsewhere; though the unclad males howled with laughter, Chaldrin made no sound when my teeth sank into his flesh and he found it necessary to force his hand free. I had drawn no more than a small amount of blood, yet was I prepared for the outraged anger the male would surely show. He rubbed

308

the pain from his hand with his dark eyes squarely upon me, brushed lightly at the many-colored circle about his bruised eye, then stepped the closer to me with faint amusement rather than deep anger. His fist came to my hair, and his lips took mine so quickly it was done before I knew what he was about. When the deep, demanding kiss was accomplished to his satisfaction, he turned to the unclad males.

"There is ever a danger in causing a wench such as this to squirm," said he in a voice which all might hear. "She is reserved for victors by cause of the sharpness of her temper and teeth—and the fact of her helplessness in the arms of a man. She is female, and easily brought to heat—and will not thank you for forcing her to writhe in any manner other than the one I was thanked. Do you wish me to offer you another slave?"

"No!" came the shouts of nearly every male within the area, so loud that I was nearly deafened. And then the laughter came, rivaling the sound of the shout, raising my fury so high that it was nigh unto madness. I fought the chain which held my wrists behind me, and nearly pulled free of the two white-clad males who held me, and Chaldrin no longer showed the amusement he felt. He directed that I be taken from the area of fighting males and left awhile to myself, yet even uninterrupted solitude failed to cool my rage for more than a hin. I smoldered through the rest of the fey, made no comment when I was returned to the chamber I was to pass the darkness in and the shackle was removed, then struggled uselessly when the male Treglin came to claim my use. When he was done and gone and quiet spread throughout the caverns, I left the chamber and attempted escape.

The following fey matched the humiliation of the previous one with pain. Though I had been able to avoid the watchers set over me by Chaldrin the darkness previous, it had proven impossible to pass all of the guards who stood watch upon the corridors between the inner caverns and the outer. The males proved themselves as deaf as all city males, yet even city males will see that which is pushed before their eyes. I avoided some and outdistanced others, yet were there too many ahead of me as well as behind. When I was trapped at last between the two groups, I was taken to the place called the wall of judgment, chained there by the neck, and left for the balance of the darkness. When the unseen new light brought Chaldrin to stand over me, I merely leaned back against the stone of the wall and refused to acknowledge his presence. Chained as I was, bereft of all covering, still did I consider myself unbeaten—and determined to act so. This the male must have seen and understood, and quickly took steps to change the situation.

The second whipping he gave was indeed more painful than the first, and meant to be more humiliating as well, as it was given before nearly every slave in the caverns. Remaining silent during the ordeal was somewhat difficult; afterward I found myself unable to stand, and not solely by cause of the countless strokes to the bottoms of my feet. Waves of pain washed over me as I was carried to a fur in the punishment chamber and again chained by the neck, yet Mida sometimes sees to her own, even in the depths. When the first male came and attempted my use, darkness closed in and removed me from the agony.

Consciousness returned me to the fur in the punishment chamber, and naught else removed me from it for the balance of the fey. Slave females brought pots of warm broth which I was unable to refuse, and white-clad males came without number, this time even more unrefusable than the broth. No salve was vouchsafed me to withstand their use, and all took care not to send me to the darkness again. At fey's end I was removed from the punishment chamber and returned to my usual place for the darkness, a place I could not stir from even though I tried. I lay upon the fur spread for me, encased in pain, grimly pleased that it had not been deemed necessary to chain me nor set guards over me. Chaldrin thought me sufficiently punished to keep me from again attempting escape, yet was he mistaken. I closed my fist about a handful of old, used fur, and swore to myself that the following darkness, with pain or without, I would again attempt escape. In that I, too, was mistaken; the following darkness, I was given to a victor.

That the entire fey was spent restoring me meant naught till two white-clad males came and chased the slave females from their task. With my wrists chained behind me, a pale red cloth tied about my hips, and a length of leather knotted about my throat, I was led limpingly through corridor and chamber till we came to the corridor which led between the rows of cells. I had not seen the male Chaldrin, and I thought it possible I was to tend Aysayn again, yet we halted a good distance from the cell I had first been taken to. This second cell was untenanted, and when the bolt had been drawn back and the door opened, I was taken within.

"For what reason have I been brought here?" I demanded of the male who held the throat leather. "For what reason. . . ."

"Silence, slave," interrupted the male, pulling me to the left of the cell door, to the side wall. Once there, I was forced to my knees, the throat leather was brought behind me and looped through the wrist chain, then tied about my ankles to keep me as I had been put. With the leather in place, my hip cloth was straightened and my hair spread out all about, and then the male stepped back to survey his handiwork.

"What think you, Falisan?" said he to the male who awaited without. "Think you Vanadin will find pleasure in the sight of his waiting gift?"

"He will do more than find pleasure in the sight of her," chuckled the other, leaning one hand upon a line of metal. "So wild was he for the use of her, he attempted to refuse having his wound seen to."

"To be willing to bleed to death for the use of a wench," sighed the first, turning to leave the cell. "I remember the feeling well, and am inordinately pleased to have it no more than a memory."

"And I," said the second, throwing the bolt after the first was once more in the corridor. The two cast me a final glance and retraced their way up the corridor, where soon even their steps faded to naught.

I found I was able to pull at the leather with my chained wrists, yet freeing it from about my ankles was totally impossible. It was clear from the words of the males that I had been won by the first of their fighters, and the thought of the thing brought my fury on with such strength that the red mist of battle lust nearly floated before my eyes. I, who had won countless battles, was to be given to a male who had triumphed but once! Again I struggled where I knelt, bruising my knees through the thin hip cloth, yet no more came of it than one would expect. The single torch flickered and burned upon the wall, the stale, heavy odor of many males came to me, the silence dinned upon my ears; I remained bound and kneeling where I had been placed, awaiting the arrival of a victor.

The sound of footsteps was not long in coming. Surely had I expected them to be hurried, yet no more than a steady pace brought two males, one white-clad, one without covering save for a length of white cloth bound about his left arm. He who was unclad was light of hair, with light, burning eyes which held to me throughout his approach and the opening of the cell. He entered slowly, this large, lean fighter covered with scars, and stopped before me where I knelt, to stare for a long, silent moment. Then he crouched and reached his hands out to the cloth at my hips, untied it and allowed it to fall from me, and lastly reached between my thighs.

"Indeed are you worth the pain and effort you cost," he murmured, continuing to touch me till I could no longer kneel without movement. "Your dark, lovely eyes say you cannot be tamed, yet will I teach you differently throughout this darkness. You will weep and call me master, and beg to give me whatever pleasure I wish. By the blood I have spilled and the blood I have shed do I swear to conquer you."

The white-clad male in the corridor chuckled and departed; those other unclad males later brought one by one to their cells also found amusement in my presence. He who crouched before me showed no amusement, not then and certainly not throughout the darkness. When the white-clad ones came with the new fey to remove me from the cell, even they lost their amusement.

"It can only have been his vow," said the white-clad male, a weariness to his voice. "I recall I laughed when I heard it, after I brought him to his cell."

"I find naught at which to laugh," growled Chaldrin, bending over me. "What sort of vow might he have made, to do this wench so?"

"He vowed to conquer her," sighed the other, stirring where he stood. "He swore that she would call him master and pleasure him at his bidding. With this one— Perhaps he was unable to keep his vow."

"Perhaps!" spat Chaldrin, straightening and turning the glare of his anger upon the other. "Have you no wits, man? Have you not seen the stubbornness of this wench? It was mindless to have left her there after hearing Vanadin's vow, left with no thought for what he might do! Where were your wits?"

"Perhaps they were with yours, Chaldrin, when you spoke to the fighters of her need to be tamed," replied the male, quiet bitterness in his tone. "Had I known Vanadin would savage her, I would not have left her with him. I, in his place, would merely have enjoyed her. Perhaps I should have paid closer heed to his vow—and perhaps you should not have given such a challenge to the fighters."

A silence came, one during which no more than breathing was to be heard, and then Chaldrin sighed.

"The fault is indeed mine," said he, all anger drained away. "I, too, would not have responded to such a challenge in such a way, yet it is now clear that Vanadin's sort would do no other thing. Go and see why the medications have not yet been brought."

"Chaldrin," began the other, yet the male refused to hear his words.

"Go!" he thundered, and when the sound of footsteps had left the chamber, he again crouched beside me. "Do you sleep, wench?" he asked very softly, putting a gentle hand to my hair. "Or is it merely that Sigurr, in his kindness, lends you some portion of his blessed darkness?"

"Neither," I whispered, spending the effort to raise my arm so that I might push his hand away. I made no attempt to open my eyes, however, for in some manner the light seemed to increase my pain.

"We—will soon have the pain eased," he ventured, making no attempt to touch me a second time. "It was not my intention to have you beaten nearly to death. This was not foreseen, and will surely not occur again."

I lay as still as possible upon the pile of furs added to that which had been mine, feeling the ache that simple breathing brought, echoing the deep pain from blows to body and face, twists of fingers in flesh, use without care or end. Jalav had been taught what came from association with males, yet Jalav, ever a fool, had not yet learned to shun their company. Males would be the death of Jalav, and surely that would see the problem solved.

"Do you hear me, wench?" asked Chaldrin. "You have my word that this will not occur again."

"And you have my word," I breathed, the whisper trembling from the pain of speech. "Should I ever succeed in escaping this accursed hole, I will find a sword and return to seek you. I will have your life, male, immediately after I have that of the female Ladayna. Though you be Sigurr's, I will not allow him to deny me your life."

A whirling illness came to my middle then, undoubtedly caused by the vehemence of my vow. I should not have allowed fury to take me with such weakness and pain abounding, yet Jalav continued to be a fool. I twisted to one side, prepared to clear the fur if I could not hold back the heaving swell behind my gullet, yet there was happily little within me to demand exit. After a moment I again lowered myself to the furs, shamefully voicing a small groan for the pain. I immediately looked to where Chaldrin had crouched, certain he would show ridicule for my weakness—yet Chaldrin was no longer there.

The slaves came with their salves and liquids and promised compassion, but they were required to stand aside till Treglin touched me all over, searching for cracks within to match the bruises without. The probing was necessary yet agonizing, and by the end of it I swam in a sea of swirling dark and many-colored pain. Two of the slaves wept as they tended me, this do I remember, yet little else of the time. A liquid was spilled down my throat which first caused me to choke, then caused me to sleep.

Upon awakening, I felt that a good deal of time had passed. I moved about upon the furs, determining which of the pain remained and which had fled, then lay still again. I could not move with sufficient ease to attempt escape again, yet when all the pain had gone, I would undoubtedly be given to another male or males, to reward them for having survived a battle. A slave female brought provender and timidly urged me to feed, but I turned my back upon her and sent all thought from my mind. It had been a considerable time since I had last called upon Mida for aid and solace, and I did not do so then. I merely mourned the fact that I could not.

The slave female left the board of provender and departed, yet only a few moments of solitude were vouchsafed me. I heard the sound of footsteps, clearly not those of a slave female, and then a hand touched my shoulder.

"You will not be allowed to refuse nourishment, slave," came the voice of Treglin, disapproval clearly to be heard. "You must heal and grow strong again, and this cannot be accomplished without food."

"I am to assist in healing and growing strong, so that I might be used again?" I asked, making no effort to turn to face him. "Jalav may be a fool, male, but is she scarcely so great a fool as that."

"Wench, you are a slave," said the male, his hand tightening somewhat upon my shoulder. "What was done to you was regrettable in that you were damaged, yet was it naught that a slave might not expect. You will indeed be healed and strengthened so that you may be used again, for you are far too valuable to lose for all time. Far too valuable a slave."

Though the overall ache I felt was scarcely an aid toward glowing dignity, I turned to my back and gazed up at the crouching male as a war leader might look upon a foolish warrior.

"Jalav is no slave," said I, uncaring that I lay bare and nearly helpless before him. "Jalav is a warrior, born to be no more than captive to males, sworn to give no aid to her enemies, no matter the pain they inflict. Speak of me as a slave if you will, male, yet the truth will not be changed by words. I will accept naught save freedom from my enemies, that or an agreement to face me in challenge. How will you have it?''

"Not as you do," said he with a headshake, his darkly browed eyes continuing displeased. "A man need not waste his time answering the challenge of a slave wench, one who knows not what she speaks of. Those of us who dwell in this domain are not as easily met as you apparently believe. You, slave, will eat the food brought you of your own accord, else will the slave gruel be fed you. Were the decision mine, even this choice would not be given you, yet does Chaldrin wish that food rather than gruel be fed you. With the gruel your recovery will be slower, yet will it come sooner or later.''

"Neither chains nor gruel will assist you, male," said I, continuing to hold his gaze. "Come the fey I have weapon again in hand, your life will be mine no matter the recovery—or lack of it—that I have made.''

"It is impossible to speak with one who is totally beyond all reasoning," said the male, rising from his crouch. "I will inform Chaldrin, and arrange for the gruel to be brought.''

He turned then, and left the chamber without a backward glance. Anger burned within me, a near-fury which threatened to consume me with lack of venting, yet there was no manner in which I might satisfy it. I struggled about to sitting upon the fur, thinking to use pain to dampen the flame, and a slave female entered and halted briefly in startlement. I knew her as the taller, thinner slave who had first accused the male slave upon my arrival, she who had been first to be beaten of the two; she looked upon me where I sat leaning upon one arm, my other hand to my middle, and slowly moved the closer.

"I am to take this tray of food from you now, sister," said she, her voice and odd smile striving for soothing gentleness. "Allow me to assist you in eating from it first, and should they ask, I will say I, myself, ate from it. No one need know save we two, and I shall certainly not speak of it.''

"One does not feed from the provender of one's enemies," I said, taking a breath as I arched my back. My muscles strongly protested such a movement, yet was I determined to recover all strength before the males knew of it.

"In no manner am I your enemy, sister," said the female, bringing herself to kneel upon the fur before me. "I feel naught save deep admiration and love for you, a love which would give you great comfort. Allow me to comfort you in your pain, sister, and show how great my love is.''

Her voice, low and coaxing, lulled me, yet her hand upon my

thigh brought an instant return of fury. Without pausing for thought, my left hand took her right and twisted, and my right hand gripped her throat with a strength which caused her to pale and gasp.

"So you, too, think to use me," I growled, bending her painfully down to the fur. "Without a weapon I may do naught with these males, yet I have no need of a weapon with one such as you. You were foolish to think I might be used with impunity, slave."

"I did not mean you harm, sister!" begged the female in a choking voice, her eyes filled with fear as her hand strove ineffectively to loosen my grip upon her throat. "It is no more than fitting that we who are used so brutally by men should take comfort in each others arms! Were we ones who lived with none save sisters about, such a doing would be commonplace!"

"Such a doing would be idle," I denied, feeling little pity for her lack of understanding. "To have a sister to speak with, to hunt with, to have at one's back in battle, yes; yet, to take a sister in one's arms? To what purpose? One cannot increase one's clan in such a way, nor may one find the strength and hardness which brings joy to a warrior. To prefer a sister to a male strong with seed is to bring disaster upon one's clan. A warrior lives for the glory of her clan in Mida's eyes, a thing which might not be achieved without new, young warriors to replace those fallen in battle. My true sisters find comfort in their place before Mida, and have no interest in the sort which you offer, nor have I. Take yourself from me, slave, and do not return."

"An excellent recommendation," said a voice as I released the female, and we both turned to see Chaldrin standing within the doorway of the chamber, his leather-bound wrists hidden beneath his folded arms. The slave I had released quickly and tremblingly put her head to the floor, and Chaldrin came closer to look grimly down upon her.

"Again good fortune attends you, slave," said he to her. "Had you attempted this other slave at a time when her temper was high, she would surely have ended you rather than merely frightened you. Return to your duties without delay, and perform them with this final thought in mind: should I ever find you attempting to force yourself upon one of your sisters, the manner of your ending will not be as swift and pleasant as that which you would have found at this one's hands. Though this has been told you before, it will not be told you again. Now, go."

The trembling female rose to her feet and attempted to take the board of provender she had come for, yet Chaldrin stood himself before it and gestured her away without it. When she had fled in misery from the chamber, the male turned to me.

"Treglin has told me that you again refuse the food I have sent," said he, crouching down to send me his dark-eyed consideration. "My brother feels that there is naught we may do save pour the slave gruel within you, yet I do not agree. I believe that you will eat the food, and of your own will."

"Your brother sees more clearly than you, male," said I, moving slowly till I sat cross-legged upon the fur. "Jalav does not partake of the offerings of enemies."

"Not even so that you might face them with weapons?" said he, his stare unwavering. "The slave Jalav would make a poor showing against me as she now is, thin and weak and growing ever weaker. The gruel would do little to improve this."

"I am to believe that you would face me?" I scoffed. "You, whose litany is that I have not yet earned the right? Do you think me so gullible as to believe that the opportunity would be given me once I had done that which you wished?"

"You will have my word upon the matter," said he, a stiffness to be heard in his tone. "And above that, there will also be the bargain we agree to. The bargain without which there will be no meeting."

"So you seek again to bargain," said I, straightening myself a bit where I sat. "What is it that you this time wish to offer me?"

"Woman, you do not now sit in a council, with power aplenty behind you," he growled, faint anger beginning to fill his eyes. "The reason I offer anything at all is beyond even my under-standing, and will not be continued forever. Should I agree to allow you to face me, you will also agree that your defeat will require you to pledge yourself as a full slave, to obey without question all commands given you, just as the other slaves do. There will be no further attempts at escape, and you will freely pleasure any man you are sent to. For this, I will have *your* word upon the matter."

I considered the male in silence for a moment, understanding at last the reason for his bargaining, then allowed myself a faint smile.

"And should victory be mine?" I asked, knowing the male considered no such eventuality. "If I am bested, I will be bound to you in full slavery, yet naught has been said concerning the possibility of my besting you. Should such a thing occur, I will then demand full freedom. Do you agree?"

"Your offer seems reasonable," nodded the male, sharing my

faint smile. "The opposite of full slavery is indeed full freedom, therefore do you have my word upon the matter on both points. And you?"

"I, too, will gladly give my word." I smiled, then spat upon the back of my hand. He immediately duplicated the gesture, and we pressed the backs of our fists together, binding the agreement. With this done, the male twisted about and drew the board of provender nearer to my fur.

"You may begin to uphold your end of the bargain with this," said he, gesturing to the provender. "Now that we have come to agreement, I would see us meet as soon as possible."

"And I," I nodded, reaching toward an overdone cut of nilno. "Come the new light, we shall face one another."

"Come the new light *after* the next new light," said he, rising to his full height. "And then only if you are fit to hold a weapon. I will not have you believe you were bested by cause of your own lack of fitness. I wish you a hearty appetite."

He then turned and quit the chamber, wrapped in the satisfaction I, myself, felt. No other save a male would be foolish enough to allow a Midanna war leader the opportunity of reclaiming her full strength before facing her, yet were these indeed males who knew no better. It was now to be my pleasure to teach them better, and teach them I would. I chewed upon the cold, grease-covered, overcooked nilno, and vowed to Mida that I would.

12 Victory—and bitter defeat

The two feyd passed too slowly for my eagerness, yet upon the second even the male Chaldrin was forced to agree that a further delay would be unnecessary. The pain and weakness had passed from me, chased far into nothingness by the prospect of long-desired battle, and I was again able to stand tall and straight to answer a challenge.

Two white-clad males came for me in the middle of the fey, disdaining the use of wrist chains, yet insisting upon the presence of the pale red body cloth about my hips. The point was too unimportant to allow it to cause a delay, therefore did I wrap the cloth about me and accompany the males through the corridors and chambers to a barred area where I had never yet been taken. The lines of metal were withdrawn and I was pushed within, and then was the metal quickly closed behind me so that the males might hurry away. As I looked about the area, it was clear where the males hurried.

The chamber was clearly larger than the previous barred areas I had seen, and more than that contained only three walls of carved stone. The fourth was no more than a partial wall, stretching half again as high as I stood, above which were row upon row of carved steps, stretching back away from the half wall. Upon these broad, wide steps sat many of the white-clad males of the cavern, their eyes following me as I stepped farther out upon the carved rock floor, their voices raised in high good humor and coarse jest. Clearly did they expect to see Jalav made slave this fey, yet such a thing would never be. Sooner than be enslaved, Jalav would allow the point of her enemy to reach her.

"Are you prepared to face me, wench?" came a voice, and I turned to see Chaldrin already upon the field, a sword held in each of his hands. He stood in no more than his white body cloth and leather wrist wrappings, perhaps five paces from where I stood.

"Indeed am I prepared," said I, reaching to the cloth about my hips, untying it, and allowing it to fall. "There will be naught to hamper my blade as it seeks your blood."

"Should you think to distract me with that doing," he grinned, moving nearer, "do not feel too deep a disappointment when it fails. When you find yourself full slave, I will be the first man you are sent to for the purpose of pleasuring him. Which blade would you prefer?"

"It matters little." I shrugged, reaching for the blade he held in his right hand. "So long as I find it well balanced and honestly keen. I will also require it for my freedom, you see."

"Ah, indeed," he nodded, releasing the blade to my grip. A surge of pleasure touched me at the feel of a well made blade in my fist again, and I looked upon the male as I stepped back.

"This weapon will do me," said I, cutting at the air between us to accustom myself to the preferences of the blade. Each sword has its own preference as to how it wishes to be wielded, and the wise warrior will accede to those preferences rather than attempt to defy them.

"Then we may begin," said the male, setting himself with the words. He had taken his own blade into his right fist, and he stood with it held before him, prepared for serious attack despite his belief that victory would be easily his. I, too, stood so at his words, yet not for long. I had not come there with the purpose of posing with sword in hand.

I swung gently at the male, seeking the manner in which he would reply, yet he made no reply other than turning my blade from him. I swung again and found the same result, then understood that the male sought to study my own movements before launching an attack of his own. I continued striking at him as though I knew naught of his purpose, yet did I show considerably less strength and speed than was my wont in battle. It had somehow been clear to me from the first that this male would not be as easily defeated as the others, yet defeated he must be if I was to regain my freedom.

The shouts of the white-clad males who watched from above the wall were both encouraging and derisive, but all voices were eager for the battle to go forward more quickly. Chaldrin paid them no more heed than did I, calmly accepting that which I sent to him till the moment he felt himself prepared to do more. When that moment came he moved quickly indeed, halting my blade then immediately striking at my head. I kept his swing from reaching me easily, too easily, for he had not put strength into the blow. The male laughed softly at the flash of anger I felt; he had forced me to show him some part of the speed I was capable of, despite my earlier resolve.

Without warning, the male then launched a series of attacks at me, his blows full strength, his speed startling. Had I been anything less than a war leader, I would surely have been taken in by the deceit behind the attacks. Chaldrin's aim was to weary my sword arm, wear down my strength till I might no longer fend off attack. His blows were like unto the rock of the entire ceiling falling upon my blade, heavy and unstoppable, resistible only for a very short while. My body wore a sheen of sweat from the attacks I had launched against him, my sword rang and vibrated clear through my arm from his blows, the dirt of the rock floor clung and ground itself into the bottoms of my feet. Two blows I took, then a third, then suddenly slid the fourth and attacked with the speed born of battles without number. Chaldrin had overextended himself in his attempt to put truly great strength into his attack, an error rarely made by any other than a young, inexperienced warrior—or one who was sure she had the measure of her opponent. No matter one's speed and strength, one cannot return from a wide swing till the top of the arc had been reached and the stroke is then directed downward or upward in return. I had not halted Chaldrin's stroke, merely assisted it upon its way, and then was my blade seeking the male's middle, intending to cut into his flesh and free the flow of his blood, so that I, too, might be free.

Straight for the center of the male's body did my blade flash, eager to taste him, yet the male proved himself a worthy opponent indeed. To block the stroke was not possible, therefore did he take the only avenue remaining open to him. With frantic haste he threw himself to his left, twisting as he went, taking no more than the edge of my blade along his left side. I moved quickly after him, intending to spit him to the rock floor should he falter, yet with his third roll was he returned to his feet, his sword held up and ready, his left hand pressed to his side, bright red flowing between his closely held fingers. Those who watched screamed and stomped with deafening frenzy, and Chaldrin himself looked upon me with a gleam in his dark eyes which I had no understanding of.

Though many another male would have ended the battle there, Chaldrin did not. He came at me again, more slowly and warily, attempting to reach me as I had reached him, yet was such a thing not possible. Had he lacked the wound in his side, the matter would surely have been in the hands of Mida; with the blood flowing so freely from him, no more than a hand of reckid passed in brisk, blinding exchange and the clash of metal before Chaldrin stumbled and went to his knees, dizziness and lack of strength taking their toll. I stood before him wide-legged upon the rock floor, raised my sword high in tribute to a warrior of merit, then took it two-handed and raised it high again, preparing to send him to Mida's chains, where he might pleasure her for all of eternity.

"Hold!" came a shout from among those who watched, and I glanced back to see that ropes had been let down the half wall, and males now stood upon the floor, one of them Treglin. Above them, standing upon the lip of the wall, three males with drawn bows stood poised to loose. I snarled an oath and stepped clear of Chaldrin, turning instead with sword raised toward those who advanced slowly across the sandy, blood-marked floor.

"I see again clear evidence of the honor of males," I called in fury to Treglin. "Order those above you to loose now, male, for I shall not again be taken as slave!"

"We have no intentions of taking you again as slave, you ignorant savage!" shouted Treglin, anger boiling truly high within him. "The vow Chaldrin made will be kept by us—yet only if he lives! Stand aside and allow us to tend him!"

"My vow will be kept in any event," came a hoarse croak from my right. I turned my head to see that Chaldrin had again risen to his feet, unsteadily, blood-covered, yet nevertheless standing straight. His sword lay upon the stone at his feet, and he made no attempt to recover it.

"Chaldrin, you are a fool!" stormed Treglin, hurrying forward to take the other male's arm and pull it across his shoulders to brace him. "Had you not allowed her to wound you. . . ."

"Allowed?" barked Chaldrin in a pain-filled laugh. "Are you blind, brother? I underestimated the wench, and nearly lost my life by cause of it. Had I not been wounded I might have held her, yet only through Sigurr's will might I have claimed clear victory. It would please me to face her again—yet only with practice swords."

I understood none of the male's amusement at being bested, yet I felt no insult at the attitude. He had fought with great skill and strength, and had not begged for his life even when it was clear it had been lost. I tossed my head to force my free-flying hair back from my arms, and Chaldrin looked full upon me.

"Freedom is yours, wench," said he, "fully earned as even Treglin knows. In accordance with our bargain, we will now take you to the outer caverns, where you will receive a torch to accompany that sword."

"*I* will take her to the outer caverns," said Treglin, gesturing others of the white-clad males to him. "*You* will be taken to the healer, where your wound may be bound up. And do not attempt to argue, for I will hear none of it!''

The male Chaldrin did indeed attempt disagreement, yet was his strength insufficient to best that of the others. Two males took him from Treglin and began to assist him in quitting the chamber, yet he forced them to halt and twisted about in their grips.

''Do not allow any in the outer world to set eyes upon you, wench!'' he called, able to pause so no more than a brief moment before the others again forced him ahead. ''It is instant death for any who attempt to depart the Caverns! Leave the city at once and do not. . . .''

His words fell away as he was taken from the chamber, and the male Treglin turned from the empty doorway and looked upon me with a great deal of sourness.

''Had that been one of our fighters,'' said he, ''the healer would have been visited with considerably less delay—at that fool's insistence. That he cares less for himself comes as no surprise to one who has known him as long as I. Once he is fit again, we will have words over the loss he has caused for us. Follow me quickly, wench, lest I succumb to the temptation of causing my brother to be forsworn.''

He turned then and strode toward the doorway of the chamber, making no effort to see whether I accompanied him. I glanced toward the three bowmen who had lowered their weapons, saw that those who stood upon the floor kept their distance, then followed Treglin at my own pace.

Treglin impatiently awaited me in the area beyond the chamber, and immediately led the way toward a corridor when I appeared. I followed from corridor to corridor and area to area, aware of the slaves who shrank back from me and the white-clad males who frowned at the weapon I carried, alert for an attempt at treachery which never came. Fully to the heavy metal door of the entrance was I taken, and there did Treglin pause among the males who stood before it.

''Stand back from the door so that we may take within any who have been left chained for us,'' said he, gesturing to the right of the door. ''Once they are sent deeper into the Caverns, we will then give you your torch. Had I been you, I would have taken the slave cloth to cover my body. There is naught here which you might use.''

''I shall make do without,'' said I, moving to one side of the door as he had indicated. I recalled the presence of the green cloth which had been taken from me among the boulders, and knew that it would be easily found with a torch to guide me. I made no mention of my intended halt beyond their precincts, and merely awaited my release.

Two of the males turned to put their shoulders to the door, and it quickly began moving outward. Suddenly, it moved considerably faster than it had, and all the males who were able to see beyond it frowned in surprise.

"So, you have come at last," said a voice from without, a male voice filled with impatience. "There are none here for you to take within, yet are you to take instructions to your leaders. The Shadow was present when the blasphemer sent to you a few feyd earlier fought upon the Shining Sands this fey. The Shadow was much displeased that he did not fall, and directs that he be sent forth again in two feyd, no sooner and no later. My contingent and I will remain here the while, to enter your domain should the word of the Shadow be disobeyed. You may now reclose this door, yet not as fully as previous."

"Wait!" called Treglin, disbelief clear upon him. "I do not understand! What are you. . . ."

"You need not understand," interrupted the voice from without. "You need only obey. Close the door."

Without the aid of those within, the heavy metal door again began to close, though this time there were heavy braidings of leather tied to the bar within and trailing past the edge of the door, keeping it from closing with its previous smooth fit. Had those without wished to open the door, they had only to pull upon the leather. Treglin and the others stared till the door had closed as best it might, then did they turn and begin to walk from it.

"Hold!" said I, halting them before they took more than a pair of steps. "Where do you go?"

"I go to consider what those above are now in the midst of," said he, looking upon me with distraction. "Should it be your wish to depart with twenty warriors on guard beyond, feel free to do so. One of your skill will easily best a hand or more of them before the others strike you down."

"What of another means of egress?" I said, taking a step toward them. "I care not where it may lead, so long as it takes me from *here*."

"The only other means of egress from this domain is death," said he, looking upon me in an odd manner. "You seem distraught, girl, yet you need not be. Freedom was promised you, and freedom you shall have—in two feyd, as it cannot be now. I go now to speak with Chaldrin, and you may return with us or remain here, as you please. No man will attempt your use the while you carry that blade.''

He turned then and led the others away, and after three heartbeats of hesitation, I followed. There was little reason to remain before a door I could not use, and it had come to me through waves of anger and frustration that the males without had spoken of Aysayn. That the female Ladayna and her cohort now sought his life in a more active manner was clear, and this purpose I would halt if I were able. To take pleasure from the female's grasp before I took her life would be satisfying, and this I might accomplish by assisting Aysayn.

Treglin left four of his males to keep watch over the door from a distance, then led the last through the corridors into the inner caverns. I had learned a small number of corridors and areas in the time I had been there, yet the corridors Treglin chose were not among them. He continued on till he came to an area with all further entrances barred save one, then entered the unbarred chamber. When I entered behind him, he was already engaged in speaking with Chaldrin, whose wound was being seen to by another male.

''. . . clearly more important than a mere blasphemer,'' said Treglin, frowning toward a Chaldrin who sat as he was being tended. ''The Shadow's warriors stand without, and we are to send the man to the Shining Sands in precisely two feyd. I dislike being commanded by those above, yet what choice have we?''

''For free men, there is ever a choice,'' grunted Chaldrin, ''and in this domain we are free men. It would please me a great deal to know the reason behind such strange doings. Never before has the Shadow been known to do such a thing.''

''The reason is clear,'' said I from where I stood, perhaps two paces within the entrance. ''It is not Sigurr's Shadow who commands the strangeness.''

Each of the males jerked his head about to gape at me, and Chaldrin stared in surprise.

''Wench, why have you not departed?'' he demanded, then looked again upon Treglin. ''The Shadow's warriors—they were there when you went to release her?''

''Aye,'' nodded Treglin, yet he looked at me rather than at the other male. ''What do you know of this, wench? How is it possible to say that the Shadow does not command, when it is his warriors who stand poised to enter our domain?''

''His warriors are commanded by another,'' said I, crouching down before the wall so that I might take some rest. ''Aysayn, the true Shadow, is here, condemned by treachery to a death which fails to come soon enough for those who wait. Aysayn must be put beyond aid before the return of Mehrayn.''

"What do you know of Sigurr's Sword?" demanded Chaldrin with a frown. "It is well known that he and the Shadow are near brothers, yet—what would a slave wench know of these things?''

"Chaldrin forgets that Jalav is no slave," said I, rising straight again at the tone of the male. "It was Jalav who freed Mehrayn and the others from capture in a city to the north, Jalav who returned with them here to bring Sigurr's word to the Shadow Aysayn. For this reason was Jalav taken captive, and for this reason will Jalav have the life of Ladayna, from whom all this evil has arisen! Are you fool enough to doubt me, male?''

All four of the males looked upon me in silence, none moving, till he who had been tending Chaldrin recalled what he was about. He turned again with dampened cloth to the wound, and Chaldrin straightened in pain at the touch, drawing his breath in sharply. The sound brought Treglin from his stare, and he turned to the white-clad male who stood beside him.

"Have the new fighter brought here," said Treglin, grim determination having taken him. "I will know the truth of this matter before I consider what may be done for it.''

The other male nodded and hurried from the chamber, passing me with an uneasy glance. I stood with swordpoint resting upon the stone of the floor, yet the male undoubtedly knew how quickly that swordpoint might be raised.

"Chaldrin, you should not have taken sword in hand again," said the one who tended Chaldrin's wound, spreading a salve upon the bloody gash. "Of all those who dwell in this domain, I find you the most difficult to tend. You must rest a full hand of feyd at minimum, else will the wound be overlong in healing.''

"I will see that he takes his rest," said Treglin, crouching down to assist with the cloth the other male would use to bind the wound. Chaldrin halted his breathing till the last of the salve was upon him, then looked toward me as the cloth was raised.

"It would be no more than fair if she who wounded me also tended me," said he with a faint grin as his wound was covered. "I would then remain upon my furs a good deal longer.''

"A neck chain would also see to the matter," said I, discounting the chuckling of the other two. How odd were these Sigurri, always and forever accepting strangers and enemies to tend them. Truth to tell, I knew not how they had managed to survive.

"Here," said Treglin, rising from his crouch before Chaldrin and turning to throw a square of white cloth to me. "It is plain you care naught for whether your body is covered, yet do we run perilously close to your reenslavement as you are. As there are weighty matters to be considered by us, use the cloth so that we may consider them with full attention."

Chaldrin and the male tending him chuckled, yet Treglin clearly meant the words he spoke. Resting my sword against the wall, I opened the square of cloth and wrapped it about me, then reclaimed my sword before crouching again.

A number of reckid passed in silence, during which time Chaldrin lay back upon the fur he had been tended on. The wound I had given him was not gravely serious, yet had he lost a goodly amount of blood, which ever took one's strength. I thought perhaps he slept, yet when Aysayn was brought within the chamber, he again moved himself to sitting. Sigurr's Shadow remained bare of all covering, and when he was brought past me, I was able to see the traces remaining of the lashing he had taken.

"There is a matter I will have the truth from you on," said Treglin when Aysayn stood before Chaldrin and himself. "For what reason would Sigurr's Shadow concern himself with you? For what reason would he wish your life?"

"Sigurr's Shadow is very fond of the fighter who stands before you," replied Aysayn, folding his arms as he looked upon the other. "Though I was lashed when last I spoke of it, allow me to repeat myself: *I* am Sigurr's Shadow."

"I am able to see sense in the thing no other way," said Chaldrin, gazing up at Aysayn. "He fought with high skill of the Sands, far beyond all nestlings and most victors. The sole point I cannot reconcile is the failure of him who replaced you behind the Golden Mask to challenge you before the entire city. How may a man who yearns for the highest place think to face Sigurr as his Shadow, when he has not earned that place?"

"The prime mover behind this treachery is not male," said Aysayn, his voice hardening. "No man would fail to realize the demands of the position; I have found it necessary to defend my place four times with the sword blessed by Sigurr. The wench schemed long and well to have me as I am now, yet would she regret it if she were suddenly faced with challenge a fifth time. He who now stands behind the Mask would fall, and she with him."

"We are commanded to have you upon the Shining Sands in two feyd time," said Treglin, eyeing Aysayn sourly. "For what reason would we be given such a command?"

"It is clear Ladayna means to have my life before the return of Mehrayn," shrugged Aysayn. "She undoubtedly has other plans to keep the Sword from discovering the truth, yet will she find difficulty in such a doing. Mehrayn is not so great a fool as I."

"You have none of you touched the topic of main concern," said I, rising from my crouch as they all turned to look upon me. "We are all aware of their intentions; what are we to do to halt those intentions?"

"That, wench, is a problem not easily solved," said Chaldrin, grimacing as he moved about upon the fur. "Perhaps Sigurr will appear at the last moment, and confront the wrongdoers with accusation."

"Such is foolishness!" I snapped, gesturing away the nonsense of the male. "There are no more than four hands of Ladayna's warriors stationed at the door which gives egress from these Caverns; your white-clad males number greater than that. For what reason do we not fall upon those warriors and then seek Ladayna in her lair above? Have your males no skill in doing battle? Are they able to do no more than watch others?"

The males gazed upon me in unexpected silence, their faces showing naught of expression, and then a faint smile touched the lips of Chaldrin.

"It is clear you know naught of our circumstances here, girl," said he. "Each of us here has considerable skill in battle, for each of us here was a victor when he fought upon the Shining Sands. Should a man live two kalod as a victor, and be as weary of battle as we, he is then given white cloth to cover himself with, and the position of training those who are sent to us as nestlings. Should we do as you suggest and return to the city above, our lives are immediately forfeit. To attempt to run to another place would be idle, for where would we go? This has become our home, as well as our place of exile. You would have me ask my men to turn their backs on it for certain death? I think not."

"Perhaps you have not considered the Shadow's pardon," said Aysayn, turning again to look down upon Chaldrin. "Should you assist me in regaining my freedom, yours would be regained as well. Yours, and that of your men who fought at my side."

"And what if you were to fall?" asked Treglin, the while Chaldrin's broad face grew disturbed. "If you were lost and your cause as well, what of us? Would our lives not then be forfeit for certain?"

"Should it be that Sigurr's face has turned from me, such a thing may well occur," said Aysayn, his voice heavy with a sigh. "I cannot demand your assistance, for I no longer stand behind the Mask. You must each of you do as you think best, and I will trust in Sigurr to set my feet upon the path to victory."

"Ah, Mida! Why must males be such great fools?" I demanded of the air above me, unable to keep silent any longer. "What glory is there in merely living? What dignity in merely accepting punishment and exile? These are brothers, these males, all of a city as we are of the sister clans; how may brothers deny one another so easily, as sisters of the Midanna would never do? This is surely the reason they will fall before us, for they will enter battle as strangers to one another, uncaring of glory and bereft of dignity. So much for the followers of Sigurr."

"We cannot all of us be as bloodthirsty as you, girl," said Chaldrin, the dryness of his tone bringing amusement to the other males. "Unlike a young, glory-seeking female, a man must think before he throws his life away."

"To find those who will assist this one will require more than thought," said Treglin, the sourness having returned to him. "There are matters which require my attention, and I go now to see to them. Do not leave that fur, Chaldrin, else I will heed the wench and have you chained there."

Treglin then took himself off, gesturing the male who had brought Aysayn with him, he who had tended Chaldrin following after the first two. Chaldrin took a pile of furs upon which he might rest his back, and Aysayn again folded his arms as he studied me.

"I had not expected to see you here, Jalav," said he after a moment of silence. "When I entered and saw you crouching by the wall, I thought I was to be given the gift I had been promised for victory."

"I, too, have had a victory," said I, aware of the amusement Chaldrin made no effort to conceal. "I have not received the gift for victory I was promised; for what reason must you be?"

"The promise was given me first," said Aysayn, beginning to share Chaldrin's amusement.. "And there you stand, clearly with no other task assigned to you. Chaldrin—may I borrow one of your furs?"

"Certainly," said Chaldrin with a chuckle, his dark eyes continuing to rest upon me. "A victory such as yours has ever earned a man a new fur."

"Perhaps this one has not been told the penalty for a slave attempting to overstep himself with those who are free," said I, watching with some small interest as Aysayn turned and began to take a fur from the pile beside Chaldrin. "A pity his last defeat will come as soon after his first victory by cause of the lack."

"Defeat?" snorted Aysayn, straightening with a folded fur in his hand. "Who is to supply this defeat? And what is this of slave and free? Do you think yourself above me, wench?"

"There are three of us within this chamber." I shrugged. "Two are covered and one is bare. Of the two who are covered, one is armed and the other would be armed if he wished to be. He who is bare has not been given the choice concerning arms. Surely must he who is bare be considered a slave."

"I see," said Aysayn, nodding judiciously with lips pursed. "And do you believe, wench, that the presence of a sword in your fist assures a knowledge of its use? One must hold a sword for many kalod—and use it—before such knowledge is available."

"The wench's knowledge of a sword is sufficient for most," said Chaldrin, looking upon me again with the gleam he had shown during our battle. "There is, of course, considerable room for improvement, yet is she adequate. However, only with a sword."

"Jalav is also no stranger to the dagger and spear and bow," said I with stiffness, displeased with the gall of the male. There he lay, his blood flowing free by cause of *my* sword, and he dared to speak of merely adequate?

"The dagger and spear and bow, like the sword, are merely weapons which may be lost—or taken from one," said Chaldrin, his calm undisturbed by my obvious annoyance. "One must learn to defend oneself without such weapons, else is one no more than a helpless female child."

"Let those who think me helpless face my sword," said I to Chaldrin, standing tall before the male. "They will learn—as you have—that Jalav is not war leader of all the Midanna for naught."

"Ah, then it was you who did him so," said Aysayn, eyeing me as he continued to hold the fur. "I had wondered, for I have seen this man with a sword. And yet he speaks the truth, wench. A full leader must know *all* methods of defense and attack."

"Jalav's knowledge is—adequate," said I with some sourness, weary of these males and their constant thirst for teaching. Surely had Mida abandoned them to the dark god for their failure to leave well enough alone.

"Adequate only for my purposes," said Aysayn, a slow grin taking him. "For your purposes, you will soon see their worth. I mean to claim my victory gift, wench, and would have you know my purpose before I attempt it."

"Your purpose is to throw away your life," I shrugged,

turning with sword up to face him. "The doing will surely send Ladayna's males from the door, allowing me to quit this place. Therefore will my purposes indeed be served."

"It is I who will be served," said he, moving forward with the fur in his hands. "And by you."

The male, continuing to wear a look of amusement, came forward slowly with the folded fur held before him. I slashed at his head, and then at his side, yet each time my blade met naught save the fur. The male used it as though it were a shield, his hands to either side safe through the speed of his movements. Twice I tried for his arms, and each time was my sword muffled in the fur. A straight thrust at his heart resulted in his quickly jumping to one side with a twist, and my sword passed harmlessly by. I threw a backstroke at him and retreated a step, yet the backstroke was avoided as easily as the rest. Chaldrin chuckled where he lay leaning upon a mound of furs, and the warmth of the cavern chamber began to slick my body.

It was not many reckid before the male's advance put my back to the chamber wall. I had attempted to attack as I had ever done, with speed and no quarter, yet the male had dipped and bobbed and jumped, and had once nearly trapped my blade in the folds of the fur. The feel of the stone at my back made me know there was no farther I might go to escape the advance, therefore did I essay a double cross-stroke at the male, to drive him back and perhaps reach his flesh at last. The male retreated at the attack, holding his fur before him, and I immediately followed to press my advantage. Fully half the distance already covered did he retreat, narrowly saving himself from my strokes, and then, when I thought him bested at last, he abruptly disappeared from before me. Down to the floor of the chamber had he thrown himself, not to beg for mercy as another would, but to tangle his legs in mine. I raised my sword to hack down at his unprotected body, yet the stroke was not to be. In some manner were my feet abruptly no longer beneath me, and the rock of the chamber floor struck my back hard.

"I had best take this now," panted Aysayn, immediately grasping my wrist and freeing the sword from my grip. I felt deeply dazed from the fall, and before I might force myself to stir, the weapon was gone.

"She nearly had you there, a time or three," remarked Chaldrin with the chuckle now to be heard in his voice. "Had she done as she intended, we would indeed be free of unasked-for difficulty."

"I am all too well aware of how near she came," said Aysayn, kneeling across me before pulling his forearm over his forehead. "Had she been familiar with this method of doing battle, my blood would have joined yours."

I fought to move myself where I lay between his thighs, yet my efforts did no more than cause me to stir. The dazedness left me only slowly, not nearly soon enough to halt Aysayn's hands from taking the white cloth which had been wrapped about me.

"There are now two who are unclothed in this chamber," said he, running his hands easily over my body after he had put the cloth aside. "I will, of course, take the loin cloth for my own use when I am done with you, as part of my victory spoils. And, as the possession of a sword gives you such pleasure, you may now have possession of this one."

His hands took my thighs as his knees parted them, and then was he entering me with such strength that I gasped. I attempted to raise myself from the stone in protest, and his palms came to my shoulders as his weight increased.

"Do you feel him deep within you, wench?" came the voice of Chaldrin, a lazy satisfaction to his tone. "Had you taken the effort to learn more than sword use, he would not have been able to put you to man use. You now reap the bitter seed of those who will not learn."

Moving in fury at Chaldrin's words did no more than cause Aysayn to hum with pleasure. His lips tasted me as his deep stroking brought the first moan to my throat; I lay upon the stone of the floor, beneath the sweat-covered body of the male, forced to feel pleasure as well as to give it. My fury did not abate, yet was it as useless as my attempt to take the male with a sword. Well used was I by Sigurr's Shadow, and made to writhe with ease.

13 The Shining Sands—
and an impostor is revealed

"See the manner in which he stands," said Chaldrin, speaking of the male who faced two others like him to one side of the circle of black sand. Beyond the farthest male were daggers, beyond the daggers swords, beyond the swords crescent spears. The three males fought a bout of elimination, the sort of battle I had already seen twice that fey.

"His balance allows him to move immediately in any direction, and his balance is due to his stance," pursued Chaldrin. "He is the most promising of the nestlings, and will one fey have the skills to equal a warrior—should he live."

Again I made no reply to his words, merely looking about at the city folk who shouted and screamed and stamped their feet high above the countless torches which lit the circle of sand. Fully half of the upper cavern beyond the circle of black sand had been stepped to look down upon the combatants, and upon these steps sat hand upon hand of Sigurri, male and female alike. At their front, surrounded by warriors, sat a male who wore a long black covering—and a golden mask.

"You have sulked about for two feyd now," said Chaldrin, turning to look down upon me with faint impatience in his dark eyes. "My loss to you was of greater consequence than your loss to Aysayn; do you see *me* sulking about like a child, refusing to speak to those about me?"

"Your loss was not one of dignity," I replied, beginning to turn from him. "Sooner would I have lost lifeblood."

"Indeed," said he, taking my arm in his great hand. "I am the foremost fighter in these Caverns, never having been bested by any since my arrival. What dignity is there in having been bested by a wench, and one who would have taken my life had she not been halted by others?" He paused a moment to allow his question to hang between us, then put another. "Do you mean to deny us your swordarm when we stand in defense of the Shadow? We know not what we will face, yet are we sure to require your aid. Do you mean to refuse to stand with us?''

"You dare to speak of requiring my sword?'' I demanded, attempting to pull my arm from his grip. "Was it not you who first pointed out what small use a sword was against those of true skill? Was it not Aysayn himself who reached beyond my blade to defeat me? Do to those who come what was done to me, and victory will surely be yours.''

"Do not attempt to pull against my hand to free yourself,'' said Chaldrin, frowning at my struggles. "Instead, swing away from the hand and through the fingers. Use your body weight and movement to assist you. And we cannot hope to defeat those who come with unarmed skills alone. Too few of the men in these precincts have chosen to stand with us, therefore will we require weapons of our own, as well as those to wield them. Will you fight at our side?''

"An excellent question,'' came the voice of Aysayn, and then the male himself appeared out of the dimness of the corridor which led to the masked opening in the rock we stood at, one of more than two hands of such openings which led to the fighting sands. "As the battle of the Shining Sands is next,'' said he as he halted before us, "and I am to fight in the following bout, a reply now would be most timely.''

"Perhaps she feels entitled to words of regret,'' said Chaldrin, looking upon the other male with sobriety. "To use a free woman so—ah—freely, undoubtedly grates upon her sense of dignity.''

"Is this so?'' asked Aysayn, sending his dark-eyed gaze to me. He had surely been loosening his body in practice, for sweat covered him and his light hair reached for his eyes. "Perhaps it would be best to ask by whose pardon she was freed,'' said he. "I have never heard of a single victory setting a male fighter free.''

"Aysayn, such caviling is not wise,'' began Chaldrin, yet I held my hand up to halt his words.

"What he speaks is truth,'' said I to Chaldrin, recalling my own thoughts upon the selfsame subject, then did I turn to Aysayn. "In these precincts a single victory does indeed mean naught, however I would have Sigurr's Shadow recall the fact that Jalav was never slave—merely a captive. Under those circumstances, a pardon was unnecessary from any source.''

"Excellent,'' said Aysayn, laughter in his eyes. "I do indeed recall the fact of your captivity rather than slavehood, and therefore stand corrected. And yet, I cannot speak words of regret for having used you. Ask of me words of pleasure and praise, and I will gladly speak them; words of regret would be lies, and I will not lie. You are more than worth the taking, wench, and this I will maintain whether you stand with me or no.''

"Honesty is to be admired," said Chaldrin as I gazed silently upon Aysayn. "We must keep that truth firmly in mind when our handful go down before the warriors of the impostor.''

"Ah, Chaldrin, I find myself fond of you despite all," laughed Aysayn, reaching past me to clap the other male upon the shoulder. "Your use of her was more extensive than mine; will *you* speak words of regret?''

"Certainly," agreed the other male, folding his arms across his chest. "I deeply regret the need to have spent two feyd upon my furs unable to claim her again. As we are soon to die, I, too, shall indulge in honesty.''

The two males laughed together, sharing a common amusement, yet I had ceased giving them heed and had returned to examining the distant form of the male in the golden mask. He sat at ease upon his step, watching the doings of those upon the sand, seemingly pleased when Chaldrin's nestling threw his dagger into the thigh of one of his opponents, then turned and made for the swords. Those others all about the masked male screamed out their delight, and when the furor faded to less than it had been, a hand came to my shoulder.

"Perhaps words of regret would not be out of place after all," said Aysayn, his amusement apparently done. "It was not our intention to make sport of you, wench, and I would offer my apologies for any insult given. You do not merit insult.''

"Again you are mistaken," said I, turning to look upon him. "I do indeed merit insult, for I have been inexpressibly foolish, sightless beyond words. So great was my pride in my ability with a sword, I thought myself undefeatable by cause of it. To have learned the truth was a bitter blow, and one I shall not forget.''

I attempted to move past him into the corridor he had come from, yet this time Chaldrin's hand was upon my shoulder.

"So that was the dignity you spoke of," said he, his voice returned to calm. "The dignity lost when one is defeated in the area one has the greatest pride in. It should not be necessary to speak of this to you, wench, yet you were not defeated sword to sword. Had you been, your bitterness would be understandable; as you were not, you need only concern yourself with learning the discipline which was your bane. Should I survive the coming battle, I will be pleased to school you in its tenets.''

"Yet what of the battle itself?'' I stormed, turning upon him with the fury which had so twisted me about those past two feyd. "How might I presume to bare a blade against my enemies, when that blade may be so easily taken from me? Am I to continue in vanity, and allow those who fight at my side to fall through my failure? Am I to lead others into the final darkness, when only I so richly merit it?"

I twisted past him to stare again at the figure in the golden mask, my need for enemy blood so strong that I would have willingly taken it with my teeth. In what other way was I to spill the blood of my enemies, with the truth so achingly clear in my memory?

"Jalav, I find myself nearly at a loss for words," said Aysayn, something of upset to be heard in his tone. "You spoke of how easily the blade was taken from you—you must pardon me, wench, for I recall no such easy accomplishment. When it was done, even Chaldrin spoke of the number of times you nearly had me. Your skill has not been bested by any swordsman I have yet come upon."

"And even were you the loss and hazard you now believe yourself," put in Chaldrin, "think you that one blade less would be to our benefit? We are scarcely likely to live through our attempt, and I am sorely tempted to lock you in slave chains to insure your survival, yet do I feel that survival as a slave would be worse than death for you. We but offer you your freedom again, wench, in one manner or another."

I continued to gaze upon the golden-masked male for a moment, then I turned to look upon the two who stood behind me. Their eyes were filled with the calm of truth, and it was not difficult to nod in agreement.

"Very well," said I, looking first upon Chaldrin and then upon Aysayn. "As you merely seek a death with dignity, I will raise my sword beside yours. And should Mida grant me more than a moment's use of it, we may not march to the final darkness unescorted."

"I do not mean to march there under any circumstances save that Sigurr himself comes before me and demands it," said Aysayn with a short laugh. "It is barely possible that Ladayna means to best me with no more than her concept of a superior warrior."

"Even were that so," said Chaldrin, a quick grimace crossing his features, "it is scarcely likely to be all that is attempted. I feel sure that Jalav will have considerably more than the moment she wishes."

"Undoubtedly we will all have the same," said Aysayn,

looking more closely upon Chaldrin. "And should you wish your own way with the foe, brother, it would be wise of you to rest a few reckid. Your strength has not yet returned in its entirety."

"For which I will take Sigurr to task when I face him," sighed Chaldrin, stepping to one side to lower himself carefully to the stone of the floor. "As I mean to stand in the cause of his rightful Shadow, his continuing anger with me should clearly have been withheld for the time."

"Continuing anger is rarely withheld, even for a moment," said Aysayn, and then his eyes came to me. "Truth to tell, I had expected naught save anger from this wench here. Though we meant no insult, our words and actions with her were rather—abrupt. Do you feel no burning, justifiable anger toward us, Jalav?"

"For what reason would I waste thought and strength in anger against you?" I asked, unconcerned with the gleam of amusement which lurked in his eyes. "The two of you are merely male, and therefore unable to do other than as you do. Should you ever find yourselves among my Midanna, you will be shown the proper matter of things."

Aysayn had seemed prepared to find deeper amusement in whatever words I spoke, yet even when I had turned from him to look again upon the fighting sands, his laughter had not rung out. Chaldrin, where he leaned against the stone of the wall, chuckled deeply.

It took no more than another hand of reckid before the male Chaldrin had favored saw to his last opponent. The matter was decided with swords, for neither had been able to reach the waiting crescent spears. Though the first male eliminated had merely been wounded, the second was run through the heart by his opponent when he attempted to press with too much vigor. The body collapsed to the black sand with bedlam sounding all about, and the victor stood with arms and sword held high, his bare, sweat-glistened body proud beneath the acclamation. Then, even before the screaming approval had faded, the male threw his sword to the sand, turned his back upon the fevered throng, and made his way back toward a corridor recess to our left. He paid no mind to the slavies who saw to the wounded and dead beneath the bright glare of torches, yet the slavies shrank back till he had passed on his way.

"He is one of those few fighters I have enlisted to stand with us," said Chaldrin from where he sat, speaking of the victor he had not had to see claim his victory. "He is an excellent fighter with great potential, and is more than willing to risk his life to regain his freedom.''

"Indeed," said Aysayn in a thoughtful manner. "He is indeed an excellent fighter. For what reason was he condemned to the Caverns?''

"That is a question we do not ask of those who come," said Chaldrin, his voice empty of all emphasis. "If we are told, by others or the man himself, the information is allowed to slip from memory. We are concerned only with that which a man does here, not with that which was once done elsewhere.''

"I see," said Aysayn, a quiet acceptance in the pair of words. No further was said upon the matter, and the Shadow and I returned our attention to the sand.

The two remaining combatants, one living, one gone to the final darkness, were removed from the black sand, along with every one of the weapons. The weapons were taken up by white-clad males, the slavies being forbidden their touching, and then two unclad fighters appeared to the ringing of small, thin-sounding bells. These two had not fought previously, yet their bodies were glistening bright, more so than the sweat of exertion would account for. The two males carried swords, yet they halted perhaps two gando-strides from each other, plunged the points of their swords into the sand, then put themselves into the sand. The two rolled about in the black sea of sand till they were well covered, then did they rise to their feet, reclaim their weapons, and stand at the alert without closing with each other. I knew not why the battle had not begun and was about to remark upon the matter, when the many torches about the Cavern began being covered.

"Watch closely, wench," said Chaldrin, remaining where he had seated himself. "You will soon see the reason why Treglin and I were able to follow you into the darkness when you first attempted escape.''

I turned from him to look again upon the sands, and felt my frown as the torches, by the hand, were covered with solid metal brackets. The heavy darkness closed in quickly, and only then did Chaldrin's words come clear. Rather than melt into the darkness, the two males and the black sand they stood upon now glowed as though torches burned within and below. The swords, too, I now saw, were marked with single lines of glowing yellow-white upon each of their sides, from broad hilt to pointed tip. Only the sharpened edges were unmarked, deadly hazards in unseen dark.

"When exposed to the light of torches," said Chaldrin, "the

black sand becomes the Shining Sands, easily seen in deep darkness. That thick mane of yours was well-enough dusted so that Treglin and I were able to follow you with ease. Those two who battle out there will not find a comparable ease, no matter that they are clearly marked for each other.''

I studied the two upon the sand as Chaldrin spoke, and realized that he spoke the truth. Midanna warriors are taught to know the length and breadth of their blades as well as they know the same of their arms, yet the males who now closed with one another to the encouraging screams of unseen onlookers had not been taught the same. They swung clumsily at one another, as though unsure of whether or not the strokes would find their targets, unsure of whether they stood too near or too far, unsure whether they, themselves, would be touched. They moved in hesitation in a small circle, their glowing forms touched with odd gaps where the sand had fallen away, and then one had further sand removed from him by the tip of his opponent's sword. A gap appeared across the chest of the male, from left shoulder to right ribs, and the male so struck shuddered and staggered backward away from the single glowing line which had touched him with pain. The other, encouraged despite the lack of visible lifeblood, pursued the first and struck at him again, this time attempting a head blow. The blow was more a crushing than a cut, and the first went down beneath it, to return the glowing sand from whence he had taken it. The second turned somewhat and plunged his sword into the first, and the screaming shouts again crescendoed into chaos. As the remaining glowing form raised his arms in victory, the torches began to be unbracketed again.

"And now comes the time for the blasphemer to face his fate," said Chaldrin, raising himself from the stone of the floor with less agility than usual. "You had best remove that loincloth, Aysayn, else will there be notice taken by those whose notice we wish to avoid."

"I find the need distasteful, yet you are undoubtedly correct," said Aysayn, his hands going reluctantly to the white cloth about his loins. "To be forced to go about unclothed is a great humiliation for a man, and highly insulting as well. This should not be."

"In our domain, it is necessary that all fighters be instantly recognizable should there be difficulty during training," said Chaldrin. "I also find it extremely demeaning, yet they must be marked in some manner, and this course changes them the least. To be consigned to these Caverns is change enough."

I turned away from the two as Aysayn grunted his agreement,

finding it unnecessary to waste words in comment. That they spoke so showed them as true males, unreasoning and concerned only with self. Had it not been so, they would have seen that their dislikes might perhaps be shared by others.

The vanquished fighter and the victor were gone from the sands in less than two hands of reckid, leaving behind an eager stir and mutter among the watchers. He who sat behind the mask of gold continued to laze negligently, yet an odd stiffness seemed to have entered his body. He gazed out upon the empty sands which had returned to their original black, unconcerned though clearly awaiting the next bout, and it came to me to wonder upon the whereabouts of the female Ladayna. I had hoped to see her there, within reach of dagger or spear; how was I to be sure of surviving the coming battle, to seek her elsewhere?

"In another moment, the spears will be set," said Chaldrin, watching as two white-clad males carrying crescent spears walked to the center of the sand, then turned with backs to one another and paced away from each other. They continued on till they stood perhaps three gando-strides apart, then did they turn to one another again, thrust the hafts of their spears into the sand, and walk from them toward the crevasse they had entered by. They slowed as they passed the slavey who had been about setting a large oval metal shield into the sand by its rim, waited till he had completed his task, then hurried him out before them. The slave, trembling with fear at being upon the sand, required little urging to depart as quickly as possible.

"You must recall," said Chaldrin to Aysayn, "that there is a choice before you. You and your opponent will enter the sands at the same distance from the shield, yet will only one of you find it possible to claim it. Should you try for the shield and fail to secure it, you will then be some distance from a weapon, the while your opponent will already have a weapon in his hands—the shield itself. Many an excellent fighter has gone down with the back of his head crushed in, long before a spear was in his reach. At the same time, you must understand that you will find it nearly impossible to keep your opponent from his spear even though you reach yours first."

"Yes, yes, I am well aware of these things," said Aysayn, interrupting what had promised to be a lecture of considerable length as he gazed out upon the sands. "The chimes are about to ring, and my presence will be required elsewhere. Before I go, there is a thing I must do." He left the crevasse opening, strode to the dim corridor he had emerged from, reached within to grope at the right-hand wall, then returned to me. "I return this to you more easily than I took it," said he, placing a sword in my hands. "Use it with all the skill you possess, and we may yet win free."

His hand then came to touch my face gently, yet before I was able to speak a word in answer, the tinkling sound came which summoned fighters to the sand. Aysayn lifted a fist toward Chaldrin, kicked his discarded body-cloth aside, then trotted through the crevasse.

"He believes he is aware of his options," muttered Chaldrin, moving to stand beside me at the opening. "To witness this battle from the seats is not the same as fighting it—which he is about to learn. We had best ask Sigurr to see that he survives the lesson."

"Ask naught of Sigurr that you are not willing to pay a price for," I muttered in turn, yet the male made no reply, for a second tinkling had sounded. Aysayn and his opponent had stood upon the sand, awaiting the signal to begin, and when that signal came, each moved immediately with the speed of life-threat—yet each moved differently.

Aysayn's opponent, with hair as dark as Aysayn's was light, raced directly for the beckoning shield, while Sigurr's Shadow set himself for the more distant yet equally beckoning crescent spear—upon the other's side. Those watching from above gasped out their surprise and delight, yet Chaldrin made a sound of disgust.

"Had he spoken to me of his intentions, the fool, I would have brought the greater distance to his attention," said he, a bitterness in his voice. "He is quicker than most, that I'll grant him, yet is he scarcely quick enough to keep his opponent from the second spear. Watch."

Just as the male spoke, so it came to be. Aysayn's opponent, divining that something was afoot from the exclamations of the watchers, glanced across to see where the Shadow ran. With scarcely a falter in his stride, he scooped up the shield without slowing, set it upon his left arm as he ran, then made directly for the crescent spear which was to have been Aysayn's. Aysayn reached the spear which had been his goal, tore it from the sand as he whirled, then ran on no more than five paces before slowing in defeat. The second male, not yet having reached the other spear, had nevertheless run to intercept Aysayn's line to the spear. He side-stepped and backed in the treacherous sand, nearly losing his footing, yet succeeding in keeping the shield and his body toward Aysayn. He had not yet reached the direct line Aysayn would have taken to the second spear, yet had

Aysayn pressed the matter, the second would have reached the line before Aysayn reached the spear. I raised one arm to move the heat-dampened hair which clung to my back, and Chaldrin stirred where he stood.

"Hear them howl for blood," said he, referring to the growing frenzy of the watchers. "They now count Aysayn done, for his opponent all but has both spear and shield in his possession. Should it be Sigurr's will, they shall find themselves mistaken."

I, too, felt highly doubtful upon the subject of Aysayn's position, and my fist tightened about the hilt of the sword I held. The dishonor I had been given might be washed away only in the blood of my enemies, no matter whether I survived or no. Should Aysayn die before full battle was joined by we who waited, there would undoubtedly *be* no battle.

"The spear is now his," said Chaldrin, his observation coming but heartbeats before the second male wrapped fist about haft. Aysayn had closed and swung his spear in graceful arcs, attempting the head, feet and arms of his opponent, yet the presence of the shield had shortened and blocked his attempts, allowing the second male to put groping hand to weapon. With a single pull the spear was freed of the sand and lowered, and then it was Aysayn who knocked thrusts away and backed in haste, too concerned with defense to mount an adequate offense. The bodies of the two males glistened nearly as much as those of the two who had rolled in the sand, their grips were precarious upon their weapons by cause of that, and those who watched screamed themselves into frothing madness. The glare of the many torches fought with the natural darkness of the cavern, much as those upon the sands fought.

Perhaps two further hands of reckid passed as the males attempted one another; though it had seemed at first that Aysayn would be quickly done, it soon became apparent that the Shadow was easily the superior of the second male. Had the second not had both spear and shield, he would have been upon the sand at their first exchange. With the added advantage came little more than added life for the male; Aysayn swung, blocked and attacked so swiftly and skillfully that the second was hard put to keep shield up, spear in place, and threatening edge from his body. His occasional spear thrust was able enough, yet overcaution slowed and shortened his attempts which Aysayn was then able to block with the haft of his own weapon.

The end came unexpectedly, for the two males as well as for those who watched. The second male, desperation having entered his movements and stance, abruptly seemed to decide upon a last, equally desperate attempt. He jumped at Aysayn in attack, causing the Shadow to back in proper defense, then himself moved rapidly backward before Aysayn began to counter. The spear which had been held for thrusting was suddenly held for throwing, and just so quickly was it on its way toward its unshielded target, mere paces away.

"Sigurr!" gasped Chaldrin, clutching at the stone of the wall, his exclamation drowned in the rolling screams of the watchers, yet he need not have feared. Aysayn twisted quickly away from the thrown spear, striking out with a two-handed grip upon his own spear as the enemy weapon hurtled past him, sending it away and down before it might approach any more closely than it had. His opponent now stood shielded yet weaponless, a condition which had proven to his opponent's advantage earlier; clearly did it seem that it would be so again.

And again were we who watched mistaken. Though his opponent was now able to concern himself only with defense, Aysayn seemed abruptly intent upon an end to the bout. He faced the other male and deliberately closed with him, struck at him repeatedly with both blade and haft, then swung far left and immediately back, catching the far edge of the shield with the knob of his spear and driving it away from before the male with the strength of the swing. Disconcerted, fearful, and thrown off balance, the other male staggered backward through the sand, his free arm flailing in vain, for the blade of the crescent spear already swung toward him, following the strike of the knob. Soundlessly the blade passed across the male's middle, leaving behind it a rapidly widening stream of red, which flowed just as soundlessly toward the sands. The male continued on down toward the sands himself and then lay still, the shield he had won still in place upon his left arm. There was little need to ask whether life remained within him, and the approval of the no-longer-seated watchers echoed and thundered from every wall of the cavern.

"It is now clear why Aysayn has survived as Sigurr's Shadow," said Chaldrin, shouting so that he might be heard above the din. "To have the dark god's approval is important to a man, yet not quite as important as battle skills such as his."

"Which he will soon require in large measure," said I, indicating the frenzied gesture of the male in the mask of gold. It was not immediately evident as to whom he gestured toward, and then my fist tightened again upon the hilt I held. Eight lines of knotted leather whispered down from the high reaches, and then black-clad males appeared and descended quickly, hand over hand, filled scabbards slung at their hips. Three males to each leather line appeared, and Chaldrin took his weight from the wall he had leaned upon as Aysayn turned from the still body of his opponent and became aware of his new opponents, some of whom had already reached the sands.

"Two dozen to less than a dozen of ours," growled Chaldrin, stepping to his left to take up the sword which awaited him. "By their loincloths they are all warriors, yet our fighters are all experienced; we may survive this set-to yet."

He then led the way onto the sands, signaling with a sweep of his arm that the others who waited at other crevasses were to join us. The watchers high above now buzzed in puzzlement over the unexpected turn of events, yet I paid them no heed as I ran toward those who hastened toward Aysayn. I had not yet grown used to the feel of the coarse body cloth upon me, yet such an unimportant thing would not distract me from the coming battle. The stains upon my honor would be away, and then the final darkness might be faced without regret.

As I had started forward first, I was able to reach Aysayn before the others and stand myself beside him as the black-clad males drew near. The attackers had slowed their forward charge as they approached, giving Aysayn's gracefully circling crescent spear the respectful distance it merited. Their swords were tight in their fists, the points jerking here and there as they sought an opening in the Shadow's defensive movement, their leather-clad feet following the same directionless path through the sands. I remained beside Aysayn no more than a moment before moving off again to the right, luring two of the males into following my steps. Surely did I then seem the more desirable target, for I held a sword rather than a spear, and I was clearly no fighter. The males paced me a short distance and then attacked, intending to clear Aysayn's right of protection, yet the deed was not so easily done. He who stood to my left attempted to spit me, foolishly overextending in the attempt; a step farther to the left and a bit forward brought his throat within reach of my blade, and as he sank to the sands with lifeblood gushing, I was able to face the one to the right with undivided attention. Again did I feel the joy which battle brought, honest battle with honest weapons, and easily did I move in straightforward counter-attack, striking all about before knocking his blade aside and burying my point in his belly. He, too, fell to the sands, and I turned with deep satisfaction to see how the others fared.

All about were white-clad males engaged with black-clad, and easily might it be seen that more black-clad males littered the sands than white. A second look showed me that *only* black-clad males were down, and then came a thought filled with strangeness: these Sigurri warriors were not so poor that their defeat should have been accomplished so easily. The two I had fought had been scarcely better than ordinary city males, scarcely worth the attentions of a warrior. Aysayn accounted for two together, one to each side of his crescent streak of silver, and he, too, wore a frown. Our forces were clearly victorious, and such a condition met the full approval of none save the wildly shouting watchers. The victory we had hoped for should not have been so easily attained.

And then we turned to see that others now stood upon the sands, below the leather, fully as many as had stood there earlier, yet with a difference. These males began to move toward us with slow deliberation, uninterested in rushing forward as the others had done. These males were warriors in truth rather than in covering only, fresh, able—and fully aware of our numbers and abilities. Those who had been sent first had been used to lure us out and expose our strengths and weaknesses; those who followed were meant to destroy us. He who sat behind the Golden Mask seemed well pleased with his doings; we who stood upon the sands growled our fury.

"Move more closely together and form a circle," called Chaldrin from where he stood with dripping sword. "We must guard each other's backs and deny them easy access to us. Do it now!"

The others moved quickly to obey his word, yet I looked upon the advancing males and wondered how many I might slay if I were to attack them before they reached us. How long I stood depended upon Mida's will, yet how many might be reasonably accounted for? Enough to justify the loss of another sword to those who had circled in defense? Was I able to judge truly when I knew not how those males fought?

"Jalav, come to the circle!" shouted Chaldrin from behind me, interrupting my thoughts. "Should they cut you off from us, they will pause to slay you before continuing on!"

As that would be the logical doing on the part of the attackers, it was clear that Chaldrin spoke the truth. With some reluctance I therefore backed through the sands to the circle, then awaited the arrival of the attackers, which was quick in coming. The torches glinted off their readied swords, as yet unstained with the red which touched ours, and the sands warmed the bottoms of our feet beyond comfort as we waited.

These new attackers were indeed of a higher caliber than the first set. As soon as they were near enough they began to press

us, the single fortunate circumstance being that our circle pre-
cluded their all being able to approach us at once. Three of their
number went down quickly when they attempted to crowd their
way forward, one by my sword, and thereafter they faced us
singly, the others behind the first line and prepared to step
forward should any of their set fall. Swords flickered and danced
in all directions, even Aysayn having taken up a blade to use in
place of his spear in the restricted area of the circle, the watchers
thundered screams and shouts to echo from the walls, and all
seemed much like a dream sent by the dark god to liven his
existence and darken ours.

Those of us in the circle, two hands of males and myself,
quickly found our strength being drained through the deliberate
actions of the attackers. Bathed in sweat, there was naught for us
to do save stand our ground, even when the attackers stood turn
and turn about against us. Then before our swords tired, he
gestured to the male behind him and was immediately replaced
so that he might catch his breath and renew himself. When this
was done before me for the second time, I quickly slashed left
and then charged the retreating male, catching both the circle
male on my left and he who retreated, unawares. The two went
down as I backed to the circle again, and not again was the
warrior before me replaced in so off-hand a manner.

Two of our number went down nearly together, and we who
remained were pressed even harder. Chaldrin, who stood to my
right, showed red upon the cloth about his ribs, yet not from the
warriors we faced. His visage was pale and glistening, strain
showing clearly, yet he continued to stand his ground. It seemed
equally clear that we could not stand much longer, and I determined that I would charge forward through their ranks when
Chaldrin fell, making a final effort toward taking as many of the
enemy with me as possible to the final darkness. My left arm
throbbed from the slice I had taken at some time, my hand slick
with the slowly running blood, and it would be foolish to wait
till I no longer had the strength to move as I would.

And then groaning sounded from those who stood farther
about the circle to my right. Needing to know what was afoot, I
stole a quick glance in that direction, then intensified my efforts
to down the male before me. He, also having seen the sudden,
on-the-run arrival of fresh black-clad males, backed and spent
his efforts upon defense. The new males poured from the crevasses,
obviously having come through the caverns, and our efforts were
surely done. The group of attackers about our circle withdrew
and massed together, prepared to charge against us from one side

as the newcomers came from the other. At Chaldrin's hissed commands we flattened our circle to two back-to-back lines, determined to resist till we fell, yet the attack never came.

"Hold!" came a voice from among the newcomers, a voice which somehow seemed familiar. "In the name of Sigurr, I command you to hold where you are!"

"Who commands in the name of Sigurr?" demanded a male from the earlier attack, moving forward a single step as he spoke. "We are here in the name of Sigurr, obedient to the commands of his Shadow."

"It is not Sigurr's Shadow whom you obey," said the first voice, now much nearer behind me. I felt a great desire to turn and look upon him, yet my strength was ebbing and I dared not take my eyes from those males before me. "He who sits behind the Golden Mask is an impostor, a would-be usurper. The true Shadow is among these men, sent here so that you might slay him all unknowing. As you know me, so must you know that I speak the truth."

"Aye, I know you now," allowed the second male, clearly filled with confusion as he gazed upon the other. "Never before has there been doubt cast upon the word of he who wears the Golden Mask, and I know not what to do. I have also never before doubted the word of Sigurr's Sword."

Mehrayn! Despite all, I turned then to look behind me, and it was truly he who stood there. Broad and red-haired, sword held in one large fist, his eyes touched me for the briefest instant and then looked again toward the male he spoke with.

"The matter may be settled to the satisfaction of all," said Mehrayn. "Though you, unlike I, do not know the face behind the Mask, you know well enough whose face it cannot be. Let us look behind the Mask, and see what we will see."

"Too late, brother," said Aysayn, from where he stood, a number of paces to my left. "He who sat above is no longer there."

We all of us turned to look upward, and Aysayn had spoken truly. He in the Golden Mask no longer sat among the now-silenced throng who had shouted so lustily just a short while earlier. A growl of anger arose from some of those who had stood encircled with us, and he who had spoken for the black-clad attackers turned again to Mehrayn.

"Never would the true Shadow behave so!" said the male with anger, his free fist clenched. "Never would he send warriors forth to do battle, and then fail to remain to assist in the outcome, should he be required! I need not see whose face is behind the Mask to know him for the impostor he is!''

A rumbling growl of agreement came from those who stood behind him, and those swords which had continued to seek hungrily in our direction were lowered at last. My sword remained as it had been, as did many another upon our line, yet Aysayn lowered his point and stepped forward.

''You have my thanks for those words, warrior,'' said he, looking upon the male with a warm smile which he then sent to the others as well. ''You all have filled me with great joy, to know that you have come against me in ignorance rather than deliberation. There is only one author at whose feet our ills may be laid. Shall we pursue him?''

''Aye!'' rang from many voices all about, with swords raised high to underscore the word. He who led the attackers stepped briskly forward to raise his sword hilt upward to Aysayn, followed immediately by the others of his males who did the same. Beside me, Chaldrin went to one knee with a grunt, his head hanging from the fatigue and pain which rode him.

''I thought never to take an unlabored breath again,'' said he, looking up as I crouched where I had stood. ''For one so poor with a sword as you, you gave a good account of yourself, girl. You undoubtedly took nearly as many as I.''

''I took more,'' said I with a glance at him, ''yet only by cause of the presence of your sword when my back was unprotected. Were you female, male, I would proudly call you sister.''

Silence touched him for a moment, then he said most gravely, ''It has become most clear that you are chosen by the gods, wench. My sword was meant to aid you, and shall do so forever more. It is the will of the gods.''

His dark eyes held to me with deep calm, declaring the truth of the words he had spoken, and I knew not what words I had yet come across, making it difficult for a warrior to know how she was to deal with them. I became overly aware of the discomforting warmth of the sand beneath my feet, and then another presence happily came to interrupt the awkwardness of the moment.

''Jalav, how badly are you hurt?'' demanded Mehrayn, crouching to my left and reaching for my blood-streaked arm. ''You should not have involved yourself in this; the battle was not yours.''

''So you are more closely acquainted with Sigurr's Sword than you spoke of,'' said Chaldrin as I stiffened against the flash of pain brought by Mehrayn's touch upon my arm. "I find myself unsurprised. As to your comment, O Sword of Sigurr, the battle was as much hers as ours, for she, too, fought for freedom. And without her presence, there would have been far fewer of us remaining erect to greet you upon your arrival."

"Which should have been sooner," growled Mehrayn, displeased with the deep slice I had taken, yet unable to do aught for it. There was not even so much as a cloth about to bind it, and I had gestured his hands from me in impatience with the useless pain he gave. Mehrayn was displeased with my decision as well, yet he made no attempt to go counter to it.

"Your arrival was considerably better than no arrival at all," said Aysayn as he came up to place a hand upon Mehrayn's shoulder where he crouched before me. "To take you to task for being tardy would be the act of a fool. Shall we go now to seek out he who attempted to stand in my place? After we have settled with him, you may tell me how you happen to be here at all."

"Which is an interesting tale in itself," nodded Mehrayn, rising to his feet. "I would suggest first, however, that you find cloth to cover your body with. We would not wish our mission of vengeance halted by cause of your being attacked by the fair ladies of this city. Their appetites for victors of the Sands are more than well known."

"At another time, I would consider it my duty to grant them their demands," laughed Aysayn with sparkling eyes. "As we have already taken enough time before setting off in pursuit, I will adopt your suggestion immediately. Chaldrin, remain here and see to those who were wounded, yourself and Jalav included. I will return as soon as I have tended to the last of this business."

"Jalav, too, has business elsewhere," said I, rising immediately from my crouch. "Should the male Aysayn find difficulty in agreeing to this, he may recall that he continues to hold sword in hand."

"And Treglin will see to those who are wounded," said Chaldrin, rising somewhat more slowly than had I. "This business was begun together, and will end the same."

Mehrayn made no comment as Aysayn looked upon Chaldrin and myself, yet his expression was frowning confusion where Aysayn's was frustrated indecision. And then the indecision melted away, and Aysayn stood the straighter.

"You both have been loyal in my defense, and I shall be equally loyal in return," said he, looking now toward Chaldrin. "Jalav, continuing for the most part in good health, may join us. As for you, friend Chaldrin, despite your indomitable will, you are all but falling from your feet. I will not permit you to go longer untended, and you may look upon that as a command from Sigurr's Shadow. I intend having you beside *me* during our victory feast, not beside Sigurr. Remain here till Treglin sends those who will aid you.''

He turned and strode away then, taking Mehrayn with him, disallowing all argument from an outraged Chaldrin. I followed quickly along to avoid any further discussion, relieved to see that we moved toward the crevasses leading to corridors rather than the knotted leather leading to the watchers' steps. I would not have allowed myself to be left behind, yet climbing leather so high with no sheath for my sword and my left arm as it was would have been difficult.

Aysayn paused no longer than the moment it took to retrieve his body cloth and urge Treglin to see quickly to Chaldrin, then we led the large group of black-clad males from the caverns. Mehrayn also paused briefly, for he had found a cloth with which to bind my arm, and insisted upon doing so. I allowed the doing with a good deal of impatience, yet spoke no word which would have given him insult. The concern the male felt was clear, yet he had made no attempt to keep me from that which I felt was necessary. These males continued to fill me with confusion, but happily there was little time to ponder the point.

When we reached it, we saw that the large metal door from the Caverns stood well open. In the small cavern beyond the door were others of Mehrayn's males, standing above the still forms of those who had brought us word from the attempted usurper. Mehrayn ordered them to remain at their post, then turned to Aysayn.

''We must offer our thanks to your enemy for having sent his men here,'' said he, gesturing to those who lay sprawled upon the sand-covered rock. ''Had they not put their leather in the door to keep it ajar, we would not have been able to enter.''

''We will thank him in the most appropriate manner possible,'' returned Aysayn, taking a tighter grip upon his sword hilt. ''Let us take torches and hasten to the doing of it.''

Many of the males took torches, and then we traversed the darkness to the steps which led upward. Up and up we climbed, each wrapped in the silence of thought, my own silence touched with pain and growing fatigue as well. The white cloth wrapped about my left arm was no longer white, and it was necessary to thrust the awareness of it from me. Had I allowed myself to dwell upon the wound, I might well have slid to the steps I climbed and not moved again for quite some time.

After an eternity of climbing, there were at last no further steps. Mehrayn led the way with Aysayn through the corridors of the large dwelling, gesturing back those black-clad males who attempted to step in our way. From one corridor to the next did we walk, gathering many who followed to see what we were about, at last appearing before the doors which led to the chambers of Aysayn and Ladayna. Those black-clad males who stood before the doors frowned at sight of Aysayn, yet Mehrayn and the others quickly explained the truth of the matter. Within reckid we were through the doors, led by those who had first attempted to bar our entrance, making straight for the doors to Aysayn's apartment—and then through.

The chamber we entered was large and entirely untenanted, as were the next two which Aysayn led us through. Greater and greater anger gripped the male with each new untenanted chamber; he strode from door to door, throwing each open, halting only when he reached the fourth. Those of us behind him stepped up to see what the chamber contained, and Mehrayn snorted in disdain.

"At the least, Ladayna is now accounted for," said he, faintly amused at the glare sent toward him by the female. She lay upon a low, padded platform to the left, much like an altar, sccured to the thing by the silver chains she wore. Her long covering of black seemed more worn than fresh, her light hair hung in disarray, yet her arrogance appeared totally undiminished.

"Why do you merely stand there and gawk?" she demanded, apparently addressing all who stood in the doorway. "One of you release me immediately, and be quick about it!"

"Indeed," murmured Aysayn, moving forward till he stood above the female, looking down upon her. "And for what reason would I have you released?"

"For the reason that I ask it," said she, resting back upon her elbows as she gazed up at him with unconcern. "You know as well as I that you will not refuse me forever, Aysayn, no matter how angered you now fancy yourself to be with me. You will undoubtedly wish to use me later; wisest would be to release me now so that I might freshen myself for you."

The smile the female sent upward to the male above her was thick with invitation and self-assurance, half insulting and deliberately so. Aysayn slowly folded his arms as she spoke, and at last nodded his head.

"You are entirely correct, Ladayna," said he, a mildness in his tone. "I will indeed wish to use you later. Tell me: where has your confederate gone?"

"Him!" sniffed the female, shifting angrily so that her chains clinked. "I have not seen the fool since he chained me here, hind ago. For feyd he has kept me a virtual prisoner in these apartments, refusing to allow me to walk free since I told the guardsmen that you were not the Shadow. Without me, his schemes would have quickly gone to naught, and how does he repay me? Like this!"

She shook her arms to indicate her bound condition, and again Aysayn nodded.

"The man knows as little of proper way to repay a wench as he knows of facing his enemies squarely," said he, bending low to Ladayna. "When I return, I will be sure to give you all you have earned."

His fist went to her hair and his lips took hers, both gestures silencing the words she would have spoken. No more than a moment did he continue so, and then he left her side and rejoined those who awaited him, leading them from the chamber. Ladayna looked after him with considerable indignation, yet a shade of doubt had entered her sharp, light eyes. I remained where I had been, leaning upon the wall to the right of the door, and when all sound of the males' retreat faded, the female looked to me with a frown.

"Why do you remain when the others have not?" she demanded, raising up again as far as her chains permitted. "And what has happened to your arm? I was told that female slaves in the Caverns are not permitted the use of weapons."

"Female slaves are not," said I, leaving the bracing assistance of the wall so that I might move the nearer to her platform. "How well skilled are you with a sword, city slave-woman? Even as I am, it will take a deal of skill to best me. Tell me if the effort necessary to release you will be repaid in battle pleasure."

"Are you insane?" she cried, attempting to back from me upon the platform. "I know naught of swords save the men who wield them. What is it you intend?"

"I mean to have your life," I replied with a frown, halting at the foot of her platform. "Did you believe I would return with thanks for having been twice sent to slavery by you? I have come to repay the debt I owe."

"You cannot!" she choked, wide-eyed with terror. "I am a high lady and the chosen of Sigurr's Shadow! It is impossible for harm to come to me, I am too beautiful and desirable! No man would ever harm me, so has my father always sworn, and so has it been!"

"I see," said I, comprehending at last the full foolishness of males. "You have been taught that you are untouchable no matter your actions, for you are greatly desired for use by males. Perhaps it has escaped you that I am no male."

Her terror-filled gaze then came to take me in, the once-white body cloth I wore, my left arm again beginning to be streaked with blood, the sword held steadily in my right fist, the battle-readiness of my wide-legged stance. With this before her, the female began to tremble, and then came a voice which interrupted my clear intent.

"And yet I *am* male, and know that one's true value," said the voice, causing me to turn quickly toward the still-open door. There the male Pinain stood, he who had taken me to the Caverns, he who had used me first before the others who had accompanied us. He stood with sword naked in his fist and easily smiling visage, no indication of fear touching him.

"She will be worth a good deal where I intend going," said Pinain, his light eyes filled with amusement. "Wenches such as she are bought by those who have no wenches, to be locked away in seclusion and used only with secrecy and shame for that which they do. They dwell to the south and worship the obscene Oneness, and will give me whatever I ask for her."

"Pinain, no!" whimpered the female from my right, misery and fear clear in her voice. "Do not take me to that place of abominations, do not sell me to . . ."

"Silence!" commanded the male, his gaze unmoving from me even while he spoke to the female. "You need have no fear that you will make the journey alone, for I have now decided that this one will accompany you. She, too, will fetch a good price, even should it be necessary for me to spill a bit more of her blood. The others protected her upon the Sands, yet they no longer stand with her."

The male then took another two steps into the room, facing me more fully before rushing forward with sword raised high. His intent to disarm me quickly was clear, as clear as my response to his rush. My blade avoided his and slashed for his face, nearly connecting as he threw himself backward and out of reach. As I set myself for another rush I cursed the clumsiness of my limbs, for the slash I had attempted should have had him. I was not as I had been earlier in the fey, and this the male was able to see.

"You throw away my time and your own strength, wench," said he, eyeing me and flexing his grip upon his sword. "Put that weapon aside and surrender to me now, else shall I forgo your price and end you immediately. Those others will not long bay upon a false trail, and will discover that I hid in that female's apartments. I intend to be gone before that occurs."

"You shall indeed be gone," said I, my voice near to a whisper. "Sooner will I be slain than forgo the vow I made. Stand ready to defend your life, male."

He knew not what vow I spoke of, yet I recalled clearly my time with him and his males in the cavern sands. I snarled away the weariness and pain which attempted to drag me down, and attacked with no further warning. The male backed no more than a step before defending against my strokes, at first with sureness and lethal intent, after a pair of moments with growing doubt. It was clear to the male that I was close to dropping where I stood; what was unclear was the fact that no more than my blood dropped to the floor cloth. That I would not allow myself to fall was beyond his understanding, as was the source of the strength which swung my blade. An edged bar of silver streaked with dark red continued to seek his vitals, and doubt was rudely pushed aside by fear. The female Ladayna whimpered where she lay, a counterpoint to the clash of metal, ignored by she who attacked and he who sweated in defense.

Despite my resolve and intent, it slowly came to me that I could not long continue as I was. The weight of my sword began to increase, much the same as the weight of my head. Behind my eyes a throbbing increased as well, all acting to make leaden my legs and anchor them to the floor cloth. The wetness of pain covered my face and body, negating even the roughened grip of my weapon, and seeing much of this put instant delight upon the face of Pinain. He disengaged from my blade and then charged forward, driving me back from where I had stood so long, intending to spit me. A dark fog had begun to close in on me as I retreated three steps, nearly unsure of what was next to be done, and then was it proven that Mida continued to watch over her warrior. As he rushed forward, Pinain's leather-shod foot came down in the small pool of blood which had run from my arm and hand, and the male slipped. Had he been barefoot, as was proper, it would not have happened; shod as he was, he slipped so far that his arms flew up, flailing wildly to recapture balance. Without thought I drove forward again, the point of my sword aimed for his belly, and then did my metal plunge through him, tearing a screaming gurgle from his throat. His falling body plucked the sword out of my strengthless fingers, and once I saw that he lay still upon the floor cloth, I turned in the midst of thickening grayness to look upon the female Ladayna.

"Sigurr be praised," she whispered, her chains clinking as she wiped the wetness of tears from her face with the back of one hand. "Sooner would I be slain by you, than be sold to monsters by another of their kind. Take my life and be welcome to it, sister, for you have saved me from far worse."

Ladayna lay back upon her platform and closed her eyes, her small fists trembling as they wrapped themselves about a length of silver chain. Her slender body trembled as well, undoubtedly anticipating the touch of sharpened metal. I took one small step toward her, then fell into solid gray fog.

14 A feast—and the concern of males

The skies were gray, as though considering rain, and a sharp breeze had sprung up to cool the heat of the fey; I stood with face up and body alive, drinking in the unmatchable majesty of it all. I felt as though I had been indoors and underground forever, and the sensation of such openness was nigh unto ecstasy.

"Should you stand there much longer, wench, Aysayn will think us missing," came the voice of Mehrayn from behind me, more amusement than impatience to be heard. "As there is food awaiting us, I would reach his apartments as soon as possible. I have not eaten as recently as you, nor as well. This porch will continue to be here even after the feast."

I sighed at the thought of provender and turned away from the skies, feeling a lingering trace of the deep, gnawing hunger which I had felt earlier. Though I had already eaten a full fey's provender less than a hin earlier, I felt as though I were nearly ready to do the same again.

Mehrayn walked beside me as we entered, the large dwelling containing Aysayn's chambers, his hand upon my neck beneath my hair toying with the leather of my life sign. That life sign had been upon me when I had awakened at first light in Mehrayn's dwelling, vital and alive and entirely unwounded after the passing of no more than a single darkness. Mehrayn had awakened as I moved about and sat up, and had given thanks to Sigurr that he had surmised correctly. After he and the others had found me in Aysayn's chambers, it had been he who had forced the whereabouts of my life sign from an hysterical Ladayna, and then replaced it about my neck. It had come to him that my previous wound had been healed when the life sign had been upon me, and he had hoped to see the same thing done again. That bruises and light wounds were not similarly healed mattered not; it was the deep wounds which affected me most. He had then put his arms about me and pressed his lips to mine, thereby confirming a second surmise: I felt naught from his arms and lips, and had not

356

the least desire for him. The strange life sign given me by Mida
and Sigurr assured my survival even gravely wounded, yet also
assured that I would find no interest in any male. The first
condition was easily understandable; the second was not.

Those black-clad males passed in the halls gave Mehrayn
small bows of respect and some, to my surprise, gave the same
to me. The guardsmen standing without Aysayn's doors allowed
us immediate entry, and we quickly traversed the corridor which
led to his chambers. Both doors stood widely opened, and a
goodly number of males already made effort toward filling the
large chamber. Platforms laden with fresh-cooked provender
lined the walls of the chamber, tended by red-clad female slaves
who hurried to and fro, seeing to the needs of the males who
stood and sat about. Aysayn sat upon a seat to the right of the
doors, other unoccupied seats near to his, and when we appeared,
his eyes came to us immediately. Mehrayn wore the same thigh-
length black covering as did he, therefore was the inspection of
Sigurr's Sword brief; I, clad in reclaimed breech of leather,
Mida's sword to my left and dagger in right leg bands, life sign
swinging gently between my breasts, was accorded a longer
inspection. This inspection too, however, was also relatively
brief, and then Sigurr's Shadow rose and came to greet us with a
smile.

"I see you spoke the truth, brother," said he to Mehrayn, his
hand touching the smooth, faintly marked skin of my left arm
lightly. "She must surely be sent by Sigurr, to be cared for by
him so well. Come and sit with me, and partake of our victory
feast."

His arms about each of us, he conducted us to the seats which
awaited us, then turned to the slaves to order that boards be filled
for us. When he sat again, with Mehrayn to his left and I to
Mehrayn's left, Chaldrin appeared in the doorway, followed by
three black-clad males. The large, broad male wore the white
body cloth which was usual with him, and an unmarked cloth
about his ribs covering his wound. He moved slowly, more by
design than by need, and stopped at last before Aysayn, no
expression to be seen upon his face.

"Chaldrin, why did you walk?" demanded Aysayn, rising
again from his seat to look closely upon the other male. "Do you
seek to open your wound again and end yourself? The six slaves
I sent would have carried you here."

"I am scarcely so frail that I need to be carried," replied
Chaldrin, folding leather-covered wrists across his chest. "And
yet, should it be your wish, I will return to the Caverns and

allow the slaves to carry me. I would not care to offend Sigurr's Shadow."

"I have no doubt that you would do just that," grinned Aysayn, clapping the male upon the shoulder. "Yet not in fear of offending. Come and seat yourself, brother, and partake of our feast. The release of the others has been seen to?"

"Aye," said Chaldrin, making for the seat to my left. "All save Treglin, who chooses to remain the while to see to those we leave behind. We have cared for them too long to merely abandon them."

He crossed to his seat and lowered himself into it, then looked upon me where I sat stretched long in my chair. His eyes briefly examined my left arm, then a faint smile touched his lips.

"Chosen by the gods, indeed," he murmured, leaning carelessly back in his seat. "Should you find the opportunity and desire, perhaps you would speak a word on my behalf."

"Certainly," I murmured in return with a nod, keeping my eyes from him. "Think upon the possible price and your willingness to pay it, and then ask me again. Should your choice be the same, I will gladly speak upon your behalf."

"Price," he echoed with a frown, at last hearing the requirement before falling silent. At last it had come to him that the favor of the gods was not without its drawbacks. Slaves came and handed to us boards of provender, and Aysayn turned to Mehrayn.

"Now that you are adequately provisioned, brother," said Aysayn, "I would appreciate hearing what brought your expedition so quickly back to the city. From what Jalav had told me, you should not have returned till it was far too late to aid us."

"So would it have gone had Sigurr not intervened," nodded Mehrayn after tasting of the baked, pressed meat upon his board. I tasted the same, then set it aside in distaste. "We were fully prepared to travel the full distance to the city of our enemies, yet the third fey of our journey saw us face to face with them—for they journeyed to bedevil us. The battle was short and decisive, and few of them remained to lose themselves in the forests. Nearly did I continue on to their city despite all, yet too many of my warriors had been wounded by the numerically superior force we had bested. I waited two feyd to allow my men to regather strength, then led them home.

"Rather than ride directly into the city, I thought to save myself a bit of time and went in search of the place I had directed Jalav to wait. I intended taking her back with me and seeking you out again, yet I found not a single sign of her presence. Again I nearly rode directly into the city, yet vague suspicions upon many odd happenings caused me to send a single rider in instead, to go to my house and fetch forth Hesain, in whose keeping I had left Jalav. The rider returned with word that Hesain had been found emptied of lifeblood, and no further word had been heard of Jalav."

Mehrayn paused to take a goblet of drink from the slave who offered it to him, and drank deeply under Aysayn's sober stare. I, too, took a goblet and drank, yet only after assuring myself that the drink was not the thrai I had previously been offered. I discovered it to be nearer to daru than the renth of the northern cities, yet still unbrewed. Brewed daru would have gone down well just then, yet what may one expect when among males?

"It was then necessary to consider what next should be done," said Mehrayn, putting his goblet aside in favor of a leg of roast. lellin. "The rider I had sent had found that 'Aysayn' had returned to his apartments, yet had not sent me private word of his return as he normally did. Also, word had traveled among the warriors, telling of the blasphemer who had attempted to present himself as the Shadow, foolishly thinking the Shadow still absent. It was mentioned how fortunate it was that the lady Ladayna had been there to consult, as the guardsmen approached were new to their posts, having only recently been appointed. Learning that the blasphemer had been sent to the Caverns, I dismissed the idea of taking my warriors to demand an audience with 'Aysayn,' and sent instead those who would watch over both the entrance to the Caverns and the gallery. I was considering in what manner I might force action of some sort from the enemy, when a rider returned in haste to inform me that a large number of warriors had appeared in the gallery early this fey, and had put themselves out of sight. Knowing that whatever battle was fought would be fought upon the Sands, I led my warriors to the Caverns. What occurred then, you are already aware of."

"Indeed," nodded Aysayn, sipping from his own goblet. "The thing was done with sickening ease, requiring no more than your absence and Ladayna's assistance. It will not again be so easily done, especially through Ladayna. The time has come to teach her the consequences of spiteful, petty vindictiveness."

"Perhaps you should not have taken her unwilling to your chambers," said I, regarding no more than the goblet I held and drank from. "Had you left her to her own devices, she would not have been able to betray you—nor me."

"Ladayna—unwilling?" scoffed Aysayn, stirring in his seat

beyond Mehrayn. "Ladayna was most willing when she came to me, seeing herself with power and station far above any other wench in the city. The station was hers without question, yet power does not belong in hands which will abuse it. She attempted to ignore the restrictions placed upon her, and gave orders which were not hers to give, thereby attempting to usurp my rights and privileges without formally challenging me for the position. For this reason was she placed in silver chains, to remind the warriors about us that her word was not as final as she believed it to be. I now realize it was Pinain urging her to these actions, that he might replace me without having to face me. It was he who changed the guard before my apartments, intending to snare me upon my return. Had Ladayna not been so concerned with her anger toward me, she would have seen through Pinain and his urgings."

"And yet," said Mehrayn, "this fails to account for her having sent you to the Caverns, brother. Spitefulness does not condemn a man to a place from which there is no return. The emotion behind such an action is more often hatred."

"Hatred was indeed the reason behind my condemnation," said Aysayn, pleasure in his tone. "Pinain, not Ladayna, had my warriors take me to the Caverns; Ladayna merely named me impostor, childishly thinking that I would be thrown into the streets as though I were a beggar. After she returned to her apartments, Pinain gave the orders he had intended the entire time. This was told me by the warriors he commanded as my chief guardsman, all save my supposition concerning his thoughts."

"Then Ladayna was a pawn," said Mehrayn, his voice containing the same satisfaction which Aysayn had shown. "Her betrayal was no betrayal at all, merely foolishness."

"Foolishness which nearly took my life, and her own as well," said Aysayn with a good deal less pleasure. "I will be a long time punishing her for that foolishness, Sigurr take me if I do not."

"An excellent beginning," laughed Mehrayn, adding his amusement to that of the other males within the chamber. I moved my gaze from the goblet I held, and immediately saw that Ladayna had entered the chamber with a black-clad male as escort, yet was she considerably altered from the Ladayna I had last seen. Gone was the long, black covering she had worn, replaced by the red half-covering of a slave female. Too, the tips of her breasts had been dyed the red of a slave, and no longer was she draped in silver chain. No chain whatsoever restricted her movements, yet was she constrained by the trappings of a slave

and the hand of a guard male upon her arm, which hurried her
forward despite her deep consternation. Directly to Aysayn was
she taken, and put to her knees before him.

"Have you completed your tasks already, wench?" he asked
with visible approval, smiling down upon the female. "As you
work so assiduously to please me, I shall now allow you to join
the feast."

"Oh, do not force me to remain here!" begged the female
from where she knelt, mortified by the laughter and amusement
about her. "Have I not been punished enough? Aysayn, I am in
agony!"

"Agony of the soul is no more than that which you have
earned," said the male in a low voice, his hand beneath her
upturned face. "You will learn to think and behave as an adult
rather than as an overindulged child, else shall I release you to go
elsewhere, likely as a slave. My patience with you is now
exhausted. You will remain here at the feast, and will serve my
guests and myself if your services are required."

"Aysayn, you must recall your promise!" whispered the female urgently, reaching up to grasp with both hands the wrist
above the hand at her face. "By cause of your other punishment,
I am desperately in need of easing! You promised to see to me
when my tasks were done! You promised!"

"Wench, I spoke of the possibility of seeing to you when your
behavior was to my satisfaction," he corrected, holding her
anxious gaze with the steadiness of his own. "No promise was
given you, for no promise need be given a slave. Should I find
myself displeased, the time will be longer yet—which is all too
likely to occur. How have you been addressing your master?"

The female's gaze widened at the words spoken to her, and
her full lower lip trembled. A long moment passed during which
she seemed unable to look away from Aysayn, and then, at last,
she ventured, "Master?"

"Excellent," smiled Aysayn, releasing her face and leaning
back in his seat. "Now let us see if there will be any services
requiring your performance. Should there be any, I shall expect
to feel satisfaction over that performance."

"Perhaps there is one already awaiting her," said Mehrayn,
looking down upon the female as Aysayn had done. "Jalav was
considerably inconvenienced by cause of her actions; does she
not owe an apology over the matter?"

"Indeed, brother, indeed she does," agreed Aysayn with a
grin as Ladayna shook her head pleadingly, stricken. "We must
see to the omission immediately."

"I was not inconvenienced," I interrupted their amusement, swallowing the last of my drink before turning to my right to look upon them. "I was offered deadly insult, the sort which may only be wiped away with blood. Is it this wrong which you seek to redress?"

The two males quickly lost their laughter, stirring in discomfort in the same manner that Chaldrin stirred in his seat at my back.

"Should you count insult, wench," said Chaldrin, "Aysayn and I are equally guilty of such actions. Do you mean to hold us accountable as well?"

"You two and this one beside me," I said, nodding toward an expressionless Mehrayn. I then rose to my feet, pushed my eating board at a nearby trembling slave, then turned to face the three males with goblet in left hand. "Which of you will be first to face me?"

Aysayn and Chaldrin exchanged a glance the while Mehrayn studied his eating board. Another moment of silence ensued, one which spread throughout the entire chamber, and then Aysayn made a sound in his throat.

"Come, wench; surely you know we may none of us face you," said he, great discomfort upon him. "Mehrayn and I, loyal followers of Sigurr, would be committing sacrilege if we were to draw weapon against his proven messenger. Chaldrin, believing as he does that Sigurr has turned from him, nevertheless also knows you as chosen by the gods. Even were he in full health, he would not again draw against you. Should you wish to end us all where we sit, you may do so; it is otherwise pointless to pursue the matter."

"Indeed is it pointless," I agreed, looking upon all of them and seeing their surprise. It was not known to them that all blood debts had recently been consigned to oblivion by another, one they were unacquainted with. "It is as pointless as offering apology for a blood insult. Had I considered the matter one to be pursued, apology would not have sufficed. Should it be your wish to continue tormenting this slave female, involve another in your foolishness. Jalav has matters of greater import to concern her."

Now was it embarrassment which touched the males, turning their skin ruddy and their eyes from my gaze. I reached my goblet to my lips and attempted to drink, only then recalling that I had drained the thing a moment earlier. I looked upon the empty vessel with annoyance, and suddenly the female Ladayna was before me.

"Allow this slave to refill your goblet, mistress," said she, her voice as quiet as her gaze was steady. "I offer no apology for doing that which was beyond forgiveness; I merely thank you for my life, and for considering a poor slave who has lost all right to dignity. Never will I forget what was taught me when you slew Pinain."

"And what was that, wench?" asked Aysayn when I made no reply to her words. The female smiled faintly, then took my goblet before turning again to the male.

"I have learned that there are those about who do not, after all, consider me too beautiful and desirable to be called to account for that which I do," said she, looking upon the male. "You are stern with me now, Aysayn, yet you have been stern with me before for no great length of time. I have learned that your leniency is caused by your love for me, yet I have also learned that there are those who feel naught of that love—and who would do me great harm in your place. Should you consent, later, to hold me in your arms, I will allow myself to feel the terrible fear such a realization brings. For now, a slave has been given a task to perform."

The female put her head down and hurried away with my goblet, and Aysayn turned to stare after her before slowly turning forward again. The male seemed touched by that which the female had said, as touched as every fool of a male within hearing. Ladayna had professed herself slave, yet she, in her own way, was no more slave than I. Had I had my preference in the matter, I would have preferred that her well-announced lessons had been in sword skill. I returned to my seat and sat again, hearing the return of conversation in the chamber.

"These matters of greater concern—" said Mehrayn to me, turning in his seat to reach a hand out to my hand—"they cannot be concerned with your mission, for our Sigurri will be prepared to return with you to Bellinard within a hand of feyd. The ceremonies must be gone through with Aysayn presiding, yet they are mere formalities. Do you chafe at the added delay?"

"I do not face your delay." I shrugged, slipping my hand away from his. "I depart with the new light, yet not for Bellinard."

"Not for Bellinard?" echoed Mehrayn with a frown, Aysayn and Chaldrin also suddenly attentive. Ladayna returned with my goblet, now refilled, and I took it without giving attention to the female. I had expected some indication of annoyance from her at the brusque dismissal, yet she, too, was aware of the attention of the males, and merely withdrew to kneel again at Aysayn's feet.

"For what reason will you not return to Bellinard?" asked

Aysayn, leaning forward past Mehrayn even as he put a hand to Ladayna's hair. "Have you not been awaiting the completion of your mission so that you might rejoin the others of your wenches? What has occurred that has caused you to change this intention?"

"The decision was not mine," I shrugged, swallowing from the near-daru. "While I slept, Mida walked my dreams as she has done many times in the past. She has reminded me of a boast and a lack, and commanded that I fulfill the first by mending the second."

"Jalav, you must speak more plainly," said Mehrayn, his light eyes concerned. "For what reason must you leave so soon, and where do you go?"

"I go to claim the war leadership of the enemy clans of Midanna," I informed him, faintly saddened that I no longer felt desire when I looked upon the broad strength of him. "Many times I have named myself war leader of all the Midanna, yet this is not so. Fully half of our clans fail to follow me—as they must if we are to find victory over the strangers."

"But—they are your enemies!" protested Mehrayn, deeper concern growing with him. "You cannot merely ride into their midst and announce your intentions! They will have your life! I will accompany you, and my warriors as well."

"They are Midanna," I denied with a headshake. "Were I so foolish as to allow you to accompany me, they would have other than your life from you—taken willingly or elsewise. You will remain here, Mehrayn, and see to your males the while I see to my own tasks. Mida willing, we shall meet again at Bellinard."

"Should he decide to remain, I shall not," came Chaldrin's calm rumble as Mehrayn's broad face set in lines of stubbornness. "I cannot aid you if I am not beside you."

"It is not possible for a male to aid me among the Midanna," I insisted, turning to Chaldrin to see that he wore the same expression that Mehrayn did. "Do you wish to be used more harshly than a female slave in the Caverns? Do you wish to place me in greater jeopardy than I would find alone? The penalty for leading free males to Midanna home tents is harsh; I would not care to add that to the enmity which will already be awaiting me."

All three males began speaking at once, then, in argument rather than in disappointed agreement. The males saw only that which they, themselves, wished, and I raised my goblet to my lips and drained it quickly. Had I been wise, I would not have spoken of my intentions, yet the time was well past to consider the point. I must instead consider the best way to avoid the well-intentioned concern of those about me, and be about this further task given me by Mida. I had seen to the raising of the Sigurri; how much more difficult the raising of enemy sisters would be was best not contemplated till face to face with it. Face to face alone, without the presence of males!

A GALAXY OF SCIENCE FICTION STARS!

LEE CORREY Manna	UE1896—$2.95
TIMOTHY ZAHN The Blackcollar	UE1959—$3.50
A.E. VAN VOGT Computerworld	UE1879—$2.50
COLIN KAPP Search for the Sun	UE1858—$2.25
ROBERT TREBOR An XT Called Stanley	UE1865—$2.50
ANDRE NORTON Horn Crown	UE1635—$2.95
JACK VANCE The Face	UE1921—$2.50
E. C. TUBB Angado	UE1908—$2.50
KENNETH BULMER The Diamond Contessa	UE1853—$2.50
ROGER ZELAZNY Deus Irae	UE1887—$2.50
PHILIP K. DICK Ubik	UE1859—$2.50
DAVID J. LAKE Warlords of Xuma	UE1832—$2.50
CLIFFORD D. SIMAK Our Children's Children	UE1880—$2.50
M. A. FOSTER Transformer	UE1814—$2.50
GORDON R. DICKSON Mutants	UE1809—$2.95
BRIAN STABLEFORD The Gates of Eden	UE1801—$2.50
JOHN BRUNNER The Jagged Orbit	UE1917—$2.95
EDWARD LLEWELLYN Salvage and Destroy	UE1898—$2.95
PHILIP WYLIE The End of the Dream	UE1900—$2.25

NEW AMERICAN LIBRARY,
P.O. Box 999, Bergenfield, New Jersey 07621

Please send me the DAW BOOKS I have checked above. I am enclosing
$_____ (check or money order—no currency or C.O.D.'s).
Please include the list price plus $1.00 per order to cover handling
costs.

Name _____

Address _____

City _____ State _____ Zip Code _____
Please allow at least 4 weeks for delivery

TANITH LEE

"Princess Royal of Heroic Fantasy and Goddess-Empress of the Hot Read."

—**Village Voice (N.Y.C.)**

- ☐ THE BIRTHGRAVE (#UE1776–$3.50)
- ☐ VAZKOR, SON OF VAZKOR (#UE1709–$2.50)
- ☐ QUEST FOR THE WHITE WITCH (#UJ1357–$1.95)
- ☐ DRINKING SAPPHIRE WINE (#UE1565–$1.75)
- ☐ VOLKHAVAAR (#UE1539–$1.75)
- ☐ THE STORM LORD (#UE1867–$2.95)
- ☐ NIGHT'S MASTER (#UE1657–$2.25)
- ☐ ELECTRIC FOREST (#UE1482–$1.75)
- ☐ DAY BY NIGHT (#UE1576–$2.25)
- ☐ THE SILVER METAL LOVER (#UE1721–$2.75)
- ☐ CYRION (#UE1765–$2.95)
- ☐ DEATH'S MASTER (#UE1741–$2.95)
- ☐ RED AS BLOOD (#UE1790–$2.50)
- ☐ SUNG IN SHADOW (#UE1824–$2.50)
- ☐ TAMASTARA (#UE1915–$2.50)

Presenting JOHN NORMAN in DAW editions . . .